THE MACRO EVENT

AMERICA'S SURVIVAL

ANDREW R. ADAMS

Fulton Books, Inc.
Meadville, PA

Published by Fulton Books 2019

ISBN 978-1-63338-964-9 (paperback)
ISBN 978-1-63338-966-3 (hardcover)
ISBN 978-1-63338-965-6 (digital)

Printed in the United States of America

To my lovely and dedicated wife and the best family anyone could ask for. A family who starts with a hug and finishes with "I love you." You guys are the paracord that binds, the crazy glue that keeps the pieces together, the first aid kit to heal any wound, the GPS to keep me on the right path, the LED light at the end of every tunnel, and the nourishment for my body and soul.

Prologue

Day Zero, 0817, Glendale, California

Dayyan Imaad Shalah arrived at his appliance repair shop in a small strip mall on Pacific Avenue a short distance from the 134 Freeway. His shop provided appliance repairs on small items such as vacuum cleaners, microwaves, toasters, and other small needs of the gluttonous American lifestyle. Not a profitable business in any sense of the word, but the small business provided him a convenient occupation seeing little scrutiny from the city, state, or United States government. The business also provided a method to receive funds under the guise of "cash sales" without any bank or tax agency taking a closer look. Dayyan did not care about profit. His chosen place was to be patient and wait for the calling.

His phone vibrated and then played the silly tone announcing a new text message. Thinking it might be his friend Naseem, he withdrew the phone from his belt pouch and looked at the screen. The message was a simple line of eight characters, A-T-5-2-Z-Q-H-3. He tensed up when he read them. *Was it time? Has the day finally come?* Dayyan thought. *Or is it a simple test?*

He clicked on the display that opened the message. The sender phone number was "000-000-0000." Whoever sent the message was using a cloaking device to hide the sender phone number. He got out a small notepad and quickly figured out the correct reply. Using the small keyboard of the cell phone, Dayyan typed a simple reply: B-V-8-6-E-W-O-1. The formula was simple. Add one letter alphabetically or numerically to the first character, two to the second, and three to the third and so on. He double-checked the formula and pressed the Send button.

Although the shop was cool immediately after reading the first message Dayyan had started sweating. Seeming like an eternity, but in reality only thirty seconds, the phone again played the text message tone. Dayyan looked at the screen. "God is great. Remain at your shop. Some customers shall join you shortly. You should be receiving a package. We shall seek your services today."

Dayyan realized his long-awaited activation had just occurred. For what exactly he did not know. The word "Today" in the text message had the first letter capitalized. This simple hidden key told Dayyan whatever would happen would do so before midnight tonight. Spotting misprinted words in a document was part of training he once received.

Dayyan Imaad Shalah was an Iraq immigrant. Before the Iraqi Freedom campaign, his father was one of Saddam's high-ranking officials. This position of importance landed him on the "Most wanted" deck of cards as the ten of spades. This deck of playing cards, an evil creation of the Coalition forces was issued to the combat troops during the invasion and used to identify the most valuable human targets. Nevertheless, his father was a traitor. When it became obvious to his father Iraq would lose this war quickly, he defected, and using a mole, he contacted the American Central Intelligence Agency.

For self-preservation, his father did not consider the fate of the other loyal Saddam officials. This included Dayyan's favorite uncle Ammar. His father had traveled extensively for the government, and his uncle had done more to raise him that his father. Dayyan's father would beat him savagely for minor infractions. Ammar, the opposite of his father, was a kind man, never once laying a hand on Dayyan.

So when the American Army with its CIA advisers came for his Uncle Ammar and four other high-ranking officials who were in hiding, it was obvious that Dayyan's father had turned them in. Several of those faithful to Saddam died when they fought back during the brief battle with the US Special Forces. Dayyan was only seven years old when he ran out into the yard and stayed with Ammar while he was bleeding out from the multiple gunshot wounds. Dayyan was kneeling over his dying uncle when an American soldier came up and kicked him out of the way. He then began to torture Amman during his last few moments of life, asking the dying man for locations of other officials. Dayyan would never forget that day, and his hatred for the Americans and his traitor father would sizzle for years.

Shortly after the death of his uncle, the CIA removed his parents from Iraq. Officially, Dayyan and his father were listed as killed. Both received a new identity and life when they arrived in the United States. The two were given new lives in Los Angeles. Their handlers provided his father employment at an auto repair shop owned by another Iraqi. After finishing high school and while attending the University of California, Dayyan received notice that his aunt, who had remained in Iraq, was ill. He asked his father for permission to go to Bagdad to see her before she passed away, and his father begrudgingly gave in.

He remained in Iraq, nursing his aunt through her lengthy but terminal illness. The CIA handlers had no suspicions, and his ailing aunt was a reasonable excuse for him to remain there for an extended time. With the growing threat of Al-Qaeda and ISIS, the CIA had bigger fish to fry, and they paid no attention to him. Ignoring him was a serious mistake. Once in Iraq, a Syrian immediately realized Dayyan's potential shortly after introductions. After careful vetting, Dayyan was introduced to an unknown man. Someone described as "very powerful." For the next five months, Dayyan met with various people, who provided training in skills including weapons, electronics, radios, warfare tactics, and other skills of warfare. The need for some of his training made little sense, but he remained loyal and worked hard to learn. His new friends continued to provide him help in many ways after returning to the United States. Introductions and training continued for an unknown and undefined mission.

Funds provided by his handlers could be explained as money his aunt had left him. He used that money to open the small appliance repair store. He faithfully followed instructions others had drilled into him in Iraq. Money arrived sometimes in simple mailed envelopes or sometimes by a "customer" who would pay a large bill in cash. With the cash, he bought various items from a list that he had forcibly made to memorize. He bought an old seventies vintage Chevrolet Suburban and an even older Dodge crew cab pickup truck. His father passed away a few months after he returned, so he did not have to worry about the "traitor" asking questions. He took the trucks to the auto repair shop his father had worked at and, using cash, had them restore the trucks to near new condition.

He bought a few guns but not enough to raise suspicion. He started to develop a cell of wolf terrorists. He would not be a lone wolf as the American media was fond of naming terrorists. Lone wolves were known to perform stupid acts, usually resulting in their arrest or death. Dayyan was extremely careful. Vetting would occur on any new acquaintance or unknown people. Dayyan simply provided basic information on them. If there were any doubts or worries, he would ignore them and push them out of his life. Dayyan's cell consisted of five direct "soldiers" besides himself and his friend Naseem. The other five men vetted others and built their own network of loyal followers of Islam. Each added other loyal soldiers. For added safety each group kept, their members secret for the other groups to add another layer of protection against discovery.

Dayyan now sent each of his soldiers a coded text message directing them to meet at his shop as soon as possible.

Dayyan did not have to wait long before his best friend, Naseem, showed up. Soon after Naseem's arrival, two others from his cell showed up. About a half hour later, a FedEx driver walked in and handed a small package to Dayyan and held out the electronic tablet, which Dayyan signed. After the driver left, Dayyan took the package behind the counter and examined it. The box was about eighteen inches square and ten inches deep and heavy for its size. He opened the outer cardboard box and found a tactical plastic case with a sealed envelope taped to the top lid. The top of the envelope had a large bold message that read, "Do not open until contact arrives to verify." There was also a set of numbers and letters under the message "3-7-H-U-8-3-S-T."

About thirty minutes later, a man walked into the shop, Dayyan asked him, "Can I help you?"

The man answered, "I have an envelope for you."

Dayyan looked at a set of numbers on the front of the envelope, "4-9-K-Y-3-9-7-B." Then using a notepad, he compared the numbers to the ones in the FedEx package and he confirmed the same code.

When Dayyan finished confirming the code, the stranger asked, "Okay, my brother?"

"Yes, it appears to be," Dayyan replied.

The two men then shook hands and exchanged names. The new man's name was Adham. He told Dayyan he was from Syria but did not freely exchange any more information. He appeared about twenty-five years old. He was clean-shaven like Dayyan, and his English was excellent. Dayyan wondered if Adham had undergone the same training as himself. Part of Dayyan's training was always to remain clean-shaven and dress, act, and speak as close to American English as possible. He had even taken an advanced English language course focusing on accent and true American ways of speaking. Dayyan assumed that perhaps Adham had done the same.

Adham took out his cell phone and called someone. The call was answered quickly, and he simply said, "God is great." And he hung up.

About two minutes later, three other men of Mideastern-looking descent entered the shop. Within twenty minutes, the balance of Dayyan's own cell arrived. This brought the count of men to ten. Dayyan locked the front door and put out a Closed sign, and the group all retreated into the back of the repair shop and started preparing for their mission.

Chapter 1

2245, Day Zero, Las Vegas, Nevada

L ee Garrett woke suddenly from a sound sleep. An eerie quiet had triggered a nerve. Yes quiet. A loud noise had not stirred him, but instead the lack of noise. Lee awoke thinking, *Something is odd.* The hotel room air conditioner was no longer drumming out its constant low rattle-infused sound. The symphony of music and noise from the popular Las Vegas downtown area was gone. He looked at the digital clock on the nightstand next to the bed. The clock face was dark.

Lee was on the nineteenth floor of a hotel room at the Double J hotel on Fremont Street in downtown Las Vegas. Having gone out to dinner, he returned to his room at around 10:15. He had phoned his wife, Madison, spoke with her for about ten minutes, and then undressed, climbed into bed, and was fast asleep within moments. Now Lee guessed the time was around 11:30 to 12:00 a.m. This weird awakening displayed how humans become so familiar to noise that a sudden lack of noise can be alarming. Lee's internal alarm had sounded loudly and clearly.

Lee climbed out of bed, found his way in the pitch dark to the window, and pulled open the curtains.

"Shit," Lee said aloud to the empty room.

Las Vegas was dark. There were no lights as far or wide as he could see. The only lights Lee could see below were car headlamps and taillamps. There was no building, marquee, lamppost, or any common Vegas overlamped signage.

"This is not good," Lee added as he stared from the window.

Suddenly and horrendously, a massive fireball erupted on the other side of town. Lee knew the explosion was on the other side of Interstate-15. As the fireball erupted, it grew into a monstrous red and yellow glowing inferno. Then the shock wave hit. The windows rattled and the building shook. Lee stepped back from the window fearing perhaps the glass would shatter. Nevertheless, the large windows held. He moved back in closer again and watched as the fireball climbed high into the black night and dots of fire and smoke arose around the main explosion. The glowing fires spread, all of them getting larger and burning more furiously by the second. The glow from the flames lit up the surrounding city, providing light to the pitch-black enveloping the rest of the city.

So what the hell is happening? Lee thought as he went to the table lamp and tried it. "Nothing," He said while trying another lamp. "No go. Okay, power is definitely out."

In the dark, Lee felt his way back to the nightstand. Lee always had a small flashlight with him when he traveled, and he kept it near the bed. He fumbled for the flashlight and his cell phone and found both on the nightstand. Lee pressed the button on the phone, and it lit up like normal. Time was 10:47. The signal meter was flat with no bars showing, and the "No signal" symbol was on. Calling 9-1-1 was pointless, Lee figured. Thousands of Las Vegas Residents and guests alike had surely seen and felt the explosion. So instead, he selected his wife's number from the favorites list and hit call. Nothing happened. There was no noise, no recording, no ringing, just nothing.

This is bad, really, really bad, Lee thought.

He started to consider the cause, which he was starting to, but did not want to accept. Lee had studied and planned, but doubted it would happen. *Maybe the power outage and the explosion are related.* Lee was overcome by the feeling this event was bigger. Much, much bigger. The room was already getting stuffy from the lack of air-conditioning. Lee stood and considered the impossible.

Lee Garrett had come to downtown Vegas for his work. He was there to oversee a new fireworks and special effects project for one of the large Freemont street casinos. He had driven up the day before from his home in Agua Dulce California, which was a small rural community outside Los Angeles, north out of the San Fernando Valley. It was roughly two hundred miles by car. The trip would normally take Lee around four hours. Staring out at the darkened Las Vegas city, however, gave Lee a chilling feeling that Agua Dulce was not going to be four hours away for the return trip home. The large fire was still burning and appeared to be spreading. He could tell that flames and smoke were overrunning many tall buildings.

Lee noticed something else. Many of the cars below had headlights, taillights, or even some hazard flashers, but he saw no cars moving. He could see flashing lights frozen in space on some type of emergency vehicle. Surely hundreds of emergency vehicles and First Responders should be screaming full speed to the giant inferno on the northwest side of town. He saw none in any direction. Was Lee's nagging hunch correct?

Lee's full name was Lee Andrew Garrett. Most people knew him as Lee, but a few friends and an Uncle who shared the name knew him as Andy. At the age of fifty-two, Lee's occupation was that of a special effects consultant and engineer. Married with two sons and a daughter. Lee was hoping his family all had made it to his house. He had insisted sometimes against pushback the family plan for emergencies, so he hoped and prayed they were all safe.

Although not a military veteran himself, Lee had involvement in the defense department for years. He consulted on their MOUT training facilities around the country. MOUT stood for Military Operations in Urban Terrain. MOUTs were fake towns or villages that units would attack or defend as part of intensive training. The Army had tapped into the special effects industry to bring more reality to the training bases. Lee's company added realistic but safe explosions using natural gas or propane and pyrotechnic devices. Also added were other types of booby traps, bullet hits, and special effects to keep soldiers on their toes and make training more realistic and even scary at times. When any explosion goes off near you, safe or not, it will definitely get your attention or as special effects people say, "pucker up your asshole."

Besides Lee's love for his family and friends and his rewarding professional life, he had a hobby which now may be of paramount importance to his survival. Prepping. Yes, Lee was one of those nutcase doomsday preppers. He took preparation seriously in his work, and he took it to a new level in his prepping. He spent hours planning for different types of natural or man-made disasters. With his wife and family members, Lee spent hours on hours, plus a fair amount of money on plans, and equipment all in case of the worst scenarios. They had stockpiles of prepper supplies at their home. Both of them read everything they could find on the subject, bought tons of stuff, and stockpiled crap to the point of driving the rest of the family nuts. Lee and Madison both religiously carried oversized backpacks in their cars just in case. A popular name for a prepper backpack was "Bug Out Bag." Other names used were G-O-O-D, or "Get Out of Dodge Bag," or W-T-S-H-T-F, as "When the Shit Hits the Fan Bag." Lee preferred BOB. It was simple. Lee kept two bags ready always. He carried a three-day bag daily in his SUV, going to and from work and around the Los Angeles area. Madison and the kids carried identical bags in their cars. For longer trips, Lee would put a larger seven-day bag into his Ford Explorer. He had loaded the larger bag for the trip up to Las Vegas. Lee was not sure of the situation yet, but he thought, *Thankfully I bought the big bag*.

Lee picked up the flashlight and hit the power button. It illuminated and lit up the room. "Well, at least it is working." Years of traveling with a flashlight in his luggage just paid off. Lee used the flashlight to find his duffel, inside which was a small lockbox containing a Ruger LC-9 small automatic pistol. Being a gun owner in California made it tough. The laws on weapon carry were strict. To legally carry a pistol inside a car within California, you had to unload it and lock it inside a box separate from any ammunition. The small lockbox fulfilled the requirement, and Lee had simply put the box with the pistol in his duffel when he unloaded it and other items from the car while checking into the hotel. Knowing the gun held an empty magazine, Lee had taken two fully loaded magazines out of his BOB and tossed them in the bottom of the duffel bag. Lee now fished a loaded mag from his duffel bag, ejected the empty from the small pistol, inserted a full, pulled back the slide, and sent a round into the chamber. The gun was ready to fire. Not having extra shells, he placed the empty mag back into his duffel. Lee was not sure why he felt compelled to load the weapon, but he had a bad feeling.

Lee quickly put on some shorts and a long-sleeved shirt. He was now hearing noise from the hallway. He went to the door and listened. Someone was pounding on a door, and a male voice was raising all kinds of hell.

"Fucking electric door locks are out. Goddamn it. Nineteen fucking floors of stairs and the door is locked. This sucks!" the loud man shouted.

Another male voice chimed in, "Let's kick the fucking door in."

Heavy pounding and kicking followed. Other doors in the hall started to open. Lee did the same, slowly opening his door, but keeping the Ruger at his side as he leaned out to look up and down the hall. Emergency lights were on at each end of the hall, casting an eerie glow up and down the long corridor. Lee saw two middle-aged, semi-overweight men dressed in the typical American Vegas tourist clothing consisting of golf shirts, long shorts, and sneakers. The two loud and probably half-drunk men were in the hall a few doors down on the right, furiously kicking at their room door. Other heads and partial bodies were leaning out several doors, watching the two irritated patrons doing their best to break into what Lee only hoped was their room.

A middle-aged woman, who reminded Lee of Peg from the *Married with Children* TV show, was standing in her door across the hall in between his room and the two pissed-off drunks. She spoke up directing her question to them, causing a temporarily pause of their determined breaking and entering attempt.

"What's going on?" the woman asked.

One of the men turned and answered, "Power's out all over. The casino TVs came on with the emergency broadcast system but then just went black. We heard someone say that one of the TV news stations said something about a nuke going off in Washington. Bout then all the stations went out. And there was a big ass plane crash North of here. We heard the screaming noise of the plane just before the explosion. There is a big fucking fire burning. We walked up here from the Freemont Street. Now these goddamn electronic locks are busted too. Cell phones are all dead. Everyone is getting really pissed downstairs."

"Is that your room?" the woman asked.

"No, lady, we are just kicking in the door of some other room. Yes, this is our fucking room. You better not let your door close or you will be in the same shit tuna boat as us," said one of the irritated men.

Without another word to the two angry men, the woman in the doorway turned back into her room and closed the door. Many conversations were starting up and down the hall between various guests all standing partially in their doorways. Lee closed his door and went back to the window. Looking outside, he could see there was no real change outside. It was total blackness except for vehicle lights and the big fire. The headlamps of the cars provided some light at street level. Lee could see many cars had the hoods up and people leaning into the engine compartments. As much as Lee was hoping for another explanation, his suspicion was starting to make terrible sense. This was not just a power outage. This was far worse. This much damage was an EMP, or Electro Magnetic Pulse. An EMP was a high-power surge of energy, which theory agreed was capable of taking down the power grids and sensitive electronics. There were two main EMP scenarios. First was a massive solar flare. Few scientists and engineers thought a solar flare could inflict this kind of damage on the power system plus kill nearly every car in Las Vegas. The other cause was a high-altitude nuclear detonation. Many experts feared the effect of a nuke EMP. The government had been studying EMPs since the late 1940s. It was generally accepted the United States and Russia had EMP weapons in their respective arsenals. Most studies recognized the possibility of vehicle and electronics damage. Some even feared that modern aircraft would fall from the sky if hit with a nuclear blast produced EMP. The military spends billions of dollars to protect their equipment; that alone might prove the likelihood of

EMP damage. Well, maybe all the facts are now proven. What the angry door kickers said about the TV broadcasts and then emergency broadcast signals all fit. It felt likely to Lee the United States was at war.

Lee went to the desk, opened his laptop, and hit the power button. The small PC booted up as normal.

Perhaps being unplugged saved it? Lee thought.

Lee selected the icon for wireless networks, and nothing showed up. That was no surprise. He turned on his small cellular hot spot wireless but ended with the same result as his cell phone. No signal.

Decision time. Do I wait until daylight? Lee asked himself.

If the United States was now at war including the use of an EMP, power was not coming on soon. Dead cars would not miraculously start running. Lee's car was in the garage. Was it possible his car and other cars avoided damage because they were inside the multilevel concrete structure? Lee needed to find out. He thought, however, that down nineteen floors would be a one-way trip. If he got to his car and found it electronically cooked like the ones visible from the windows, he would be forced to become a serious survivalist. Lee would be walking. Moreover, if the EMP had happened, this city would die a quick death. Thousands of visitors and residents would be in dire trouble. Adequate help would not be coming anytime soon. Food, water, and transportation would be a commodity ordinary people would start killing for. A running car could be a death sentence if you stayed in this town.

Lee decided. He packed his duffel with clothes and bathroom stuff. He would scrounge useful items from the room and sort the stuff out at his car, which he hoped against all odds was running. He stuffed the bag full including the computer. He put on sneakers, jeans, T-shirt, and a loose-fitting overshirt. It was early September and warm outside, but he went for jeans versus shorts. He then stuck the LC-9 in his right pocket and the other full magazine in his left rear pocket. He went to the window and took one last look out. The fire was still raging and continuing to spread consuming more and more buildings. The smell of smoke was penetrating the room. Lee guessed it was coming through the simple window air conditioner units that adorned most hotel rooms.

Lee put the duffel over his neck and one shoulder, put the flashlight in his left hand, palmed the Ruger one more time, went to the door, and cautiously opened it. The two drunks had seemingly gotten their door open, as they were gone. A couple of people were talking between rooms further down the hall. Lee put the security arm out to keep the door from latching, moved out into the hall, and headed toward the stairs.

The stairs were crowded with people—some coming up, some coming down. People were talking among their groups or to strangers while passing in the stairwell.

"What do you think happened?"

"Plane crash."

"Terrorists."

"Hoover dam broke."

"Nuclear war."

"Emergency broadcast was cut off."

"Washington nuked."

Lee heard all kinds of talk and guesses. However, not a single person said EMP. Lee knew from his own discussions with people and friends the public was mostly naive to EMP. Partly because the government rarely brought it up. Most serious preppers feel the government has no solution, so why talk about it? So most Americans had no clue. Of course, Lee was still assuming an EMP was the cause. Lee did not talk much to anyone in the stairwell, and he surely did not say EMP. Hell was going to break loose in Las Vegas, and Lee wanted to be out of town as soon as possible. *Is it selfish?* he thought. No, he had prepared for this possibility. Even after constant reminders about being ready for an emergency most people did nothing in preparation for the slightest hiccup in their cozy lives.

Lee came out of the stairwell and into the casino, lit by emergency lights. Hundreds of people were milling around. The employees were trying to keep calm and answer questions, but they looked even more fearful than the civilians. They probably knew they would be vulnerable when these pissed-off people started taking out frustration on anyone with any authority.

Lee kept moving. He kept the flashlight off and hidden, not wanting to lose it. He made his way to an exit, out, and down the street to the parking garage. It was a warm fall evening in Vegas. Temperature was in the eighties, Lee guessed. Dry as usual for the desert. Thankfully, Lee thought about how he had parked his own car and not used valet. He would usually park his own car. What good would a bag full of survival gear be if he could not even find his car, was something Lee considered whenever tempted to use a valet. It was quite dark outside, but dozens of emergency lights produced a glow from buildings making navigating easy. Most stores had closed and pulled down security shutters. He did see a commotion at the pharmacy on the corner. Security was trying to usher out the crowd to lock the doors. It was not going well. Two Las Vegas police officers were heading toward the pharmacy.

Lee started up the stairs to the second floor of the garage. Now it was really dark. The garage emergency lighting was either minimal or not working. Car lights shined from a few locations, helping Lee to navigate the dark interior of the garage. Lee saw people in some cars lit up by interior lights. He heard a couple of cars "cranking" over but heard none starting or running. Hoods were up on several cars, and people were discussing and trying to discover the problem. Lee kept moving.

Please start, Lee thought. But he honestly did not have much hope. Older cars were theoretically more EMP proof than newer ones. He had already seen several cars much older than his that were not starting. Lee's nearly new Ford Explorer had all the bells and whistles with all kinds of modern electronics including engine controls. "Good luck," he said quietly under his breath.

Lee got close to his car. He decided to forgo trying the remote door locks. His remote key Fob had a real key attached to it. Hoping to stay out of sight and the minds of others, he moved slowly and carefully to his car. He used the real key to unlock the driver's side door and slide in, throwing the duffel in the passenger seat. The car smelled of burned electronics, which Lee considered a bad sign. He pulled the Ruger from his pocket, placing it one of the cup holders. He put the key in the lock of the steering column and, looking around to ensure no one was close, turned it to the first position. Nothing happened. The normal array of various indicator and warning lamps on the dash panel did not light up. Neither did the GPS entertainment screen. He then turned the key to the crank position. Nothing. Obviously, the electronics in this model even controlled the starter motor. "Well, that answers that. Looks like I am walking," Lee mumbled as he sat there in the dark, worthless pile of metal that used to be a car.

Just to be sure, like everyone else, Lee did get out and open the hood and used his flashlight to look around. Nothing was obvious. Battery was still there. He could smell the same burned odor as the inside. Otherwise, it looked normal. Lee's high technology automobile would probably not be running anytime soon, if ever. The country had perhaps become a massive wrecking yard, with thousands or millions of cars sitting useless. "Five thousand pounds of scrap," Lee said to no one.

Lee climbed back into the car and by hand unlocked the rear door and climbed into the backseat to prepare his gear. Keeping out of sight would minimize the number of people that may see him while getting ready. Lee folded down the right rear seat, slid the Bug Out Bag forward, and opened it up. He pulled out a pair of tan-colored cargo pants and a vacuum-sealed bag containing a tan military undershirt. Lee packed many items, including some of the clothing, in vacuum bags. The vacuum bags shrank bulking clothing down, saving room and keeping everything clean and dry even if the backpack got wet. Quickly he changed into the clothing. He reached over the rear seat for a pair of combat boots he stored loosely in the back. He pulled out two pairs of heavy thick socks, which were kept in the boots. One pair he pulled on and the other pair he stuffed into his BOB with items from his duffel bag. Lee stuffed as much clothing as possible into the main bag. He was expecting a long walk. The BOB had a main bag but also a smaller detachable "chest" pouch. The smaller pouch would strap on over his chest after placing the main bag over his shoulders. Inside were various items, of which

Lee looked through, placing some in the pockets of his cargo pants, including a couple of gas lighters, a multi-tool, a small roll of para-cord, a compass, and an extra flashlight.

Also, loose in the back of the car, Lee had a waterproof plastic EMP proof electronic case. Inside were two five-watt Ham-Band radios, extra batteries, a dipole antenna, a Garman Etrex GPS, and a Samsung Tab3. Lee turned on each of the electronic items to ensure they were working. He did not wait to see if the GPS satellites were working, knowing the garage could slow down that process. The Garman Etrex would be worthless without GPS satellites. The Samsung tablet contained a program which displayed high-resolution Google Earth images, which he had painstakingly downloaded onto micro SD cards. This would provide him close up detailed maps of the entire region from Las Vegas to home in Agua Dulce. The photo images could be of utmost importance for getting home in one piece. As a backup, he had a California map book, which contained detailed maps of the entire state. His maps overlapped from California to Las Vegas. He also had a Vegas city map. Out of the atlas, Lee took the relevant maps and the Vegas city map and folded them with the immediate area on top. He put them into a plastic map case from the chest rig bag.

Lee gathered the electronics, slid them into a special Mylar anti-static bag, then placed the bag into the BOB. He discarded the heavy plastic box. The Mylar would provide protection in case another EMP occurred. Lee dug into the bottom of the BOB and found the fifty-round box of 9 mm cartridges and then pulling out ten rounds and reloading the empty mag. He put the mags into the chest rig. The last loose items were a fanny pack, a heavy jacket, and a "Boonie" hat and a cardboard box. Inside the cardboard box was two plastic half-gallon jugs of water and four square-shaped Fiji bottled waters. Lee always kept the square Fiji bottles as they compacted better into tighter spaces in the bag. The bag had a unique expandable bottom section. He opened it up to full expansion and stuffed in the four small water bottles. Opening one of the large bottles, Lee started to chug down the water as fast as he could. Lee drank the water as if he were preparing for a colonoscopy, sucking down the fluid in large gulps. The second bottle Lee would tie onto his bag. With a possible 250-mile hike home from Vegas to home, water was his most valuable commodity. He knew many tricks to scavenge water, but the more he had to start, the better he would feel.

Lee performed a mental check of the contents of his bag. The bag included about every suggested item the survival prepper community could dream up. There was a variety of food items, including military-style MREs, or "Meals Ready to Eat," high-protein power bars, and emergency survival bars. Spread in various compartments and separate bags were hygiene items, tools, defense, first aid, water treatment, a lock pick, and all kinds of utility stuff from rope to clothespins. Lee did not pack a sleeping bag but instead he preferred the "stay dressed" with a blanket and jacket method. He did carry a hammock so he could rest suspended off the ground and away from bugs and snakes. His preference would be to take inventory and sort out the contents, but he did not want to spend the time. He tied his heavy jacket on top of the bag with the extra bottle of water.

Lee looked around the car for other things worth taking. He had leftover snacks from the ride up. He removed the phone charger and placed it into an outside pouch on his bag. He removed an extra flashlight from the glove compartment and added that to his pack also. He also found a half bottle of Gatorade, which he downed even though it was warm.

When he finished packing, Lee scanned over the car and remaining items once more. He had remorse about just walking away from his car. *Bummer!* he thought. He had extra keys and, for some reason, decided to leave them under the seat. "Never know," he said aloud. He looked at the new Toshiba laptop and sadly stuck it back into the empty duffel bag that he shoved down behind the second and rear seats. The weight of a worthless laptop computer was not something he wanted to add to his load.

Lee pulled the map case out of his chest rig and studied his way out of Dodge. A part of good prepping was to plan routes out of places you may find yourself. Lee had done so for the best route out of downtown Vegas. This was another prepper pastime. Using a sharpie, Lee marked his planned route, memorized as much as he could, and returned the map back into the chest pouch. While in the pouch he retrieved a strap-on headlamp and put it around his fore-head but left the light off. The headlamp, as well as all his flashlights, were dual-lamp type, with white and red light. The red lamps were usable in the dark without losing night vision, and they were not nearly as noticeable from a distance. Lee made sure he was familiar with the red lamp button versus the white lamp button.

It was time to get moving. Lee looked around, and not seeing anyone, he slowly slid out of the rear seat and started putting on the various bags. He did so while trying to remain hidden. First, the fanny pack went on and around his waist, hanging in the front, then the main pack. Once the main bag was on and adjusted, the chest rig went on, attaching to metal rings on the front straps. He had a leg holster for his pistol but decided to forgo wearing it while still in the city. Having a worried, pissed-off cop seeing a side arm would not be wise. He put the pistol into the fanny pack and put a rag over it. The two extra mags went in his front top pocket of the cargo pants. Some extra rounds went into the other pocket.

Shit, this stuff is heavy, Lee thought once he took the full load. He guessed it was at least fifty to sixty pounds. Lee took one last look inside the car to ensure he had not left anything behind, left the doors unlocked, and headed toward the stairs.

Chapter 2

2330, Day Zero, Garrett Household, Agua Dulce, California

Madison Garrett was woken from her deep sleep by the front door slamming and then her youngest son Logan shouting in a frantic voice, "Mom, Mom, wake up, something is wrong."

Madison opened her eyes to a bright light from the upper corner of the room. The LED battery-powered emergency lights were on. Her husband Lee had installed the lamps around the house a few years back. The few times they had come on because of a power outage, they annoyed the heck out of her. The emergency lights did provide decent light in the room. She slid her legs out of bed, arousing the two family cats sleeping on the bed near her legs and feet. She heard Logan again. "Mom!"

"I'm coming, Logan. Calm down," she replied while pushing her feet into her plush house slippers. She looked back to see the time but found the digital clock to be dead. She thought, *Well the power is definitely out.*

Madison came out of the room, finding Logan standing at the bedroom door. She could see him clearly in the living illuminated by another emergency light. She also noticed two plug-in emergency flashlights were shinning up the walls above their respective wall sockets. Emergency socket lights all around the house were another one of Lee's safety items.

"What is it, Logan? You scared me and the cats half to death," Madison asked.

Logan was huffing and puffing and sweating prolifically on his forehead and chest. His shirt was soaking wet. She knew it was not a hot night outside, "So what gives?"

While trying to catch his breath, Logan explained, "I was on the 14 freeway, and all the cars just stopped suddenly, even mine. I managed to pull over to the center divider okay, but a lot of people crashed. I guess they lost control of the cars without power brakes and steering."

"All the cars?" Madison asked.

"Yes, Mom, all of them. After I pulled over and started looking around, I could tell the powers out as far as I could see. I have never seen it so dark. The glow from LA over the mountains is gone. It is pitch-black outside, and you can see a zillion stars."

"Where were you when the car quit, and what did you do?" Madison quizzed Logan.

"I was just about to the Agua Dulce Exit. I did not have to walk far. I grabbed my Bug-out Bag that Dad gave me and walked—well, ran mostly home," Logan answered.

Logan was the youngest of the Garrett children. He was eighteen and still living at the Garrett house while attending college in the San Fernando Valley and working part-time at a restaurant in Santa Clarita. Madison knew he had been working that night and was on his way home from work. Like the other Garrett males, Logan was about 5'11" and lean. He still had a huge head of dark wavy hair, which was out of control at most times day or night. It was a massive mess of tangles after his jog from the freeway. He tried to push it into place, but it was pointless as the thick locks fell as they may around his face.

Madison said, "So it may be all this crazy stuff your dad has done for years might have just paid off. Speaking of your dad, I hope he is all right. I spoke to him earlier tonight before bed."

Logan answered, "It seems like it. Everyone on the freeway was standing around wondering what to do. Most people did not even have water. The people that were a long way from home looked really worried. There was nothing I could do. I gave my water, emergency food, a couple of lighters a flashlight and my emergency blanket to a couple with two small children. After that, I did not stay around. I grabbed my bag and headed here."

Logan continued, "While I was hiking up here, I turned on the little two-way ham radio Dad put in all our bags. I turned it to the FM channel but could not pick up a single radio station. That is not right. I guess with the power out, our TV and satellite are not working either," Logan answered.

"I think it has to be much more than a local power outage Mom. Some of the people on the road said they had heard news broadcasts on the radio just before everything died. The news was saying there was an unconfirmed nuclear explosion in Washington, DC."

Madison froze when she heard Logan's statement. It took her a moment before she could even speak again. "Logan, your dad has some electronics packed in metal boxes out in the main storage shed. One of the boxes says emergency radios. Go get that box. We can see if our base station radio works and try calling the other kids."

Logan headed out the door with a flashlight, and Madison went to the kitchen to check on the refrigerator. She opened the refrigerator door, and it was dark. No light was on, and she heard no sound. She knew Lee had installed a battery system, which was connected to the solar panels. The batteries powered some kind of "converter." She knew it was meant to keep the refrigerator and freezer in the garage running if a power outage occurred. But it was not working.

Logan returned shortly with the large metal case. He sat the heavy box on the dining-room table and he and Madison looked at the label taped to the top.

Emergency radios:

> 1 Ham radio—Preprogrammed to match all por-
> table radios
> 1 battery powered AM-FM-Weather-Short Wave
> 1 crank powered AM-FM-Weather
> 1 spare wire type antenna

1 roof mounted magnetic antenna
Copies of all instructions and manuals

They opened the metal box. It had metal Mylar tape around the seam, which they peeled off. Inside was a lining of thick plastic material, which they folded back, exposing several smaller Mylar bags. Inside one of the bags with a label marked "Ham Radio." Madison pulled out that bag as well as one labeled "battery-powered emergency radio." Logan removed the small ham radio from the shiny protective bag and carried it to a corner cabinet of the dining room. Lee had given the family members instructions of how to install the radio. The cabinet had a power cord and an antenna cord inside one of the upper cabinets. The top of the radio had a taped on laminated card containing instructions.

1. Connect antenna to the back
2. Plug in the power connector
3. Turn on power.
4. Display should read "3-13"—This is the preset frequency that matches all the portable radios.
5. If display does not read 3-13, read the detailed instructions on the back of this card.
6. Once radio is on, press button on mic and talk. Use our planned call signs:
    a. Home = Garrett Base
    b. Melinda and James house = Garrett East
    c. Lawrence's apartment = Garrett West
    d. Portable radios = Garrett mobile 1–6 (age before beauty)

Logan continued to connect the circular connector on the antenna and then the power plug. Both were tricky, but he did so easily. Then he turned on the radio. The small digital screen lit up and after a bunch of random flashing, it stopped and displayed "3-13" just as the instructions said it should.

"So far so good," Logan said.

While Logan had been hooking up the two-way radio, Madison had been rotating the dial and flipping between AM and FM on the small battery-powered radio. She was trying to find a station that was broadcasting. Similar to Logan's experience with the small portable radio, she was not having any luck. She switched to the Short Wave setting and started scanning those frequencies slowly.

Logan then said, "Well, this radio seems to be working, so let's try calling the other kids."

Logan picked up the mic, but just as he did, the radio came to life. "Garrett Base, this is Garrett West. Do you copy?"

Startled, Madison and Logan looked at the radio in shock and then realized that it was Lawrence calling from his radio. Logan answered, "Lawrence, is that you?"

Lawrence called back, "Yes, Logan, it is me. I have been calling for about ten minutes and hoping someone would answer. Are you guys all right? Are you there with Mom?"

"Yes, I am here with Mom. My car quit on the freeway and I jogged here and woke her up. Is the power out at your apartment?" Logan asked.

"Yeah, power is out. Cars and other electronics are dead. My car will not start."

"I just got this radio hooked up and working. I have a hunch Dad might have been right about a lot of this. We are worried about him. He called Mom from Vegas a few hours ago. I hope he is okay," Logan said into the radio mic.

"Don't worry about him. We know he has more stuff and plans up his sleeve than most anyone in the country. He will be okay."

Madison asked for the mic from Logan and said, "I imagine you are right, Lawrence. If your car is out, Lawrence, how will you get here?"

"Richard Silva and his wife live about two miles from here. I am going to pack up some of my stuff and make my way to their house. I will use my mountain bike. My roommate has already left to go to his parents' house that is close to here. I am not sure what they will do from there."

Lawrence was the oldest of the Garrett children. He had enlisted into the Army at the age of eighteen, became an Army Ranger, and had numerous deployments to Iraq, Afghanistan, and other places. Many missions and deployments were so top secret he never told the family about them. He, like Logan, was now attending college working on a criminology degree with hopes of joining one of the three-letter federal agencies. He and a friend from school had rented an apartment in Newhall about fifteen miles from the Garrett house.

Richard Silva was a non-active-duty marine who worked for Lee. He was a stocky 5'9" who believed completely in the saying "Once a Marine, always a Marine." He worked out regularly and went to the range frequently to keep up his shooting skills. Richard and his wife, Dena, had a standing invitation to the Garrett house if a major disaster or emergency occurred. Dena was a short, frail brunette who looked as if a weapon would knock her over if she ever fired one. But Richard was always joking about how Dena could whoop him if she wanted, and Lee figured being a marine, he would be of great help in defense of the house. Richard was agreeable to the arrangement and stored certain things at the Garrett house. The couple had also contributed to the emergency food supplies and other prepper equipment.

"Are you using the large radio or one of the small ones?" Madison asked.

"This is the larger one. I hooked it up like Dad showed us, and I guess it works," Lawrence replied.

"I will bring it with me. I have a large pack. I will bring as much stuff as possible. I will try the smaller radios once I am outside and in a clear spot. Leave your large one on. I guess you have not heard from Mel and James?" Lawrence asked, referring to his younger sister Melinda and her husband James who lived in Acton, about ten miles in the other direction from Lawrence.

"No, we just turned on the radio when we heard you. I think if their radio was on and working, they would have chimed in by now. Maybe they are sleeping and do not even know about the power outage yet."

Lawrence replied and then asked, "You might be right. I guess they will find out in the morning. Have you tried starting up Dad's Mustang yet?"

"No. We did not even think about it. I will have Logan go try right now and call you back. If it is running, we could come and get you and then go see about Mel and James," Madison said.

"No! If it is running that is great, but whatever you do, do not go out in the car. I just witnessed a big knife fight out on the street in front of the apartment over a running old Nissan pickup. It will be nuts on the roads with all the dead cars and stranded people. Crazy people may kill you for that running car. If it is running, lock it up in the shed out of sight. When I get there tomorrow, maybe the roads will have cleared up. Then we can think about going out for Mel."

"Okay, Lawrence. I guess you're right. But if we don't hear from the kids by tomorrow sometime, I am going to be very worried," Madison replied.

"I think they will be okay. You know that James has more guns than Dad does. Melinda is an expert with her 1911. Lawrence said referring to the common military version of the .45-caliber semiautomatic handgun. I bet you hear from them in the morning when they wake up and find out what happened."

Madison then said, "Okay, Lawrence, go and get yourself ready to head out. You be careful also."

"I will, Mom. I will call you back when I can. Keep the radio on. Try to make sure the small solar panel on the outside of the house is charging the radio battery. Logan can check it in the morning when the sun comes up. I think he knows how. If the battery goes dead, you can use one of the car batteries. Bye for now, Mom. Logan, you keep things safe until I get there. Love you, guys," Lawrence said.

"Love you, Lawrence. See you soon. Mom out."

Chapter 3

2245, DAY ZERO, GLENDALE, CALIFORNIA

D ayyan and the rest of his cell had been busy all day. After his cell members had arrived at the repair shop plus the four new men, Dayyan had opened the two envelopes. The Fed-Ex package contained one, and Adham had brought the other. Both the envelopes contained a USB flash drive. Dayyan pulled a laptop computer from a locked cabinet and placed first one and then the other flash drive into the ports. The flash drives had various files, photos, and miscellaneous junk on them. File comparison software confirmed they were identical. The duplication was another safeguard used for operational security. All but one file was worthless junk just used to mix in and make the real file less noticeable.

Dayyan found the file he was looking for. The file had an .mp3 file extension. An icon had been created to make the file appear as a simple music file. He changed the extension to a .txt extension and opened it. It was just a garbled mess. Therefore, he opened a Symantec encryption program and opened the file again using software. The file turned to usable text.

Dayyan saw three locations listed as "immediate targets." The first two were gun stores. The third location was undisclosed. His handler would call and provide him the third target only if the first two targets were attacked successfully. The instructions sternly reminded Dayyan, "Do not open the box until the Time." What time, he did not know, but he suspected it would be sooner than later.

He suspected that clearly, he would know when the time arrived. The file was lengthy with instructions and other useful information. Immediately, Dayyan started giving the men instructions.

Dayyan sent all four of his cell members except for Naseem to the two separate storage lockers Dayyan had rented in other parts of Glendale. The group took the two older trucks, loaded up the contents from both lockers, and returned to the shop. Dayyan gave the men strict instructions to leave all the crates and boxes closed and locked and just return them to the shop. Dayyan did not want to disclose his "stash" to everyone until the event happen. Three of his cell members who had men in splinter cells of their own made phone calls directing the faithful go to three different locations immediately and wait for instructions. Additionally, they were ordered to remain until further contact was initiated.

The shop was hot and smelly with the eleven men remaining all afternoon and evening. Dayyan collected all cell phones and placed them on a center table. For necessary phone calls, the caller would use the phone speaker with others nearby listening. No one was permitted to leave alone. Even when using the small restroom, the door had to remain open. A large order of pizzas ordered from Dominoes arrived early in the evening. Dayyan had used the time to read the more detailed instructions. A list contained a large number of hard and soft targets labeled as "Targets of Opportunity." Another list contained names of sympathizers who may be of value. Dayyan committed as much as his brain could hold to memory. Boredom was setting in while the men waited.

At 10:30 p.m., something did happen. WNN was playing on the Satellite TV. Suddenly an obviously shaken-up newscaster came on and interrupted the scheduled financial show. The newscaster was in the large editorial room instead of the fancy news set. People were running in all directions behind the worried-looking newsman. All of them looked scared and shaken. Something big was happening. The female newscaster spoke in a shaken voice, "Reports are flooding into the newsroom of a massive explosion in the Washington, DC, area. We are trying to get witness reports now, but communications systems are not working…"

The newscaster paused as an assistant handed her a slip of paper which she started reading, "We have reports from outside the metro DC area. People are describing a huge mushroom cloud. Some are also reporting a massive flash as far away as Baltimore. Other reports are coming in of large-scale power fai—" The screen went blank for a moment. Naseem picked up the remote and change to Fox News. The screen was displaying "Fox News Alert" and it appeared as if technical difficulties were confounding the network as it tried to switch to a live person. However, it also went black. Naseem pressed the previous button on the remote and it switched back to WNN. Scrolling text was the only thing on the screen: "Stand by for instructions… this is the emergency broadcast system…this is a real emergency…"

Naseem switched to the local channel 7, Eyewitness News. A newscaster was broadcasting from the news set, "We have many reports of a massive explosion possibly nuclear in Washington, DC. We are trying to get our affiliate correspondents on the phone."

The female to his right broke in, "Phil, we have Eyewitness reporter Gail Sanderglass on the phone. She is calling from Annapolis Maryland. Gail, what can you tell us?"

A broken and static-filled response came, "Diane, we were driving back to our hotel in Annapolis and the entire sky to the west lit up. We then saw an ominous glowing cloud start to form. A shock wave hit us about thirty seconds ago. Our car was rocked strongly. We can now hear dozens of sirens in the background. Three police cars just wen—"

Then that channel also went black.

A few seconds later, the power in the room went out. Dayyan made his way to the workbench and turned on a large lantern style flashlight. His men were standing silent and staring at him and one another. Everyone seemed stunned. The room was silent. Dayyan found several more flashlights and handed them out. Dayyan went to the front of the store, and the others followed. The men lined up at the windows and looked out to a pitch-black street. Dayyan opened the front door and stepped out. No lights were visible except for a few car headlights down the block to the left. Cars were stopped at various places in the street. Many at odd angles and places. None of the cars were moving. He could hear many of them cranking over as the drivers tried to restart the engines. He listened but did not hear any of them restart. People were getting out and opening the hoods of the dead cars.

Dayyan looked at the group of men now surrounding him and spoke. "Well, my brothers, it has begun. A great blow has been delivered to the Great Satan. Our mission now begins. We shall now rise and join the extermination of the infidels. You have been trained for this mission, and it is time to begin."

Dayyan went back inside with Naseem following. Slowly turning one by one, the new army reentered the store.

Chapter 4

2345, Day Zero, Las Vegas, Nevada

Lee walked down the exit stairs of the parking garage and out onto Carson Street between 3rd and 4th streets carrying the backpack, chest rig, and fanny pack. He was trying hard to get a stride going and balance the heavy load. The September night was cool, but he was already sweating from the heavy weight of his pack. Having the packs surrounding him added to the heat buildup and sweat. Sweating this much meant his water use would be high.

Lee turned to the right and headed west toward the railroad tracks. The tracks ran east and west between him and the Interstate-15 freeway to the north. The tracks would be Lee's route out Downtown Vegas. Railroad tracks in general took a straight line and were the shortest and most level routes. Lee knew the streets and freeway were going to be a dangerous place. The stranded people from the electronically fried cars were now without water, food, and help. His large survival bag would be a natural target. Railroad tracks, normally being the last place a person would want to go, would now be the ideal place.

Lee tried to stay in the shadows as he moved along the buildings passing people on the street. The moon was about three-quarters full, having been full a few days earlier. Now high in the sky, it was casting plenty of light, which made walking without a flashlight easy. However, the uneasy feeling of walking down a mostly dark Las Vegas street was haunting. He continually looked around and kept close eye on anyone nearby. People were moving around aimlessly. For the most part, people he saw looked stunned and shocked and were staying with their cars or lurking in small groups talking.

It was about thirteen short blocks to the railroad tracks. When Lee reached Main Street, which was parallel along the tracks, he saw a lot more people. Several stalled or parked taxis were ahead, and a large group of drivers were gathered near them. To avoid them, Lee moved as far out of the street as possible. One of the drivers did call after him, but Lee ignored him and dodged between several broken-down cars as he crossed Main Street.

The smoke from the massive fire was bad and starting to sting Lee's eyes. The orange glow over the freeway was ominous and huge. Lee kept to Main Street for about a block until he found a debris and junk-ridden path that seemed likely to lead to the tracks. The path was worn and littered with broken wine and beer bottles and other trash. As well-traveled as it looked, Lee guessed it to be a homeless path to the railroad tracks.

When Lee reached the tracks, he stopped, took a knee, and remained still for a minute or so to survey the scene. Seeing no one, he got back up, shouldered the pack, and started to move west along the tracks. A service road provided an easy path as long as he watched for litter, debris, or large rocks. Lee worried about being in the open with the moonlight, making him easy to spot. He would need to remain vigilant and keep his head on a swivel. His pack created a large blind spot to the rear, forcing him to spin every fifty paces or so. He would spin to his right then left, looking back for any danger coming up from behind.

Lee walked for about a mile without problems. But his luck ran out. Suddenly out of some debris-ridden buildings on the right, three figures emerged moving out to block his path. Lee slowed but kept moving and, at the same time, reached into the fanny pack and placed his hand on the Ruger. A round was in the chamber and ready to fire.

As Lee got close, one of the dimly lit figures called out, "Hey, bro. Where you heading?"

"Nowhere that is any of your business," Lee said back.

"Shit, man, that is not the way to be with the fucking world falling apart. We might all need to help each other, man."

"Well, I do not have time for chitchat, so you guys need to just move out of my way," Lee said.

"Like, why the fuck should we do that, asshole?" Another of the figures stammered out, obviously half-drunk or stoned.

"Because if you don't, I will blow your dumb-ass heads off," Lee said while pulling the pistol out of the fanny pack and pointing it at the three figures.

"Shit, man, like what the fuck," replied one of the men as they moved back down the bank.

"What an asshole," the other druggie said.

Moving rapidly, Lee walked past them turning and keeping the gun trained on them. Being careful not to stumble, he moved in a sidestep motion. The druggies stood facing him, watching his retreat south. When about forty yards away, Lee turned forward to move faster, figuring they would not follow. He also thought if they did the noise, they would make walking in the rocks and gravel would be loud as hell. He had moved another twenty yards when *thud*—something hit the backpack. Lee spun back around in time to see one of the sleaze balls throw a rock in his direction. In the dark, it was impossible to see it coming, so he did the best to shield his face and head. He dropped to one knee, brought the LC-9 up, pointed it in their direction, and squeezed off six rapid shots: *bang, bang, bang, bang, bang, bang*. The little Ruger spit out the nine-millimeter rounds without any problem or hiccups. Lee never expected a hit at this range with the small short barrel pistol. It surprised him when one man screamed out and fell over into the gravel. The other two turned and ran quickly, leaving their friend lying in the rocks. Lee fired two more shots for good measure, turned, and double-timed down the tracks.

Lee moved rapidly down the tracks. He pressed the release, dropping out the near-empty mag and sliding it to his right pocket while he was moving. He pulled out a full mag from his left pocket and shoved it into gun. After running for several hundred yards, he slowed and stepped behind a signal box and peered back to see if anyone was stupid enough to follow him. Winded and panting hard, he waited a couple of minutes before moving on. Lee thought about the druggies running to the cops. But he thought the police had a hell of a lot more important things to worry about right now. Stoned-out druggies reporting someone had shot at them would be a minor problem for the police right now.

Crouching to catch his breath, Lee stayed put for a few minutes. He pulled one of the water bottles out of the pouch on the fanny pack and took a long drag of the stale water. Lee made a mental note that he should have changed out the stored water more often. "I guess I will do that for the next EMP event," he said aloud, thinking it amusing. It took Lee about five minutes to lessen his heavy breathing. He was still in good shape, but he was not an exercise nut and had not done any serious hiking since a two-day hike up Mount Whitney with some friends. That was about ten years ago. His leg muscles were in decent shape for his age, and that helped. Being out of breath, he decided would be the worst problem on what might be a very long walk home.

Chapter 5

0030, Day 1, Glendale, California

Dayyan waited about an hour after the EMP before opening the sealed box. He had received some training on EMPs and he had read several articles about them. He knew that for this powerful of a pulse, the only real possibility was a nuclear blast at high altitude. A solar eclipse or Coronial Mass Ejection, known as a CME, would not have the power for this level damage. He was convinced an EMP was the cause of the power failure and the dead cars. He had waited to open it to prevent damage if another weapon was detonated.

He pulled the plastic tactical case out of the cardboard box. The high-tech container was sealed with a strip of silver foil tape wrapped around the full perimeter of the seam. He used his knife to cut the tape, opened the box, and found it lined on the inside with the same type of foil tape. A coiled metal-type seal had replaced the normal rubber O-ring. Inside the box was a large plastic bag that contained another Mylar bag, which in turn contained one last plastic bag. Dayyan thought this might be overkill for EMP. But he had gathered a lot of knowledge after reading various technical articles, including the latest Air Force report to Congress. The best scientific minds in the world were not sure how much damage electronics would see during an EMP event.

Inside the final bag was a new Iridium 9505 Satellite phone plus a car charger and four extra batteries. Dayyan installed a battery, powered on the phone, and went outside to check for a signal. It read full strength. He pulled out a list of numbers he had written down from the USB document. He punched in the number listed as "Number One."

A moment later, a man with a thick Middle Eastern accent answered, "Yes, my brother. God is great. Please tell me your status."

Dayyan briefed the man on the situation. After listening, the man said, "You have done well so far my brother. Use your list tonight to start building your supplies. Report to me when you have gathered what you need and have completed your first two target missions. Remember, you will need far more supplies than you and your brothers currently can use. Get as many supplies as you can. Contact me in the morning after your raids. God willing you will do well tonight. God is great, my brother."

The call disconnected.

Dayyan and his team of ten men then opened all the crates and sorted out the equipment. There were plenty of assault rifles, pistols, and ammunition. There were also radios, clothing, tactical vests, and other combat equipment. The men all dressed into plain black pants and black long-sleeved shirts, which each person had brought with them. Each man was issued a semiautomatic pistol and tactical leg holster. Everyone had extensive weapons training, so they went to cleaning and inspecting the guns and loading up the illegal high capacity magazines. Four 12-gauge pump shotguns were distributed.

Two of the newcomers including a skinny, nerdy-looking man named Walter, brought in another large crate, and placed it in the back room without opening. Walter explained that it would be best to leave it closed until needed. Dayyan did not argue. He assumed there was good reason.

They had five running vehicles. Both Dayyan's Suburban and old Dodge were fine. Naseem had bought an old Ford tilt-cab box truck. Like Dayyan, he had previously taken it to a truck shop and had it gone through carefully. Adnan, one of Dayyan's soldiers, had an old Chevy Van, and Ghaith had an older Chevy Suburban. The van the four new brothers had arrived in was a new Ford rental and like millions of other cars nationwide was dead as a doornail. Dayyan assumed the men arrived by airplane and had no choice but to rent a new car. Dayyan had an amusing thought. *Wonder why they did not call "Rent-a-Wreck."*

The men loaded up two to each truck plus three in Dayyan's Suburban. They caravanned on backstreets to the two locations where other men were waiting. Three men were at a home just two miles north. Four other men were waiting at an office building near the Burbank border. Those men also had an old running Chevrolet station wagon. Weapons were provided to all the new soldiers. After everyone was ready, the six-vehicle convoy with sixteen fighters headed to the first target in Burbank.

Chapter 6

0030, DAY 1, RAILROAD TRACKS NEAR DOWNTOWN LAS VEGAS

After the few minutes of rest and reflection, Lee started back down the railroad tracks. Staying to the side of the track and in the shadows, he stayed alert in case the druggies were stupid enough to come looking for him. Lee thought it doubtful; however, the two cowards even came back for their friend. The unlucky drug addict may have bled out from his wounds or would before getting medical help. Lee had some remorse, but right now he could not worry about it. Maybe it would hit him later, but the important thing right now was to keep moving out of town. His family and his home were the reasons driving him now.

Lee walked under several overpasses without issue including the Interstate 15 freeway. At Tropicana, the tracks went over the roads. He did not like the extra exposure, on the overpasses, but he pressed on cautiously. When he reached Hacienda Avenue, it changed back to an underpass, making him relax. But as he approached, he could make out dozens of people on the bridge ahead. He stopped and studied the scene on the overpass for a bit. Too many people had a vantage point on the bridge, where they would probably see him moving by. He looked around and saw that to the west was a large empty field. It was a clear dirt field, but the moonlight would surely expose him. Lee wanted to move southwest, but to do so, he would need to backtrack. To the east, industrial buildings bordered the tracks, and Lee could see a gap between two large buildings. He decided to divert down the trail between buildings. The trail ended at a road, which also headed south under Hacienda. So once again, Lee moved further east into the industrial area. Once he hit Valley View Boulevard, he turned back south across Hacienda, keeping to the west side of the street as much as possible. He tried to stay within the shadows cast by the moon, which was moving closer to the western horizon. Lee continued on Valley View toward Russell Road.

Somewhere after crossing Russell, Lee was approaching an intersection when he saw someone ahead. The dark shadow of a person was moving along the cross street ahead. As Lee tracked him, he made the turn onto Valley View Boulevard and headed south, the same direction as Lee. He came out of the shadow as he turned the corner. In the moonlight, Lee could tell the man was of medium build and height and in good shape. His backpack was smaller, and he was moving faster than Lee. Lee thought he might be someone from the military or a real health nut. He just had that look and was moving like a soldier. As the man turned the corner, he glanced over and spotted Lee. The two were diagonally opposite at the intersection. Lee suddenly realized he too had moved into the moonlight, disclosing himself to the other man. So Lee simply raised his hand in a "Hey there" gesture. The man did not appear as a threat, and he gestured back and kept moving. Lee followed, remaining on the opposite side of the street. The man was gaining distance quickly, convincing Lee he must be active or ex-military. Therefore, Lee gave him the mental name of "Cap" (for Captain) as a way of identifying the man in his mind.

As much as Lee tried keeping up with the man—or Cap, as Lee now kept thinking of him—he was moving too fast. The guy was younger and in much better shape, and with the smaller pack and load, he increased the distance between them as the two moved along Valley View Boulevard.

After a few minutes, Cap was a good block and a half ahead. Suddenly the street lit up. The lights startled Lee. His first thought was the power came on. Quickly, he realized the bright lights were the headlights of a car sitting in the middle of the street near the Captain. Lee moved closer to the right side of the street and deeper into the shadows. Cap was lit up brightly by the lights as he stood midway across the street. Seemingly, the car had occupants, and when Cap walked by, they had turned on the lights. Two figures exited the car from the sides and walked to the front, facing Cap. Cap had turned around, facing the headlamps.

Three other men appeared from the left side of the street and moved behind Cap. He twisted slightly and backed away from the three men approaching from his right rear. Lee was close enough to make out angry voices, sensing immediately this was not good. He continued to move forward slowly and as stealthily as possible, staying in the shadow and using parked cars and bushes to hide his approach.

When Lee had moved to within a half of a block, he started consider that he should divert around what was starting to look like a one-sided confrontation. He did not know these people. Why risk his own exodus from Vegas by jumping into this mess? He was now close enough to hear the conversation and make out words, so he listened as he slid down behind a parked car. With bright headlights facing away from Lee, spotting him would be difficult if not impossible. The lights would be blinding to the men facing them.

Straining to listen, Lee could make out the various people confronting the Captain. One of the men at the front of the car was a tall, skinny black man around thirty years old. Next to him was a shorter figure Lee could tell was an overweight black woman. All three of the figures behind the Captain were skinny young blacks. Lee guessed them to be early twenties or maybe even teenagers. One was very tall, the two others slightly shorter. The three were wearing baggy pants hanging below their butts, high-top athletic shoes, layers of various bright-colored shirts, and ball caps at odd angles. Everybody appeared nervous as they inched their way toward Cap. One man behind Cap was holding a club or bat. Another had a medium-sized knife that he was flipping around in his right hand. The sagging pants forced the three idiots to keep one hand on their waistbands to keep from losing the ugly shorts as they approached the Cap. Otherwise, they would probably trip and fall to the ground. *What a bunch of dipshits*, Lee thought.

"So just what in fuck you doing in our hood man?" The tall man at the front of the car spoke out in a heavy ghetto slur.

"Just passing by. I mean you no harm," replied Cap.

"This hood is my hood cracker man. Me and my woman here was just getting down with things you know. Then you, out-of-place white boy, comes strolling along and ruined our mood. And what's you got in your army bag?"

"Like I said, I mean you no harm. I will be on my way now," Cap said as he started to back across the street, expertly keeping all five men in front of him.

"Well, if you'z gunna be unsociable like man, then perhaps we just gunna take what you gots," the tall man at the car said as he reached behind his back and pulled out a large shiny silver pistol.

The thug pointed the gaudy pistol at the Captain and continued, "Now I asked nicely, but howz 'bouts you just drop that bag down. If you'z lucky, maybe I will not pop a cap in you'z dumb-ass cracker head…muthafucker."

The skinny dipshit held the gun sideways like the movies, so Lee mentally gave him the name of "Hollywood."

Cap froze and put his hands forward in a nonthreatening manner. "Okay now, man, just calm down. If you want this bag so bad, you can fucking have it. It is just my dirty laundry."

Lee was having bad visions of how this would likely play out. He figured this was going to get ugly fast. He doubted they would let the Captain go unharmed. In fact, Lee was certain they would probably shoot him regardless. Therefore, he slowly crouched down and moved slowly and quietly along the parked cars. He made his way around two cars getting closer to the confrontation going on in the street. He slinked up behind the trunk of a parked car and drew the 9 mm. He considered removing his pack but did not want to risk losing it. Keeping the bag on, he felt for the extra mags in his left pocket, making sure they would be easy to retrieve.

As the Captain slowly removed his pack an ugly blathering of racist and slang words came from the five thugs. The assholes were talking shit now as Cap surrendered the pack. While removing the pack, he had continued moving slowly back from the three younger idiots. Lee guessed the Cap was hoping to drop the pack and haul ass. The Captain probably decided it was better to be alive without anything versus just plain dead.

As Cap slid off the pack and set it down, Lee positioned the 9 mm on the trunk of the car and steadied it with a two-handed pistol grip. Hollywood was twenty-five to thirty yards away, making for a difficult shot for the little Ruger LC-9. Nevertheless, Lee figured he had to try. Lee hoped if he could get off a few shots, the idiots may all run like the druggies on the railroad tracks. If the group all started running from the gunfire, Cap might just get away without getting shot. Lee hoped with the car as a shield plus Hollywood, not knowing how to aim a pistol would give him an advantage. At least for several seconds. Lee steadied the gun and aimed it at the side of Hollywood's head. Knowing the LC-9 trigger pull was a foot long, Lee made a mental note to squeeze the trigger. *Don't jerk it.*

Cap was still slowly trying to move away, but just then Hollywood said, "Where you fucking going, man? We aint'z done with you'z honky chicken shit gleaming white ass yet."

"Say goodbye, fucker." Hollywood lifted the silver pistol up directly at Cap.

Hollywood was going to shoot, so Lee held his breath and squeezed the trigger on the little 9 mm. His grip was steady on the trunk lid, and the iron sights of the pistol lined up with the side of Hollywood's head. However, just as the trigger snapped and the pistol went off; the fat, ugly woman moved forward and into the line of fire. That was her shitty luck as the round was already heading down range. Blood and screams erupted. The round removed most of the fat woman's nose off her fat round face as it flew by at high speed. Not hitting a major bone on the woman's face, the bullet continued straight, hitting Hollywood right below his right ear. His head flew sideways as the gun dropped from his hand, and he slumped over headed for the asphalt. Lee squeezed off another round in the same direction, hitting Hollywood again as he slumped to the ground. The fat woman fell back against the front of the car blocking one of the headlights while screaming like hell and holding her now noseless face. Lee slid the gun quickly right and lined up the sights on the closest of the other three thugs. As soon as the sights of the small gun lined up, he squeezed off two quick rounds and that asshole dropped to the ground.

The remaining two men were too close to the Captain for Lee to safely take a shot. It did not matter. When his first shot had gone off, the three had frozen in place, not understanding what had just happen to their dipshit leader. Cap reacted quickly moved forward, grabbing the arm of the club-wielding thug and yanking him forward and past. Expertly, Cap pulled the arm back and around thrusting it up behind the man. The shocked idiot screamed out in pain from the probable dislocated or broken shoulder. The last man did not wait around. He turned and ran like a running back of the NFL and headed into a large parking lot of a store.

Hollywood was lying motionless and did not appear to be breathing. Lee assumed he was dead. The woman was screaming like a banshee, and blood was spurting from her face like a showerhead. Lee ran from behind the car heading toward Cap. Cap looked at Lee holding the 9 mm and the two throbbing jerks lying at his feet. He realized this stranger had intervened just in time. Lee moved close to the screaming woman and Hollywood. The side of his head was a mess, and a large pool of blood was forming. The low-life bully would not threaten anyone again. Lee reached down, picked up the chrome pistol, and moved toward the Captain.

"Thanks, man. I think you saved my ass," the Captain said.

"No problem. These crap sacks were already assholes. But they decided to become super assholes because the shit has hit the fan," Lee replied.

Cap reached out his hand to shake the savior's hand, but instead Lee handed him the ghetto pistol and said, "Take this. I assume you know how to use it."

"Shit, yes," Cap said.

Cap examined the semiautomatic pistol pulling back the slide to see if a round was in the chamber. Then popping out the mag, he examined it to find it had a full fifteen rounds. This meant Hollywood never got off a shot.

"Nine millimeter," said Cap.

"That is lucky, same as mine," Lee replied.

Lee and the Captain heard a commotion from the store parking lot the thug had run to. Loud shouting was coming from a large group of people who were gathering. The crowd was building and starting to move toward Lee and Cap. The woman on the ground had quieted some as shock set in, but she stirred as she heard her fellow losers heading over.

"We best get the fuck out of dodge," Lee said while turning and heading down the street.

"Agreed," Cap said, as he scooped up his pack and took off alongside Lee.

They heard the loud voices from the approaching crowd. "Those mothas killed YZ."

"Let's go fuck them up," another from the mob chimed in.

The angry yells and screams started rolling together, but nothing sounded good.

Cap and Lee were double-timing west down the cross street. Lee's age was quickly becoming a hinder to the younger and faster man. He was too old for running at speed for long with sixty pounds of gear. Cap was starting to pull ahead, but he slowed, and then reaching back, grabbed Lee's chest strap, helping to pull him along. They continued running down a long block, making a left turn on the next cross street. At the next corner, they turned to the right and across the street, heading toward a row of industrial buildings. Looking back as they made the corner, they could see about ten people, including a couple of people on bicycles chasing them.

Lee and the Captain ran along past several buildings. They were crossing a driveway between two large buildings leading to the back parking lot. A large chain link gate was open slightly. Cap stopped abruptly and pointed. "This way."

The two men slid through the gate, and Cap closed it behind them. Cap stopped and wrapped the lock chain around the two gateposts. He hoped this would fool the chasing thugs into believing the gate was locked. Lee had already started down the driveway, and Cap closed the distance behind him. As they ran between the buildings, they could see flashlights bouncing off buildings in the street and shouting at the mob as they kept up the pursuit.

Making it to the rear parking lot, Lee and Cap slowed as they came to a tall brick wall, running along behind all the rear lots. Cap hesitated, and then seeing a dumpster against the wall, he pointed and led Lee in that direction. Cap obviously had a plan, and he was taking Lee along.

"On the dumpster and over the wall," Cap said to Lee.

Cap jumped up on the lid, turned, and reached out helping Lee do the same. With the pack on Lee would have a tough time trying to climb on top, but Cap grabbed the pack and, with a swift pull, just reeled Lee up alongside him on the lids. They both moved toward the brick wall and looked over. The wall separated the lot from a large dirt field. The drop was about eight feet. Both men swung over the wall. Cap landed first turned and slowed down Lee's fall as he plummeted down rapidly with the heavy pack.

Standing against the wall, the men looked around the barren field to assess their choices.

Lee spoke first. "It is getting light out. If we head across this field, we will be in the open."

Cap replied, "Let's stay near the wall then keep moving along as far as we can. We will be harder to spot."

Without further discussion, the Cap, followed by Lee moved along the wall to their right. They slowly and quietly moved about a block. The wall ended and a small side street crossed in front of them. The wall stopped twenty yards short of the street. Shrubs bordered the field to the edge of the street creating a visual wall. Both men moved forward, keeping below the bushes. The men knew the cross-road fifty yards right of them was the same road they had left when ducking between the buildings. As they watched the mob entered the intersection, meaning the phony lock on the gate must have worked. People were yelling and pointing of flashlights in all directions. Obviously, the thugs wanted to find the men who had killed their fellow crap sacks. Daylight was coming rapidly now. Lee and

Cap stayed low and hidden behind the thick bushes. Alternatively, they could retreat to the wall, but that seemed like a bad idea.

After much pointing and yelling, the two thugs on bicycles turned and headed down the street in Lee and Cap's direction. Someone had thought about looking behind the buildings. The two bike riders came down the street, looking toward the bushes where the two men were hiding.

Without any discussion or warning, the Captain sprung from his crouch and ran along the bushes just as the first rider was passing an abandoned car near the curb. The hood was still up and this offered Cap some shielding as he sprinted at full speed toward the bike and rider. He hit the stunned rider with the force of a bus. Cap lifted the surprised thug right off the bike and, using his weight and momentum, tossed the small teenager through the air for about twenty-feet. The shocked kid skidded on his face and hands and rolled into a pile. With rider gone, the bike to continue rolling upright for about thirty feet and fell over against the curb.

The next biker had no time to react to the surprise attacker. He tried desperately to stop or steer around. He stopped just short of the captain. That was a bad mistake. Cap reached over the handlebars, yanked the stunned teen up and over, slamming him into the pavement with a sickening thud.

Lee had followed out behind Cap. As Cap was body slamming the second man, he moved over to the first just as the stunned teenager tried to stand up. Lee did a running drop kick on the side of the kid's head, knocking him over and out.

"Grab the other bike." Cap said while staring to mount the one he had just abruptly stopped.

Without answering, Lee ran down the street pulled the first bike from the curb, and climbed on. Both he and the Cap started pedaling and gaining control of the bikes. Several shots rang out from the intersection. They did not look back. They just pedaled as quickly as possible, hoping the rest of the hood had nothing but pistols and not any more bikes. Lee and Cap rode down the street heading southwest and turned the corner to the right on what Lee guessed was Sunset Street.

When they got close to Decatur, Lee yelled forward at Cap, "Turn left."

Cap waved and complied, and they both made the turn south on Decatur, heading toward the 215 overpass. The number of people outside kept increasing as they rode. Some were standing around dead cars. People were walking solo, or in groups of two, three, or more. With no wish to stop for any purpose, Lee and Cap kept up their speed and momentum. The light made everything visible now. As they cycled out of the 215 overpass, one man from a group of three moved into the street toward their path. Cap did not veer. Instead, he pulled the large chrome pistol up in his right hand and pointed it at the man, heading toward him and Lee. The surprised man stopped dead in his tracks and then stepped back, raising his hands as he did. Cap, with Lee following, cruised by not slowing or looking back. The man yelled some obscenities at the bikers but did nothing else.

As they rode, the two men occasionally looked over to their right, where they could see a huge column of smoke. A massive fire was out of control and growing rapidly. Lee remembered there was a large mall west on the 215 a couple of exits; he guessed that it was burning. This probably meant that more assholes like the ones that they had just faced were taking advantage of the dire state the city was in, looting and burning buildings as they went. Lee wondered what drove thugs and looters to burn down stores and buildings after stealing and looting anything of value?

The two men kept riding silently for a couple more miles, occasionally looking back. They started to enter residential subdivisions and now saw dozens of people out, mostly talking in groups. However, Decatur remained clear of people and abandoned cars. The ride was starting to wear down Lee exhausting him. He started falling back. Picking a place along the road, bordered large fields on both sides, the Captain rolled off the pavement into the dirt field on the right. They both dismounted the bikes and, for the first time, had a chance to talk and formally meet.

Cap held out his hand. "Jake Rodriguez. I can't thank you enough for what you did back there."

"Lee Garrett, not a problem. Those shit bags deserved what they got," Lee said, returning the hardy but now sweaty handshake, thinking he now had a real name for the Captain.

"No argument with me. I am sure glad you came along. I spotted you behind the car but was not sure what you had planned. Sure thankful you were armed. You seem to have everything, including the kitchen sink. Geez, that is a huge pack!" Jake said.

Lee explained, "Yeah I am one of those nutcase preppers. I carry this crap with me all the time, but I sure wish I had brought along an AR. I didn't think those thugs were going to let you walk away. You look like military?"

Jake replied, "Good guess. Actually, it is Sergeant Rodriguez, 11th Armored Cavalry out of Fort Irwin. I am not a captain as you have been calling me. I work for a living. I was in Vegas just for a couple of days of fun and excitement. I got more excitement than I had planned. I think something big has hit the fan. Might be world war three. What about you? You seem to know what you are doing around guns, and the way you pack looks military to me."

Lee continued his introduction, "No, just a military buff. I do work with the DOD on military projects. Stuff like pyro and special effects for training centers. I did some stuff for Fort Irwin a few years back for one of the MOUTs." Lee assumed the soldier would know the terms DOD for Department of Defense and that a MOUT was a training center resembling a real town.

"No shit. Well, you move well for an old dude who is not a vet. What do you think happened?" Jake asked.

Lee answered, "My guess is the US has been attacked with nuclear weapons. The power outage and the cars being damaged had to be an EMP. An EMP is the only thing that explains it. There was some talk of a nuke from people in the casino, and I heard the TVs went to the emergency broadcast signal just before the power quit. I hit the bricks as soon as the shit storm started."

Jake replied, "I was at the Luxor playing craps in the casino when the lights went out. I guess you can call that crapping out. Took me a while to get to my room and jimmy the door open. I grabbed my bag and decided it was best to get out of Dodge. People were already fighting in the casino, and it was getting real fucking scary. I figured I'd be needed back at base if World War III has started."

"So where are you heading now, Jake?" Lee asked.

"One of the civilian employees from the base lives in Sandy Valley. He lives there with his wife. I visited them a couple of times on weekends. I am hoping he was home. I figure to head there and see if he and I can figure out a way back to Fort Irwin. As I said, I had better get back to base. What is your plan?" Jake said.

"I live in a small town called Agua Dulce, near Valencia. Have you ever heard of it?" Lee asked.

Jake nodded and said. "Yeah, I do. It is by those funny looking rocks along the 14 freeway south of Palmdale. I had a buddy whose parents lived there. I went a couple of times and did some horseback riding. They had a nice ranch with horses and other livestock."

Lee continued, "Exactly right. Lots of horse property and large spreads. I have five acres, but not any horses. I do have a shit pile full of prepper stuff. Getting back home is my goal. Funny, however, is that I have planned for this event just in case and my plan included heading to Irwin as a stopping point. I figure the 15 freeway is a death trap. The people on the roads are stuck, out of food, water, and most Americans are too fat to walk a mile let alone twenty or thirty. They will look at our bags like a Wal-Mart. I am not going near the freeway. I have planned to use the power lines roads that run from north of Stateline near Sandy Valley due west and pass along near Irwin and on to Barstow. The power line road is a straighter shot than the freeway, although it is dirt and probably goes up and down hills a lot."

Jake looked amazed. "You have this planned out in advance?"

"I always say better to make a plan and not need it than need a plan and not have one. I have the route all scoped out and loaded on a Garmin. I also have satellite images of the entire route on a Samsung tablet. As I said, I am one of those nutcase preppers. I am smart enough not to plaster my face and house on that TV show. That would just let all the lazy shits in town know where I am and what I have," Lee said.

"Man, you are prepared," Jake said with wonder and followed with, "All I have is a road map I got at a gas station on the way out of town. What was your plan for transportation?"

"Well, I have a few ideas floating around, including construction equipment, such as utility carts, front loaders, or even off-road type forklifts. I plan to look for whatever mode of transport might still be running. I figure most diesels should still be running. Maybe not one of the newer ones in passenger cars like the VWs or Ford Trucks. They rely too much on electronics. Another alternative I was thinking of was a bike. Well, thanks to those scumbags back there who loaned us these. By the way, these look brand-new," Lee said as he reached over and found a price tag hanging on the one he was riding.

Jake laughed. "Yeah, I don't think they need them anymore. Thankfully, they look like decent mountain bikes. I bet they busted into a bike store ten minutes after the power went out. They being scumbag assholes is lucky for us now."

Lee pulled out the Samsung and showed Jake the Google Hybrid map images he had painstakingly stored on the device. The maps were by areas, on removable Micro SD cards. After showing Jake the tablet the two of them compared notes on water and food. Lee had a large stash of food and a few gallons of water. Jake had six one-liter bottles and a bunch of snacks and fast food that he paid cash for at the same store he got the map.

Jake explained, "I'm was lucky to have a lot of cash. I had been doing well in the casino and cashed out a bunch of chips an hour before the power went out. The convenience store was about to be overrun. Most people did not have cash they were pissed off because the owner would not give them credit or pass stuff out free. It looked to me like a group of young thugs was getting ready to rush the place when I left."

They decided their chance meeting was a great break for both of them. Jake offered to carry some of the extra load Lee had. That was a blessing for Lee. He started by giving Jake one of the half-gallon jugs of water. Lee gave Jake one of the twenty-five round boxes of 9 mm so he would have extra rounds if they ran into further trouble. Lee had two large knives, so he gave Jake one with a belt holster.

As the two of them looked over the map, Lee pointed out the dirt road that turned off state Highway 160 to Goodsprings. Lee thought it would be safer and shorter than following Highway 160 around to the north. The paved road would be easier but longer. The route they would take would be a dirt road, but Lee guessed the dirt would be hard packed and suitable for the bikes. Both bikes were heavy-duty style mountain type. With the fat tires and fifteen speeds, the bikes would work well except in deep sand or steep hills. The two new friends agreed riding the bikes most of the time beat walking all the time. From Goodsprings, they would continue west toward Sandy Valley. The only worry Lee had about the planned route was they would first have an eight-mile ride north on Highway-160, a major road that headed from the southern part of Vegas to Pahrump.

The men looked to the east to see the sun coming up over Vegas. They could see no fewer than thirty large dark columns of smoke. As they watched, new columns started. Jake said, "Well, it looks like all the zombies are out rioting and looting." The two agreed, getting out of Vegas was the right call.

They mutually decided to take a short break and suck down some water-and-energy-drink mix and eat some of the snacks and power bars before mounting back on the bikes. Lee dug into his bag and pulled out two small handheld radios with headsets. He checked the power, frequency, and then attached the throat microphones and handed one to Jake.

Lee said, "They are not as good as military or police stuff. But they are definitely better than those cheap GMRS radios that you can get at the sporting goods stores with those bogus claims of thirty-mile range. Those radios are lucky to reach thirty yards."

Lee explained the operation of the radios to Jake. "I have the frequencies preprogrammed into the radios. They have a low power and high-power setting." Lee pressed the keypad and other buttons, setting the A frequency for low power on a channel. Then he set the B frequency for the same channel but high power. "While up close, we use the lower power to keep discreet. They have privacy codes, but it might be best to remain discreet. If we get separated by distance or obstacles, switch to the higher frequency."

Lee then explained the other frequencies and how he based the numbers on months. "For example, January was 1, February 2 and so on. If you want to change frequencies, use any hint to signal a new month for example, go to Independence Day. That would mean switching to July or frequency 7. The privacy codes for each month are the month plus 10. So, frequency 7 uses a privacy code of 17." The starting frequency that Lee set on the radios was March or 3, with a privacy code of 13.

Lee replaced the short antennas with longer ones and put on a throat microphone. He showed the separate push to talk buttons on the throat mic then tested the radio with Jake responding on his own. Jake did the same. Both radios and microphones worked loud and clear. Lee gave Jake an extra battery pack. Lee had a pouch on his utility pack for his radio. He had an extra small utility bag hanging on his backpack shoulder strap. Lee undid the small pouch, and they rigged it to Jake's bag to hold his radio. Now the men could talk while riding.

Chapter 7

0115, Day 1, Burbank, California

Dayyan led the convoy through the streets of Burbank. They had to avoid dead cars and, more importantly, people who all tried to stop them for help. Many times, they resorted to pointing guns out of the truck or car windows to move people back from the vehicles. They had only seen two police officers. They were on foot and turned to watch the convoy of running trucks and cars. The officers tried flagging down the convoy, but Dayyan sped up and drove by the policemen with the rest of his convoy of vehicles following closely behind. This stunned the two police officers, but they did not know how to react.

The convoy finally arrived at the gun store on Magnolia Boulevard, and Dayyan pulled around the back into the alley. He ordered the men over the tactical radio to keep two vehicles in front and to take up defensible positions to guard against any police or nosy intruders. The other four vehicles, including the box truck, pulled down behind the store. Two of the smaller trucks took up positions to block and defend the small alley.

While most of the men stood guard, two men took a large gas-powered abrasive saw to the rear door of the gun store. Fire departments and rescue workers nationwide used the same design saw for entering burning buildings or performing rescue operations. The heavy steel door with multiple locking bolts was no match for the huge saw blade, and it opened within two minutes. The alarm system was blaring as they opened the door, obviously working off a battery. Dayyan did not care. No power, phone, or radio signals would go out to warn the police of the break in. If the police received the burglar alarm, which Dayyan doubted, with their own cars dead, how could they respond?

Just after getting the door open, a man yelled loudly from a wooden fence on the other side of the alley. "Hey, what the fuck are you guys doing?"

Dayyan looked at the man and then calmly drew his .45-caliber pistol and shot a round closely over the man's head. He fell back into the yard. Loud screaming came from behind the fence.

Dayyan turned to one of his sentries and said, "Keep an eye on that yard in case someone else is that stupid."

With the door open, four men plus Dayyan and Naseem went into the store. Using bolt cutters and the saw as needed, they cut into all the interior security locks, cables, and safes and removed the items they came for. They took all the assault weapons, including AR, AK-type, or any other military-type rifle. They took tactical 12-gauge shotguns. They also swept up all the semi-auto pistols. They gathered ammunition for the types of weapons they had taken and tactical gear such as vests, packs, chest rigs, etc. It took about twenty minutes to load up what they wanted in the four rear trucks. When the men finished, Dayyan brought back a gallon can of gasoline from his truck. He opened the can, poured it on the shelves of remaining ammunition lit a road flare, tossed it in, and returned to the truck.

The convoy formed up again and drove east. Once they cleared the Burbank downtown and found an isolated parking lot the convoy stopped and redistributed the weapons and gear. While they were sitting in the parking lot, moving things around, an old 1950s vintage flatbed truck came down the street. Dayyan signaled two men who quickly ran out and pointed their AK-47s at the front of the truck. The driver slammed on the brakes and desperately tried shifting to reverse. Before he could move backward, the first soldier was at the right-side window, shooting into the cab, killing the two men inside. Two other men jumped off the flatbed and ran.

Dayyan told his men to drag the two bodies out of the truck. The two soldiers who captured it jumped in to drive the newly gained truck and the convoy once again headed east. Their next target would be a larger gun store in Pasadena.

They were once again working their way through small streets and trying to avoid dead cars. Twice the convoy was forced to make a U-turn and go a different route. As they were getting close to the store on Arroyo Parkway, Dayyan saw a huge Pasadena Police Department armored truck cross in front of them on California Street heading west. Dayyan recognized it as a Bearcat brand. It had large letters "SWAT" on the sides.

Dayyan radioed Naseem in the Dodge crew cab behind him. "Did you see that running armored truck. I want to follow it for a bit. Let's see what it is doing. You and the others fall back. I will follow it at a safe distance."

Dayyan followed, staying about two blocks back. The truck had working headlamps and taillamps, making it easy to keep track of. Dayyan had shut his lights off and was navigating by the little remaining moonlight. Suddenly the big armored truck slowed and turned into a parking lot. Dayyan carefully moved closer and stopped about a block away.

Dayyan said to Adham, "Move over and take the wheel and stay alert. If something happens, take off and find the others."

Dayyan stepped out of the truck and walked slowly up the street. When he got to the parking lot, he could see the armored truck in front of a supermarket. There was a couple dozen people in the parking lot. Dayyan at first thought the police might be trying to quell a potential riot or break in at the market. People were probably getting anxious about the situation and out looking for potential food and water sources.

As he watched, the back door of the big truck opened, and three cops got out. They were all dressed in military-type gear. One was carrying an AR-style rifle. They moved around the truck, joining another cop who climbed out of the driver's front door. They moved to the front of the store and started talking to employees from the market.

Dayyan got on the radio again. "Naseem, bring three cars and park with Adham. Then move up to my location on foot with your guns and extra magazines. Bayas, take two trucks and circle around the back on Palmetto Street. Park and come around the west side of the store. Let me know when you are in position on the side of the building. Do not expose yourselves."

When Naseem and four other men got up to Dayyan, they handed him a rifle, and they all moved quietly down the street using the Bank of America building for cover. The men had AR15 rifles with low-light scopes. Dayyan signaled the men to follow him, and he moved along the bank building keeping low. They used parked cars for cover. Dayyan moved to a place in the parking lot, where he had perfect visibility of the armored car and the four SWAT officers who were standing with a large group of people.

He now understood the reason the police had come to the store. Several people who looked like employees were pushing shopping carts full of stuff out of the store to the back of the truck. It was clear to Dayyan the police were gathering supplies for themselves. The cop with the AR15 rifle climbed into the back of the truck, sat down the rifle, and stepped back out. All four cops were near the rear of the truck and in clear view of Dayyan and his men.

Dayyan whispered to his men who had lined up behind two parked cars, "Target your man from left to right by the same order we are standing here. "Bayas, are you in position?"

"Yes, we just got here. I can see the armored car and the police," Bayas answered over the radio.

Dayyan was using an earpiece and throat mic, so he did not have to worry about the radio transmission alerting anyone near the store.

"When you hear us fire, you shoot and attack," Dayyan said into the radio, and then to his men, he said, "Ready to fire in 5-4-3-2-1... fire!"

All five men shot at once and kept shooting. Three of the four officers went down hard. Only one cop managed to take cover behind the large truck. The civilians ran in multiple directions. Dayyan kept firing at the cops on the ground. He also kept shooting at the one behind the truck. Shooting started from the west side of the store, and Dayyan could see his other soldiers pouring out from behind the building and putting the last officer in a cross fire.

"Follow me," Dayyan now shouted, and he ran forward, shooting as he moved. His men followed. The police on the ground had all fell silent. Their ballistic vests had protected them initially, but as Dayyan's soldiers got closer using headshots, the surprised officers had no chance. They had fought hard with only their service pistols. The man behind the truck also went down. Dayyan's men from the corner of the building had flanked him.

Dayyan quickly checked out the truck to ensure there were not any other police hiding inside. He looked into the cab and found the keys still in the ignition. "Naseem, take this truck and drop us off at the other vehicles. The rest of you back to your cars. Quickly! Meet three blocks east just past the railroad tracks."

Dayyan and his group jumped into the back of the armored car and sped away, leaving the four Pasadena Police officers lying in pools of their own blood. The big truck alone was a big victory. Inside, Dayyan found five assault rifles, four shotguns, and six tear gas grenade launchers, plus hundreds of rounds of ammunition. One of the men opened a large Pelican case and found four sets of generation three night vision goggles. These were a huge added score to this deadly raid.

When the now larger convoy arrived at the Pasadena gun store, Dayyan pulled the armored car up to the side door. He was stunned when the door opened and two armed men walked out approaching the truck. Dayyan guessed they had looked through a view port in the heavy door, saw the Pasadena Police truck, and assumed it was the police coming to help secure the store. The mistaken assumption would cost them their lives. Naseem jumped out the right door, and Hamden jumped out the back of the Swat truck.

Before the men from the gun store could react, bullets were flying. Both men went down with multiple gunshots to the torso and head. One managed to get several shots off from a .45-caliber carbine rifle. One of those shots hit Hamden in the chest, knocking him back several feet. After making sure the two guards were dead,

Dayyan and Naseem went to the fallen soldier, who was lying on the ground clutching his chest. Dayyan looked down and said, "This is a serious wound, my brother. You may not survive."

Hamden's eyes met Dayyan and he said, "I should have taken one of the vests from the policemen we had killed, but we did not have the time. I am...proud to have served with you my brother." He tried to speak further, but blood started running from his mouth and nose. Dayyan knew he would die. He reached over and rubbed Hamden's forehead. His eyes closed, and he took in one last breath and was gone.

"Go with God, my brother," Dayyan said.

Dayyan stood and directed two men from another truck to move him out of the parking lot and cover him with a tarp. They did not have time to deal with a burial.

The Pasadena gun store was a treasure chest of arms. With the newly confiscated flatbed and the armored police truck, they took hundreds of new assault rifles, pistols and thousands of rounds of ammunition. They did not face any more resistance as they loaded the loot and headed back to Glendale. And as in Burbank, Dayyan set fire to the store and its remaining weapons and ammunition.

Chapter 8

0830, Day 1, Garrett Household, Agua Dulce, California

Madison and Logan had been up most of the night. Using the battery powered two-way radio system Logan continued trying to contact Melinda and James but had no luck. He asked a couple of times about taking the Mustang and going for them, but Madison was still against that idea. She was convinced the roads would be hell and very dangerous.

Logan looked through a binder Lee had had created containing a multitude of instructions to follow for emergency situation. Husband and Father Lee had been nothing less than anal on making lists of things to do and ways to prepare.

Logan found a section containing instructions for the power inverter. "The solar panels are connected and will provide AC power to the house whenever there is sunlight. There is a DC power system to run the 8000-watt inverter. The inverter is disconnected, removed, sealed, and inside the EMP proof metal cabinet in the storage shed. I keep it protected to prevent damage from an EMP or massive power surge. The solar panel inverter and battery charger are hooked up at all times. There are extras of both of those items in the large metal cases in the shed."

Instructions explained how to handle a complete power failure:

1. Power down the main breaker.
2. Turn off all the main house circuit breakers.
3. Plug the inverter into the large battery connection and the large AC connector. They are different, so you will not be able to mix them up.
4. Turn on breakers for the large kitchen refrigerator and extra garage refrigerator.
5. Turn on the breaker for the smaller house water pump. The pump and refrigerators run off the batteries.
6. Unplug all the electrical appliances in the house unless they are specifically needed. If needed, only use them during the day or turn off the refrigerator
7. Only use the LED lighting systems.

Additional Instructions explained other things to do:

- During the daytime, the power inverter should be shut off to allow the batteries to recharge.
- If the water tank is getting low:
  1. Turn off the refrigerators.
  2. Turn on the well pump and let it replenish the water tank as needed.
  3. Once filled, turn it back off and turn the refrigerators and house pump back on.
- The solar panels should be able to keep up on a daily basis and keep the batteries charged. If not, there are extra twelve-volt solar panels that can be set up in the yard to charge single batteries. Extra batteries could be scrounged up. Once charged, any two of like size can be connected in series to provide another 24-volt bank. The inverter runs on 24VDC.

There were detailed instructions on testing the solar inverter and battery charger. This testing would need to be completed during daytime. Logan would do that later when the sun was out in full. For now, the refrigerators and house water pump were working.

There were other instructions for all kinds of things. An index in the front of the binder had the following chapters:

1. Security
2. Water Conservation
3. Septic Considerations
4. Food Items: Storage Locations and Use
5. Electronics
6. Vehicles
7. First Aid and Medical
8. Contact Information for Families and Friends
9. HAM Radio Information
10. Garden Preparation
11. Survival Manual Listing (Manuals in Survival Storage Shed)
12. Miscellaneous Items in the Survival Shed

Logan and Madison perused the binder to see what other information was contained. Madison commented, "I sure hope your dad is home before we need to figure out this stuff."

"I am sure he will be rolling in anytime, Mom," Logan said. "Meantime, we might as well get working on stuff. Dad will be unhappy when he gets home, and all we've been doing is sitting around eating Bonbons."

Madison laughed. "But it is his fault we have Bonbons because the freezers are still working. Or we could tell him we decided to eat all the ice cream in case the freezer convertor gizmachi or whatever it is called quits working."

Chapter 9

0845, Day 1, Highway 160, West of Las Vegas, Nevada

Jake and Lee rode along at a comfortable pace, keeping in touch on the radios. They both wished like hell the bikes had storage racks for the backpacks or at least some of their gear. But they agreed they could not be choosy about the free bikes. Lee joked to Jake that he guessed the two shit bags that had stolen the bikes did not look for ones with accessories. They discussed that not having spare tires or patch kits was worrisome. Lee told Jake the story of how a pro motorcycle rider had once finished the Baja 1000 with a blanket (borrowed from a local Mexican family) wrapped around his front wheel. Jake laughed and said they should keep their eyes out for a blanket.

They had seen a few people walking. People acted leery and were keeping their distance from one another. This was resulting in little interaction between strangers. They lost count of the numbers of abandoned cars they passed on the roads. Occasionally, they would see a running car, but only older cars, trucks, utility diesels, and a couple of older school buses. The trucks and the buses were crammed full of people. Jake and Lee suspected the packed vehicles had been picking up stranded motorists along the highways. Lee commented to Jake, "It's good to see some good people are helping out others."

Lee and Jake decided to keep the bikes and stick to their plan. Abandoning the bikes for a ride to somewhere did not make sense.

Lee kept an eye on the Garmin, checking the programmed route. After about an hour on the highway, they came to the dirt road, and Lee radioed Jake to turn to the left. They turned onto the hard packed and level road. The road quickly worsened into soft dirt and up and down hills. The riders used caution, carefully steering around strewn broken glass all along the road. Clearly, the users of this road just tossed out glass bottles as they drove along.

Both men had to dismount the bikes several times and push them up hills or through deep sand. It was grueling, but they still figured the easy parts made up for the hard parts. They stopped several times to rehydrate and snack on something light. They knew the importance of keeping up their energy and body fluids. Lee determined on the Garman GPS that this dirt road was about sixteen miles long. Thankfully, the design of the mountain bikes was well suited for loose soil and dirt and had fifteen gears to deal with the steep hills. Luckily, neither bike suffered any flat tires, which was great considering all the crap on the soft dirt road.

Finally, around 12:30, the road improved, and the two riders headed down a hill and reached a paved road. Lee's GPS identified the road as the Goodsprings Bypass, and they could see the buildings of Goodsprings in the distance.

Chapter 10

0915, Day 1, Glendale, California

Dayyan and his small army had returned to Glendale just after dawn. After leaving the burning gun store in Pasadena, they had seen few people and faced no resistance or police. Dayyan split his small army into three groups. Naseem drove the armored Bearcat to a furniture store that one of the men managed. Several other vehicles went with that group. Naseem drove the SWAT truck inside the back warehouse to hide it.

Dayyan had just returned to the appliance store when the satellite phone rang. He answered, "Yes, my brother?"

"I trust your first missions have gone well?"

"Yes, better than expected. We have hundreds of weapons and thousands of rounds of ammunition, and God rewarded us with a police SWAT truck," Dayyan said.

Dayyan went on recounting the story of capturing the truck and killing of the police officers.

"Yes, my brother, you have done well. Now I have another mission for you that should greatly strengthen your army."

Dayyan took out his notepad and wrote down two addresses as he listed intently to the man on the phone. When the man finished, Dayyan simply answered, "God willing this will go as well as our last mission." The call disconnected.

Dayyan used one of the tactical radios to call Zufar with the third group. They had gone to a large secluded house about a mile north in the foothills. He relayed the first address and told Zufar to take his force and go to the location. "Look for four men in an old Ford van to pick up. Once you find them return to the furniture store, where we will form up for the next mission."

About forty minutes later, the entire convoy was ready to roll again. Their fleet now consisted of nine odd trucks and cars, including the SWAT truck. Dayyan's men used paint, tape, and cardboard to cover all the lettering on the police truck. Foolish or curious people were chased away at gunpoint. The now larger group of twenty-two men loaded up into the various vehicles and moved out to the new target. Dayyan told the men the target was in an industrial area off San Fernando Road near the Hollywood Burbank Airport.

The convoy pulled up to a large concrete tilt up industrial building. Dayyan read the main sign on the front, "Ve-Safe Industries." Below the large sign was a smaller sign reading "Brinks Repair and Storage." An even smaller sign just below read, "Brinks trucks in this location carry no valuables." Dayyan smiled and said to Naseem and Adham, "Any running armored truck is now worth far more than all the worthless money it would normally hold."

As the rest of the convoy pulled up, the small front door opened, and a man in a security guard uniform exited and moved toward Dayyan in the stolen Pasadena SWAT truck. "As-salamu alaykum wa rahmatullahi wa barakaatuhu," the man said as Dayyan exited the passenger door of the large truck.

"Wa-Alaikum-Salaam," Dayyan said back to the man as they shook hands.

"I have carried out my mission as directed. This facility is secure. I have eliminated the other guards. My name is Uday. Have your men bring your trucks around to the side lot. I will open the large door. You may follow me."

Dayyan followed Uday, who told him he had been working at this company for over a year. "No one ever suspected anything. These stupid infidels." The two men went through a lobby where Dayyan stopped for a moment to look at large photos and publicity type prints along the walls.

Dayyan asked Uday, "What is the purpose of this company?"

"The main company Ve-Safe Industries is a specialty armored car builder. They build custom trucks and cars for many customers from politicians to movie stars. They are also a main Los Angeles distributor for a large armored car company back east. The new trucks come here for outfitting with the final accessories paint and lettering. This company maintains armored cars and trucks. The Brinks Armored car company use part of the building for storing and repairing their own armored trucks."

"Interesting," Dayyan answered.

The two continued through the offices toward the back of the building. As they passed one office, Dayyan could see a large pool of blood on the floor and could sense the smell of death. Dayyan sensed that Uday killed the other guards here. The two men exited the offices into a massive high ceiling building. Rows of armored cars lined both walls. Dayyan quickly counted to himself about thirty trucks. Uday moved over to the nearest roll-up door and unlocked a padlock, securing the lower door lock. "With no power, we have to roll the door up by hand." Uday started tugging on the chains that ran up to the lifting gears and pulleys above the door. The door slowly started rising.

Naseem entered, followed by two other men. Dayyan quickly barked out orders, "Bring the trucks inside that will fit. Have the other men set up security on all sides of the building. Send in Walter with the special crate. He knows which crate."

"Yes, General," Naseem said back.

"General?" Dayyan questioned Naseem.

"You are leading our army, and you are our general," Naseem answered.

"I am honored to lead all the faithful," Dayyan answered. Then he turned and asked Uday, "Have you tried to start any of these trucks after the EMP?"

Uday pointed to four large heavily armored trucks that sat together on the opposite wall. The trucks had a flat black paint job but no lettering. "Those four run. They just came in and were scheduled for delivery to the Homeland Security base at LAX. These trucks are equipped with the latest in EMP protection. Perhaps the same protection the Pasadena Bearcat truck you acquired."

Dayyan looked over the impressive armored trucks. He opened the bullet-protected door and looked inside. The latest in new technology adorned the inside, including things like exterior cameras. A rotating gun turret was located behind the driver's seats. Weapons would not be found in this fabrication and repair facility. But Dayyan knew if he could find a suitable gun, it could be adapted easily to the turret.

Naseem and Walter walked up. Two other men followed, carrying a crate that they sat down on the floor near the group. Walter said to Dayyan, "I have had technical training on these trucks. Some of the newer trucks have EMP protection. Homeland Security insisted on it, so the company manufacturing them has decided to only produce one electrical system. However, there was a California needed module added for pollution control. The added modules have no shielding against EMP, so they have probably failed. We have new ones in the crate, which have multiple layers of protection from EMP."

The group walked to one of the Brinks trucks parked further along the row. Walter examined the serial number on the door jam and compared it to a list that was inside the box. "Good, this truck has the latest EMP protection. Let's see if it runs." Uday jumped up into the driver's seat and flipped a large toggle marked "Ignition" and then pressed a round button marked "Starter." The large diesel motor cranked over for a few seconds and started. It was running, but the motor was rough and producing a large cloud of black smoke.

Uday called down from the cab, "The 'check engine' lamp is on."

Walter told the group, "You can tell the electrical system has been damaged but not the main engine controller or the truck would not have started." He signaled Uday, who then turned off the key, and the truck engine shook to an abrupt stop.

Walter opened the crate, pulled out one of the sealed Mylar bags, and tore it open. Inside was another plastic wrapping, which covered a second Mylar bag. He tore both open and extracted a metal cased electrical module. Naseem and Uday opened the front hood, and Walter climbed up on a small stepladder and peered into the engine compartment. A few minutes later, Walter had the module changed out, and they started up the truck again.

This time, the truck started and ran smoothly. The exhaust no longer contained excess smoke. Walter spoke up. "It has worked, my brothers. Let us see how many more of the trucks we can fix. I have twelve of the replacement modules."

Chapter 11

1315, Day 1, Goodsprings, Nevada

Lee and Jake rode into Goodsprings from the North. They looked around constantly for any sign of trouble. Neither man knew what to expect out here in a small town. The bypass road turned to the east, so they followed another paved road south into town. Lee knew they had to pass all the way through the old mining town and pick up the road continuing west toward Sandy Valley. When they turned left onto Spring Street, up ahead was a large group of people and some cars, trucks, and other assorted vehicles. Lee remembered from being here years ago the Pioneer Saloon was up ahead. Now he could see the one-hundred-year-old bar and café was a buzz of activity. Originally built around 1910 during the old mining days, it now had become an organized relief center. Lee and Jake saw several firemen and a policeman or sheriff out in front of the bar. After a short discussion, they decided to approach the bar. They rode their bikes near the front of the bar. They dismounted the bikes and walked over to a table by the front door. Several people sitting or standing around looked up and nodded at the newcomers.

"Good morning, Sheriff," Lee said to the officer.

"Hey, guys. Where have you two come from?" the sheriff replied.

"Vegas. We headed out early last night. I am Lee, and this is Jake. Jake is active duty at Irwin," Lee explained.

Jake and Lee decided earlier not to discuss their experiences in Vegas, so Lee kept it simple.

The sheriff shook both Lee's and Jake's hand and introduced them to several others around the table. More handshakes followed.

"I am Carl Burrows, county sheriff's office. I live here in Goodsprings. How was Vegas?" Carl said.

"It was starting to implode," remarked Jake. "We made a trade for these bikes and got the heck out of there."

Jake also ignored all the details of the shooting and how they actually got the bikes.

"What's happening here?" Lee asked.

Carl explained, "The old Pioneer saloon is the perfect spot to set up a temporary shelter for all the refugees we are getting. Most of these folks were stranded on Interstate 15, which is seven miles south. The saloon owners have graciously opened it up for refugees. They are cooking up the perishable food for the stranded people. Most of the refrigerators and freezers are not working, so the food is going to spoil quickly anyway. We do have some small generators running a few of the coolers so we can stretch out the food as long as possible."

Lee and Jake could see a large group of people in the patio area of the bar.

"Did these people walk here from the freeway?" Jake asked.

"Some, but we scrounged every running vehicle we could find. Volunteers are making trips back and forth to pick up stranded people," Carl replied.

"That is great of you. You are the first people we have run into that are trying to help," Lee said.

"So what is your plan now?" Carl asked.

"We are heading to Sandy Valley. A civilian worker from Irwin lives there. I am hoping he is there, and we can figure out a plan to get to Irwin," Jake explained.

"What is your friend's name?" Carl asked.

"Rick Hardwell," Jake answered.

"I know Rick. He is a member of the VFW in Sandy Valley. I am also a member. I'm ex-army reserve. I did a tour in the first Gulf War," Carl said.

"That is a weird coincidence." Lee slid into the conversation.

"Not really. Only a couple of thousand people live in this area. Everybody knows everybody and well. Everybody knows everybody's business too," Carl said with a slight laugh. "We have a couple of high-power handhelds that are working between us and Sandy Valley."

Carl was referring to a portable police radio. "One of my buddies is on the other end and he knows Rick also. Let me see if I can reach him."

As Carl picked up the handheld radio and started to call out, Jake and Lee turned to look over the scene at the old tavern. About seventy-five people were milling around. It appeared locals were helping with the refugees. People were cooking food and handing it out. Others were lining up, folding chairs, cots, and patio lounges adding to the odd assortment of furniture already on the patio. Jake and Lee watched about a dozen people setting up tents in the field on the side of the saloon. They assumed this effort was to provide places to sleep for the refugees. The sad looking group of refugees were gladly sitting or lying down. Most looked tired and all looked worried and scared. The patio was filled with conversation. The crisis befalling the United States was the most common subject. Many were telling tales of experiences since the power and cars died.

Carl came, found Lee and Jake, and told them he had reached his friend in Sandy Valley. "My buddy Joel says that Rick was at Irwin when the power went out. His wife Lucy came by the Mormon Church that has become the refugee center. Sandy Valley does not have a direct paved road to the highway, so they are not getting many refugees yet. However, we plan to take some refugees there if we feel we are reaching our capacity. Anyway, Lucy told Joel that she was going to take their old VW dune buggy, which was running, and head to Irwin along the power lines. Apparently, she and Rick had made that run a few times just for fun. She knew the way and figured it was better to get to Irwin and be with Rick than stay at home alone. She guessed Rick was needed at Irwin and not coming home any time soon. She had packed up stuff and headed out about an hour ago."

"Well, I guess we are about an hour late," Jake commented to Carl. "Had we gotten here sooner, we might have hitched a ride."

Jake then looked at Lee and said, "Well, I guess we will have to keep pedaling our asses all over town."

"Oh well, I can sure use the exercise," Lee said while laughing.

Jake said, "Hey, Carl, is there any hardware store where we might be able to buy or barter for some spare tubes for these bikes?"

"No, not really. I will ask around the people here. And is there anything else I can do for you guys before you ride off into the sunset?" Carl replied.

"In case we end up walking and taking several days, is there any food you can spare? Lee here is stockpiled well, but I did not bring much to the party," Jake asked of Carl.

"Well, you guys should go grab a burger before you head off. I will ask the kitchen to make some sandwiches for you also," Carl said. "But you know you two guys are welcome to stay here and see what develops. We could even put you to work."

"We appreciate your hospitality, Carl, but I know Lee wants to get home, and I am certain they are going to need me at Irwin," Jake replied.

Jake and Lee then went to the counter, where a cheery middle-aged lady handed each a plate with a cheeseburger, fries, and salad. Knowing it might be a long time before they would have fresh beef again, the two travelers cherished their meal.

Carl came over as they were finishing eating. He was carrying a small box containing six sandwiches and six bottles of water and some emergency food packages similar to the ones Lee had in his BOB. Jake packed most of the stuff into his backpack. Then using triple layers of plastic bags, he and Lee duct-taped some stuff to the handlebars of both bikes.

Lee and Jake said their goodbyes and thanks to Carl. The men wished one another good luck for the uncertain future. Hearty handshakes sealed the respect all around. Carl was one of the good people the country was going to need desperately in the coming days, weeks, and months. Lee wondered if perhaps he felt the same about Jake and him. Jake and Lee then climbed on the bikes, and as they started to ride off, Jake saluted Carl, who returned it and said, "Stay safe out there."

Lee and Jake rode off and worked their way south out of the town, picking up the Sandy Valley highway and turning west. Just as they got on the road, an old or vintage military truck known as a "two and a half ton," or "deuce and a half," roared past them headed to town. Behind that was an old Ford pickup truck. Both trucks were packed with people. Some waved, but most looked stunned and desperate. Lee and Jake kept moving.

Chapter 12

1330, DAY 1, GARRETT HOUSEHOLD, AGUA DULCE, CALIFORNIA

Melinda and James reached Madison with the two-way radio at around 9:30 a.m. The couple had slept through the EMP unaware until morning and waking up to no power. Going outside and finding their neighbors milling around, trying to start their cars was all Logan needed to know that something drastic had occurred. He and Melinda pulled the two-way radio from a closet and set it up using Lee's instructions just as the other family members had done. Once working, James contacted the main Garrett house.

The two-way radios provided the Garrett family a lifesaving advantage as a method for the three households to communicate. Although the Garretts were not yet aware of the extent of power and communication outage countrywide, they knew the radios Lee had set up provided their family a link for communicating. Cell phones were as dead as landlines, and widespread panic was surely occurring. Fear for loved ones gripped everyone. James and Melinda began to realize how important this HAM radio was. The two felt bad about all the kidding and harassment the family had given Lee over his obsession with setting up the radios at the three households.

Using the radios, a discussion of choices went back and forth. The final agreement was for Melinda and James to sit tight until later in the day. Then assuming Lawrence and Richard Silva made it to the house, they would send out a rescue party the ten miles, driving Lee's old Mustang.

Meanwhile, Logan and Madison started taking stock of their emergency items and food supplies. A mostly buried shipping container up the hill from the house contained most of the emergency food. Although only under a few feet of dirt, the buried container remained at a nearly constant sixty-eight degrees. The hard volcanic rock of the Garrett property had proven difficult to excavate, but once completed, the nearly solid rock provided for strong walls and minimal reinforcement for the sides of the container. Steel beams and an added layer of galvanized sheet metal added strength to the roof. Besides food, the container had a large supply of other essential items including ammunition, batteries, stoves, fuel, medical supplies and about everything any well-versed Prepper would have a supply of. The container also had air ventilation pipes coming from two remote locations into a void below the floor. An air intake in the floor provided filtered air for one of three different air systems. The primary powered unit was an added HEPA air pump. If the outside environment became contaminated, the pump and filter combination created a slightly positive pressure in the container, ensuring no contaminants could leach into the container. A small dehumidifier and a portable air conditioner were also inside the container. A bank of 12-volt batteries powered a 48-volt inverter that could run any of the ventilation units. Solar panels arranged on the hill kept the batteries charged and ready. The ventilation pipes contained HEPA filters at the hidden intakes. HEPA filters could stop a multitude of dangerous things, including chemical, biological and even radioactive dust particles. Lee had designed the container for possible use as a short-term "survival shelter." He argued there was little chance of using it for something like a nuclear or biological event. However, its use as a fire shelter in the fire-prone Southern California high desert was a real possibility. The buried, insulated, and dual entrance door shelter would be impervious to any raging fire and could easily provide clean, cool, and filtered air for a dozen people if needed.

The Garrett property was a constant rising slope from the entrance gate up to a rocky ridgeline along the north end of the plot. The highest point of the hill was eighty feet higher in elevation than the house. Large rocks at that point provided a perfect and natural location for an observation point. Lee and Logan had taken bags of premixed concrete up the hill with the tractor and poured and smoothed out the mix between the rocks to create a flat floor. They drilled into the rock using a concrete bit and hammer drill and installed eyebolts using a chemical two-part epoxy.

Logan found a tarpaulin and net in the storage shed he and his Dad had put together at the same time they built the OP. It consisted of a brown metallic tarp with a military camouflage net layer over the outside and connected to the inside layer with plastic wire ties. The combination unit would provide both shelter from rain and some concealment. Logan hiked up the hill and installed the net over the makeshift observation point. Then following instructions contained in the emergency book, Logan rolled out a multiconductor wire from the top of the OP down the hill to the house. Lee had already prepared a "phone" system using two old dial telephones. Following instructions available on Prepper sites, Lee rewired the phones and installed a lantern battery on each one. To make them quick and easy to set up and use, Lee had installed simple plastic connectors on each end of the cable. Once plugged to the phones at each point, simply lifting one phone's handset caused the other phone to ring. The cheap phones provided clean, easy, and undetectable two-way communication similar to expensive military field phones.

Logan also took other items up to the OP, including bottled water, a large pair of binoculars, two small folding chairs, blankets, and a spotting scope. Plus, he carried up a small ammo-box of AR15 rounds and another of AR-10 rounds. He wanted the ammo and other items preplaced. If someone needed to man the post, they would only need to take weapons and personal items.

Madison had started looking over the short- and long-term food stores. She wanted to conserve the fresh and perishable food as long as possible. So she planned to supplement all meals with the long-term freeze-dried, canned, and dehydrated foods from the food container. The food container did contain a mixture of canned and bottled items, which they periodically rotated out of their daily diets. Far more importantly were the long-term products. These items had shelf lives of up to twenty-five years. She also found ten cases of MRE meals. The MRE meals did not have as long of shelf life but were quick and easy to use. She brought two cases of the MREs down to the house.

One of the sections in Lees emergency manual said to "prepare to bug out." The instructions contained a list of priorities to stockpile in the garage. If the Garrett home became unlivable, they would evacuate using whatever running cars they had at their disposal. Currently, that included the old Mustang, which Logan backed up to the garage door, plus two Yamaha dirt bikes. Logan had retrieved both bikes from their respective shed and had drained and refueled them. Using a car battery power air compressor Logan topped off the air in all the bike tires, the Mustang, and even the Kubota tractor. The bikes would not carry large supplies, but they could traverse rugged terrain and would be valuable scout vehicles if the family was escaping to other places. He also found a tool bag made special for the bikes, which contained spare parts such as spark plugs and tire tubes plus an assortment of the needed tools. If the time came, forcing the family to flee, everyone knew the plan was to head north toward Lone Pine California. Lee's Aunt Betty lived North of Lone Pine California in the foothills of the High Sierra Mountains. It was a perfect retreat spot should the need arise. Aunt Betty welcomed the idea of the family bugging out to her house in the mountains.

Madison also found a large box, which contained ten battery powered LED motion lights. They were small flat lights with 120-degree motion sensors. They contained small solar chargers to renew the rechargeable batteries during the daytime. Lee's instructions said to install new rechargeable batteries in each unit and then place them around the property, hiding them within bushes or rocks. The small LED lights would provide warning for anyone trying to move around the property at night. Madison installed the new batteries in each unit and tested them, but she would let Logan do the placements later.

The five acres was only fully enclosed with three-wire metal post fencing. This fencing was more of a border marking, which did little to keep out people or wild animals. A portion of the yard around the backyard and side yards of the house had six-foot tall wood fencing. Madison knew that Lee had been working on a "sensing" wire, which he planned on running around the three-wire fence. Lee had explained to Madison how the extra sensor wire would run on electrical insulators close to the center bare metal fence wire. Most people would not notice the small wire. However, if a person tried to cross under the top wire, there was a good chance they would squeeze or bump the sensor wire into the heavier metal wire. When the sensor wire touched the fence wire, this grounded the circuit and sounding an alarm. If anyone cut the sensor wire, the alarm also sounded. Madison knew it was pointless, as Lee had not finished running the sensing wires around the property. So with the large open property, the family needed to be vigilant day and night.

An electric gate protected the main entrance to the property. The gate motor was a low voltage motor, which was powered by a pair of RV type batteries. The control panel had a simple solar panel above it to keep the batteries charged. Logan had already confirmed the gate was working except for the keypad. EMP waves had apparently damaged the small controller used to store and confirm keypad entries. Logan figured out how to jump the wires inside the control box to open and close the gate. He found two simple toggle switches in the workshop. He wired them up, and after testing them, he used duct tape to adhere them inside the control box. A padlock on the control box secured it. Logan found four keys that fit the lock. He tagged them all with paracord. He kept one, gave one to Madison, and placed the extra in the kitchen. The last one he placed near the gate under a large lava rock.

Around 4:00 p.m., Logan was partway up the hill above the house when he spotted two old Honda three-wheelers coming up the road toward the property. A single person was on the lead bike, towing an odd-looking trailer behind it. The unwieldly trailer tilted side to side from the large pile of boxes, and bags secured to it rope and straps. The second bike with two riders was trailing back a bit, obviously trying to avoid the dust kicked up by the lead bike. Gear and bags dangled from the handlebars of both bikes. Logan could see what looked like rifle cases tied on top of the gear. Both bikes looked way overloaded with weight.

Logan ran down to the house and yelled for Madison. They both moved to the kitchen window just as the bikes stopped at the gate. The rider on the lead bike climbed off and started punching numbers into the gate keypad. He removed a full-face motorcycle helmet, which allowed Madison and Logan to see it was Lawrence. Logan sprinted down the hill, with Madison trailing behind at a slower pace.

Logan yelled out as he got closer to the gate, "Hey, Lawrence, keypad is out. I have to override it."

Lawrence replied, "Hey, little brother."

Logan was close enough to see his brother was wearing a military combat leg holster filled with his 9 mm Barretta 92FS. The FS was a civilian version of the M9 pistol Lawrence had carried as an Army Ranger. Richard and Dena Silva stopped the second three-wheeler behind the trailer and climbed off. Logan arrived at the gate and opened the metal control panel and used the new switch he had installed to open the gate. The motor hummed, and the gate swung open. Logan and Lawrence met as the gate opened and hugged each other. Richard and Dena moved up and hugged Logan. Lawrence and Dena both had on bulky, overstuffed backpacks. Richard was the only one of the three not wearing a backpack. Lawrence assumed this was a need for Dena to ride behind him on the small old ATV. Both of the bikes sat idling as the four chatted a moment before Madison arrived. Madison repeated hugs for each of the newcomers.

"Where did you get these antiquated three-wheelers?" Logan asked.

"Richard's old neighbor had them since sometime in the eighties. He was the owner of some ATV company back then. I guess he did lots of racing on three-wheelers and buggies. But he is barely able to ride his little electric scooter now days, so he offered them to us. He told us he had no plan of bugging out. He had his 357-revolver strapped to his scooter and was just daring anyone to come take his stuff."

Richard chimed in, "Yeah, that ornery old bastard will probably go down, but only after he reloads that revolver several times. He helped get these two running. He had two newer Yamaha 4-wheelers, but they would not start. Carburetors had plugged up from stale gas. These old Hondas just needed a shot of starting fluid and some air in the tires."

Lawrence added, "Frank did not have any premix for these old two-strokes. None of the neighbors did either, so Frank convinced us that power steering fluid would work. We drained gas out of his Lincoln Navigator and mixed in power steering fluid, and here we are. They smoked a bunch but started running better and better as we went. The new gas and steering fluid must have cleaned out the carbs."

Lawrence pointed at the tires and said, "Look at those tires. They have so many cracks we did not think they would make it here. They were so out of round they about shook our teeth out for the first few miles, but they eventually smoothed out. I just knew we would be walking sooner than later."

Madison asked about the trailer.

"Frank also had that old garden wagon. It is actually a dump trailer. His ex-wife used it in the garden. But now that she is gone, I think Frank does not care much about trying to survive. We told him we would come back for him in the Mustang, but he said don't bother. Said he ain't leaving his house. Been there for forty-plus years. Told us he buried his wife's ashes in the rose garden and is not leaving."

"God rest the first people who try to rob or loot from old Frank."

As the group stood talking, the second three-wheeler engine suddenly started running faster and then coughed and quit, producing a large cloud of white smoke. The group looked at each other and started laughing hysterically

Chapter 13

1710, Day 1, Sandy Valley, Nevada

L ee and Jake rode their borrowed bikes into Sandy Valley in the early evening. The sixteen-mile ride was uneventful although tiring because of numerous hills and valleys. Both men were dead tired after the long walk and two long rides. The rough terrain and the uncomfortable packs were taking their toll. Thankfully, the ride to Sandy Valley was all hard pavement. As they approached the town, Lee spotted the familiar steeple of a Mormon Church ahead, and after telling Jake on the radio, they rode toward it. Like the fire station in Goodsprings, this place also had refugees milling around although fewer because of its isolated location. It appeared the Mormons were the ones setting up the camp here, and again, like the Pioneer Saloon, tents, cots, and chairs abounded. Someone was using a barbecue to cook up what looked like beef, and people were lining up with paper plates for their turn at the food.

Lee pulled up first, followed closely by Jake, and they both got off and parked the bikes against the building. Then they started asking around for Joel, but he walked up and found them first.

"You guys must be Lee and Jake?" a medium-height balding middle-aged man said as he approached.

"We are. Are you Joel?" replied Jake.

"Yep, that's me. So are you the two nuts from Vegas planning to ride bikes to Irwin?" asked Joel.

"Well, unless a yellow cab pulls up looking for fares, I guess that is our only choice," Lee chimed in.

All three men laughed at Lee's comment and shared handshakes.

Joel then said, "It is too bad that Lucy left for Irwin. She couldn't find anyone to go with her. She was driving one of those four-seat VW power dune buggies. You guys could have ridden with her. I can tell you that sure would have made me feel a whole lot better. Having that stubborn woman heading out on her own has me worried. I did all I could to talk her out of it, but she insisted that Rick would be stuck at Irwin, and she wanted to be with him. She is a Class A gutsy woman."

"Yeah, our experiences so far have not been great. I hope she stays alert and safe," Jake said.

To which Lee added, "That's an understatement."

"She is tough," said Joel. "At least she is packing. She took along a 1911 forty-five. She also took along some supplies. I just hope that old buggy gets her there."

"Well, we are heading the same way, but it sure would be nice to be driving versus riding these motorless mopeds," Lee said, pointing at the mountain bikes.

"Well, we will be in good shape after riding to Irwin across the mountains," added Jake. "I just wish they had some kind of rack to hold our bags. Our shoulders will be a blistered mess when we get to Irwin. And Lee's bag is a lot heavier than mine," he said as he pointed at the two bags sitting next to the bikes.

"Well, at least my bag has decent shoulder straps and a good lap belt," Lee said as he rubbed his shoulders and then pulled back his shirt to see the condition of the skin. "Not blistered yet."

Joel then said, "You know, these Mormons have an entire bike shop in the back. They have a bunch of mountain bikes the missionaries have used over the years. Let's ask if they have any racks or baskets."

Joel turned and looked around, obviously trying to spot someone in the group of people milling around. He spotted the person he was looking for and started that way. "Let me see what I can do."

Joel came back in a couple of minutes with a tall skinny guy about forty years old, who was wearing a white shirt and one of those Mormon name badges. Joel introduced him to Lee and Jake as "Brother Walker."

"You gents can call me Johnnie," said Brother Walker.

Jake and I looked at each other, trying not to look amused.

Obviously use to this response about his name, Johnnie said, "I know, I know, a Mormon named Johnnie Walker is an oxymoron name, but it might be what keeps me a good tea drinker."

Everyone laughed.

The men shook hands, and after a minute or two of discussion about Lee and Jake's ride from Vegas and their plan to head to Irwin, Brother Walker addressed the two new friends' concern. "Let's go see what we can find in the back. I think we might have something that will make your travels a little easier, but let's see what your tire sizes are first."

Brother Walker knelt down and read off the sizes of the tires to us. "Well, thankfully, they are both the same size. That makes it easier to have spare tubes."

Johnnie led Lee and Jake around the church to a rear storage shed and opened it. It was full of bikes of all conditions plus various parts and pieces. Johnnie walked inside, pulled a two-wheel cart from behind bikes in the corner, and manhandled it to the door. He also handed Jake two new tubes in boxes and two bottles of green slime tire sealant. He looked around for a moment, and he found a little tool kit and air pump, which he brought out with him.

Lee and Jake looked at the cart design and determined it should attach to the rear axle bolts of a bike. With the cart, tools, and parts, the three men returned to their bikes in front of the church. Johnnie explained how to attach the trailer to Lee and Jake, and the two took to installing it, which took no time at all. The parts and hardware needed to attach the cart was in a ziplocked bag taped to the cart. Both bikes were similar, so it made no difference on which bike they installed the cart. They discussed putting the heavy stuff in the cart to lighten up their backpacks and the strain on their shoulders.

While Lee and Jake fixed up the bike and stowed their gear, Johnnie came back and suggested then men "chow down" before leaving. Some of the Mormon volunteers were cooking chicken plus various side dishes. He explained that with the power out, they were going to use up their frozen stuff first as they did not want to rely on the single small gasoline generator that was running. Johnny explained to Lee and Jake the church had recently installed a large diesel generator, but it would not run since the EMP.

Lee asked, "Can I take a look at it?"

Johnny said, "Sure, that would be great. Follow me."

The generator was a new diesel generator. Johnnie opened the access panels, and Lee started to look it over. They could all smell a burned odor coming from the control panel compartment.

"It smells just like the inside of my car in Vegas," Lee said.

"The panel is dead, and it does nothing," said Johnnie.

Lee finished looking over the generator, and he turned to the men. "Lucky it is an older type Kubota diesel with a mechanical injector pump, unlike some newer technology with electronic fuel injection. Mechanical injection does not need much to run. All you need to do is get it turning over and give it fuel."

"Why do you think it is dead then?" Johnnie asked.

"Well, they probably added this electronic panel to control the fuel solenoid and even the starter motor. It probably controls the glow plugs, and likely it's tied into the oil pressure and temperature. If it is cold outside, the electronics activate glow plugs before cranking over the engine. If the engine overheats, the electronics shut down the motor to prevent destruction. My guess is the electronic board was fried from the EMP, but I doubt the engine or the starter motor is bad," Lee said.

"It is well beyond me," answered Johnnie.

"Me too," said Jake.

Lee then asked, "Do you have any small jumper wires? You know, the ones with alligator clips on them?"

"I don't think so," said Johnnie.

"Okay, no problem. I have a couple of them in my bug-out bag."

"Why do you have jumper wires in your bag, Lee?" Jake asked.

"Well, like I said, one of my choices for wheels was construction equipment or older tractors and stuff. Jumper wires make it easy to borrow them," Lee said back to Jake with a wink. Lee then headed back around the front to his bag and returned shortly with four jumper wires.

"Okay, first, let's see if the starter motor will go," Lee said. He hooked a wire from the small terminal on the starter solenoid mounted on the side of the engine compartment. Then he touched the other end to the positive battery terminal. The starter motor instantly turned over the engine, but it failed to start.

"That is a start in the right direction. No pun intended," Johnnie said, excited the motor turned over.

"Yes, that is good. Now let's see if we can get fuel going to it," Lee said.

Lee then looked over the motor and found the wiring going to the fuel shut off solenoid. He unclipped the plastic connector. Taking another jumper, he attached one clip onto one prong in the solenoid end of the connector and the other to a metal bracket on the motor. He attached another jumper to the second prong being careful not to short the two clips together. If this worked, Lee figured they could make a more permanent attachment. Lee took the end of the second wire and attached that to the battery terminal, creating a small spark. A clicking sound emanated from the solenoid.

Lee said to the two men, "The small spark means the solenoid still has continuity. A large spark might indicate a short circuit."

Now with the fuel solenoid hot-wired, Lee again touched the starter solenoid jumper to the same terminal on the battery. The starter motor started turning over the engine again. This time, after a few seconds, the diesel motor sprang to life, producing a roar and a cloud of black exhaust.

The men shouted out hoorahs over the noise of the diesel motor. They exchanged high-fives all around.

"This is fantastic, Lee," said Johnnie.

"Nice job, man," said Jake.

Lee showed Johnnie how to shut off and restart the motor. He suggested they get some wire and connectors and, if possible, a toggle switch that they could wire to the fuel solenoid and maybe a push button for the starter motor. Johnnie said he would see what they could scrounge. Lee reminded him to keep an eye on temperature and make sure to keep it full of oil. There would not be any safeguards now.

The men left the generator running for now. Johnnie went into the church and came back to tell Lee and Jake the multiple refrigerators and freezers were all working.

"Now we don't have to use all the fresh meat right away, which is good. But I guess some people will not like that. Let's go get you two heroes some of the barbecue chicken before it is gone," Johnnie said.

Jake replied, "Lee is the hero. I would not have figured that out."

The three men walked back around to the front of the church.

Although Lee and Jake had eaten only a few hours earlier at the Pioneer Saloon, they figured they might as well fill up with the fresh food and protein. It might be days before they see real food again. As the two men were being served the great-looking chicken and side dishes, Johnnie was telling the others how Lee had repaired the generator. Several of the other Mormons came up and thanked the two men. Jake just pointed at Lee and told them he did it all.

Lee and Jake finished their second scrumptious meal of the day, consisting of barbecue chicken, potato salad, and some canned tomatoes from storage, plus fresh cucumbers that one of the local farmers had brought over. They ate while discussing their next step. It was nearly 8:00 p.m. and would be getting dark soon. They discussed and weighed the choices. They could wait until morning and continue in daylight. That probably made sense as tired as both men were. Lee pointed out how exhausted he was. With little sleep, a long walk out of Vegas, two separate deadly encounters, and the long bike ride here, both men were wearing down. On the other hand, they realized being on the roads tomorrow in daylight posed more danger. As each hour and day passed, stranded, desperate people on the roads would become more of a threat. Their supply of food and water was a valuable target. Some people may feel the men should share. Others may try forcibly to take what they wanted. Neither man wanted another battle. It was going to be dark soon, but maybe they could get down the paved road to the dirt power line turnoff and move inland a ways and camp. They knew leaving now was the safer bet, but both men were exhausted.

Finally, reaching a compromise, they decided to take a five-hour break, get some sleep, and when the nearly full moon was out, they would take off.

The next part of the route would be to take Kingston Road southwest from Sandy Valley. The road was paved and straight for the first five miles as it passed through rural desert farmland. After five miles, it changed to a maintained gravel road and worked its way up over a mountain range. After crossing the mountain range, the road turned south and intersected the power line road that would lead the men to the south of Fort Irwin. They would try to get at least down past the paved portion tonight and then find a safe place to camp out.

With the decision made, Lee and Jake found Johnnie, told him their plan, and asked if they could sleep here for a few hours. Johnnie not only agreed but also took them into the church and found two military cots for them to use. With the plan of leaving later in the night, Lee and Jake decided to move the cots outside. They did not want to disturb sleeping people when getting up to leave.

"If you are going to leave in the middle of the night, allow us to say a blessing now," Johnnie asked the two men.

"We would appreciate that," Lee answered, with Jake nodding his approval.

Johnnie then gathered several of the Mormons and about two dozen of the refugees, and they all gathered in a large circle and grasped hands.

Johnnie recited the blessing, "Oh, Father in heaven. Bless these brave men, Jake and Lee, as they continue their long journey to reunite with their families. Make their journey safe and quick. Provide them with shelter when needed and food to nourish and strengthen their bodies. Also, Lord, please provide for all of your children who have gathered at your house here in this beautiful valley. Please provide for those who need your help in this terrible time. Please help those faced with desperation and need throughout our great country. We ask this in the name of Father, the Son, and the Holy Ghost, amen."

"Amen" sang out from the entire group.

Lee and Jake placed two cots next to their bikes and bags, and they both collapsed onto the cots. Lee was fast asleep in little time. The prayer got Jake thinking and kept him awake for a time. He thought about this situation and his new friend Lee. He also thought about his family and what he had done that had brought him here to this place during this tough time.

Chapter 14

0300, Day 2, Sandy Valley, Nevada

Lee had set an alarm on his watch to wake him and Jake up at 0300 hours. It felt to Lee like they had just lain down, but the two got up reluctantly. Lee shared baby wipes with Jake, which they used to clean up. They also brushed their teeth using some bottled water, gathered their stuff, and readied the bikes. They put the backpacks in the cart with some loose water bottles, tools, and other heavy items. Lee tied his chest rig on the handlebars of his bike with some wire ties and put on the fanny pack. Jake said he would pedal the bike with the cart for now and they could trade off later.

The two men quietly pushed the bikes out of the parking lot, mounted them at the road, and headed out. The moon was high in the sky and providing acceptable light for riding on the paved roads. Lee and Jake moved along at a slow pace, not wanting to exhaust themselves any further. The ride was easy on the paved parts of Sandy Valley Road, but soon it gave way to graded gravel road where it met Kingston road. The loose gravel made riding a lot more difficult. Both Lee and Jake were improving their skill at navigating loose dirt and gravel. Neither man crashed as they had done many times the day before.

The road up out of Goodsprings was good, but started climbing steeply. Both men had to dismount the bikes often and push them up steep climbs. It was grueling work. They would continue to ponder dumping the bikes but knew the road would be flat and downhill after they got up and over this pass, so they just kept pushing and moving, resting often.

The setting moon decreased the light and made navigating more difficult. Lee put on his headlamp and rode in front to mark the way. Jake followed along closely behind him.

Around 5:00 a.m., Lee and Jake both felt they were far enough up in the mountains and felt secure. They decided to rest for a bit and wait for daylight. Lee got out his tablet stove and heated some water for coffee. They shared the hot drink. Both men ate a sandwich received from Carl, plus a couple of the remaining snacks from the convince store in Vegas. Wanting to hydrate, both men finished off a bottle of water with added energy-drink powder. They discussed various things while they were eating and drinking. Lee told Jake about his involvement at the training facilities known as "MOUTs" at Irwin. He explained how he had worked with the General's Chief of Staff, a civilian named Steven Rollinson. Jake knew Steven, and he was still at the base. The talk soon waned as Lee and Jake both relaxed and fell asleep.

Chapter 15

0330, DAY 2, SYLMAR, CALIFORNIA

Dayyan sat with Naseem, Uday, and a new soldier, Arman, who had brought his own small army to join with Dayyan's force earlier that evening. They sat on the 210 freeway behind a dead flatbed truck. Their position provided them a vantage point overseeing the new Sylmar National Guard base that lie below them. It was just off foothill Boulevard near the Hanson Dam Recreational Area. The base had just opened in spring.

A new target was provided to Dayyan after the successful mission at the armored car factory. The new target was astonishing to him. His handlers were expecting his small force to take on a real military base, which likely would have superior forces equipped with superior weapons. Such a bold attack could result in annihilation of his small force. But as the plan was revealed, he could see potential for a huge victory. A successful mission could strengthen his army and deliver a terrific blow to the infidels and nonbelievers.

Dayyan had kept the force at the armored truck factory until just after sundown. He then split up the convoy, including the new heavy armored Homeland Security and Brinks trucks, into three groups, and they all made their way to the North San Fernando Valley. After getting nine of the Brinks trucks running plus the four Homeland Security trucks, they now had the same number of cars and trucks as men. This meant each man would need to drive alone.

His handler had told him there would be more men at the new target to strengthen the army.

One of the three groups of trucks ran into trouble heading to the rendezvous location. There assigned route was up Wentworth Street toward Foothill Boulevard to the north. The lead truck was one of the DHS trucks taken from the Brinks shop. Near Foothill, they met a large group of police and firefighters at a large relief center set up at fire station #24 on the left side of the road. Many civilians most likely rescued from the 210 freeway were milling about. There were also police in the mix of people, who instantly turned toward the large impressive convoy of trucks, probably assuming they were coming to help.

Zohar was driving the lead DHS truck, and at first, he did not know what to do. He slammed on the brakes, and the six trucks behind him did the same. A group of police officers headed down the street toward him. Not being comfortable backing up or trying to turn the big armored truck around, he just floored the gas and headed toward the police officers. At first, they looked shocked, but they all ran and jumped for cover. Zohar sped by, and the other vehicles followed. They roared past the stunned people and police, chasing many out of the street. No shots were fired by the confused police as the convoy sped by and disappeared under the 210 freeway.

The convoy of trucks made the left turn onto Foothill Boulevard and continued to their destination. Zohar had a concern about leading the police to their meeting point, so he radioed Deshawn, a skinny African-American, who was driving one of the original suburban trucks. "Stay at the tail end of the convoy and watch for a response from the police."

Deshawn remained on the side of Foothill Boulevard for about fifteen minutes. He reported that an old ford sedan came up Foothill and stopped. Two policemen climbed from the car and looked up Foothill Boulevard before getting back into the car and heading back. The police probably did not want another meeting with the hostile force, who tried to run them over. They probably did not feel they had enough men, cars, or firepower for a real shootout.

Dayyan was worried before this latest encounter that reports of meetings with a hostile group and the attacks on the guns stores plus the murder of the Pasadena Swat team was going dangerous. He felt it would start getting broadcast over whatever communication net was working. This incident would add credence to the other sightings and put the authorities on high alert.

Dayyan's group that had come up Sunland Boulevard had arrived first at the rendezvous location. Zohar's convoy showed up a few minutes later. The third group led by Arman arrived last, having the longest route up Osborne Street around the west side of Hanson Dam. They scattered the large trucks in numerous locations around the recreational area using heavy brush or trees to hide them. Stealth was paramount to this operation. Dayyan walked on foot to a point overlooking the National Guard Center. His handler had given the location to him, and there he found a single man.

Dayyan approached the man who introduced himself. "Hello, my brother. I am Arman Ridwan Bousaid. I guess we are here for the same purpose."

"It appears so. How has your success been so far, my friend?" Dayyan answered.

"I have gathered about twenty-five men to add to your army. Unfortunately, we have not had near the success as you with weapons and vehicles. We assembled east of San Bernardino. As directed, I have been here with three men since yesterday watching the National Guard base below. The rest of my men came in a large old school bus a few hours ago. They are waiting at the golf course below the dam."

Dayyan continued to get the report from Arman. "Originally, when we arrived there were about twenty soldiers. Some firefighters and police also arrived on foot. For the last day, men have left taking the large six-wheel trucks in and out of the compound. I think they are picking up stranded motorists along the freeway and other roads. Some trucks have returned and left again, but so far, this base does not appear to have become a refugee camp. Currently, we think there are only about five or six soldiers inside the main building. I have two men hidden down close in the brush watching and the third man is acting as a runner giving me reports."

As Dayyan thought about the mission to take the base, he had concerns. Just a few men could effectively stand off his army if they were to lock themselves into the heavily built and secure main building of the armory. They surely had radios and would call for more army help if attacked. However, he had an idea. It was gutsy and could fail just as easy as succeed, but rewards for success were huge. *God willing it might work*, Dayyan thought.

Chapter 16

0515, Day 2, Sylmar, California

Lieutenant Dale Allen was sipping coffee as he sat at a small desk in the main office of the new high-tech National Guard base. He was one of five men currently at the site. After the EMP, only about twenty men and two female soldiers made it to the base. Four stranded LAPD officers joined them at first. Their Ford Explorer police cars had died like millions of other civilian cars, forcing them to walk to the base on foot. Eventually, they hitched a ride on one of the rescue trucks to the LAPD Foothill Station.

The National Guard base commander did not make it to the site, and no one had heard from him. Dale was the highest-ranking officer. He had been in charge since arriving several hours after the EMP riding one of his older Yamaha quads from his house in Granada Hills. The ten-mile or so drive on the quad was not terrible. Being single, he did not have to worry about a wife and kids, only two dogs that he convinced a neighbor to watch for him.

As soon as the soldiers started wandering in, the two civilian security guards bugged out. One of them drove an old Chevrolet Camaro that was still running, so the two men asked to leave to go back and tend to their own families. Dale did not see any reason to keep them.

The first job the men undertook was to send out teams of four men in the large 6×6 trucks to rescue stranded motorists off the 210 and Interstate 5 freeways. They had been doing so for over twenty-four hours, mostly taking the motorists to fire stations, hospitals, or police stations. The trucks returned for fuel and supplies and after loading, headed back to different parts of the freeway and main roads. They loaded up cases of MRE meals and bottled water, which was divided up to the truckloads of refugees.

Dale and the remaining men were using the one working radio network to stay in contact with the main National Guard base in downtown Los Angeles and another large base in Van Nuys. So far, the main priority was picking up the stranded motorists. However, longer term plans were in the development stage. Orders for most bases was, pack up and move to a working airport such as Van Nuys or Hollywood Burbank. This would provide a quicker method of resupply. Also, the forces were to protect the airports and ensure they remained open. Dale received instructions they would be transferring to either Hollywood Burbank airport or the small private Whiteman Airport on the other side of the Hansen Dam Recreation area.

Dale had the remaining men start doing inventory and loading up trucks even though they were currently short on drivers. He decided that if needed, he would ask for civilian volunteers to drive the trucks during the move. They had not started loading weapons yet, but he would do so soon. He was currently looking over the handwritten inventory. Obviously, all the guns including the large machine guns and tear gas systems would go plus all the ammo. However, he had a huge problem. "Those fucking mortars!"

The lieutenant did not think for a moment he would need mortars for this national emergency, and hoped like hell that he was right. Normally, no way in hell would a National Guard base have any short-range artillery weapons, but they were here and it was his problem. A "cluster fuck," as Dale called it by the Army Supply Depot resulted in him having the mortars.

While outfitting the base earlier in the year, a large private delivery truck showed up at the base and unloaded its cargo. Included in the mix of supplies were four 60 mm mortar launchers and 240 rounds of high-explosive shells. The colonel went nuts. When he ordered his to men to put that "shit" back into the truck, the driver refused.

The driver told the colonel, "Had I known these explosive rounds were in the load, I would not have transported it here from Nevada. I am in violation of about a dozen state, federal, and national highways traffic safety laws and rules. If you put that stuff back in my truck, I will leave it here and fly home."

It took about two weeks for the Army to discover the cause of the screw up. The paperwork stated the base was to receive a new design tear gas launching system that fired cardboard gas canisters in a similar fashion as a mortar. The Army, in its infinite wisdom, had named the new tear gas system "TGM224." The current model standard 60mm mortar was a M224A1 System. So for the new base TGM224 systems were part of an inventory of riot control equipment. However, when the paperwork moved through the military bureaucracy, someone messed up. While transferring numbers and quantities using an old computer system and not finding the new designation, a clerk just dropped the "TG" and used the older number, which was in the database. This resulted in the order unintentionally changed to the M224 Mortar System. To compound the mistake, a supply clerk added the A1 to the order, figuring some idiot had used the older part number that did not have the "A1" versus the new name.

The next part of the mistake was another shipping clerk, who thinking it weird someone had ordered the M224A1 systems, but the round designation was incorrect. Therefore, he fixed the "mistake" changing the cardboard canister tear gas cartridge to the M720HE rounds. He had made the determination any unit ordering the M224A1 units needed the correct rounds for it.

The civilian truck picked up the load in Northern Nevada and arrived in Sylmar the next day. Only after unloading the cargo was the bureaucratic mistake found. The driver would not take them back. The Army started a paperwork war, trying to figure out how it happened. Meanwhile, the launchers and rounds were placed in a heavy-duty weapons bunker. The mortar tubes and explosive rounds had been at the base about three weeks. Command placed an order for a special weapons truck with escorts to pick up the dangerous rounds and the launchers. The truck was scheduled to arrive two days from now.

Lieutenant Allen decided leaving the mortars and high explosive rounds here was not a choice if they were moving. The equipment had to go with him and his command. Once he got to an airport, he would try getting them onto a military transport plane and the "hell out of his sight." So with this plan, Alan ordered his men to load one of the big trucks with the launchers and all 240 rounds. As an extra level of caution, they kept that truck inside the large bay. Parked outside were six more trucks stuffed with weapons, food, water, and other supplies. He wished he had more men to help guard the base and the trucks, but the orders to pick up stranded motorists left a skeleton crew. Allen wanted to be ready to move as soon as the order came down.

Chapter 17

0615, Day 2, Garrett Residence, Agua Dulce, California

L awrence had awoken a few minutes earlier and found Madison in the kitchen using one of the small gas camping stoves to make a large pot of coffee. As Lawrence walked through the dining room, he looked out the window and froze. "Shit, someone is down at the gate."

Madison came over to the window to look. Down near the front gate, there was a large bright fire engine red truck. It was a van or panel truck. Lawrence said, "That is an old truck. Looks like late fifties vintage." On the sides of the truck was the lettering "RESCUE 8." They could see two people near the truck. An older man and woman were moving around the truck. They were working on something.

"Get everyone up," Lawrence said, and then he started putting on a khaki shirt and boots. When he had dressed, Richard came in the house from the motor home that he and his wife living in.

The rest of the family and friends soon arrived and took turns looking out the windows at the truck and two people. Now it became obvious that round-the-clock guards were essential. They had discussed it, but a shortage of people made a 24-7 post in the bunker on the hill difficult. The group now knew they needed to remain vigilant. This truck had driven right to the gate without detection.

Lawrence said, "I think they have some kind of problem with the truck."

Richard asked the group, "Do you think we should just wait and see what they do?"

Lawrence replied, "I think we should go see what is up. Better to surprise them and control the situation versus waiting to see what they do. They look to be in their sixties or seventies. I do not think they will be any trouble. Richard, you take the AR-10 sniper rifle, go up the hill, and provide cover just in case. James, you stay here at this window and provide added cover. I'll go down there. Everyone, get a radio. Arm up with the guns you have been assigned. Take various positions around the house and property. Keep your weapons out of sight unless of course you need them."

Everyone quickly did as Lawrence instructed. They gave Richard a few minutes to get up on the hill in a concealed spot that provided him a clear line of sight to the van and its occupants.

Lawrence went out the opposite side of the house and circled around to approach the van. He was carrying the Mossberg twelve-gauge pump shotgun and his Father's Glock-21 .45-caliber semiautomatic pistol. He slowly walked toward the front gate.

When Lawrence was about seventy-five feet away, he stopped and yelled to the couple, "Hello!"

The man had been crouching down by the right rear tire of the van. The woman was standing behind him looking over his shoulder. She turned quickly to face Lawrence, and the man stood up. The woman had a big revolver and she pointed it in Lawrence's direction.

"Whoa, hold on, lady, I don't mean you any harm. This is my property, and I just wanted to see what you two are doing."

"Don't come any closer!" the woman yelled back.

"Look, I will put down my guns if you will do the same," Lawrence said as he sat the shotgun down and laid the 45 next to it.

The woman turned to the man, who nodded. And exchange of words between the two strangers took place, which Lawrence could not understand from where he stood some thirty feet away. Relief came over him as the lady slowly turned and let go of the gun after placing it on the hood of the truck.

Lawrence now moved toward them slowly with his arms out in a nonthreatening manner. As he got closer, he said, "My name is Lawrence. As I said, this property belongs to my families. By the way, other family members are in hidden positions watching, so please don't do anything to spook them."

"Okay," said the man. "Come on over."

Lawrence moved to the gate and placed his hands on the top rail. He was now close enough to size up the couple. They appeared to be in their mid to late sixties. Both seemed in decent health, except the man had a pronounced limp. Lawrence noticed it as they moved forward to greet him. "My name is Barry, and this is my wife Holly." He then stuck out his hand. Lawrence shook Barry's hand and then Holly's.

"What are you guys doing here?" Lawrence asked.

"We came down this road to hide ourselves. A group of assholes took potshots at us on Soledad Canyon on the other side of the freeway. It looks like they must have hit the rear tire. I drove here on the flat. I don't think I could have gone much further. Tire is junk now. To top it off, they hit the spare tire also. I am trying stop the leak in the spare with some of those tire sealer cans, but it is not working. The hole is too big."

"Where did you guys come from, and what is this truck?" Lawrence said.

"We live down in Sylmar. There are fires everywhere in the Valley. Last night, one of the fires started heading our way, so my wife and I decided to get out while we could. This old truck is the original prop truck used in an old TV show called Rescue 8. I bought it about twenty years ago from a guy that had bought it from the prop house. I was sure glad I had it. Our new Lexus was dead as yesterday's communion wine."

"I think my dad mentioned that show. Kind of like the show *Emergency*, right?" Lawrence asked.

"Yep, that is right. Filming took place in 1958 for a couple of years. It starred Jim Davis as one of the firemen. He is the actor that played Jock on the TV show Dallas. Anyway, we loaded up all our emergency supplies and headed out. The freeway is a permanent parking lot, so we went up, over Little Tujunga Canyon Road, and through Sand Canyon. We were planning on heading North to Big Pine, where my brother lives. We were on Soledad Canyon and someone tried to roadblock us. I spun the truck around, and we headed up Agua Dulce Canyon road. Whoever was blocking the road took several potshots at us. The rear windows were also shot out. I say we lucked out not getting hit in the back of the head."

Lawrence moved left along the gate until he could see the back of the truck. It was an old one-ton Chevrolet Suburban with a beautiful bright fire engine—red paint job. Both of the small rear door windows were mostly gone. Only a few shards of glass stuck out around the frame of the windows.

"Wow, you guys are lucky to be alive," Lawrence said. "I want to let everyone know you guys are not a threat."

Lawrence slid the radio from its belt pouch and said, "Everyone can stand down. I think these people are okay. Mom, you should come down here. Oh, and bring that pot of coffee and some extra cups please. Richard, stay there and keep an eye out. Someone was chasing these people, and they may have followed."

"Roger that. And can you have Sandra bring me a jug of coffee?" Richard answered

A few minutes later, Madison, Melinda, James, and Logan all arrived at the gate. Madison was carrying a large steel pot that had the coffee, and the others were carrying cups including extras for the couple and Lawrence.

Lawrence went over and punched a code into the keypad, and the gate slid open.

"How come this gate is working? Do you people still have power?" Barry asked.

"Batteries power the gate. My dad wanted it to work if the power was out, so he built it with a solar panel and a couple of car batteries."

Lawrence pointed to the control box and solar panel near one end of the gate. "We also have solar power for the house and a battery bank that provides us some power at night."

The Garrett clan arrived, moved through the gate, introduced themselves, and shook hands with Barry and Holly. Lawrence prodded Barry to retell the story of their trip to the rest of the family. Madison handed out coffee cups, and she poured a cup for everyone as they listened to Barry recount the adventure.

Lawrence took the time to explain to Barry and Holly the state of things at the Garrett house. He also explained about his missing father, Lee. He did not have to say they were all worried, but he explained how Lee was resourceful and quite well prepared.

Madison said, "I expect Lee to pull up driving a forklift or backhoe any minute now."

Logan responded, "Knowing Dad, it will be more like an old Mach-1 Mustang."

Barry answered, "Hate to be negative, but I think all the roads must be treacherous. Too many people out there had no preparation at all, and they will do anything to survive. The locals are going to create roadblocks like the one we experienced to stop anyone strange. We have no idea what they would have done had we stopped, but we did not want to find out."

Madison responded, "Yes that is the biggest worry we have. However, we are confident Lee will think of some way to make it home."

Then Madison changed the subject, asking, "So tell us a little more about yourself, Barry."

Barry told the story to the group, "Well, we're both retired. Before that, I owned an automotive repair shop over in North Hollywood. I had the place for about thirty-five years. I opened it when I came back from Nam."

"So you were in Nam?" Lawrence asked.

"Yep, I almost did two tours for the 1st Air Cavalry. I was part of an L-R-R-P team. You know, Long-Range Reconnaissance and Patrol," Barry said to explain what LRRP stood for.

"Well, I'll be," Lawrence said. "I am an ex-75th Ranger Regiment, 1st Battalion. I've been out about a year now. I know what the old L-R-R-P teams were. They eventually molded into the 75th Ranger Regiment."

Barry answered and saluted in perfect form, "No shit. Rangers Lead the Way."

"All the Way, Sir," Lawrence replied, returning the salute, completing the Ranger Ritual typically exchanged between Rangers and Officers.

"Yeah, you are right about the 75th Ranger Regiment absorbing all the LRRP teams in seventy. 'Bout then, I was being medically discharged. A week before my second tour was to end, I stepped on a Viet-Cong booby trap and had part of my left foot removed by one of those wooden spears. I could have stayed in, but that war was a political crap trap, and I was glad for a way out. I have no problem fighting a war, but I did not like fighting a bullshit police action where the rules changed daily. We should have just parked the battleships New Jersey and Missouri right in Hanoi harbor and shelled the fucking Chinese backed north until they surrendered."

Barry continued, "So I got out and a couple years later opened the shop down on Lankershim Boulevard. I always was a car nut, and my dad owned a repair shop before he passed away in sixty-five. Then I met my lovely wife, Holly, at a Mexican restaurant down the street from the shop. We married a year or so later and have been a happy couple since. Right, honey?"

Holly spoke up. "We married in seventy-five. We just celebrated our forty-some odd anniversary."

Madison then asked, "So you said you were trying to get up to Big Pine?"

"Yep, that is where my brother lives. We figure a small town out in the middle of nowhere might be the best place to be. The emergency radio says the power is out all the way past the Mississippi River and that Washington, DC, was nuked."

"An EMP took out the power," Logan said.

Barry continued, "I figured so, having lived through the Cold War. So Holly and me loaded up as much of our survival stuff as we could into the old Rescue 8 truck and headed out."

Lawrence asked, "Survival stuff?"

Barry and Holly looked at each other, and Barry asked, "Yeah, do you guys ever watch that show *Doomsday Preppers*?"

The entire Garrett clan laughed, and Madison said, "Watch it, we live it every day. My husband, Lee, should be on the show. But he always said the dumbest thing a real prepper could do was plaster their face and property all over the TV. So yes, we are Doomsday Preppers."

"Well, me and Holly are the same. Hated to leave the house, but it's probably nothing but ash now. The fire was out of control, and without fire, trucks, or water, there was not any way to stop it. We crammed the most valuable stuff in the truck. We took most of our supply of survival food, camping stuff, extra gas cans, a small generator, guns, and ammo. Let me show you our stash," Barry said.

Barry led the gang around back of the truck and opened the double rear doors of the old suburban.

A wide variety of items filled the truck nearly to the roof. The Garretts could see dozens of square emergency food supply buckets, gallon bottles of water, gas cans, and a huge variety of stuff all piled on top the buckets and cases of food.

"Did you have other guns besides that big revolver that Holly pointed in my direction?" Lawrence asked.

"Yep, there are a couple of Mini 14s in there, a couple of 12-gauge pumps, and a slightly illegal B-A-R," Barry answered.

"You got a working Browning?" Lawrence asked.

"Yep, had it buried in the backyard in a watertight canister 'bout twenty-five years. Still like new. We had one in our squad in Nam. I had to look long and hard to find one in the States. Actually, I found a nonworking one and did a makeover on it and made it like brand-spanking-new. I got about two thousand rounds of ammo for it. I also put in full auto kits into my Mini14s before we left the house." I'm figuring at this point, if I am busted for full autos—well, so be it, but I want all the firepower I can get. Wishing I had kept the BAR handy when we got ambushed."

"I am surprised you did not stand and fight when you guys were attacked?" Logan said.

"We had the long guns buried under our stuff in the back of the truck. We did not know if the cops, army, or Homeland Security would have roadblocks and searching vehicles. Besides, Holly here is a crack shot with that 357. Hell, she is a regular Dirty Harry with that thing. Plus, her eyes are much better than mine anyway. That is why I need the full auto. I can just spray and pray," Barry added, at which point they all laughed.

Barry then showed Lawrence and Logan the flat spare tire. It had been standing vertically inside the truck when the shooting occurred. The brand-new tire had a clean hole in the middle of the tread. A bullet had passed through the back door penetrating the tire. The rim stopped it, leaving the slug inside the tire.

Logan spoke up. "Hey, Dad has one of those tire plug kits. I bet it will work on this clean hole. I will go get it."

"And bring along that 12-volt air compressor. We can hook it to Barry's truck battery or to the batteries in the gate box," Lawrence said to Logan.

Logan and James turned and headed to the house and garage and returned shortly. The two of them took to plugging the tire using the pistol-type tire plug tool. It only took them a few minutes. Lawrence hooked up the alligator clips to the batteries inside the gate box, and the compressor starting chugging. They rolled the tire over to the compressor and attached the clip-on tire chuck. It took several minutes for the tire to fill up to the rated pressure.

Meanwhile, Lawrence and Barry used a large off-road type jack from the back of the truck to lift and take off the destroyed right rear tire. The now-repaired and filled spare was lifted onto the hub. The lug nuts were snugged, and the truck was lowered down. Logan used the cross-shaped lug wrench to tighten the lugs again once the tire was on the ground to ensure they were not loose. While doing this work, Logan thought to himself how his dad had taught him to plug tires and the trick about dropping the truck before the final torqueing of the lugs. He sure hoped his dad was okay and headed home.

While Logan and Barry were finishing installing the tire, Madison and Lawrence stepped away from the group to have a private conversation. When they were out of earshot, Madison said to Lawrence, "Are you thinking what I am thinking?"

"You mean how maybe we should offer to let Barry and Holly stay on here?" Lawrence replied.

"The fact they made it to our gate without us knowing proved how we could use some more help. They come well-supplied, which will minimize added drain of our own supplies. At least let them stay until things calm down on the road and they can then head off to Big Pine," Madison explained.

"I am totally on board with that. Do you want to have a group meeting to see what everyone else thinks?" Lawrence said.

Madison answered, "I think everyone will be in favor of it. Everyone knows we do not have enough help to stand guard twenty-four hours a day. They might be pretty old, but I have a hunch they can both take care of things pretty well."

"Okay, let's go see what they think," said Lawrence as he and his mom went back to the truck.

Madison explained their idea to Barry, Holly, and the others. Barry was a little hesitant, but Holly reiterated that they had only gone about twenty-five miles and "were almost killed." Making it to Big Pine was going to be difficult or impossible. So they agreed. No objections were raised from any of the Garrett clan. Lawrence radioed Richard and Sandra in the bunker on the hill and let them know the plan. They did not have any objections.

Barry and Holly were now official members of the Garrett Clan.

Chapter 18

0900, DAY 2, POWER LINE ROAD WEST OF KINGSTON ROAD, CALIFORNIA

As the sun was rising, Lee and Jake mounted their bikes and headed out. Two hours of hard riding, pushing, and swearing and they were at the top of the pass. They were thankful as they started down the other side of the pass on a long straight road. Once they hit the straight downhill, it was possible to see the power lines in the distance, and they arrived at them about forty-five minutes later.

The riders turned right and started heading west along the power line service road. They had changed bikes several times, but now Jake was leading and Lee was riding the bike with the small cart. Lee found riding the bike with the wagon was easier because of its extra rear wheels. He pointed out to Jake on the radio that he thought it acted like a set of training wheels. This amused Jake who agreed with the assumption. They had been on the power line road only a short distance when Jake stopped. Lee pulled up next to Jake, who was looking down at the dirt road.

"Look at these tracks," Jake explained. "These look new, and they look like some style of off-road tire. Maybe the buggy that Lucy is driving left these tire tracks."

Lee agreed with Jake's assumption. They decided to keep looking for the tracks. Assuming these tracks were from Lucy's buggy, knowing they were following the same road was a positive. They paused for a few minutes and drank some water and then kicked off again and kept moving west.

The road was still straight as an arrow, but it started getting steep again as it headed up the east side of another California desert mountain range. Eventually it got too steep, forcing them to dismount and walk the bikes for about the thirtieth time. As they had a dozen times before, they second-guessed about keeping the bikes but, just like before, would decide they would be well worth it in the end.

Arriving at the crest of the latest mountain range required pushing hard for most of the morning. When Lee and Jake arrived at the summit, they stopped, sat, and relaxed and ate the contents of an MRE from Lee's bag, washing it down with water-infused energy-drink powder. Both men knew the importance of staying hydrated. Since leaving Goodsprings, there had been no signs of trucks or cars or vehicles. The exception being the dune buggy tracks which were visible in the soft dirt along the road the men continued riding.

Lee and Jake decided to take about a two-hour break after eating. The sun was high and bright in the clear blue desert sky. Lucky the temperature high in the mountain range was cool. They laid out a poncho and a blanket on the soft sand, and both men slept for about two hours, awaking around two thirty in the early afternoon. They loaded up and headed out.

It was downhill, now making moving easy but dangerous. Both riders took several spills in the soft dirt and ruts of the service road. Concerns about either injuring themselves or damaging the bikes was high in their thoughts, so they constantly slowed.

They made the descent down the mountain range into a small valley and started up another. This climb was not as steep as the last, allowing them to ride more and push less. They reached the top of that summit around 6:00 p.m.

Just as Jake was climbing onto his bike to start down the west side of the latest summit, Lee noticed something in the distance on the power line road. Jake got back off his bike as Lee pulled out a pair of small binoculars from a pouch on his chest rig.

"This is interesting, Jake," Lee said. "It looks like a dune buggy like the one Joel described to us. It is sitting in a ravine."

Lee handed the binos to Jake, who looked down the hill at the buggy.

"You might be right," Jake said. "I don't see anyone around it though."

"Wonder if Lucy had to abandon it?" Lee asked.

"Could be. I cannot think of another good reason for it to be sitting there," Jake replied.

The two men climbed on the bikes and headed down the hill, looking for any sign of trouble. It took them about ten minutes to reach a point about fifty yards from the buggy where they stopped the bikes and dismounted. They turned in all directions, viewing the area carefully, and then made the final approach to the buggy slowly pushing the bikes.

The buggy was empty, and they saw footprints all around it plus a clear single set of prints continuing to the west in the direction of travel. Lee started looking over the buggy, trying to figure out the reason it had been abandon. The old Volkswagen-powered four-seat buggy did not have an ignition switch, only toggles and push buttons, so Lee removed his chest rig and fanny pack and climbed in where he determined the problem quickly. When Lee went to press down the clutch pedal before starting the buggy, he found it already sitting down at the floor.

"Clutch cable is busted," Lee said to Jake and then continued using a slang term for the Volkswagen dune buggy. "Common problem on these old V-dubbers. Cable probably broke when she downshifted for this ravine. She must have headed out on foot."

"Is there any way to fix it?" Jake quizzed. "You are the MacGyver of the group."

"Thanks, but I am just handy," Lee replied. "I have an engineer buddy whom I call Inspector Gadget. I even have the *Inspector Gadget* theme song as a ring tone on my phone for him. Or I guess I should say I had it."

"Well, you probably still have the ring tone, but I doubt he is going to call you to help out," Jake replied.

Lee wondered how his engineer friend was making out in the post-EMP world. He was pretty well-prepared like Lee, so he was optimistic that he and his family would weather this out.

Lee was still in the seat when he said, "Let's make sure it is running first." After determining it was in neutral, Lee hit the toggle marked Ignition and pressed the red button next to it. The VW motor sprung to life. It sounded fine. Fuel gauge said three-fourths full, oil pressure was good, and the voltmeter was in the green. The four-seat buggy seemed okay other than the broken clutch cable. The great condition of the buggy impressed Lee. Someone had taken great care of it.

Lee climbed back out of the driver's seat and stood staring and thinking. "I doubt there is a way to fix the cable, but we might be able to jury-rig something to allow us to drive it."

The braided steel clutch cable had snapped at the pedal end. It was a straight pull from the pedal through the center of the floor and up to the clutch arm. The clutch arm protruded from the side of the transaxle. Lee said, "I might have an idea." He started looking around the buggy to see what they had to work with.

"We need something like a pipe or bar and some tools. Every serious off roader has some tools," Lee said to Jake. Lee discovered the passenger seat tilted forward, and there was a neat little toolbox under it. Inside he found a bunch of tools and small parts, including a handful of worm-drive type hose clamps.

"These clamps will work, but we still need a bar or pipe for my idea to work," Lee said.

"What about a tire iron?" Jake asked.

"I saw one of those four-sided ones bolted to the top of the spare tire, but we need something straight," Lee answered.

"Well, if you are sure you can make it work, we could always use one of the sidebars on our bike trailer," Jake said while pointing at the small trailer behind the one bike.

"I guess if we get it running, we won't need the trailer or bikes. That might work," Lee said, looking at the bars on the little trailer.

"What is your plan?" Jake asked.

"My plan is to clamp a bar onto the clutch arm. One of us can work the clutch while the other drives," Lee said.

"Are you kidding?" Jake asked with an amused look. "That seems like it will be a real coordination challenge. A little like rubbing your stomach and patting your head."

"We only need the clutch when stopping and starting. I can drive without using the clutch once we get moving. I drove a buggy like this back from Baja California one time without a clutch. My buddy and I just made sure always to stop on a steep hill so we could roll-start it," Lee answered.

"Can we push-start this now?" Jake asked.

"I don't see how you and I can push it out of this ravine. There is not a way to roll downhill unless we get out of this ditch," Lee said as he pointed around. Lee and Jake could see that huge boulders blocked the ravine in the downhill direction, and both directions out were too steep for the two men to push the VW.

Seeing no other choice, Lee and Jake used the tools from under the seat and removed the tubing from one side of the bike trailer. Concerned it was too light, Lee suggested using both sides and taping them together to make it twice as strong. After removing the two bars, Lee held them in position on the clutch arm. The tubes were too long, causing them to collide with one of the buggy frame tubes. Lee had found a hacksaw under the seat, providing a way of cutting the tubes.

"Once we cut these tubes, we risk taking our little trailer out of commission," Lee said to Jake.

"Well, like I said, I was doing well at the crap table when the lights went out. Let's hope my luck is still running good," Jake replied.

While Jake held the tubes one at a time, Lee sawed them off to the length they needed. Then they wrapped them together to form one stronger tube using duct tape also scavenged from under the seat. As they were doing the work, Lee said, "Good thing Rick kept the basic MacGyver stuff in here."

After taping the tubes and with Jake holding them, Lee screwed four small worm drive clamps around the combined tubes and cast steel arm. He had removed the broken cable first to make more room. It was a tight fit, but the tubes fit between the motor parts and the horizontal roll bar tube. After Lee had the clamps secure, he gave it a tug to try out the new clutch arm. Lee pulled the arm forward to see if it would release the clutch without bending or breaking the makeshift prybar.

"I think it works. Let's give it a try," Lee said to Jake. "You sit in the backseat behind me. I will drive, and you work the clutch."

"I bet this is going to be fun," Jake said.

"Let's use two simple audible commands of *clutch* and *out*," Lee said to Jake. "When I say *clutch*, you pull it down. When I say *out*, you release it slowly, as you would do if you were working a clutch pedal. Got it?"

"Got it. Let's give it a try," Jake replied.

They moved the bikes and trailer out of the way and climbed into their assigned spots in the buggy. Lee called out "Clutch," and Jake pulled down on the handle. Lee started up the buggy and put it into first gear.

"Okay, here we go. *Out*!" Lee yelled over the motor. Jake let out the clutch, and Lee eased the throttle. The buggy jerked a few times, jumped a few feet, and stalled.

"Shit," Jake said loudly.

"No big deal. I think we are close. Try again," Lee said.

Jake pulled in the clutch, and Lee restarted the buggy and yelled "Out" again. This time, the buggy did not jump but rolled forward smoothly, so Lee drove up the incline out of the ditch in first gear. He started down the flat road. When RPMs were up, Lee eased the throttle back and moved the gear shifter toward second. It stuck at first, ground a little, and then fell into second. Lee drove along the road for a few hundred yards to a place with enough clearing to make a U-turn. He returned to the starting point, passed by it, and again found a place to make a U-turn, turning back in the correct direction. Lee passed their bikes, continuing up the slope out of the ravine onto a flat spot.

Once on flat ground, Lee yelled out, "*Clutch!*"

Jake pulled the lever, and the clutch disengaged, causing the motor to rev up. Lee backed off the throttle and the RPMs dropped.

He stopped the buggy and killed the ignition. "Bitchin'," Lee yelled out and turned, giving Jake a high-five.

"Shit, boss, we are riding in style now," Jake said. "I am the clutch man. You is the gas man."

Lee and Jake climbed out of the buggy and started loading up the gear. Jake would ride in the back, so they placed Lee's larger BOB in the right front seat and Jake's bag in the right rear seat. Extra loose stuff was piled on the floorboards.

"Do we take the bikes?" Lee asked.

"I think we better just in case something else goes south on our new ride," Jake answered. "We should leave the trailer, however. It is too large, and besides, we vandalized it. We can tie the bikes on the top of the roll cage."

Lee removed a bundle of half-inch diameter rope that was secured to the outside of his bag, and using "trucker" knots, the two men tied both bikes to the top of the roll cage. When finished, they climbed into their seats. Because of his awkward position, Jake could not put on a seat belt. Lee decided he would forgo his belt also. They were in this together, so if they wrecked, they both wrecked big.

Chapter 19

0530, Day 2, Sylmar, California

Dayyan was in the second of four of the large black DHS armored vehicles. William was driving the lead vehicle. Born and raised in California, he was in outward appearance and speech the most "American" of his men. In the previous few years, William had turned toward Islam and eventually the dark side of the religion after meeting Naseem at a local Mosque. Dayyan's handlers carefully vetted him, and he was now a trusted brother. His California accent and his white look and actions made him look as American as apple pie. William and the others in the four trucks were wearing black uniform shirts and DHS hats that they had scavenged inside one of the older trucks at the armored car shop. The drivers and front seat passengers were all clean-shaven. William even sported a badge that read "Sullivan" and two rows of military type ribbons and several other items. He looked as much like a DHS officer as any actual officer would.

The four trucks rolled in tight formation right up to the locked gate of the National Guard compound. Two M4-equipped soldiers moved toward the gate, shining flashlights at the big black trucks lighting up the "Department of Homeland Security" emblems on the side of the lead truck. The heavily armored trucks did not have roll-down windows, so William opened his door and stood on the step. Leaning around the door, he said to the two guards, "Evening, gentleman, Captain Sullivan, D-H-S. My unit was sent from Burbank

Airport with orders to access the situation here in the North Valley. Is your commander available to have a meeting?"

Without answering directly, Specialist Alton Haynes spoke into his radio mic, which was hanging from his right shoulder strap. "Lieutenant, four D-H-S trucks from Burbank Airport are at the gate and asking to see you."

Allen said back over the radio, "Are you sure they are D-H-S?"

"Sir, the trucks are all armored type, and the men appear to be the real McCoy."

"Okay, open the gate and send them up. Maybe they have some information or can tell us what the hell we should be doing."

Specialist Haynes unlocked the gate lock and slid the large heavy steel gate open. William saluted, climbed back into the truck, and drove the first of the four big trucks into the yard up to the main building. Dayyan smiled. It appeared his plan was working. As the four trucks moved in, the rest of his men would be assaulting the base from two other directions through holes they had cut into the fences quietly during the last hour. The last truck in the convoy held back slightly, and only when the first trucks were near the main building did it start to move forward. This forced the two guards to leave the gate open waiting for the last truck.

When the lead truck arrived at the front of the HQ building, Lieutenant Allen had already come out of the building with Sergeant Claude Sutton. Both men kept their pistols holstered as they approached the trucks. Dayyan had his driver pull up on the opposite side of the first truck with the third truck pulling behind the first. Blocked from view, four men exited Dayyan's truck from the rear door and made their way quietly around the back of the lead truck. Allen and Sergeant Sutton reached the first truck, stopped, and stared into it. William fumbled around in the truck, wasting time before flipping a switch on the dash. The left side of the truck lit up, brightly casting a blinding light into the eyes of the two unsuspecting National Guard Soldiers. They never saw the four terrorists who came around the truck until it was too late.

As the fourth truck turned into the driveway and was partway through the gate, the rear door opened, and four men jumped out.

Unlike the soldiers, Lieutenant Allen and Sergeant Sutton did not see; these soldiers at the gate spotted the men coming around the truck. It made no sense to either man, and they raised their M4 assault weapons but not quickly enough. Dozens of rounds sprayed out of the rifles of the four ISIS thugs, cutting down the soldiers instantly.

At the sound of the gunshots, the lieutenant and the sergeant jumped and started to pull out their side arms, but like the gate guards, they had no chance against multiple rifles. As his men shot down the soldiers, Dayyan sprinted for the door to ensure the two men had not locked it when they came outside. It had not been locked. Dayyan flung open the door and signaled his men inside. A brief one-sided firefight occurred as three more soldiers charged to the front of the building at the sound of the gunshots. Those soldiers had been loading trucks and had not bothered to retrieve their rifles. One had a sidearm, but the other two were defenseless against the onslaught by the rebel soldiers and their AK-47 assault rifles.

Only two National Guard soldiers would survive the attack. The men were out in a rear storage lot planning to bring up two more trucks when the shooting started. Both the unarmed soldiers crouched down out of sight behind one of the big 6×6 trucks. They could see the shooting at the gate and front of the main building. They decided to charge up into the fight, but just as they decided to move, a group of about twenty men ran from behind the storage building heading toward the main building. Knowing it would be suicide to run into the fight unarmed, the two slid under a truck and remained hidden. Eventually, when it was obvious dozens of armed terrorists had overrun the base, the two men crept into an area behind the storage building where they hid among stacks of large 250-gallon water tanks.

At the main building, Dayyan was smiling to himself. The plan had worked flawlessly. Dayyan and his men had taken the base without a single of his men being injured or killed. Now he had large trucks, plus other weapons such as machine guns. God had been kind to his small but growing army.

Chapter 20

1930, Day 2, Power Line Road, Somewhere in California

U sing the "buddy" clutching method, Lee and Jake headed out in the buggy. "Clutch...out...clutch...out..." Lee would yell out, and Jake would comply, working the clutch lever using the aluminum tubes from the bike trailer. They were getting better at the odd routine, only stalling or grinding gears a few times while navigating a deep ditch or ravine or when climbing a steep incline. As it was starting to get dark, Lee turned on the front mounted "bugeye" headlamps. Lee was keeping the speed down using third gear for the top speed, considering that neither he nor Jake was wearing seat belts. As they moved along at a decent pace, Lee suspected they must be getting close to the Death Valley Highway. That highway ran at a right angle to their path from Baker North out to Death Valley.

Lee looked back to see how Jake was doing. Just as he returned his gaze forward, he froze in shock. A lone figure was standing in the road right in his path. Lee slammed on the brakes, yelled "Clutch," and the buggy stopped. Lee and Jake could tell it was a woman and she was pointing a large pistol right at them.

"Lucy!" Jake yelled out just as Lee raised his hands from the wheel.

Lucy slowly lowered the pistol, and as she shielded her eyes, she called back, "Who is that?"

"It is me, Jake. Jake Rodriguez."

Lee reached out, flipping off the headlights which had surely had been blinding Lucy.

"Jake...what the...what are you doing here? How did you get my buggy running? Where did you come from?" Lucy started spattering out question after question.

Jake climbed out and ran up to Lucy. They hugged as Lee climbed out and joined them.

Jake introduced Lee, "Lucy, this is Lee. He saved my ass back in Vegas. We have walked and ridden bicycles out of Vegas and were heading to Irwin like you. We found your buggy back up the road a ways, and Lee came up with a slick way to make the clutch work."

"Hi, Lee," Lucy said as she moved forward and gave him a big hug. "I am so glad to see you guys. I was getting scared shitless out here. I had just decided this was a stupid idea to drive that old jalopy to Irwin."

Lucy was wearing what looked like an old Vietnam era knapsack. She tucked the .45 pistol back into a waist holster. They all walked back over to the buggy, and Jake showed her the neat trick Lee had come up with for the clutch arm.

Lucy laughed and said, "Wow, I would have never figured out how to do that. I guess Joel was right that I should have waited for someone to go with me."

Jake replied, "Hell, Lucy. I don't know anyone who could have figured out this clutch thing. Lee here has saved my ass, fixed the Mormons generator, and fixed your buggy. He is not army. He must be some superhero and should be wearing a cape."

"I never wear my cape out in public anymore," Lee responded.

The three of them sat for a few minutes and talked as they drank water and munched on power bars and trail mix. Jake asked Lucy if she figured on walking the rest of the way to Irwin. She told him and Lee that she did not know. She said she had first thought about going on but now had decided to walk down the road to Baker. She figured Baker would be a huge mess with many stranded travelers. However, she did not feel she had enough water for a long several days' walk to Fort Irwin. When seeing the buggy coming, she did not know what to think and just reacted, pulling out the 1911. Thankfully, she had not shot at the two men.

Everyone was happy about finding one another, so they sat for a bit discussing the terrible calamity facing the nation. Eventually, they decided it would be best to get going.

"If we hit the road, we should make Irwin in a couple of hours in the buggy," Lee said.

They stuffed Lee's huge bag and Lucy's smaller rucksack into the backseat with Jake. Then using bungee cords holding everything satisfactorily secure, they loaded up.

Lucy found the loose seat belt ends and started to put them on.

Lee spoke up. "Jake cannot wear the belts, so I am not either. This will keep me from doing something stupid."

Lucy responded, "Okay, screw it, I will go commando also." She dropped the belts, letting them fall back along the seat.

"Clutch!" Lee yelled and started the motor.

"Out!" And the newly formed trio headed down the road.

After about a quarter mile, Lee could see a road crossing ahead. He thought it must be the highway to Death Valley and started to say something, when suddenly, two people jumped in the road in front of the buggy and started waving their arms.

"Shit!" Lee said loudly to both and then "Clutch" back to Jake.

Lee skid the buggy to a stop but left it running and in second gear. The two people in front of the buggy were clearly female, and they lowered their arms and stood still in the middle of the dirt road. Lee started reaching out toward the ignition switch, intending to turn it off. As he did, another figure jumped out from behind a large bush on his side and stuck a long skinny barrel right up to Lee's face and said, "Don't fucking move."

Lee then noticed another shorter man coming out of the bushes to the right moving toward the buggy. Lee could not see any weapon.

Lee, Jake, and Lucy all froze. Lee's Ruger was in the fanny pack around his waist, and he considered it, but with the rifle barrel only six inches from his head, he dared not move. Lee raised both hands above his head slowly. Lucy looked down at her waist where the 1911 was, but she, like Lee, realized the danger. She put her arms up. Lee could not see what Jake was doing, but he assumed the clutch was released and the buggy was still in gear. Lee turned slightly to his left to look at the man with the gun. He was an older, scraggly-looking person, and the rifle seemed small, like a .22 caliber or something of that sort. It was not a military-type weapon, and its small size might have been amusing if not for it pointing at Lee's head.

The man with the rifle looked behind Lee at Jake and said, "You, what the fuck are you doing? I said get your hands up, asshole."

"I can only raise one hand, dude," Jake said.

"Fuck you! Put both hands up now before I shoot your ass," the skinny man said as he swung the gun toward Jake. As he did, he stepped in closer to the buggy, placing himself between the front and rear wheels.

"Get that other fucking hand up now!" the man said again.

"OK," said Jake.

"*Out!*" Lee yelled, and he punched the throttle.

Jake got the message, and he released the makeshift tubes, allowing the clutch arm to fly back and violently engage the clutch. The result was similar to what racers would call "sidestepping" the clutch. The buggy jumped forward. As it lurched, Lee reached out with his left arm, grabbing the end of the barrel and pushing it up toward the buggy, causing the skinny triggerman to fall forward with it. The man fell as the big rear wheels spun, grabbing traction rolling up his right side and over his chest, slamming him into the soft dirt. Realizing he was about to be flattened, the man squeezed the trigger, firing one round harmlessly into the air. He then let go of the rifle and turned toward the tire, putting both hands out, thinking he could stop it. It turned out to be a major mistake.

The buggy jumped over the skinny man and continued down the road, forcing the two girls to jump away. Lee slammed the brake pedal, sliding the buggy to a stop. He then flipped the ignition toggle switch to the Off position and jumped out with the Ruger in hand. Jake had already leapt out of the right side with his ghetto blaster pointed at the other man and the screaming girls. The man on the ground was rolling around screaming.

Jake threw down the other man and planted a foot into his neck. Lucy followed the men out of the buggy and pointed the 1911 pistol at the two girls, telling them to lie down. They both complied in lightning speed. Lee ran up to Skinny and pointed the Rueger at him as he rolled, screamed, and held his right arm with his left. His right arm did not look good. Lee could see what looked like an extra elbow sticking out between the original elbow and his wrist. Lee reached down and picked up the rifle, examining it. As he had guessed, it was a small bolt-action 22. He pulled the bolt back but did not cycle it forward.

"Why in God's name did you attack us?" Lee yelled at the man.

"I think my arm is broken, and I can't breathe," he replied.

"I should just shoot you for sticking this gun in my head, you asshole," Lee blasted back.

Jake stuck his big gun in the back of the other man and spoke. "Are there any more in your group?"

"No, just the four of us," the man replied.

"Are you fucking sure of that? Because if anyone else shows up, I am going to shoot you first," Jake asked again.

"Yes, I swear. I did not even know Howard was going to do that," the subdued man answered.

"So your name is Howard?" Lee asked the injured assailant.

"Yes," he mumbled between groans and crying.

"I am going to search you," Lee said. "If you do anything stupid, I will finish what the buggy started."

Lee looked over the man and did not see any other weapons. He patted his front pockets and found only keys and a wad of cash, which he dropped on the ground. Rolling him over, he pulled a wallet from the back pocket went through it and found a license. Howard was in bad pain, so Lee did not worry about him posing any more threat. He looked at the California driver's license. "Howard Linwood Bodner."

Lee then went over to the two girls. He judged them to be in their midtwenties. He said, "Roll over and sit up. Do not do anything stupid, or you will be back on your face. Got it?"

"Yes," one replied.

"Okay," said the other.

The two girls slowly sat up. Lee went over to the buggy and from his backpack removed several large wire ties from the MOLE webbing, which covered the sides of the pack. Jake patted down the other man also finding money and a wallet plus a small multitool and knife that he tossed off the road.

Lee returned with the wire ties, using them to bind the girls' wrists. They were crying hysterically, and by the wet spots on their tight-fitting jeans, it appeared both of them had relieved themselves.

Jake moved the other man over, telling him to sit next to the girls. Then Lee bound his wrists also, although a bit tighter than he had for the girls. Jake looked at his wallet and said, "This idiot is Jason. Jason Orville Thompson."

Lee figured the girls did not have wallets. Then he started to wonder if they had other stuff. If so, where was it? No one was carrying any type of bag or pack. They would not be out this far in the wilderness without some kind of gear or a vehicle.

"Well, ladies, what are your names?" Lee asked.

The brunette spoke up. "I am Brenda, and this is Megan."

"So what are you doing, and why in hell did you try to ambush us?" said Lee.

They both started babbling at once, so Lee said, "Megan, shut up. You tell me, Brenda."

Brenda started, "We were passing through Baker in Howard's camper. We were going to go out and camp in Death Valley. We stopped for gas, and just as we pulled in the station, the power went out. A bunch of people were watching TV in the store. We went in to see what happened, and they said the emergency broadcast signal had come on. They were talking about a real emergency and maybe a nuke in Washington. They said the TV had a message saying 'Stay tuned,' but the power went out and the TV went off."

"Keep going," Lee prodded.

"Everyone hurried to their cars, but none of them would run but ours. We did not know what to do. We had not gotten any gas yet, and we did not have much left. We decided to stay and wait to see if the power would come back on so we could get gas. We stayed all day yesterday. Then people started all getting like really weird. They started demanding that the stores give them food and water and fights started breaking out. And everyone was looking at us weirdly because our truck was still running."

"A couple of guys came over and said that we should siphon gas out of the non-running cars and put it in the camper truck and then we could drive it back to Barstow. Howard was going to do that, but then several people started saying they wanted to go in the camper, and it started turning ugly. Howard went into the camper and pulled out that gun and pointed it at everyone and told them all to get back. Then we jumped in the truck. Jason drove and we got the heck out of there. Jason started going toward LA, but there was a huge crowd of people trying to stop us, so we turned around, and the only road that was not blocked was the one to Death Valley."

"We drove out as fast as we could, and we headed up the road, looking for other roads that might double back toward Barstow. We found this road, but the truck got stuck real quick when we left the highway. It is on the other side of the road just a little ways. We have been trying to dig it out since yesterday afternoon, but it is really stuck. Then we think it ran out of gas while we tried to get it unstuck. We did not know what to do. Then we saw your lights coming down the hill and we saw you stop a ways back."

"So you made a quick plan to ambush us," Jake asked.

"*No!*" the blonde said. "Howard told the two of us to stand in the road because it was more likely someone would stop and we could ask for help. He did not say he was going to use the gun. He said he wanted it just in case someone in the dune buggy was dangerous."

"We just need help, mister," said Brenda. "I'm sorry Howard pointed his gun at you. But please don't hurt us."

"And please don't leave us out here," said Megan. "We'll die out here."

While the three were listening to Brenda's story, Lee, Jake, and Lucy saw Howard was still moaning and groaning, but he was less vocal. "Watch them," Lee said to Lucy and Jake, and he went over to check on Howard.

It was now obvious that Howard had injury to his chest as well as his right arm. His breathing was labored. "The story the girls told us? Is it true?" Lee asked Howard.

"Ye…ah…yes. I…was…just…trying…to protect the girls." Howard quietly stuttered out between hard breathing.

Lee leaned down and said, "You know, Howard, this is the third time between Jake and I that we have been attacked since the shit hit the fan, and it is getting old. People had better start working together, or we are all fucking doomed. Your dumb ass stunt has nearly killed you, and I am not sure what we can do to help you."

Lee went to the buggy and opened his BOB, retrieving the first aid kit from the top pouch. He pulled out a water bottle, which had layers of duct tape around it. Lee wrapped tape on all his water bottles in that manner. He carried the stuff over to Howard and set it down. If Howard had crushed ribs and internal injuries, there was nothing in Lee's bag that would help. Nevertheless, Lee would do what he could for his arm and pain.

Lee looked around and, by luck, saw some wooden road marking stakes. Likely stuck in the side of the road to mark a trail or racecourse, he pulled up two and returned to Howard.

"Lucy, come and help me," Lee asked. "Let's try to splint his arm."

"Howard, this is going to hurt. But it will hurt less if I splint your arm," Lee said to Howard.

Lee carefully pulled Howard's left hand away from his broken arm. Then he pulled the sleeve on his right arm up to expose a small bone that was sticking out just above his wrist. "Lucy, hold his shoulder," Lee said.

Lucy moved around to the other side of Howard, and she grasped his upper arm and shoulder.

"Now, Howard, this is going to hurt like a mother," Lee said.

Lee then held the upperpart of his forearm and stretched out his wrist. Howard screamed bloody murder, but Lee kept pulling until the bone pulled back below the surface of his skin and muscle. Blood spurted out, but it did not look like any major artery, so Lee was not too worried about him bleeding out.

Lucy held the arm straight while Lee used the two wood stakes and some self-clinging gauze to fashion a crude splint. Over the gauze, Lee used duct tape to tie it all together tight while leaving room for swelling. Lee thought, as big an asshole as Howard was, he did well with all the pain. However, Lee had concerns—his color was bad and he was showing signs of shock.

After wrapping the arm, Lee rolled Howard over onto his left side to reduce the pressure on his chest and that eased his breathing a small amount. Lee got out six Advil and two prescription pain pills that were in a small plastic pillbox inside his first aid kit. The pain pills were an old prescription given to Lee for some reason or another but never used. Hell, Lee did not even know if they were still good, but he figured they might be good even as a placebo. Lucy held up Howard's head while Lee placed the pills on Howard's tongue and held the water bottle for him to drink down as much liquid as he could. Lucy unwrapped a sweater from around Brenda's waist, folded it to use as a pillow, and Lee covered Howard with a thick multilayer emergency blanket. For the time being, it was all they could do for Howard.

Lee, Lucy, and Jake gathered out of earshot of the others to discuss choices.

"I think this guy might be bleeding internally," Lee said.

"Asshole should have just asked for our help," Jake replied.

"Probably after their experience in Baker, they were all scared that we would just kill them," Lucy added.

"Well, if we leave them, he could die. What do you guys think about taking him to Irwin and leaving the rest here?" Lee asked.

"I guess that is the only right thing to do," Jake replied. "Even the Afghanistan people help their enemy's once they are defenseless. It is Pashtun law."

"I am good with that. Might be a tight fit, but we can make it work," Lee said.

The three of them walked back over to the group and told them the plan.

Lee spoke up. "Okay, guys, we are going to load your friend Howard up and take him with us. You three are going to have to walk the rest of the way to Fort Irwin. It is about thirty miles, so it is going to take you a couple of days, but your other choice is to go back to Baker and take your chances. Personally, I would hike to Irwin. I assume you have some food, water, and clothing in your camper, so you need to pack up enough stuff for three to four days. Do you have backpacks or duffels you can make into backpacks?"

"Yes, we do have some small day packs," replied Jason.

"Come up with a makeshift way to carry as much water as possible. Take jackets and extra socks. I hope you all have comfortable shoes. Take first aid stuff, flashlights, matches, or lighters and anything else you think might help. Don't worry about cooking. Take food that you can eat cold. You do not need extra weight of cook gear. I have a map I will mark out the course and give you a compass. It is the best we can do."

"Or should do, after you tried to bushwhack us," Lucy added.

Jake and Lee carefully lifted Howard, who was getting worse into the right rear seat of the buggy. Jake did strap him in and put a jacket under his arm to help with the pain as best he could and tucked the emergency blanket around him. He was clearly in shock, and his color was getting worse. Jake and Lee did not want to waste any more time. They piled the bags and gear around him and crammed stuff into every available space.

Lee carried the 22 rifle, backed up the road a ways, and left it. After loading up Howard, Lee gave the others a map, compass, and some bulk food bars, plus four Bic lighters. Lee and Jake climbed back into the buggy. Lucy used Jason's multi-tool to cut the girls and Jason's wrists free and slid over the right side and into the front seat of the buggy.

Lee wished them luck, started the buggy, and then said, "Clutch, out."

Lee drove around the three harried and worried people. Jake and Lee were becoming experts at the clutch routine, so they smoothly motored off in the buggy. Crossing the highway ahead, they saw the stuck camper about a quarter mile down the road. The tires of the truck deeply buried in the soft silt of the Mojave Desert. It was an old Dodge Crew Cab with a beaten-up Lance brand camper on the back.

Seeing the depth of the sand, Lee was certain pulling the truck out with the broken clutch buggy would have been risky. Using valuable fuel from the buggy would not ensure the gas-guzzling truck would make it anywhere safe. Baker was obviously a disaster already. After a short discussion, they all agreed that risking the VW to save the camper was not worth the risk. They drove down the road past the camper and continued to Irwin.

They had driven for about two hours, and Lucy thought they might be getting close to Irwin. Lucy said it was only a few miles to the south side of the base. Jake agreed, saying he had been out in this area training. As the three of them were discussing the distance, suddenly the world lit up brightly, blinding everyone in the buggy. Several spotlights hit the VW from ahead.

A loudspeaker-amplified voice spoke out. "*Stop the vehicle and put your hands up or we will shoot to kill.*"

Lee did not bother to call out the clutch commands. He hit the ignition toggle switch and raised his hands. He assumed they had found Fort Irwin, or at least the army had just found them. Everyone in the buggy raised his or her hands up, except Howard.

"*You in the backseat, raise your hands,*" the voice commanded.

Jake yelled out as loud as possible, "We have an injured man here. He cannot comply. I am Sergeant Rodriguez, Eleventh Armor, Bravo Company. Don't shoot."

"*We are going to approach. Do not move,*" commanded the soldier on the loudspeaker.

Everyone sat perfectly still as two men approached from each side of the buggy. Both soldiers had military-style assault rifles raised and pointing directly at the heads of the occupants.

"You, Rodriguez, what is your commander's name?" the soldier on the left side shouted out.

"Colonel Braxton," Jake said.

"What is the Colonel's call sign?"

"Derringer," Jake said immediately.

"And why does a gringo-looking asshole like you have the name *Rodriguez?*"

"Because my stepfather is Mexican and my mother is more gringo than you, Dupree, you dipshit."

Lucy and Lee looked at one another, knowing that Jake knew the soldier and the soldier knew him. The game was up, and Lee and Lucy started to breathe again.

"Who you got with you, Roz?" Dupree asked.

"That is Lucy Harwell in the front seat. Rick's wife. This is Rick's buggy. This nutcase driving is my lucky leprechaun that saved my butt in Vegas. The injured man in the backseat got himself run over trying to hijack us. He needs medical help ASAP," Jake explained.

"Peters, get on the radio and call the gate. Tell them we have injured. Get a medic down here. Tell the colonel that his spoiled brat Rodriguez has come back home," Dupree said to another soldier.

Lee, Lucy, and Jake climbed out of the buggy but left Howard where he was. While they waited for the medics and the colonel, Jake explained the clutch problem and other highlights of the journey to Dupree and the other soldiers.

Jake asked, "So, Dupree, why are you turds guarding this back road into the base?"

Dupree answered, "General's orders. World War fucking Three has started, and talk is there may be Lone Wolf terrorists trying to inflict more damage on the country from the inside. You are lucky we did not just blow you guys to hell. Shit, Roz, you look like a dirtbag terrorist, now that I think about it. I saw cleaner assholes in the middle of Afghanistan herding sheep."

"Shit, Dupree, did they actually issue you retards bullets?" Jake said sarcastically back.

"Yeah. One each. Just enough to finish you off," Dupree said back.

"Fuck, Dupree, the way you shoot, you could not hit this buggy with a full mag of shot shells and a steady rest if you were standing on the hood," Jake said.

"I remember shooting some Taliban dude with an AK who was going to pierce your helmet while you were jacking off reloading," Dupree replied.

Jake answered, "Well, I will give you that one. I guess that means I have to take care of you for the rest of your crappy life."

Their sarcastic exchange ended as a Humvee rolled down the road, trailing a cloud of dust. It pulled up, and two soldiers with medic emblems climbed out and headed to the buggy. A couple of other soldiers helped carefully lift Howard out of the buggy and lay him down on a stretcher. The medics looked him over and took some vital signs. They wasted no time and started an IV on him. They were just starting to pick up the stretcher when another Hummer came down the road. A large-framed, short man got out and marched to the assembled group. When he was close enough, Lee could see the Bird Colonel emblem on his multi-cam uniform. He was wearing an army issue cap versus a combat helmet.

"Well. Look what the cat dragged in," the colonel said to Jake.

Jake saluted, and the colonel returned the salute.

"Permission to come aboard, sir?" Jake asked with a smile.

"What the fuck do you think this is, soldier, a fucking Navy PT boat? I always knew you wanted to be a pussy SEAL or something. Well, now that you wandered back in like a cat wanting fed, my car needs washed," Colonel Braxton replied, adding, "Hi, Lucy. Your hubby is worried sick."

The colonel then looked at Lee and said, "Who is this home-less-looking person you two have dragged in?"

Jake then introduced Lee and gave the Colonel a short story version of the meeting.

Braxton then said, "So do you guys know what is going on?"

"Well, it looks like the shit has hit the fan. We are assuming EMP and maybe all-out nuclear war," Jake said.

"You're not far off. Jump in the hummers, and we will brief you guys back at the base," the colonel said in a command-like tone.

The colonel directed Lee and Lucy to get in the backseats. Jake climbed into the passenger seat of the colonel's Hummer. The colonel told his driver to stay and help get the buggy towed back and climbed into the driver's seat. He made a wide turn through the open desert and followed the MEDIVAC Hummer.

The Hummer stopped briefly then continued through a defended gate into the southern part of the base. Lee, Jake, and Lucy could see lights in some buildings, but most were dark. Military trucks were moving about in all directions. Lee thought this was a clear sign the EMP proofing the military had spent billions on was working. However, like Jake and Lee had seen in Vegas, civilian cars were not moving around. Like in Vegas, these cars had also been damaged by the EMP. On the way to the base, he related to the colonel how Howard and his friends had unsuccessfully tried to hijack the three of them. He told the colonel how they had left the other three hijackers on the power line road and told them to walk here. The Colonel said he would send a couple of hummers down the road to see if they could find them. He wanted to send out some patrols that direction anyway.

When they arrived at a building which looked like a command HQ, the colonel parked and the group all followed him inside. As they got in the door, a tall and excited man ran down the hall and picked Lucy up, hugging her and kissing her. Obviously, it was Rick. Lucy gave Rick a quick rundown of the trip and rescue by Jake and Lee. After hearing the story, he gave Lee and Jake a hug for rescuing her, and then he started into her about trying it alone. Lucy pointed out to Rick as tired as she currently was, she was in no mood for a lecture. Rick backed off and then told the colonel he was going to take her to his apartment and get her cleaned up. She gave Jake and Lee long hugs and kissed them both on the cheek, and then she and Rick headed off.

"Mr. Garrett, I need you to wait here in this office while I debrief Lieutenant Rodriguez," the colonel said as he opened a door and ushered him in.

The colonel told a private to bring Lee some water and a sandwich. Lee went in, sat down on a leather sofa, and relaxed for the first time since this adventure started. He sat at first but then thought "What the heck" and lay down. Lee looked at his watch, and it was 3:37 a.m. Within seconds, Lee was sound asleep.

Chapter 21

0847, Day 3, Fort Irwin, California

Lee awoke to someone shaking his shoulder. Startled, he sat up, saw Jake, and looked at his watch, remembering it was the last thing he remembered before falling fast asleep. It was now 8:47 a.m. Lee had slept for five hours.

"Lee, get up. I brought some of your extra clothes from your bag. There is a makeshift shower down the hall. Go clean up and change. I brought a razor also. You look like crap. The colonel wants to talk with you."

"Man, I was done. I think I would have slept on this couch for several days if you had not rudely woken me up," Lee responded.

"We got things to do. The colonel debriefed me, now he and the general have some serious questions to ask you. Don't ask me what, just get your ass cleaned up and ready. There is a briefing at 1000 hours, and they want you to attend," Jake said as he turned and headed out the door.

Lee noticed that Jake was now wearing a fresh set of multi-cams, and his appearance made it obvious he had already showered and shaved. Lee headed down the hall and, with direction from the private who had taken him to the office hours earlier, found the makeshift shower. The shower consisted of a garden hose and wide spray nozzle running through a window into the normal but non-working shower. He assumed a lack of power was perhaps keeping pumps from running and water distribution was not working. The shower water was lukewarm, but it felt fantastic. Lee showered and shaved under the hose and then found a dry spot in the room to change into the fresh clothing Jake had brought. Lee laughed quietly when he found it to be a surplus set of old desert camo that he had kept in the BOB. Most likely this stuff was from the first Gulf War, but Lee did not care as it was clean and felt wonderful.

After leaving the makeshift shower room, an army specialist with the nametag "Ryan" was waiting for Lee and told him to follow. Ryan escorted Lee down a long corridor, passing by several offices and larger rooms, which Lee assumed was part of a military police station. His assumption was confirmed when they passed by a long folding table where the contents of his bug-out bag lay spread out as if someone had done a detailed inventory. Lee thought it amusing to see all his stuff so neatly organized. Moreover, he silently considered, "Crap, that is a pile of stuff. No wonder I am tired and sore from carrying all that shit."

Lee and the specialist exited the MP building, climbed into a Hummer, and drove a few blocks to an unmarked building that looked like a warehouse. As they approached, a roll-up door went up, and they drove in. Specialist Ryan parked the Hummer in an empty spot along a wall and said, "Follow me please, sir."

Ryan led Lee through a small man-door and down a hall. Making a turn into what one would have thought a small office or a closet was, to Lee's surprise, a large metal door built similar to a bank vault. That door opened, and the two men moved into a stairwell that descended. They walked briskly down three flights of stairs and met another metal door. This door also opened just as they approached. Several video cameras along the hallway explained the automatic operation of the doors. Obviously, someone was watching Lee and Ryan closely as they approached.

Lee and Ryan entered a large corridor bordering a large room encased behind tall glass windows. The large room was a beehive of activity with soldiers working on computer terminals and assorted electronic type stations. Massive flat-screen displays covered two walls of the room, but they were blank or powered off. Two much smaller screen flat-screen TVs were sitting on what looked like folding tables just in front of the large displays.

Inside the large room, Lee noticed a stout-looking balding officer. When the officer turned Lee could make out two stars on his collars. This was likely the commanding general and the main command center. Lee finally relaxed as arrest and confinement now seemed unlikely.

Ryan continued down the corridor with Lee trailing behind. They entered a smaller briefing room or a classroom. Ten rows of tables with fold-up chairs sat facing one end of the room. About fifteen soldiers of various rank plus a few civilian dressed men and two women were sitting at chairs or talking in small groups. Lee felt like an idiot standing here in his antiquated desert camos without any insignia or emblem. Most of the people gave him a curious look. Two nearby soldiers noticed Lee with a simple nod. The rest either ignored him or smiled or snickered at the oddly dressed Lee.

Along one wall was a table stacked with various food items, including sandwiches, fruit, bags of potato chips, and power bars. There were also large square bins of coffee and tea, and a case of bottled water sat on the floor.

"Help yourself to something to eat. The briefing will be in about fifteen minutes," Ryan said. He then shook Lee's hand and exited the room.

Lee ate some of the food items with great enjoyment. The sandwiches were dry, with slices of ham or beef and cheese. The coffee was somewhere between a triple-shot cappuccino and Cuban coffee, but it hit the spot and gave Lee an instant buzz. He saw a small ice bucket with Red Bulls, cokes, and Monster energy drinks on a table at the other side of the room. He figured the caffeine must have been helping to keep these soldiers going.

Lee had just finished eating when Jake and Colonel Braxton came through the door.

"Well, Mr. Garrett, I hope you managed some rest, food and a cold hose down. Sorry the shower is so pitiful, but we are trying to conserve generator power," the colonel said.

Lee stood and responded, "Thank you, sir, it was all great. I feel like I might just survive. I appreciate your hospitality."

"Sergeant Rodriguez briefed me about your walk and ride out of Vegas. He also told me you worked here at Irwin a few years back on one or our MOUT programs. I found Rollinson, and he remembered you. He even went to his file and found a copy of your security clearance paperwork, including your "secret" clearance status. I will assume that is still in place, and everything we now discuss comes under your agreement with the defense department?" The colonel finished with this question while looking Lee straight in the eyes.

"Absolutely, sir," Lee replied, still trying to understand where this conversation was heading.

Before Colonel Braxton further explained, the general walked in with a lieutenant following closely behind. The general did not hesitate for a moment. He walked straight to Lee and held out a large hand large and powerful enough to double as a club. Lee reached out, and the general's hand enveloped his in a powerful grip and single-motion shake. His nametag read "Stollard." He was about six feet tall, appearing framed from solid concrete. He had a look of confidence that would command respect regardless of rank. Lee was sure there General Stollard had worked up through the ranks by his ability, talent, and experiences and was good at his job.

The General wasted no time and said to Lee, "Mr. Garrett. I am glad to meet you. Sergeant Rodriguez and Colonel Braxton have filled me in on your journey and your background with the base. I have matters to discuss with you regarding Agua Dulce which I understand is your home."

"Yes sir. I do live there. At least I did. I hope my family is there and safe." Lee said.

The General responded, "What we know, so far, Agua Dulce is fine. I am certain your family is fine for the time being. However, the situation in Agua Dulce will most surely be changing. I would like to discuss Agua Dulce with you. Before we discuss in detail, I think it will be helpful for you and Rodriguez to attend the briefing this morning. The briefing will bring you up to speed on what has occurred in our country. We are having daily briefings for people who are making their way back to base."

General Stollard ended the conversation with, "Mr. Garrett, I have other pressing issues to deal with. After the briefing, we will talk again." He turned and headed out with the colonel in tow.

Another Lieutenant moved up to the front of the room and requested everyone to sit down.

He introduced himself. "Gentleman, I am Lieutenant Hollingsworth. I shall provide you with a full brief on all but need-to-know information. I must confirm again that you are bound by your security agreements either as enlisted, officers, or as contractors to the US Army and with the United States Department of Defense."

Someone in the second row burst out, "And telling anyone else carries the standard penalty of death, right?"

The room laughed out in mass.

"Yes, sir, that is probably about right and maybe truer than ever," Hollingsworth said back.

The lieutenant moved over to the end of the room and flipped a rotating board, exposing several maps which were pinned on the opposite side. He rolled the frame closer to the front row of attendees.

"Gentleman, this is the situation," said Hollingsworth. "At 0025 hours, Washington time three days ago, classified hidden radiation meters southeast of Washington, DC, detected a possible nuclear device. The detection system automatically alerted all federal and local agencies, who responded to the area immediately. Additional detectors started sounding off, suggesting a target was moving toward the center of DC. Local security forces identified a suspicious rental van driving at high speed and took up pursuit."

"President Pauline Harrold was en route to the White House on board Marine One helo, having just landed at Andrews Air Force Base. She was returning from a vacation in Martha's Vineyard. A maintenance issue with Air Force One had delayed her flight by three hours. When the detection of a possible nuclear weapon occurred, the Secret Service immediately turned around Marine One and headed back to Andrews."

"Capital police, Secret Service, and other forces kept up the pursuit of the suspect van as it drove northwest toward the capital and White House. Assumptions are the van was forcibly stopped approximately two clicks from the DC Mall just as Marine One was on final approach into Andrews. It is probable when stopped and cornered, the driver or drivers of the truck set off a weapon. A nuclear detonation occurred. Marine One was tossed out of the sky by the shock wave crashing into a hangar at Andrews. How the pilot managed to get the bird down at all is a wonder, but it crashed hard. Most on board were killed, including the president's husband and two staff members plus the pilot and copilot."

"The president was unconscious, and she was transported to an undisclosed location. She is in serious condition and in a coma. Her condition is still questionable."

"Holy shit," Lee muttered to Jake, which mixed in with comments throughout the room

Hollingsworth continued, "It gets worse. The vice president was only three clicks from the blast. He had attended a fundraiser earlier in the evening. It is unclear why he was still there. Regardless of why he was still there, it appears neither he nor anyone at that hotel survived the blast. The building collapsed with hundreds of others in the area. Rescue teams are still digging through the rubble, but hope is fading."

"Ten minutes after the blast, Cheyenne Mountain detected two missile launches from North Korea with trajectories toward the United States. NORAD activated all defensive systems. This included interceptor missile batteries plus Alaska and Washington state interceptor aircraft. Multiple launches from Iran were then detected approximately ten minutes after the North Korea launches. There were six total with two ICBMs on trajectories towards the Western Hemisphere, and four shorter range missiles with trajectories toward Israel."

The news was getting worse by the moment. Most of the men in the briefing looked stunned as they sat quietly watching the Lieutenant. Jake was silent also. Lee assumed he had already heard most of this news.

The lieutenant continued, "All our defenses went into automatic high alert. One of the Korean missiles was shot down by our new Star Wars defensive battery. Unfortunately, the other detonated at an altitude of five hundred miles over the California Oregon Border creating a massive EMP burst. Our experts believe an EMP was the plan of the North Koreans. It also seems obvious the entire plan was a coordinated attack by North Korea and Iran."

"Meanwhile the four short-range weapons fired from Iran entered Israel airspace where the Israelis managed to shoot down three of the four. Clearly, the Israel "Iron Dome" air defense is better than anyone knew. The fourth missile hit a major military target in Southern Israel with a nuclear blast of roughly 12 megatons. The two long-range Iranian ICBM rockets both suffered failures over the North Atlantic and fell harmlessly into the Atlantic Ocean. Perhaps the Iranians were not as technically advanced as they thought. That might be our salvation."

"Wow, the US might have dodged the bullet of all time," Lee said to Jake who nodded agreement.

"If the two Iranian missiles were also EMP devices, we would be in deeper shit that we already are," said Jake back to Lee in a low voice.

"Gentlemen, it could be much worse than it is," Lieutenant Hollingsworth said before continuing. "But it is still bad. With the president in a coma and the vice president presumed dead, the Secret Service found and secured the Speaker of the House Jeffrey Baylor. A federal judge swore him into the office of president one hour after the EMP detonation."

"After the swearing in, Speaker Baylor, now President Baylor, was provided our war plans and defensive and offensive choices. He immediately contacted both the Chinese and Russian leaders and discussed our situation and for them to expect retaliation against North Korea. And upon confirmation of the Iranian missile trajectories, a response would also be coming against Iran. The Chinese protested first, threatening an attack on North Korea would bring them into the conflict. Then surprisingly the Russian President told the Chinese that Russia would stand on the side of the United States and would join them if China became involved. The Chinese thankfully backed off. Some feel that the Russian president's hatred of President Harrold and his long relationship with Baylor was the reason he decided to side with the United States."

Hollingsworth added, "While the phone calls were going on, North Korean forces started to attack South Korean and US Army positions along the border. A full-scale invasion by North Korea must have been part of the coordinated attack plan."

"Speaker Baylor, now President Baylor, then ordered a pre-planned strike order. This involved a US Submarine attack from the North Pacific. Three hours after the EMP detonation over California, the USS *Tennessee* rose to launch depth and unleashed twenty-two of its twenty-four Trident II missiles, each equipped with eight independent warheads. Two missiles with technical issues were not launched. All the launched missiles made it into North Korea and deployed their independent warheads successfully. It is certain that North Korea is gone and probably will never exist again. The North Korean soldiers that were part of the invasion are surrendering in mass to South Korean or US troops. Also, US North Pacific Naval assets, including two Los Angeles attack submarines, engaged numerous North Korean warships and sunk nine of them, including two of their submarines which were hunting for our Boomer."

Lee knew the term *Boomer* was slang for the ballistic missile submarines.

The lieutenant went on, "Meanwhile, the status between Iran and Israel was intensifying. Iranian warships had moved to the Mediterranean and started attacking ports and shore positions in Israel. Most likely, part of the plan was to provide distraction and slow down or prevent an Israel response to the nuclear attack. Iranian ships launched attacks against American Naval Assets in the Persian Gulf and the Indian Ocean. Severe damage occurred, including sinking one of our frigates and damage to three other ships, including the aircraft carrier USS *Ronald Reagan*. American naval forces retaliated mercilessly, sinking sixteen Iranian ships so far, and attacks are still underway. Our ships in range were given orders to launch non-nuclear cruise missiles at Iranian land-based military targets. Over 125 missiles were launched from various US and British surface ships and submarines in the area. Speaking of the British, they have jumped into the fray fully and have committed all available resources to the battle or relief efforts.

"The response by Israel was undeterred by the naval action. Israel aircraft have launched many large-scale sorties into Iran straight over Iraq. It appears they may have even used airborne nuclear explosions, most likely suicide-type missions to clear the airspace of Iranian air force interceptors. Four detonations occurred at thirty-five-thousand-foot altitudes along the Iran and Iraq border. Follow on aircraft entered Iran and unleashed at least twenty-five nuclear weapons of various megaton sizes. We are not clear how the Israel aircraft returned to Israel without midair refueling aircraft. Our intelligence teams assume some aircraft may have been on one-way flights. Some attack aircraft crashed in Iran after dropping or launching their weapons. Others appear to have landed in Kuwait or Iraq. It is also reported some aircraft may have retreated north to Azerbaijan, one of the few non-Israel hostile countries in the Arab world."

"Once there was confirmation by both the United States and British Air Defenses the Iranian missiles were indeed targeted at the United States, President Baylor order a final blow to Iran. About twelve hours ago, twelve B-52 Bombers from Diego Garcia in the Indian Ocean attacked Iran with twenty AGM-86B nuclear cruise missiles, each from wing mount and internal rotary launchers. Out of the 120 missiles launched, eighty-two reached targets and detonated successfully. Iran, like North Korea, will never recover to do harm again."

The room broke out in applause.

"It is hard to believe that either North Korea or Iran somehow believed they would survive this fight no matter how hard their first hit against the United States and Israel was," a soldier in the second row commented.

"I don't think the fucking bastards have the sense of a dead donkey," another replied. "At least the world is rid of those two problems forever."

"It is sad to think of the number of civilians who perished in North Korea and Iran because of the actions of irrational fanatics," a third chimed in.

Hollingsworth looked up from his notes. "Yes, a lot have died. However, you will be stunned by the death and destruction unleashed on the United States. I doubt anyone will have sorrow or sympathy for North Korea or Iran after hearing the results of the attacks on us."

Lee was thinking about how most of the country considered Pauline Harrold a fraudulent president. Having the conservative Baylor as president might be saving the United States from total and final destruction. He thought back about how far-left socialist-leaning Pauline Harrold had barely won the presidency. Down in the poles until a month before the election, a massive perpetrated scandal emerged and caused the outspoken billionaire president to lose the election for his second term. The scandal fell apart, and the truth came out a month after the election. It had been a carefully crafted plan by a group of high-ranking democrats and many gullible and perhaps culpable news media giants. When confronted, the guilty admitted they knew it would be proven false, but they hated the president so much and were willing to go to jail to see him lose. The devastating damage was done and the election over when the truth came out, and a bitterly divided country watched as the socialist leaning took office. Legal challenges were still rocking the courts.

Within weeks of becoming Madame President, Harrold started reversing all the previous administrations gains in world relations. She had reinstated the terrible deal with Iran and had decided to recognize North Korea as a legitimate country. She had canceled all sanctions against both countries. She had also commanded the military and spy agencies to stop all surveillance and harassment of the two rogue nations. Even the United Nations felt the new liberal US president had gone way too far.

Next, President Harrold went after Russia in as many ways as possible while kissing up to China. The Russian president made it clear he hated the new US president, socialist or not. China, meanwhile, was getting everything they asked for. Harrold lifted all trade balance sanctions, and the trade deficit between the US and China skyrocketed.

The stock market crashed, the economy died, and inflation started to climb. None of the obvious results of her socialist-leaning ways slowed her or the Democrats down. The Democrat-controlled house and Senate passed one bill after another designed to tear up and destroy the American Constitution. Gun laws were passed by the dozens. The antigun politicians were floating the idea of firearm confiscation nationally. Many blue states and cities were already passing confiscation laws. The only thing stopping rampant changes to the gun laws was the still right-leaning Supreme Court. Thankfully the replacement justices put in by the previous president had set up a right-leaning majority which still upheld the constitution. The justices kept kicking back law after law. They reviewed several laws from anti-gun California. Never before had the court decided to hear so many gun law challenges, and in most of them, they "shot" them down. Pun intended. Everyone knew if the balance of the high court changed, the Second Amendment was sure to fall.

Most gun owners went into a "hide them" stance. Experts, including the FBI, doubted there were any less guns in civilian hands even with dozens of new laws. Many liberal states were conducting raids against law-abiding gun owners at random. Most felt the few selected raids were a strategy to scare people into turning in their weapons. Lee, like many others, still had his guns and would keep them no matter what. He had adapted to his guns by adding devices such as quick release pins and making them "featureless." These simple changes kept many rifles from being classified as an assault weapon. All the minor changes were simple to reverse. Most owners knew this and kept the parts to reverse the changes if needed.

A massive pro-gun rally took place in Sacramento, California. The liberal governor kept signing the antigun bills, and one day, the gun owners had seen enough. An estimated forty thousand gun owners showed up at the Capital Building in Sacramento fully armed. The gun-carrying public outgunned the Capital Police by 50-1. The governor ordered the National Guard to respond. For two days, a face-to-face standoff took place without a single shot being fired.

The peaceful show of force sent a stern message to the politicians. Had shooting started, a revolution by the Second Amendment backers may have started right in the capital of liberalism, Sacramento, California. The United States was overflowing with guns, and it was going to remain that way. Legal or not.

The lieutenant moved to the board with the maps pinned on it and started to explain the situation, interrupting Lee's thoughts, "This map shows the effect of the EMP detonation on the United States."

He pointed to a map of the United States, Canada and Mexico. On the map was a point near the border of California and Oregon midway between the Pacific coast and Nevada. Emanating from that point were five lightly shaded circles of red, orange, yellow, tan, and green. Horizontal lines marked a distance from the center point.

Hollingsworth explained, "The colors represent the estimated effect of the EMP on electronics, including the power grid and vehicles. This red area covers a radial distance of seven hundred miles from the epicenter. Within this area, power grid damage is one hundred percent. Vehicle damage is ninety-five percent. Damage to other electronics is estimated at seventy-five percent."

The red circle reached the California Mexico border in the south, continued east over a third of Arizona, all of Nevada, and most of Utah. It also covered a small part of Wyoming, the west part of Montana, and all of Idaho, Oregon, and Washington. Several hundred miles of southwest Canada also appeared within in the circle.

"The orange circle reaches out another four hundred miles to a total distance of eleven hundred miles from the blast center. Damage in this area to the power grids is about ninety percent, vehicles sixty percent, and other electronics thirty percent.

"The orange circle covers south over about half of Baja, California, part of Mexico. To the east it covers the rest of Arizona, half of New Mexico, and most of Colorado. It continues north through the balance of Wyoming, most of the balance of Montana, and deep into Canada.

"The yellow area reaches another three hundred miles. The power grid damage is about twenty-five percent, vehicle damage ten percent, and little damage to other electronics."

The last circle swept south, covering all of Baja and a large chunk of Mexico. It curved north, covering part of Texas, half of Oklahoma, most of Kansas, all of Nebraska, and South and North Dakota. It also covered a huge part of Canada.

"This tan portion of the country has little direct damage from the EMP blast itself. However, power is out as a result of indirect damage caused by the connections to the other more seriously affected western parts of the power grid. Damage reaches out nearly two thousand miles from the blast. Indirect damage may be easier to repair. Components such as transformers and the computer controls have not been damaged. The independent generating units simply overloaded and shut down because of the high surges. In some cases, starting those grids may be possible after being isolated from the damaged areas. However, the startup procedure is painfully slow. All power loads must be shut down to prevent more surges which may cause further damage."

"So basically, most of the country west of the Mississippi is in the dark?" someone asked.

"Yes, that is correct. In addition, a huge area around Washington is also without power due to the ground blast in DC. The only part of the country with most power on is the states southeast of the Mississippi such as Florida, Georgia, Alabama, and Louisiana."

"What was the determined trajectory of the other two Iranian missiles?" asked Jake.

"One missile was headed for Atlanta, Georgia, and the other seemed to be aimed at New York City."

"Jeez," was all Lee could say.

"Had the nukes headed for Georgia or New York also been an EMP, the entire country would be blacked out," Jake said.

"The blackout is just part of the story," Hollingsworth continued. "The casualty figures are devastating. Estimations are roughly 1100 passenger, commercial, or private aircraft were airborne in the red or orange zones at the time had massive electronic failures, and probably most just 'fell' out of the sky. Some planes managed to land, but most had devastating engine or electronic failures and crashed. In Los Angeles alone, there were twelve aircraft on final approach into Los Angeles International Airport, which crashed in populated areas or into the Pacific Ocean. Current rough estimates of people killed in aircraft crashes or on the ground is two hundred thousand, but expectations are this number will rise. Obviously, most countries lost hundreds or thousands of their citizens, and they are quite pissed off. Dozens of countries are already coming to our aid with relief or defense."

Hollingsworth added other information. "About one hundred navy soldiers are dead or missing in naval actions in the Persian Gulf. Roughly 350 United States soldiers are confirmed killed, with hundreds more wounded or missing from ground assault in Korea. Experts also estimate another one hundred thousand people may have died because of the power failures, including people with pacemakers or those on critical life support."

"The death toll estimate from the ground blast in Washington, DC, is one million directly, and radiation-related deaths will probably bring that total to about 1.5 million. Obviously, the injuries will be staggering. As you can imagine, medical resources for the entire east coast are overwhelmed."

"US command is operating out of a nondisclosed location. President Baylor activated a top-secret preplanned government response protocol. The code name for this planned response is MACRO EVENT. MACRO stands for 'Mass Casualty Relocation Operation.' The MACRO event has levels from 1 to 10, depending upon the nature of the event and the amount of the country affected. The attack on the United States has been designated a MACRO-7 event. On the shit hit the fan scale of 1 to 10, we are in a 7."

Hollingsworth paused, and a sergeant moved forward from the back with a stack of stapled reports. The document looked to be about one hundred pages long. He moved forward row by row, passing the documents to those seated at the end of each row. Those men in turn passed them two their right in their row. Lee took a copy and passed the balance to Jake and the rest of the row. Lee looked at the cover, which read as follows:

TOP SECRET
UNITED STATES OF AMERICA
STRATEGIC PLANNING DIVISION OF
THE UNITED STATES DEPARTMENT OF
DEFENSE
MACRO-7
Mass Casualty Relocation Operation-Level 7

Document to be created (by printing of electronic file) and distributed only upon order by the president (or acting president) of the United States as a necessary response to a catastrophic event either military, natural, terrestrial, or civil disruption that has caused massive casualties in isolated or wide spread areas of the United States. The event shall also be of such nature that large-scale relocation of civilian population will be necessary to save the remaining civilian population from further casualties.

Creation, distribution, in whole or part of this document prior to execution of this operation by Presidential order is a forbidden and considered an offense of treason.

Everyone was looking over the document as Lieutenant Hollingsworth continued, "You can read through this entire document after the briefing. The copy you have is a partial copy matching your mission and security level. There are copies in more detail for larger mission planning and higher security levels. If you open the document to page 8, you will see a bullet point list of the most important features of the MACRO-7 protocols."

Lee turned to page 8 and found the bullet list.

MACRO—7
BASIC ORDERS SUMMARY LIST
(Note: This is a summary only. Exact orders with full legal language are contained in further detail within this document, or attachments to this document)

The prime order of all military, federal, state, or local authority is as follows:

- By necessary means including extraordinary methods allowed by this document, authorities of all federal, state, or local levels shall deal with the threat or source that is the cause of the MACRO event. The federal government shall use all available resources, agencies, and power to neutralize the source of the event or the country, countries, or those responsible for the event. Because of the (assumed) disastrous nature of the event resulting in the MACRO event declaration, some aspects of the United States constitution may, as necessary, be suspended by the president of the United States or any acting president. Suspensions shall be clear, exact, and limited to the time needed to stabilize the situation. Only suspensions necessary for the overall survival of the remaining citizens specifically, and the United States in general, shall be made.
- Aid the civilian population with immediate medical needs in any method possible with all the resources available.
- Immediately provide security and safety for the civilian population in those areas where possible. Then develop continuing operations

to extend security and safety into wider portions of the country.

- Provide relief efforts directly in locations where possible, or provide relocation support to displaced civilians.
- Activate preplanned military operations included in addendums to this document.
- Martial Law is "at first" declared nationwide by activation of the MACRO event. By presidential or state governor orders, changes to martial law may occur as a means to improve emergency response and relief efforts. Martial Law allows for the following:
  o Curfew is in effect from dusk to dawn for all civilians except emergency response personnel. The authorities may detain people outside in public during curfew times.
  o Rioting, looting, or any activity of a person or persons considered adding to the catastrophic situation which has befallen the United States, which may cause harm or loss of property to others can be handled by the authorities in any expedient manner. This includes the use of deadly force by local law enforcement or military units. The civil rights for persons adding mayhem to the situation are considered suspended. Those persons are, by order of the federal government, considered as foreign combatants and shall be treated legally as such until such time the MACRO event is lifted.
  o Intentional hording or price gouging of existing supplies or commodities is prohibited. Those persons confirmed by the

authorities of hording or price gouging shall be subject to detention. Local
authorities shall confiscate the supplies
or commodities of the offending person
or persons and use them as common supplies for distribution to civilians in need.

- All commercial aircraft, including cargo and
passenger aircraft are now under the direct
control of the federal government. All uses
shall be controlled by a special emergency
office of the United States Air Force. This
branch of the Air Force housed in five locations has been pre-developed. The primary
use of commercial aircraft shall be for the
transport of relief supplies and for transfer
of refugees into non-affected areas. Aircraft
shall also be used for movement of government personnel or equipment.

- All commercial trucking is now under the
direct control of the federal government. All
uses shall be coordinated by a special emergency office of the Department of Homeland
Security. This specialized department, housed
in six locations, has been predeveloped. The
primary use of commercial trucking shall be
to move large amounts of relief supplies or
equipment.

- All railroad assets are now under the direct
control of the federal government. All
uses shall be coordinated by the office of
Homeland Security. This specialized department housed in six locations has been predeveloped. The primary use of rail freight trains
is to move large amounts of relief supplies
or equipment. The primary use of passenger
rail trains shall be for the transport of relief

supplies and for transfer of refugees into non-affected areas. Rail shall also be used for movement of government personnel or equipment.

- The Department of Homeland Security is authorized to open pre-existing detention facilities or, as needed, build and staff new facilities. Detention facilities shall be utilized as necessary to contain criminals or civilians who have taken part in or are planning behavior that is detrimental to stabilizing the already catastrophic situation.

- All active duty military, reserve military, federal law enforcement, state law enforcement, and local law enforcement shall make every effort possible to return to their assigned units or departments as quickly as possible and in any manner possible. Should returning to their assigned units or departments impossible, they shall report to any military or law enforcement unit regardless of departments, or agency affiliations, where they shall be accepted by those units, departments and commands and utilized in a manner conducive to their training, status, command, or expertise.

- Any physically able person who honorably dismissed or discharged from any United States Military branch within the last three years shall be considered "reactivated." They shall, if possible, report to the nearest military unit, command, branch etc. The local commanders shall have authority to accept reactivated persons into the local command. Alternatively, the commands may transfer such persons using available transport to a unit where the soldiers training, status, command, or expertise would be more effective.

- Any physically able officer (commissioned or noncommissioned) honorably dismissed or discharged from any United States military branch within the last five years shall be considered "reactivated." They shall, as possible, report to the nearest military unit, command, branch, etc. The local commanders shall have the authority to accept such reactivated military officers into the local command. Alternatively, the commands may transfer such officers using available transport to a unit where the officer's rank, status, command, or expertise would be more effective.

- Civilians with expertise and abilities considered valuable to the authorities may be "commissioned" into any United States military unit by the President of the United States, any state governor, or any active duty United States Army, Air Force, or Marine Corp General, or any active duty navy or Coast Guard Admiral. Civilians shall be commissioned at any suitable rank up to that of Captain and shall be classified as "Event Commissioned."

- Any United States Army, Air Force, or Marine Corp general or any active duty navy or Coast Guard Admiral can perform battlefield commissions of enlisted personnel to officer status as judged necessary.

- Any United States Army, Air Force, or Marine Corp General, Colonel or any active duty navy or Coast Guard captain or admiral can perform battlefield promotions of current officers as judged necessary.

- All medically trained people, civilian, or government shall report to and shall be temporarily assigned and controlled by local authorities in any manner that utilizes them in the most efficient manner.
- Each military unit nationwide, as part of this order, has been assigned a specific "Area of Responsibility," or AOR. The AOR assignments have been preplanned. Orders for each command are contained in area specific supplements to this document. Specific command documents are contained as part of the full MARCO Event Order. A full listing of all unit assignments is contained within Addendum C below.

The list continued, but Lee and Jake stopped reading when Hollingsworth started speaking again.

Hollingsworth started back up with, "The MACRO-7 Event has built in overall orders and instructions. Some of the most important are the preassigned AOR or area of operations for existing command units including this command. Next, I will go over our AOR and specific orders."

Hollingsworth moved to the rolling board and rotated it around. This side contained a more localized map. This map contained a detailed map of the area of California and Nevada.

The lieutenant then continued, "This map shows our AOR and other commands in the California, Nevada area. Our AOR runs along the 15 Freeway from North of Barstow to the Cajon Pass, actually the Cajon Summit. It then runs along the ridgeline of the Los Angeles National Forrest past the Newhall Pass and to the summit of the Grapevine or Route 5." Hollingsworth used a small wooden pointer to run along the boundary of the AOR.

He continued, "The boundary of our AOR then turns north around Tehachapi, Mojave, and then back to Irwin. The primary areas and main towns or cities falling under our command are the following: Barstow, Mojave, Tehachapi, Lancaster, Palmdale, Victorville, Acton, Agua Dulce, and Santa Clarita. Specific points that are of uppermost importance are Edwards Air Force Base, the logistics base near Adelanto that was formerly George Air Force Base, Palmdale Regional Airport, and the small Agua Dulce airstrip. These airfields are important, as they are the main airfields providing logistic support, relief efforts, and evacuation points. These bases are the first major objectives, and securing them as quickly as possible is a priority. Securing these bases and making them operational for immediate use is paramount to our mission. By the way, supply aircraft have already been flying into Edwards Air Force Base as of roughly twelve hours ago.

"Our greatest concern will be the relief effort for the thousands of refugee civilians expected to flood out of the Los Angeles area seeking help, food, shelter, medical attention. With most vehicles disabled, these people will be on foot, bicycle, horseback or improvised forms of transport. Few will be using running cars. This expected onslaught of people will potentially become the largest refugee problem in history. Los Angeles and Orange Counties are the largest population in the affected EMP zones. Los Angeles and Orange County are followed by San Francisco bay, San Diego, and other major cities in California, Oregon, and Washington State.

"Our mission includes setting up refugee centers and providing food and housing. The available airfields will be the best locations, as this will allow transport of food and supplies direct to the refugee sites with aircraft. Thankfully, with the failed EMPs on the east coast, most of the heavy lifting capabilities of the air force are still intact. Commercial aircraft will supplement the military aircraft. The airfields also allow relief aircraft from other nations to land within zones of large refugee populations. Moving relief supplies by ground is expected to be difficult at first. Trucks or trains will need to pass through less affected areas of the country where they may be stopped, hijacked or looted."

Hollingsworth pointed to the lined and colored area north of the Fort Irwin AOR and said, "The AOR to the north of ours is to be under the command of Vandenberg Air Force Base. Because the base does not have ground troops, a large force from the East Coast is supplementing it. We believe that will be two infantry brigades from Fort Benning, Georgia."

"The AOR to our east is under the command of Nellis Air Force Base. Two brigades from the East Coast are also reinforcing Nellis. Right now, they have a huge problem, as Las Vegas is in total meltdown."

Jake and Lee looked at each other. Both men had the same thought: "Glad they had gotten out of Vegas when they did."

He then moved the pointer south. "South of us is the AOR for the Marine base at Twenty-Nine Palms and the Barstow Logistics base. Further south is assigned to the Marine Base at Camp Pendleton. The military commands, as you can see, are covering the areas outside the heavy metropolitan LA basin. Metro areas are under direct control of Department of Homeland Security. Direct orders of the MACRO-7 absorbs all police and fire departments, National Guard units, and individual soldiers within the city boundaries. In a nutshell, LAPD, LA County Sherriff and all other police departments now work for DHS. The large goal in cities is different from rural locations. The basic problem is containing violence and securing badly needed facilities such as the hospitals, airports, and ports."

"To summarize our mission, we are to set up relief camps at major airfields and assist the civilian population in getting to those centers. Once there, we must care for them, treat the injured, and when possible, evacuate people to unaffected places in the country. We have two primary choke points in our AOR: the Newhall pass and the Cajon Pass. Those two passes will become human highways in the days to come."

Lee thought, *One of those human highways leads right through Agua Dulce. Shit.*

The lieutenant paused for a moment and then said, "The various tasks of our mission will require a large separation of our resources into different units. We will assign small military groups to the different locations through our AOR. We will be thinly stretched, to say the least. Our challenge is resources, and our commanders are working that issue as we speak. Each of you should now report to your currently assigned duty station. Your unit officers will provide more details and specific assignments. Currently, we are using many of our assets picking up the hundreds of stranded motorists along the highways. Our units are transporting the rescued motorists to the logistics base at Barstow. That base is already becoming a massive relief center. Cargo aircraft are being tasked to fly out people after supplies are unloaded from military aircraft. And at last word, some of the first passenger aircraft started arriving this morning."

Hollingsworth added, "Another major effort underway right now is the repair of vehicles affected by the EMP. Motor pool resources plus anyone who can turn a screwdriver have been replacing electronics modules and other parts on many of our buses and commercial vehicles."

A soldier in the front row asked, "Where are they getting all the parts?"

Hollingsworth responded, "I was about to tell you about the containers—so glad you asked. Some of you know about the containers. About two years ago, we started receiving sealed containers. The containers equipped with special locks also had metal foil tape seals over all the door seams. Our orders were to, under no circumstances, tear the seals or open the containers unless orders came from High Command. In total, we received about forty containers. As many of you know, we parked them in three different locations here on the base. None of the containers had been opened since delivery.

"Well, it turns out, someone high up must have had a concern about a possible EMP attack. One of the first orders in the MACRO event document was to unseal and open certain containers. It turns out that they contain post EMP-needed supplies. Also included is a tailored assortment of parts specifically chosen for our base. Our military vehicles weathered the EMP without damage. Someone knew what they were doing when they designed those electrical systems. But the containers included an inventory of electronic parts matching our vehicle inventory. We found boxes of parts for our civilian autos and trucks, our buses, and even our ATVs. We even have modules for our POS cars."

The POS comment received a chuckle from most everyone. They knew POS was slang for "piece of shit," referring to the Ford sedans used by MP's and officers on the base. The term supposedly had originated from a statement by Will Smith in the *Men in Black* film.

"Oh, great—that means the MPs will still be passing out speeding tickets," a civilian in the third row said out loud to a chorus of laughter.

"That is right Bob, so if by some miracle your Prius still runs, you better keep it under twenty-five," another fellow in the row responded.

Again, everyone laughed.

Hollingsworth said to the man in the first row, "One thing the containers did not have, Bob, was any Prius parts, so I don't think you will be using that hybrid anytime soon.

"However, the containers did have a huge variety of stuff including computers, printers, radios, GPS units, and other electronics, including medical electronics such as ECG machines and such. There were several containers full of nothing but portable generators. Two containers have radio gear which is fully set up and ready to use. All antennae connections on the containers are equipped with surge protection. The radio containers plus several others have secondary doors allowing you to enter thru the equivalent of an EMP air lock. You pass through one door and close it, allowing the inner door to open. This system provides protection for the equipment in case of another round of EMP.

"Orders are to keep them locked and sealed and to not to remove items unless needed. This is a precaution against another EMP attack.

"Several containers have nothing but NBC gear," Hollingsworth stated, knowing that this military crowd would know that NBC stood for "Nuclear, Biological, and Chemical." Ten refrigerator containers containing medical supplies and medicines have been plugged into power since arriving. Other commands and bases all around the country have received similar containers."

As the lieutenant finished his last statement, a private named Rudd opened the door and looked around the room. He saw Lee and Jake and then caught the eye of Hollingsworth. With a pointing action, the three men understand he needed Lee and Jake to come with him.

Lee and Jake stood and left the briefing, following the private down the hall into another smaller conference room containing an oblong table and eight chairs.

"Please sit down, gentleman. The general will be here shortly," Rudd said to Lee and Jake.

While the two new friends waited, they discussed the situation and how messed up it was. Jake was not sure what the general wanted to discuss with them. So while sitting and waiting, Jake told Lee about construction of the command center during the Cold War.

Jake explained, "Design of the building is to withstand a nuclear explosion as close as one mile away. I know if feels like four floors when you come down the stairs, but it is not. The roof direct over our heads is ten feet of reinforced concrete. Above the concrete is a radiation barrier made from lead and another twelve feet of compacted granite. Finally, a top layer is an another ten feet of concrete. We are not even using two counterweighted blast doors, which can close in fewer than ten seconds."

"The building is impermeable to EMP. The threat of EMP from the Soviets during the Cold War was quite real. Every single wire that enters the command center passes through a bunker we call the soup can room. Large cylindrical devices connect to the wires. They are some old style of suppressor which will stop the magnetic pulse. The Cold War era protection is the reason the EMP did not damage this command center."

Lee replied, "I noticed the large video screens were not working."

Jake answered with a laugh, "Those screens are off because of the large amount of power they use. They just load the power system, which is a combination of generators, solar panels, and batteries. The general says they are just for show and remind him of the movie *Doctor Strangelove*."

Jake continued, "Anyway, the government was a lot more pre-pared for EMP than everyone thought. I guess that is good news."

Just about then, General Stollard and Colonel Braxton entered the room with a female sergeant. Lee read her nametag, "Wilde." Stollard introduced her to Lee. Lee could tell that she and Jake already knew each other. She was an attractive blonde, about 5'10" inches tall. The colonel also introduced a civilian named Victor Briggs to both men. Victor was a shorter man with thick glasses and dark black hair. He had an armful of documents and folders.

"Mr. Garrett, Sergeant, I want to get right to this as time is short," the general stated.

Lee and Jake both nodded, and the general continued, "I assume after attending the briefing, you both know what we facing and what our mission is?"

Lee and Jake both said "Yes, sir," almost at the same time.

"Okay, Mr. Garrett, I have something I want to run by you. You are now aware our mission is to get control of critical sites such as airfields and somehow deal the expected flood of refugees. As you probably now know, we expect a huge number of refugees to come through the Newhall pass. Most will pass through Agua Dulce and Acton. Agua Dulce has a small airport which happens to be the clos-est airstrip to the Newhall pass. Besides this strategic airstrip, what else can you tell me about Agua Dulce?"

As the general asked, Briggs spread out a large map of Santa Clarita, Agua Dulce, and Acton. The map appeared recently printed or plotted. It was a hybrid map similar to the type Lee carried in his bug-out-bag. The map contained aerial images overlain with road names and other details.

Lee sat back slightly and said, "Well, Agua Dulce is a small community. I would guess about three thousand residents. It has a small downtown area with a couple of restaurants, a great hardware store, a market, and a veterinarian clinic. Most of the properties in Agua Dulce are two to five acres minimum. Many people have horses. Most residents are fairly well-off. It is a tight-knit community close to LA, but it feels as if you are in the middle of nowhere. The airport is small. Agua Dulce is mostly known for is the Vasquez Rocks." As

Lee spoke, he had been running his finger along the map pointing out the various locations as he mentioned them.

Lee continued, "Acton borders Agua Dulce and is very similar. It does have several downtown areas and a few freeway offramps into those commercial zones. Agua Dulce and Acton blend together."

"So tell me this, if you had to cordon off Agua Dulce and secure it, what would you do?" the general asked.

Lee pointed to items on the map. "Well, not having much time to think about this, I will give you my quick thoughts. Assuming you mean roadblocks, there are only a few ways into the center of Agua Dulce. You can come in on Agua Dulce Canyon Road from the 14 freeway or up Sierra Highway and turn up this road here, which is Davenport. Both have steep hills alongside the road, so they would be easy to block. Here…and here." Lee pointed to the points on Agua Dulce Canyon and Davenport, where choke points would work the best.

Lee continued, "If you close off Sierra Highway at Davenport, you can get double duty, as this would block Davenport and Sierra Highway. Blocking Sierra would keep people from going around the west of Agua Dulce and entering from the back or North side. As you go out the 14 freeway, the other main road that enters Agua Dulce is Escondido, which would be easy to block also. Past Escondido, the roads that cross the freeway go into the Acton areas on the north or south. Most roads do not connect Acton to Agua Dulce because of this range of hills which intersects the two towns." Again, Lee's finger did the walking on the map as he explained his thinking.

"And exactly where is your home?" Colonel Braxton asked.

Lee pointed to a location on the map on the west side of the main Agua Dulce valley and explained, "Right here, up along this hill. I have five acres that run up along this ridge. I have a great view of the Vasquez rocks, and my house is quite secluded."

The general jumped back in. "After my people studied the map, they came to the same conclusion about choke points. I'm glad you have confirmed that. From what we can see, the Vasquez rocks would make a good location for a refugee center. We can feed people and provide aid and then, as possible, move them to larger facilities we will set up in Palmdale and Edwards Air Force Base. In addition, the small airport has a runway that is 4,600 feet long. The runway is short for most large aircraft but usable for take-off and landings by C130s. Engineers already have a premade plan that can extend the runway another one thousand feet without too much problem except for a couple of pissed-off homeowners."

General Stollard continued, "Dealing with refugees is just part of the problem. Something not mentioned in the briefing. Evil crap is starting to occur in the LA area. We have been receiving reports from urban areas in and out of the EMP zones. They describe attacks by 'lone wolf' terrorists. These groups have been attacking gun stores, National Guard bases, and even police stations. They are killing anyone who gets in their way. They are picking up arms, vehicles, and other supplies at a rapid rate. Intelligence back east thinks these attacks may have been a smaller preplanned part of the overall larger plan of attack against us. These individuals and groups seem organized and ready. Some groups went active within hours of the EMP attack. The CIA had been tracking a few of these bad guys before this went down. They were hunting for more information to find their keepers."

"Often, it seems the original lone wolves are forming their own small armies and using the stolen gear to equip them. Some of these groups appear better armed than local police. One report from Oakland said that a group of armed terrorists attacked a police substation and overwhelmed and killed over twenty police officers and civilian workers. The report said they then went to jail cells and gave young inmates a choice of being shot or joining them. They just shot anyone suspicious. Many joined. Intelligence now estimates that army at five hundred strong.

"Now here is the scary part," the general said as he paused for effect. "Reports say some groups are flying ISIS flags."

That sank in for a moment, and Lee muttered, "Son of a bitch."

"No. Sons of dogs," Jake said. "I fought those bastards in Iraq. Now I have to fight them in California. Fuck."

"The rest of the situation in LA is going to crap in a short order," General Stollard explained. "The airliners that crashed have started massive fires. Looters and just dumb assholes have started dozens of other fires. The smoke over LA is intense. Many parts of the city have out-of-control fires and looting. The LAPD has made a major effort to secure primary locations. All major police forces also have copies of the MACRO plan. The police are defending LAX at all costs. Burbank airport is not secure or usable now. An operation by Homeland Security and the National Guard is underway right now to secure Van Nuys Airport."

"Some people are already heading out of LA. We need to get a team into Agua Dulce and Acton to start making plans to deal with thousands of refugees. My command problem is that my forces are stretched thin. I want to set up a choke point at Agua Dulce, but I am short on resources. Most of my troops are already at or will be assigned to Edwards, Palmdale, or Adelanto. I also want to set up a similar choke point on the east side of the Cajon pass."

"Mr. Garrett, I would like to run something by you. The MACRO event gives me the right to commission civilians and place them into critical roles."

"I read that, sir," Lee said.

"Well, I would like to do just that," the general said back.

"What do you mean?" Lee said, looking and feeling rather baffled.

"Well, I would like to offer you a commission and send you back to Agua Dulce with the job of acting as a military liaison for the community. I am not asking you to go into battle with ISIS, but take the job of coordinating with the community to gain their trust and cooperation. You see, Mr. Garrett, I need the people of Agua Dulce to help us with this herculean effort. We do not have the resources on our own. Without volunteers from the civilian population, we are doomed. I would like you to go to Agua Dulce with some of my soldiers and get the ball rolling. You might say this is a type of a Green Beret mission."

It took Lee a second to respond. "Well, sir, I am glad to do whatever I can to help. Why do I need to be commissioned to do this job?"

"I think having an army rank will gain you more respect. It also allows me to have direct command over your actions. The other side of the saber, I will be the one to blame if things go shitty," the general said.

"Well, I would be honored with the trust, sir," Lee said as he sat there almost in shock.

"From what I have heard from Sergeant Rodriguez, you have already proven yourself. Besides, his butt is going with you," General Stollard said, and he turned toward Jake and smiled.

"First, I will send you with Rodriguez, Wilde, and two others of their choosing. The five of you will be first boots on the ground in Agua Dulce," he said as he looked at Sergeant Wilde, who was nodding at Rodriguez.

"So when do we leave, and how are we getting there, sir?" asked Jake.

"We can send a couple of UH-60s out in the morning. We have concerns about a secure landing spot, but we will have to chance it and just try the small airport," the general said.

"I want to send you with a couple of four-seat ATVs the motor pool guys have running plus equipment and supplies, including squad weapons," the general said.

"Why not just sling load everything and we can do a quick drop and dust-off?" Rodriguez said.

Lee jumped in, "Sir, my family should be monitoring a pre-arranged Ham radio frequency. I was carrying two small portable radios. My family and certain friends all agreed to use a specific channel in the event of something like this was to happen. My radios are only good for about twenty-five miles at best, but if you have a large-watt radio, we could send a message. My son should be at my house, and from the way I read the MACRO orders, he has been called back to duty."

"When did your son get out and from where?" said General Stollard.

Lee explained, "He was a 1st Battalion, 75th Ranger, sir. He has been out about two years. Currently, he is going to college for a degree in criminology. So he is, I hope, at my house. I also have a friend who is a Marine whom I would imagine made his way to my house. He was part of our survivalist team or plan. The rest of the family are all experienced shooters and could provide added security."

"How do we know they get the message? Does their radio have the power to reach us?" Rodriguez said.

"I doubt it," Lee said.

Suddenly, the general stood up and went to the door. He yelled into the command center, "Jeffries, come in here for a moment. Someone get Sparky. He should be in the radio room."

A civilian came into the room as the general returned to his seat.

"Jeffries, what is the current status of our drone?" Stollard asked.

"We are over the San Fernando Valley working to help the guard troops secure Van Nuys Airport. Now we are just reconnoitering the rest of the valley. Smoke is getting so bad we may lose visibility in the next twenty-four hours," Jeffries replied.

"How is fuel?" Stollard asked.

"We are going to RTB in about four hours, sir," Jeffries answered.

Then a tall, skinny, geeky-looking soldier came into the room, and General Stollard turned to him. "Sparky, can you tune your stuff to a Ham frequency and hit Agua Dulce from here?"

"Sure, I can tune in almost any band, and I have amps that go up to five hundred watts. Hell, General, I can bounce a signal round the world from here. But anyone within about fifty miles of here will not like it when their equipment gets hit with all that power."

"Sparky, you geek, have you ever looked at where we are? There is not shit within fifty miles of this base," Colonel Braxton said in a sarcastic tone.

"Okay, so Sparky, can you drag a radio into the war room so we can see drone feed and talk at the same time? I have an idea," said the general.

"I have a remote mic and speaker I can set up. Give me five minutes to hook it up," Sparky said, and without saying any more, he turned and headed out.

"He is a man of few words," said the Colonel.

The general said, "Okay, here is the plan—Sparky will get the radio remotes near the drone screens. Garrett, we are going to fly that drone right over your house, and you are going to see if you can get someone to hear you on the radio and give us a signal. Sound like a plan?"

"Well if they are listening like planned and they have kept the batteries charged, they should hear us," Lee answered. "I better get one of my radios and make sure Sparky has the correct frequency."

"First, let's have a plan to download to your family," General Stollard said. "Sergeant Rodriguez, when can you have your team loaded up and ready to go? The right answer is zero six hundred."

"We can make that happen, sir," Jake answered.

The general laid out a plan for everyone. The sergeants and the colonel added ideas, and after about fifteen minutes, the plan was ready. General Stollard told Lee to go get his radio and help Sparky set up the frequency. Jake and Lee took off and returned shortly to the command center.

Chapter 22

0900, Day 3, Garrett Residence, Agua Dulce, California

All the members of the Garrett family and newly extended members were helping to set up for the possibility of a long haul of survival. Barry and Holly's unexpected arrival at the gate had clearly displayed the need for tighter and full-time security. The group upheld confidence that Lee would show up sooner than later. Until then Lawrence would, with input from everyone, be the final say on security, work assignments, and other issues.

Lawrence felt that security was the first and most important task. At least one person would now man the now-completed observation point. Logan with help from Barry and Richard made the OP point not only more effective but added a few more creature comforts. They brought up large plastic containers to hold several heavy blankets and more tarpaulins. Using plywood and two-by-fours from a stockpile in the workshop, Logan and Richard built a makeshift flat surface inside the OP, which would double as a table and sleeping cot. Sometimes, two people would man the post, and the cot would allow one person to sleep while the other stood guard. A thick air mattress and sleeping bags made for a comfy bed.

Included in the wide variety of gear brought by Lawrence and Richard was a Leopold LTO thermal spotting scope. Although the scope and optics were not military quality, it still provided a decent thermal image at nearly 750 yards. Logan found a small camera tripod on which he mounted the scope for better stability. Richard used premixed concrete to create four different flat pads around the makeshift volcanic rock bunker for placemen of the scope and coverage in all directions. This would allow for fast position changes of the scope. A powerful pair of Nikon binoculars provided the primary visual tool for scanning the terrain around the Garret property.

Lawrence and Madison made a tour of the close neighbors. Although none of them were as well prepared as the Garrett family, they could manage for a few weeks. Everyone had a decent supply of food, and two of the three had generators. The third neighbor had installed a solar system with a battery backup, so they had power at all times. Those neighbors told Lawrence how others further down the road who had installed solar did not put in a battery system, and their entire system was out. One of the downfalls on many solar systems was the fact that during a power failure, the solar system shut down to avoid what was called *islanding*. This feature was intended to prevent power being sent back into grid during a power failure and possibly causing a safety problem for linemen. This was probably a major problem country wide of solar systems not working without the power grid.

Three sides of the Garrett property had homesteads of similar size as the Garretts. The fourth side to the northwest-bordered vacant land, which was part of a rough undeveloped range of rocky hills, which lay between the main part of Agua Dulce and the more westerly area along Sierra Highway. Lawrence was concerned about the vacant land.

"If a group of organized, smart, or military-trained people are making their way up from the southwest and they want to stay safe and off the roads, the old mining property would make a good choice for travel. And anyone taking that route is going to be of decent shape to deal with the terrain. That makes this area a worry. Everyone on guard needs to constantly monitor these hills. And consider that anyone coming that way may be sneaky and smart. Keep yourselves concealed and monitor as far out as possible. If a trained person or persons gets close and sees the houses, they will most likely move as stealthily as possible to avoid detection."

Several of the solar motion lights were placed in the key locations approaching the property from the rocky hills. They placed the lights at least three hundred yards out on the most likely approach paths, and Lawrence used several tricks to hide the lights from approaching people. In most cases, this meant locating them behind or below an object such as a tree or rocks, which would have to be moved around by an approaching person. The goal was to keep a hiker from seeing the light while approaching. Then when they passed, the hidden light would detect the motion and activate the lights. It was a given that the intruder would immediately attempt to destroy the light, but at night in the dark, even a few seconds of the bright LED lights would be easily noticed by the sentries in the OP.

In addition to the lights, Lawrence and Richard set up numerous fishline traps. This involved tying very small monofilament wire to a solid object and across a likely path. Depending on the location and the available hiding spots, the fishing line would set off some type of noisemaker. Noisemakers were made from coffee cans, bells, or several other clever devices Lawrence and Richard had been trained to use.

Lawrence voiced his concern about the devices to everyone. "The problem with these fishing line devices is a truly trained warrior will likely spot them. Then he will know he is up against someone else who is also likely military. This may make him change direction or just increase his awareness. But they should work on nontrained hikers."

While Lawrence and Richard concentrated on security, Barry volunteered to clean and prepare all of weapons in the Garrett gun safe. His Marine Corp experience was all about respect for guns so he, Logan and Holly went through each gun meticulously, cleaning, oiling, and inspecting them. Lawrence knew his father had kept extra parts, including standard AR-type magazine releases. So besides servicing the weapons, Barry removed any of the California required modifications and replaced them. Lee had two AR15s, which were built as to the California "featureless" designation. This meant the guns did not have pistol grips or adjustable stocks. This allowed them to not fall under the California description of an assault rifle. Barry and Logan converted the guns back to the standard configurations. No one knew what would occur with the gun laws or enforcement of them during this time of great crisis. But for now, everyone agreed it was safer to have the guns as easy and lethal to use as possible.

The AR-10s in the safe were all equipped with quick-removal rear lower pins. This was another way around the worthless California laws. The pin pushed in and released the back of the lower receiver from the upper receiver. When it moved a slight amount, the magazine could be removed with the standard magazine button release. This type of modification complied by classifying the rifle as having a fixed magazine. The release pin modification was left in place, but the small modification to the magazine release which prevented it from releasing prior to opening the action of the rifle was removed. Now a rapid magazine change was possible.

The safe had plenty of magazines. All of them were the ten-round California Compliant. There were 30 AR15 mags and 36 AR-10 Mags. Logan also found magazine pouches of various designs. All the mags were unloaded, inspected, and reloaded. He then placed some kind of pouch with each rifle containing at least four extra magazines. All the remaining mags were then placed in two key locations inside the house.

Logan also retrieved several ammo cans of extra 556 and 308 ammo and placed it inside the house with the extra magazines. At each stockpile, he placed a fast reloader for both rounds and some basic tools and cleaning supplies.

The gun collection contained an assortment of other rifles, shotguns, and pistols. Some were not of much use in a real fire fight, so they were left inside the safe. There was a 12-gauge pump shotgun, which was placed at one of the ammo locations.

The two most unusual weapons were the M1-Carbine Bullpups. Lee had purchased two of the conversion kits from J&S Tactical. The kits were well-made systems which allowed you to very easily remove the stock M1 barrel and action assembly and install it into the new Bullpup stock system. The conversion system had a slick system of high-tech linkage that simply lay inside the stock trigger but con-nected it to a forward-mounted pistol grip. The trigger action was slightly harder but had good feel. The new gun was only a pound heavier, mostly due to the added features, including a tactical rail system. It took a little getting used to, but the converted bullpup was only twenty-six and one-fourth inches long and very easy to carry, aim, and shoot. It was a perfect weapon for a smaller person or as a secondary rifle.

Like the other weapons, Logan cleaned and oiled both bullpups and all the available magazines. He found eight ten-round magazines for each. He placed one of the small carbine rifles at each of the house weapon stockpiles.

When Lawrence returned to the house later in the day to see progress, he was quite impressed with what he now dubbed the "armory team." He commented that it looked like the Garretts were setting up for an Alamo-type siege.

He started to say, "Well, you know what Dad would say—"

Logan and Madison both finished the sentence, "It is better to have it and not need it than to need it and not have it."

Barry and Holly both laughed at what was obviously the Garrett family motto.

Chapter 23

1325, Day 3, Fort Irwin
Command Center

T he general and his group had returned to the command center by the time Lee and Jake returned. The general turned to Rodriguez and said, "By the way, after we try this hookup, get Mr. Garrett over to the supply officer. Fix him up with some late model camo. Get him three or four change outs of the new Multicam and get a nametag and the other window dressing for it. Every time he walks in here in that first Gulf War camo, I have a flashback to killing Iraqi tanks."

Laughter filled the room. Lee gave the radio to Sparky after explaining the frequency and privacy code settings. Sparky ran off to the radio room so he could make the necessary adjustments on his gear.

As everyone waited, Lee thought, *What the fuck have I got myself into now?*

A technical operator turned to the group and said, "The drone is leaving Burbank now. We are directing it to the coordinates of Mr. Garrett's house, sir."

"Sparky are you ready?" General Stollard yelled out toward the radio room.

Sparky came back and replied, "All set. Go ahead any time."

"Mr. Garrett, you are on. See if you can wake someone up. Do you have a call sign?" the general asked.

"Yes, sir," Lee said as Sparky handed the radio microphone to him.

The colonel handed Lee a handwritten script prepared in the last few minutes. He explained to Lee that the idea was to remain discreet but be clear enough to Lee's son. Lee needed to fill in the blanks with things such as a call sign.

Lee pressed the transmit button on the mic and said, "Garrett base, Garrett base, this is Garrett mobile calling. Garrett base, Garrett base, this is Garrett mobile calling…"

Lee repeated the call three times and then started with a message: "Garrett base, if you copy, first, do not bother to reply as you will not be able to reach my location with your radio. I need you to understand that I will have eyes on you in…"

Lee paused and looked at the drone technician, who replied, "Twenty minutes."

"Garrett base, I will have eyes on you in twenty minutes. I repeat, I will have eyes on you in twenty minutes. Eyes are high and remote. If you are getting this message, you need to send me a signal. Get a large whiteboard to use as a signal board. Go to the front of the house and stand by. I will let you know when I have eyes on the house."

Lee repeated the instructions two more times and then followed with, "Garrett mobile standing by."

The group in the command center waited while watching the monitor of the drone feed. The Colonel explained to Lee how the drone was piloted remotely from Florida. The Command Center received the camera feed by satellite. The technician in the center also used satellite to communicate to Florida.

The camera signal from the drone was clear and powerful although the drone was flying at ten thousand feet in altitude.

Everyone watched as the drone flew across the San Fernando Valley. The group could see dozens of smoke columns rising high into the air from points on the ground. The thick smoke was starting to form a heavy overcast layer, which was dropping lower and lower into the valley floor. Eventually, drone surveillance, or any airborne surveillance, would be impossible. The drone left the urban sprawl and headed over the mountains of the Angeles National Forrest. It continued over the barren mountain range and down the north side. The gathered people could see signs of civilization starting to form again. A few moving vehicles were visible among homes and people scattered in the foothills and canyons below.

Eventually, the drone image started to move around as if someone was manipulating the camera. After some random motions, it locked onto a specific location. Lee could make out structures and surrounding features, and it was enough for him to realize he was looking at his house from ten thousand feet up. The drone image zoomed in, allowing Lee and the others to see ten people in front of a house. One person looked as if they had a board as Lee had directed over the radio.

"Okay, sir, camera is locked onto the objective. Does that appear to be your house, Mr. Garrett?" the drone technician said to Lee.

"It looks like it," Lee said, holding back his excitement.

"It looks like there are ten people in front of the house," the technician said.

"Yes, I agree, and they have the large board to use for the signal," Lee said.

"Okay, hit the radio again, Mr. Garrett," Colonel Braxton said.

The general left during the delay to deal with other pressing issues.

Lee thought about how many important issues must be on his plate right now.

Lee keyed the mic once more and started, "Garrett base, this is Garrett mobile. Garrett base, this is Garrett mobile. "I have eyes on you now. If you are reading this transmission, flash your signal board three times."

Seconds later, the person with the board held it in a horizontal position then tilted it up, once, twice, and a third time. Everyone else was waving and jumping up and down. Lee got chills on his spine, and his eyes started to tear up as he realized they had just contacted his family.

Lee thought, *Thank God, some or all of my family are there.*

Lee realized he could see makeshift lettering on the ground in front of the group. It said, "LOVE U."

"Garrett Base, I got the reply. Thank God you guys are okay," he said, releasing the mic for a moment.

"I know you are all wondering how the heck I pulled this off, and you will find out soon, but I need to give you instructions," Lee said into the mic as he watched the screen through damp eyes.

"First, if you understand me, flash the board one time for yes, two times for no."

The board tilted once.

"I need you to set up and secure a spot for a sling load drop. Drop will occur tomorrow at zero seven thirty from a flight of two uniform hotel birds. Birds will drop loads and dust off after exfil of personnel by fast rope. Secure spots for the drop loads and personnel. Do you copy so far?"

Lee read from the prepared script. The use of military jargon would scramble the conversation slightly from others who, with simple radio scanners, would be listening in. This was the only alternative using open frequencies. People with military experience, including Lee's son, would know the term "Uniform Hotel" as a label for the UH-60 Black Hawk helicopter.

The board tilted once.

"You need to provide OP SEC for the operation. There is concern for the birds. Can you do that?"

Lee used another military term, "OP SEC," or Operational Security, in his transmission.

The board tilted again. This made Lee realize that at least his army son was there, as he would understand the terms used.

"Also provide smoke. Do you copy?"

Again, a single board tilt.

"That is the end of our instructions. Now is everyone okay?"

A single board flash and Lee once again could see everyone jumping up and down and waving their arms.

"Is everyone expected there?"

Another board tilt and more waving and jumping.

"Okay, Garrett base, I will see you in the morning. Everyone, take care. Garrett mobile out." Lee said for the last transmission and then handed the mic to Sparky. Lee had to wipe tears from his eyes as the drone image zoomed back out.

Colonel Braxton interrupted Lee's thoughts, "Wilson, have them fly the drone over the surrounding area and reconnoiter it. Put some eyeballs on the town and circle the airport. I want to know what we have to work with."

Chapter 24

1325, Day 3, Garrett Residence, Agua Dulce, California

Madison, Dena, Logan, Barry and Holly were standing around or sitting at the kitchen counter drinking glasses of cold Gatorade made from powder and munching on mixed nuts. The newly extended Garret family had all been helping with preparation around the house. Madison with Dena's help had completed an extensive inventory of food and other supplies in the house and the storage container. So the four decided to take a small break. Melinda and James had just walked into the room when suddenly the base unit radio blasted out loudly. As well as the base unit, two of the smaller handheld radios sitting on the counter also blared out the same message.

"Garrett base, Garrett base, this is Garrett mobile calling. Garrett base, Garrett base, this is Garrett mobile calling…"

Everyone froze. For a long agonizing moment, everyone thought Lawrence was calling using a handheld radio from the Observation Point on the hill above the property. The stunned group stood looking at the radio, but no one moved.

Logan was the first to speak: "That's not Lawrence. It's Dad."

Madison looked shocked, but she ran around the kitchen counter and grabbed the microphone from the small clip on the radio, but she did not press the transmit button.

The message kept repeating, *"Garrett base, Garrett Base this is Garrett mobile calling."*

Then there was a short pause which seemed like minutes. Lawrence burst through the front door. "Shit, did you guys hear it? I think it's Dad calling."

Now the radio call started again. *"Garrett base, if you copy, first, do not bother to reply as you will not be able to reach my location with your radio. I need you to understand that I will have eyes on you in…"*

Another short pause and then *"Twenty minutes."*

Lawrence looked at Madison holding the microphone and lifting it toward her face.

"Mom. Don't try to broadcast. You will block him."

Madison lowered the mic, and the message started again: *"Garrett base, I will have eyes on you in twenty minutes. I repeat, I will have eyes on you in twenty minutes. Eyes are high and remote. If you are getting this message, you need to send me a signal. Get a large white board to use as a signal board. Go to the front side of the house and stand by. I will let you know when I have eyes on the house."*

The message repeated as the stunned family members stood there. James and Richard came running up the backstairs and burst in as the last message came through: *"Garrett mobile standing by."*

Everyone looked shocked. At first, they just looked at one another. But almost on cue, a few seconds later, an uproar started. Everyone was yelling, screaming crying, jumping up and down, and hugging each other. Madison had to sit down as she felt weak.

Lawrence spoke first. "I don't have any idea how Dad has pulled this off, but he has. He is either flying over in a helo or he somehow stole a drone. We cannot just sit here. Logan, go get a piece of that white foam board from the workshop. Richard, go up on the hill and use the spotting scope and binos. See if you can figure out who and what is looking at us? Everyone else outside."

Lawrence then went to Madison and leaned down to her. Melinda was already sitting next to her and holding her tightly. She was crying heavily. "Mom, Dad has pulled something off. Don't ask me what. But whatever it is, I think he is safe. Let's go out there and give him a big welcome."

Chapter 25

0540, Day 4, Helicopter field, Fort Irwin, California

Lee and Jake—or Roz, as Lee found out many of his close friends called him—stood looking at the two UH-60 Blackhawks as the crew warmed up the turbine engines. Sergeant Wilde, Specialist Kirwan, and Specialist Sanders made some final adjustments on two sling loads sitting out in the open. Each of the loads consisted of a large formed plastic pallet holding one four seat Polaris ATV and piles of boxes all around and within the ATVs. The boxes were an odd lot of equipment, MREs, ammunition, gas cans, water, radio, and many other assorted items. Jake knew the loads also each contained an M240 belt-fed machine gun. Lee said he hoped like hell that was not something they would need.

Roz said to Lee, "Wasn't it you that said 'Better to have something and not need it then need something and not have it'?"

Lee answered, "Yeah, yeah, that was me. Okay, I guess we should bring it along. Can we also bring along one of those M1 tanks?"

Roz replied, "Sure, if you want to drive the behemoth from here to your house. Believe me, they are not fun to drive down the highway more than a few miles. Plus, you will need a fuel truck to follow along and keep the gas-guzzling turd fueled up. It uses about ten gallons per mile."

Warming up of the choppers was complete. "Load up!" sounded out from a crew chief.

Lee was anxious to get going. He could not wait to see his family. The hastily created unit had spent most of the night gathering the gear up and loading the pallets. Jake and Wilde had worked out the inventory list and other personnel at the base helped finding and bringing the stuff to the airfield. Specialist Kirwan had taken Lee to the supply building where a PFC issued three sets of modern multi-cam with all the trimmings. The supply building even had an embroidery machine plugged into a small Honda generator, and the private made up the small Velcro tags with "Garrett" on them. Other tags were issued to Lee, including fabric rank insignias which were a slight takeoff on the standard Captains Bars. The left bar (right if looking at it) had a horizontal bar in the middle, extending out, making a partial E shape. This was to show Lee was a "Captain, Event" versus a standard military captain. His stuff included American flags for his shoulders and unit emblems for the 11ᵗʰ Armored Cavalry division with the famous "Black Horse," which would attach to his left shoulder. That patch was like a badge of honor to Lee.

When Lee questioned Jake about getting the unit emblem, he said, "Wear it proudly. You deserve it. Jake then produced a paper tag he had made using a sharpie. On it was a scroll which said, "Viva, Las Vegas" plus two dice. Jake used a straight pin to pin it on Lee's right shoulder.

"That is your last deployment emblem, dude. It goes on your right shoulder."

Lee laughed at it. Wilde rolled her eyes and said, "You know what they say about Vegas."

Roz responded, "Yeah, what happens in Vegas makes you want to get the fuck out of Vegas."

"Sounds about right to me," Lee added.

The group climbed into the choppers and received instructions from the crew chief on where to sit to keep the load equal. After everyone strapped in, the massive rotor blades spooled up and the big machine lifted off. The noisy vibrating chopper hovered around for around thirty seconds and a ground crew member attached the heavy sling line from the belly to one of the pallets. The big motor cranked up hard, the big helo leaned forward, hastened down the flight line, and lifted into the air. The Blackhawk made a bank to the right, and Lee could see the other chopper through the open side door. Shortly after, the crew chief slid the door closed and the two Black Hawks gained altitude and headed what Lee assumed was southwest.

As Lee sat back and tried to get comfortable, he looked around at the group he had joined. Roz leaned back in the uncomfortable seat and fell fast asleep before the big bird had reached 2,500 feet of altitude. Roz had not slept at all since arriving at the base two nights ago. Specialists Kirwan and Sanders also looked like they might be trying to get some shuteye, but so far, it appeared the uncomfortable seats were a bigger problem for them.

Lee looked over at Sergeant Wilde. She had a "hundred-mile stare," Lee thought. Liz was not looking at anything in the chopper. She was surely thinking about something. Lee did nothing to interfere with her faraway thoughts.

Chapter 26

0600, DAY 4, UH-60 BLACK HAWK, ONE OF TWO, SOMEWHERE OVER THE MOJAVE DESERT, CALIFORNIA

Sergeant Liz Wilde sat strapped into the Black Hawk with the rest of the team. Exhausted but too tired to sleep, she started thinking about the crisis the country was in. She also considered the local situation she was part of. She had total confidence in Roz even though she barely knew him. He was just one of those people you knew the moment you met you could trust with your life. The two Specialists Kirwan and Sanders seemed like good soldiers. Roz had vouched for them, and she felt his picking them to join the group must say a lot. This so-called "event captain" was another story. She was surprised as hell when the general commissioned a civilian and stuck him into this mess. Could his lack of real training put them all in danger at some point? It was odd, but Roz had told her not to worry. Garrett had made it clear in tactical or dangerous situations, Roz or Wilde would be in command. Garrett's job was strictly to convince the residents of Agua Dulce to help keep the world from self-destructing. Time would tell how Garrett would do and if the world would survive or not.

She thought back to the early morning when Rodriguez had returned to the base. She had been working in the battalion HQ when he entered. He came up to her and, in a terrible Jack Nicholson impersonation said, "Honey, I'm home."

She had jumped up, surprised at seeing him. Liz did not know if she should hug him, salute him, or give him a ration of crap. In the few weeks, she had been at Irwin she had started to like Roz. She went with the more neutral approach and said, "Crap, Roz, you made it. I figured you would just stay at the pool in Vegas and sit this one out."

"What and let you deal with the crapola coming down on the United States alone? Shit, no. I stole and rode a zebra from the Las Vegas zoo here just to keep you from fucking up and ruining it for female grunts worldwide."

"That so. Where did you park the zebra?"

"Park it shit. I gave it to the colonel. We are all having zebra steaks for dinner," Jake said.

"Screw you, Roz, I never eat anything with eyes," Liz sounded back.

"Bullshit, Wilde. I heard you ate three Taliban on your last deployment."

"Yeah, but I dug out their eyeballs first." Then in a more realistic tone, she said, "Glad you are back, Roz man."

"Glad I am here, Sarge," Jake replied, also in a serious and sincere tone.

Jake slid a chair from another desk and dropped into it. He continued to tell Liz the story about walking out of Vegas and getting surrounded by a bunch of ghetto monsters and how an over prepared "civvie" came along and saved his butt. He told the rest of the story and she sat spellbound, listening to him.

When he had finished his story of the trip back to base, he said, "So listen, Wilde. Colonel is thinking of sending me and a few other unlucky bastards to a small town just outside Los Angeles called Agua Dulce. He said I could pick another sergeant and a couple of specialists to tag along. I figure this shit storm has sidetracked your new ladies' club. We are going to be spread thinner than air on toast, so you interested in tagging along?"

"Where the hell is Agua Dulce Roz?" Liz said back.

"Right next to Acton," Rodriguez said back.

"So where in the hell is Acton?" Liz said, even more irritated while rolling her eyes.

"North of Santa Clarita or Valencia. You know where Magic Mountain is?"

"Jeez Liz, you should study the map for your AOR," Roz said in a "What the heck?" tone.

"Okay, all right, I got you. Now I know where you are talking about. Some horse farmer town just short of Palmdale, right?"

"That's it. So are you in, or should I go find some retarded reject from the Marine Corps to take your place?" he said.

He stressed his question by doing the swirly circle thing around his head suggesting a Looney bird.

Liz sat for about three seconds and replied, "You know, Roz, the crapper has overflowed. I think we are either in with unplugging the toilet or just sitting and allowing crap to run all over the house. If I am going to be mopping up shit, I guess you are one of the mop boys I would just as soon be stuck with. Fuck it. I'm with you."

"That is the wild woman I know," said Jake. "Wrap up whatever Facebook or Twitter shit you are doing, powder your face, and get your butt over to CC. On the way, you might want to ask yourself how you got into this donkey parade. I have to go wake up my new guardian angel."

Roz turned and headed down the short walkway of the small office complex and turned the corner.

So now as Liz sat in the noisy and vibrating UH-60 monster, she thought, *How* did *I get into this donkey parade?*

Liz Wilde was a native of San Diego California. She grew up near the beaches and spent way too many days on them. She learned to surf at age nine. She surfed weekends or before school, after school or even during school. When in high school, she was suspended for cutting afternoon classes something like twenty-eight times and heading to the beach. She did not mind school; she just liked the beach better. When threatened with not graduating high school, she simply told the vice principal, "No problem. I will stay. I like it here." They gave her a diploma and sent her packing.

She was just short of six feet tall, with a lean build and dark-brown hair and extremely good-looking. She was already in excellent condition even in high school. After school, she took a part-time job at a gym, and she got into training and physical fitness. When not working, she attended every class the gym held for anything from boxing to yoga. If not in class at the gym or working, she went surfing.

She entered an Iron Man competition and loved it. She worked hard to train for more of them, and she excelled. She kicked butt on all females and many males. She was the first female to place in the overall top five in a local San Diego competition.

After the award ceremonies, she overheard one of the males who had placed just above her in third place say, "She must be a lesbian or a guy in drag. No chick can do what she does."

She walked over and dropped him with a hard-right jab. He fell to the floor, with blood running from his nose, and looked up at her.

"Listen, asshole. I am as straight as you wish you were. In fact, if you had any ability to get a hard-on, which I doubt since it is only steroids that gets your weak ass across the finish line, I would drop down right now and give you the best and maybe only fuck of your miserable life."

Liz held her foot just above the man's crotch, pressing hard enough to discourage him from trying to roll over or get up.

Then some friends, other contestants, and officials swarmed in, picked her up and took her outside.

It was two weeks later while walking out of a fruit smoothie joint that she saw a recruiter station.

She thought, *What the fuck.*

She went in and talked to the Army Recruiter. He suggested many job duties, but few combat jobs were open to women. They went around and around for several days, and finally, Liz settled for an 88M, which was a truck driver.

The recruiter told her, "88M MOS will get you as close the front lines you are going to get packing a pair of tits."

At first, she was insulted by his comment, but she knew this was going to be common and she better learn to ignore it. "Hell, she did have great tits."

Three weeks later, after a teary-eyed departure from her mother and dad and two brothers, she headed for training at Fort Sill, Oklahoma. She completed the ten weeks of basic training and the seven weeks of advanced training with ease, surprising the other recruits and officers of the training battalion. She scored top of class or close in almost any challenge.

Early in the training, during a ten-mile rucksack march, Liz thought the pace was too slow. She knew most of the 88M people were a bunch of out-of-shape "turds" who could barely keep pace. Liz immediately paced way ahead of the group. One of the more vocal sergeants came up alongside her.

"So what's up, Wilde, are we not moving fast enough for you?"

Liz replied, "No, Sergeant. Just trying to get the most out of this."

"Well, have you considered if you go too fast, you will be a burned-out pile of crap five miles down the road?"

"I don't think so, Sergeant," Liz said back and instantly knew that was the wrong answer.

"You don't think so, huh? Well then, why don't you just double-time your ass back to the base? When you get there, get our showers ready and then we will be along later."

Liz answered immediately, "Yes, Sergeant."

To the sergeant's surprise, she leaped forward and started running at a blistering pace, forty-five-pound rucksack and all. She lost sight of the class, and she made the remaining six miles to the base in less than forty minutes. Tossing down the rucksack, Liz ran to the men's showers and went stall to stall, turning all of them on full hot. She did the same for the women's showers. She then ran over to the sergeant's quarters, went down the hall to the private showers, and turned all of them on steaming hot.

She returned to the front of the barracks and sat on the porch. About ten minutes later, the entire class showed up. Sergeant Henderson was leading the pack.

Liz stood at attention in front of the barracks.

Henderson walked up nose to nose with her and said, "Remain at attention, Wilde, and do not move."

As the soldiers gathered, he ordered the class to "Fall in" so they were facing Liz shoulder to shoulder.

She remained standing still. The sergeant approached with four other sergeants.

"Wilde, did you have a nice run?" Sergeant said as he glared at here with his face only inches away.

"Yes, Sergeant, I did. I also did as you ordered. The showers are running. I am not sure how long the hot water will last. They have been on quite a while now."

Liz had added the last part highlighting how long she had been back.

"So, Wilde, you felt leaving your fellow soldiers was okay to do?" Sergeant Henderson said.

"No, Sergeant. I was only following orders, Sergeant," Liz voiced back.

"Well, you can follow one more order. You stand at attention here until we have all showered. Then you take your miserable butt inside and personally dry down all those showers. I don't want to see so much as a water drop the size of an ant's asshole. Then maybe you will get to shower. No, check that. You do not look like you broke out in a sweat, so you can skip showering. Got that, Wilde?"

She did as commanded. She stood at attention waiting until the entire class showered, changed into exercise clothing, and returned to formation. It took nearly an hour. The sergeant went to his quarters and returned in clean exercise clothes.

He walked up to Liz and said, "Well, Wilde. You were right. My shower ran out of hot water before I got there. Therefore, I had to take a cold shower. That is just not right. So from here on while in my class, cold is the only shower you will take. Maybe cold showers will help to keep in check all the testosterone you seem to have coming from somewhere in that dickless body of yours. I will leave it to Sergeant Landry to check in on you."

Landry was one of the two female sergeants in the training class, which had about a 20 percent female-to-male ratio.

Therefore, Liz took nothing but cold showers for the rest of basic. She almost got to where she liked them. She continued to outperform almost everyone in the class. On the shooting range, she scored expert with an M4 rifle. She was devastating in hand-to-hand training. Some thought that perhaps the men went easy on her, but whatever they did, they usually found themselves looking up at her from a prone and subdued position.

About fourteen weeks later, she graduated. She received the award for overall top recruit for the class. She was the first female to ever receive that honor. After graduation, she was assigned to 4th Infantry Division at Fort Carson Colorado. She found out her assignment to Fourth ID was because that division would be shipping out to Afghanistan in about two months. She wanted combat, and she was going to see it soon.

After the graduation was over and friends, family, and soldiers were thinning out, Sergeant Henderson approached her. She had returned to her barracks to bring back her belongings, and her family was not around.

"Wilde, I want to discuss something with you," said Henderson.

"Yes, Sergeant," Liz replied.

"When you first got here, I figured you were just another female trying to prove something to herself or someone else. We get many females passing through here who fall into that category. However, that day with the rucksack run and the showers even surprised me. I did the math on that run, and you ran times with that ruck on that most people could not have done bare-ass naked. In fact, assuming you slowed down on the last three miles, you may have broken the record for the first three miles. It was impressive."

"I also want to tell you something else. The army is changing, as you know. Political correctness is changing many things from gays in the military to the role of females. The army is now sending a limited number of women to Ranger School. I also happen to know a bunch of the officers over at 4th Infantry ID. We worked that assignment for you because they are one of the few units that are giving woman a fair shot at this man's army. When you get there, I want you to do what you do and kick butt. Then when it becomes official, I want you to put in an application for Ranger School. Most available slots will go to officers from West Point or OCS. However, I will bet a dollar to a half-eaten doughnut some enlisted females will be considered. Wilde, you are one of the few females I have met who can make it through Ranger School."

"Uh…that…I'm…thank you, Sergeant. I do not know what to say," Liz said, almost stunned at the sergeant's remarks.

"You don't have to thank me, Wilde. Just go and do what you do," Sergeant Henderson said, and then he put out his hand.

Liz shook the sergeant's hand firmly. She had not seen him since.

Two weeks later, she was at Fort Carson. Six weeks after that, she landed in Kabul, Afghanistan, and started her fourteen-month deployment. At first, they assigned her to ride shotgun, or TC position as some called it, in a large cargo truck. She did that for about three months. She worked hard and trained even harder. One of her officers plainly noticed her constant physical training, including going to the firing ranges whenever she could or just sitting and reading any military book she could get her hands on. She brought a language program with her and worked on the Arabic languages constantly. After a few months, she had learned the language so well she would have lengthy conversations with their Afghan counterparts and interpreters. One day, her sergeant approached her and told her she would be taking the TC position in one of the Humvees. The Humvees usually rode up closer to the front of the convoys. Their division had slowly been receiving newer mine resistant trucks, or M-RAPs, but the convoys still had large numbers of up-armored hummers. She jumped at the chance.

One her third trip out in the Hummer TC seat, all hell broke loose. They were taking a load of supplies to a forward operating base or FOB for short. Suddenly, a large explosion occurred. An IED devastated the lead M-RAP, flipping it over onto its side. The second M-RAP was driving close behind the first when hit by a second, although smaller, bomb. It rocked violently but managed to stay upright, injuring the turret gunner who could not return fire.

The behemoth sat not moving. All along the convoy line, gunfire started. Taliban poured from every building and hole in the small town. RPGs were raining down on the convoy of American vehicles, and machine gun and sniper fire came from windows, rooftops, and side streets.

Liz's own turret gunner was returning fire to the right side when a small teenage boy stepped out from around a corner and pointed an RPG right at the driver's side window. The up-armored Hummer was better at resisting hits, but it also put you in a box where no one but the turret gunner could return fire. Liz and the driver, a first sergeant named Torrez, watched in horror as the round screamed at them and hit the edge of the roof right above the driver's door. The round exploded with a violent impact and a ball of fire. Liz expected to be dead, but most of the explosive force deflected over the Hummer. The round hit right at the edge of the roofline, saving Liz and the driver. However, most of the deflected round slammed into the turret, killing the gunner instantly.

Torrez took a hard hit, and the explosive tore a large hole in the top of the body. Debris and shrapnel rained into the cab. Wilde saw Torrez slump forward with blood spilling out from several wounds. With the two lead M-RAPs out and her gunner down, they were now sitting ducks as dozens of Taliban streamed into the fight from every hiding spot. They were doomed if she just sat there.

She flung open her door and jumped out with her M4. She took a position behind the right front fender and starting picking targets as they ran toward her Hummer and the two M-RAPS. All the training on the rifle range paid off, and pure muscle memory kicked in. She smoothly and quickly moved the gun from target to target. Using two and three taps, she dropped Taliban attackers one after another, including the teenager who fired the RPG at her Hummer. He had just reloaded the RPG when Liz put a .223-caliber round into his neck and one more into his chest as he slumped over. Small arms fire started raining from the right side of the Hummer, forcing Liz to move back to the rear of the truck and eventually around the back. Crouching behind the Hummer, she slammed in another mag and started firing to the right. After cutting down three more

Taliban, she moved along the left side of the truck and opened the door. Torrez lay slopping over the steering wheel, moaning but not moving much. Liz grabbed the big sergeant, pulled him out of the seat and along the side of the Hummer. Lucky for her, Torrez was getting some strength and control back and could take some of his weight. Liz pulled him back past the rear door and yanked it open, pushed, lifted, and shoved Torrez into the rear seat.

Liz slammed the rear door and went back to the front hood. She could see six attackers moving toward the left side of the second M-RAP and five more on the right side. They were firing AK-47s on full automatic into the heavily armored truck as they advanced. She lined up on the left side group, flipped the selector of her M4 to three round bursts, and squeezed the trigger. One after another, the attackers dropped. Some looked her way in a display of shock as she moved the M4 from target to target. The Taliban on the right side had now moved forward of the M-RAP, blocking her from making a shot.

"Shit," Liz said aloud and, without thinking, jumped into the driver's seat.

The Hummer was still running. She dropped it in gear and slammed the gas pedal to the floor. The overloaded beast lurched forward and started gaining momentum. She kept the throttle floored and headed to the M-RAPs. She steered around the right side and could now see other attackers. This group of fighters was trying to find an opening to rain fire into behemoth. One man was holding what Liz recognized as a grenade. Just as she rounded the rear of the M-RAP, the white robed man pulled the pin and looked up at the top of the truck. His intent, Liz guessed, was to toss it into the unmanned gunner's turret and thus into the M-RAP.

The front of her heavy Hummer slammed into the first two Taliban gunners and then into the grenade wielding attacker. One surprised fighter flew over the hood and down the right side. The ten-ton vehicle plowed them to the ground, crushing them under the wheels. Three other Taliban managed to sidestep as she sped by. Nevertheless, those three forgot or did not know about the grenade. As they raised their AK-47s to fire at the truck, the fragmentation explosive went off, taking them out with hot supersonic chunks of steel.

Liz continued forward toward the overturned M-RAP. This M-RAP had American soldiers around it expertly firing at the onslaught of attackers. For some unknown reason, the overturned M-RAP had fewer casualties than the one which stayed upright. She slid the Hummer up to the three soldiers, turning right, putting them on her side of the Hummer.

She opened the door and yelled, "Use this Hummer for a shield! We need to get the guys out of the other M-RAP."

Wilde did a crazy three-point turn and started back with the Hummer and the three soldiers walking alongside, shooting at targets while using the vehicle as cover. They covered the distance quickly and went to work getting the disabled vehicle open. The gunner from the first M-RAP climbed in and, after lowering the injured gunner out, took over the main gun. He opened up with the Browning .50-caliber on any remaining Taliban and into suspected hiding places. Two other men from the M-RAP were not badly injured and coming around, so they joined the fight.

However, the fight was about over. One of the convoy tail M-RAPs came roaring up to support the front of the badly damaged column. The remaining Taliban were hightailing it out of town. The battle was over. Only then did Liz notice the blood pouring from her left leg. Shrapnel from the RPG had hit her leg, but in the excitement, she had not even noticed her wound. She sat down, and a medic came to her aid cleaning and wrapping the wound and forcing her to take an antibiotic injection. He also offered pain pills, but she refused them.

The wound was not life-threatening, but it resulted in a trip stateside, through Ramstein Air Force Base in Germany. Once reports of the battle made it to command, a Purple Heart, a Silver Star, and a promotion to sergeant were all awarded to Liz Wilde.

Liz also received a visit from the chief of staff of the army while she was at Walter Reed.

"Sergeant Wilde," he started, "I have read the reports of the battle. It is an incredible feat of bravery on your part. You may not be aware, but you are a huge inspiration for women in the army."

"Thank you, sir," was all she could think to say as she sat there nearly speechless.

The two of them—well, mostly the Chief of Staff—talked for a few more minutes. As he was turning to leave, she did speak out, "Sir, may I ask something?"

"Absolutely, Sergeant," the Army COS replied.

"Sir, I have heard the army is allowing females into Ranger School. So…well, sir, I was wondering, what are the chances of getting a shot at it?" Liz asked.

"Actually, Sergeant Wilde, we have been struggling with that issue for years now. Many people are dead set against it. I must admit, I have been one of those. However, after some great success and inspiration from soldiers such as yourself, I am now a major supporter of the program. I will call your commanding officer and suggest he has you fill out an application. Your application with those of other female applicants will land on my desk. I have already decided to approve the first group of women. I would say you have a good shot at it." He smiled, turned, and walked away.

Five months later, Liz was standing in a group of graduating soldiers at Fort Benning, Georgia. They had just completed the RTAC, or Ranger Training Assessment Course. Fifty-three soldiers made it through the tough two-week class, including Liz and four other females. About 125 had started. It was a requirement to attend and pass the pre-ranger assessment program before Ranger School. Now she and four other females would attend the next Ranger class.

The Ranger class is a sixty-one-day, three-phase struggle of mind and body, considered by many to be the hardest combat training in the world. Sleep deprivation is one tool used to beat the students down. Combined with extreme overexertion and demanding stellar performance during faux combat missions.

Liz had completed the first phase and was two weeks into the mountain training in Georgia when she started the worst menstrual period of her life. Perhaps it was the weakened condition of her body, lack of food, or the fact she had lost twelve pounds. Who knew, but it was bad. The first day she went through the allowed four feminine absorbent pads. She then resorted to combat dressings she borrowed from her fellow students. She was bleeding to the point of thinking something terrible was wrong. Nevertheless, she kept going. Painful cramps started hitting her almost constantly.

She and a squad of classmates were given a mission to set up an ambush on an expected truck convoy. They crept through the darkness in a wooded area. They knew that an OP-FORCE, or opposing force, was trying to find them before they could perform their mission. They moved slowly and quietly to avoid detection. She was second in line behind Sergeant Connors on point. Suddenly Connors dropped to a knee and signaled stop by raising his right fist in a ball. She slowly advanced closer to see what was up.

Connors used sign language to signal he had seen something ahead in the trees. Suddenly, Liz had a massive menstrual cramp. The pain was as if someone had punched her in the stomach. She doubled over with pain. Connors could see her anguish, and he broke proto-call and silence by whispering at her, "Jeez, Wilde, are you okay?"

She never had time to answer. Shots rang out from all around, and the rubber-coated simulation rounds started hitting her and Connor from several angles.

Crap, Liz thought.

The rest of her squad was quickly enveloped by the OP-FORCE, and all were considered "killed" within seconds.

She heard a booming voice from the trees, "Lay down, you are all fucking dead."

She dropped prone on her chest and lie in the damp dirt. Colonel Winnick walked up, pushed on her side, and told her to roll over. She complied. He then stepped one foot across her, placing a foot on either side of her hips. Then he surprised Liz by dropping down and crouching just above her abdomen. Quickly he reached up and pulled the top of her multi-cam blouse open and reached above the neck of her undershirt and reached in. She was stunned, thinking, *What the fuck, is he going to rape me?*

The colonel found the metal chain of her dog tags and pulled them out. He then took a large fixed blade from a pouch on his right leg and quickly and smoothly cut the chain. He then said, "I am going to keep these as a souvenir because you are dead."

She stared up in shock, not knowing what to do next. She lay there, trying with all her mental power to not break out in tears.

Then he spoke quietly and calmly. "Wilde, I want you to listen to me very carefully for a minute. You and your team are dead, because of your 'lady' problem. A problem that you had no choice in bringing into battle with you. I want you to know something else. I am one of the few old soldiers that think woman should be in the military. I am pulling for it. That is why they gave me a special assignment to follow these 'Ranger-ette' classes. I have been closely following you and the other women of this class and the previous classes. However, I do not think mixing women soldiers in with the men is a good idea. Soldiers already have enough crap to worry about in and out of combat. I do not want to toss another big problem for them to deal with into their already difficult job. The fog of war is bad enough. Men should not also have the fog of perfume added to the haze.

"The time may have come for women in front-line combat. That is fine, but make all-woman units. Battalion size, brigade— hell, create an entire Division of Women. Just keep them out of the mix of my boys. Men do not play in the woman's softball league, and woman should not play in the men's. If you want equality, get a female army unit and prove yourselves all by yourselves without having half the woman complain they were discriminated, assaulted, or insulted or some male soldier tried to hit up on them. Stand on your own. Fight on your own. I know you can do it, Wilde, and I am certain there are more like you."

He continued without waiting for Liz to respond. "So, Wilde, here is what I want you to do. I want you to get your dead ass up, take your dead-ass squad, and return to the camp. Then I expect you to finish Ranger School, which you are more than capable of doing. When the Chief of the Army shows up at graduation, which I am sure he will do, I want you to get his ear and tell him just what I told you. Tell him to create a female unit, Wilde. Then tell him you will be glad to be one of the enlisted in that unit."

The colonel stood up but looked down at Wilde and said, "I am keeping these tags, Wilde. Do you know why?"

"No, sir," she replied, trying desperately to hold back tears.

"Because you are going to be famous, and I am going to sell these dog tags on eBay or Craigslist or something," the colonel said as he turned and walked off.

Liz Wilde did graduate Ranger School. And she did get the ears of the Chief of Staff, the Secretary of Defense, and the Vice President, all of whom attended the Ranger graduation. And she did suggest an all-female unit.

Two months later, she received a letter and new orders. The letter was from the Chief of Staff, and it read as follows:

> Sergeant Wilde,
>
> I am pleased to inform you the United States Army has decided to create an experimental combat unit consisting of all female enlisted personnel and female officers. The unit will be patterned after an airborne cavalry unit. At first, it shall be a battalion-sized unit. You have shown great interest in this idea, and you have more than proven yourself to the United States Army. Because of your dedication, I have ordered, effective immediately, for your transfer to the initial formation of this unit.
>
> The army has chosen Fort Irwin for this new command. You may wonder why such a remote base. The experts feel this new command, for obvious reasons, will be under great scrutiny by other commands, the news media, the public, and our distinguished politicians. For various reasons, there is wide range support or contempt for this plan.

The remote and isolated location of Fort Irwin makes it more difficult for outside people to interfere with this controversial idea. On the reverse, it makes daily interaction with local populations by the soldiers of this new command more difficult, allowing them to concentrate more easily on the needs of this difficult job. We feel although the soldiers may not agree, it will provide the best chance of success.

Selection of qualified female officers for this new command is underway. I assure you only the most qualified female officers will be considered for this new command. Similar screening will apply for the experienced enlisted personnel. Only females who have recently enlisted or are doing so currently shall be considered. All recruits will face close scrutiny. Candidates will have the choice of changing their classifications to a new MOS, which is to be 11D. The recruiting rules will allow selection for this new MOS by only the most qualified female recruits.

If you accept this mission, which I am certain you will, you receive a promotion to the rank of Sergeant First Class. You are one of the first enlisted to be assigned to this unit. Your mission on arrival to Fort Irwin will be to start working with General Stollard to decide the logistics of this effort, gear up quarters and find out other needs. The first groups of enlisted personnel and officers that will start to arrive within sixty days. General Stollard will at first assign numerous personnel including civilian workers direct to you to aid in this planning stage. Male soldiers or civilians will fill many of these temporary assignments. This will allow people with knowledge of Fort Irwin to help in this unit start up. As other female personnel arrive on assignment, the plan is to reduce male staff members until there is zero.

During World War II, forming another controversial unit another group of patriotic Americans occurred. They performed brilliantly with honor and distinction. They were the Tuskegee Airmen. I have faith your new group of patriots will also be a valuable addition to the United States Military. I expect your unit to also perform with honor and distinction.

I am certain you are a great choice for this, and I wanted personally show my support for you and this exciting mission. Best of luck, Sergeant Wilde, and Godspeed.

Sincerely
General Robert E. Landis
Chief of Staff, United States Army

Liz had picked the letter up off her desk. She had received it at Fort Collins three weeks ago. She had arrived at Fort Irwin four days later. The first officers and enlisted personnel were according to schedule would start arriving two days after the EMP had exploded and the war started. She hoped none of them were on air flights when the EMP hit.

Chapter 27

0700, Day 4, Garrett Residence, Agua Dulce, California

The Garrett family, friends, and refugees, had gotten up at 5:00 a.m. Since the flyover the day before, nothing but excitement filled the air. Discussions went on constantly with everyone suggesting ideas of how Lee pulled off the event. None of the family had slept much since the wild drone over flight and long-distance radio call from Lee. Everyone wondered how Lee had managed to get the military involved to the point of flying him home. And topping it off, Lee was coming home as part of some military mission.

Lawrence, Logan, and Richard worked late into the evening clearing areas for the drop load and fast rope landing. They would have preferred to use the diesel Kubota tractor to clear some spots. However, Lawrence feared the tractor would tear up and loosen the dirt excessively. This would create a huge dust problem for the helo. Instead, they used a chainsaw to cut down the larger desert bushes. They chose spots that were suitable distance from the house, which were flat with short weeds and bushes. They decided not to waste valuable water on the dirt. Using some old white house paint and some precious water to dilute it, they spilled it out in two large *X* shapes. This would mark the locations for the two drop loads to be set down.

Lawrence had made up a smoke pot to use for the helos. He took several shop rags, soaked them in diesel fuel, and placed them in a metal bucket. He then soaked a few more rags in gasoline, making it easier to light quickly.

Using the gas stove, Madison and Melinda had cooked up some powdered eggs and potatoes, passing them out to the group at around 6:00 a.m. Security arrangements planning had occurred the night before, so everyone took up their assigned positions around 6:15 a.m. Lawrence had plenty of experience with this kind military landing, so he would remain near the drop zone. He would light the smoke canister and help if needed with the fast ropes. He would carry only a Glock 21, .45-caliber semiautomatic pistol in a leg holster. He placed a Bushmaster AR10 up behind a large rock near the zone. Marine Richard took a position on the highest point on the property equipped with Lee's custom-made AR-10 sniper variant with the twenty-four-inch barrel and a Springfield 6-20 X 56 scope and bipod.

Mike would remain hidden on the front deck with an AR15. Madison and Melinda both had custom M1-Carbines. Both weapons had bull-pup conversions using a kit from J&S Tactical. The M1s were light, short, and easy to use. Their weakness was an effective range of only three hundred yards. Lee's son-in-law, James, took position at the road entrance to the property sporting his own custom AR15, and a leg-holstered 1911. Logan would go with his brother near the landing zone. He would carry a Mossberg 12-gauge pump plus an FMK 9 mm also in a leg holster.

Bear and Holly would provide added security from another high spot on the property. Bear had an M&P AR-10, and Holly had her big .44 Magnum pistol.

For good measure, the Baofeng and Motorola radios were set to the frequency used to contact the house by Lee. There were enough radios to go around, although not all had throat or remote microphones. They could use the small radios to talk among themselves, and if Lee tried to contact them, everyone would hear the incoming message. Everyone was in place and eager to see what would happen next.

Chapter 28

0722, Day 4, UH-60 Black Hawk, One of Two, Nearing Agua Dulce, California

The crew chief of the UH 60 helo got up and opened the left side door. From where Lee was sitting, he could now see the terrain rolling past. He felt the distinct sensation of falling as the big chopper starting dropping lower to the ground. Suddenly, Lee knew right where they were. He could see the small Agua Dulce airfield below and the Agua Dulce valley stretching out toward the hills on the far side. He caught a glimpse of the peak behind the Garrett property. As the chopper passed the airfield, it banked left slightly, suggesting the pilots were looking around. Lee guessed they were surveying the airfield on the way by, in case they needed to use it as an alternate landing spot.

Jake had awoken from the brief nap when the door was opened and he gave Lee a thumbs-up. The crew chief held up three fingers, signaling the bird was three minutes away from the landing zone. Wilde, Sanders, and Kirwan all started shuffling around in their seats, making sure their gear was ready and squared away. Everyone checked each other's gear, and Jake checked Lee's.

Unlike Jake who had fallen asleep on the flight over from Irwin, Lee was too excited to sleep. He had been reliving the previous four days. He felt as if the EMP blast was just yesterday. The escape out of

Las Vegas and his chance meeting of Roz seemed like a crazy dream. General Stollard had entrusted Lee with such an honor by commissioning him into the army as a liaison. That was an act still hard to fathom. Sure, Lee knew a lot about the military and he was handy with a gun, but instant captain? Madison and Lee's kids were not going to believe this. His son Lawrence who made the entire family proud being a ranger for eight years would flip out.

Lee did not expect to be in battle, so he had been pondering his role of working with the local residents of Agua Dulce and Acton. He had been rehearsing a speech in his mind he would most likely need when they assembled the locals. He figured his role was going to be a lot like project management, but on a serious and complex manner. Instead of budgets and schedules, he would be working on plans that could affect the life and death of people and families. His emotions went from excited to honored to terrified.

Lee had an odd thought as they flew along: "Well, at least now I may be entitled to a flag-draped coffin."

Chapter 29

0722, Day 4, Garrett Residence, Agua Dulce, California

The Garrett clan heard the helicopters before seeing them. A low-frequency beat produced from the two large UH-60 choppers was coming from the northeast. Lawrence knew the sound well, and with his military experience, he could tell there were two birds coming. A moment later, Richard saw the two helos from his high perch on the ridgeline, and he radioed down, "Visual two inbound birds with sling loads."

Lawrence saw the two Black Hawks seconds after Richard's radio call. They were dropping down near the airport and banking slightly. He could make out the sling loads hanging underneath each chopper. After the curve around the airport, the two birds straightened and headed toward the Garrett house. He looked around to see if everyone appeared ready, and at the same time, he felt for one of the three small lighters he had placed in his pocket. He would use one to light the smoke canister sitting below in a clearing.

The two choppers raced across the valley trailing their dangling loads. From his point near the landing zone, Lawrence could see many houses down the hill. As he watched the choppers, he also noticed people coming out of the houses and looking to the Northeast toward the incoming helos. The loud noise would bring everyone in Agua Dulce out. That was certain. People would most likely believe that help was finally coming. Lawrence shared the hope this was the start of a relief effort. He bent over and lit the smoke canister, which erupted with a whoosh and large flame. The small fire quickly started producing thick black smoke from the diesel-soaked rags.

The wind was light, so the smoke rose straight. Lawrence thought that was lucky for the helos. He had personally made dozens of landings and fast rope INFIL in high winds and never liked it. He hoped his father was on one of the Blackhawks and maybe planning to fast rope. Light winds were a joy to Lawrence.

Chapter 30

0725, Day 4, UH-60 Black Hawk, One of Two Nearing Agua Dulce, California

A s they approached the Garrett property, the Blackhawk crew chief motioned for Lee and the others to remain sitting until they dropped the sling load. A series of hand gestures and movements relayed the message around. The choppers occupants understood the message loud and clear. Lee was trying hard to look past the chief through the open door to spot his family. He got a glimpse of what he thought was his son Lawrence near a large X on the ground. He also saw what looked like his wife Madison up closer to the house. Smoke was coming from a bucket or can near the X marking.

Their chopper banked around and flattened out settling over the drop zone. The crew chief was leaning out the door and talking on his headset to the pilots. Suddenly, the Black Hawk lurched hard. Lee assumed this was from the big pallet hitting the ground. The crew chief flipped a switch on the bulkhead, creating a smaller jerk, and the chopper lifted slightly, moving forward. The crew chief signaled everyone up and in-line as they had rehearsed at Fort Irwin. The chief reached over behind the door and slid out the big bundle of large diameter rope. The heavy rope fell out the door, unwinding as it did, and went taut to the mount, slightly out of the doorway.

Kirwan and Sanders were first to the door. With heavy gloves on, the two men slung their M4 rifles along one side of their chest, reached out, grabbed the rope, and dropped out of sight below the doorframe. Jake was the next to go. He also used heavy gloves, grasped the rope, placed his legs around it, and disappeared out of view. Sergeant Wilde was right behind him. Everyone roped out within seconds, leaving only Lee and the crew chief remaining inside the Blackhawk.

Lee approached the door carefully, trying to keep from falling because of the constant rolling and pitching motion of the Black Hawk. The crew chief reached over with a metal carabineer and clipped it to a harness Lee was wearing. Jake had helped Lee putting on the harness before they had boarded the Black Hawk. The carabineer was secured to a smaller diameter rope, which ran over a small pulley at the top of the door frame. The opposite end of the rope was already locked into an odd-looking figure-eight-shaped ring near the door. Lee assumed this was a rope brake or belay.

The chief pulled Lee toward the large dangling rope and yelled loudly, "Now or never! We need to get going!"

Lee reached out for the fat rope, and as he grabbed it, he felt a knee in the butt sending him out the door and down the rope. The harness pulled tight on his chest, showing he was not free-falling, instead being lowered at a slower pace toward the ground than the other four.

Chapter 31

0725, Day 4, Garrett Residence, Agua Dulce, California

Lawrence watched as the first of the two UH-60 Black Hawks came in over the landing zone, performed a quick and impressive 360-degree turn, and lined up on the first *X*. The pilots' displayed skill at their job and light wind made it even easier. Lawrence could see a man hanging out the door, which he knew from experience would be the crew chief. The big bird lowered slowly, and the large pallet holding what looked to be a large four-seat ATV hit the ground, bounced up slightly, then settled. A second later, the sling released, and the straps fell, landing slightly off to one side of the pallet.

No sooner had the sling released, the Black Hawk moved forward about fifty feet, and the big fast rope fell from the side door. Seconds later, one soldier, then three more in quick succession slid down the rope in perfect form. They hit the ground and moved away instantly. The trained soldiers knew staying at the end of a fast rope was a sure way for the next person out the door to flatten them. The four all had rucksacks, tactical vests, and various gear strapped to them. The first two had what Lawrence recognized as M4 rifles on single-point slings hanging along their right sides. Both soldiers expertly hit the ground, had their weapons up, and were ready for action within seconds. The next two soldiers were only sporting leg holsters and side arms. So far, the near-perfect show of fast roping was impressive.

Lawrence looked up, seeing another person in the doorway. However, unlike the previous soldiers, the crew chief attached a smaller rope to a harness wrapped around the man's chest. The rope slack disappeared, and the man stepped out, grabbing the big rope. Or perhaps the crew chief pushed him—it was difficult for Lawrence to tell. He slid down nearly perfectly but slower as the belay rope was paying out until he hit the ground. The last man's back was to Lawrence when he landed and unclipped the smaller rope. The second he did, the rope retracted into the chopper. The big helo turned, revved up, and lifted away from the drop zone.

The last man out turned and moved toward the other four soldiers. They all then moved down the hill, making their way toward Lawrence. Lawrence could now tell the last man out of the chopper was his Father Lee. He took off at a sprint toward Lee, where he crashed and picked up the older man. The other soldiers just watched as Lawrence spun Lee around in a dance of joy to see him.

Lee spoke out finally, "Put me down. This is not the proper way to treat a superior officer."

Lawrence dropped Lee down and then started to look him over.

"Holy crap! Where did you get this outfit? What rank is this goofy insignia?" Lawrence said about the modified captain insignia on Lee's multi-cam shirt in the center of his chest.

"It is a long story, but at the moment I outrank you," said Lee.

"How can you outrank me? I am not enlisted anymore," Lawrence responded.

"Well, that has changed. You are officially back in the army," Lee told Lawrence with a big smile on his face.

"Oh fuck," said Lawrence.

Lawrence and Lee's talk was cut short. The second chopper loudly passed near them, forcing the five of them to kneel down to reduce the wind and dust. Using the same path as the first, it continued past the now-sitting pallet holding the ATV. The second bird lowered down expertly with its crew chief guiding; it plunked a similar pallet forty yards from the first. The sling dropped, the crew chief saluted the men on the ground, and the second Black Hawk roared up and away, falling in behind the first. Both Black Hawks gained altitude as they raced back across the valley toward the airport, where they again made a sweeping turn over. Then they banked hard, hastened over the mountain ridge on the far side of the valley, and were gone.

Once the choppers were gone, Madison, Melinda, Logan, and James all came sprinting up the hill. The other members of the Garrett crew all stayed at their assigned security stations. Before taking positions that morning, Lawrence coached everyone to remain at their posts. Lee could see other people coming up from nearby properties on foot, ATV, and motorcycles. All were obviously curious about the two big army helicopters and the two loads of gear that were now sitting on the Garrett's hill. One old seventies vintage sedan came down the dirt road and stopped at the gate.

After a joyous reunion with hugs, kisses, and more hugs all around, Lee introduced the Garrett family to Jake, Liz, Kirwan, and Sanders. After an exchange of handshakes, Madison went from one to the other of the newcomers, giving them all a hug and thanking them for bringing her husband home.

"You may not thank us after you find out the job he now has," Jake said.

"I don't care what job he has, as long as he is here safe," Madison said to Jake.

Then to Lee, she said, "Why do you have that uniform and all those things?" pointing at his multi-cam uniform and all of his new insignias.

"And what is this?" Melinda said, reaching out to the paper tag on Lee's right shoulder. The paper patch and pin somehow survived the ride, the drop out of the helo, the wind, and the dirt.

"This is my badge of honor. I have a long story to tell all of you. First, we need to let all these people know what is going on. Jake, you should go with me," Lee said to the group and Jake.

"Wilde, you come with us also. Kirwan, you and Sanders start getting the stuff unloaded, and I guess down near the house," Jake ordered to his team with a nod from Lee.

The entire group near the landing zone minus Kirwan and Sanders started hiking down the hill to one of the largest groups of curious spectators. As they walked, Lee waved his arms at two other groups, signaling them to join them at one location. There were greetings from those knowing the Garrett family, and right away, questions were flying about what was going on.

"Were those army choppers?"

"What is all that stuff?"

"When did you get in the army, Lee?"

"There is a lot to explain, and we want to organize a town meeting. Because of the lack of any effective way to communicate to the residents of Agua Dulce, I need everyone to create a coconut telegraph," Lee told the group, using a term from a Jimmy Buffett song.

"This is sergeants, Rodriguez and Wilde." Lee continued pointing to the two soldiers. "We would like everyone to spread out and pass the word. We will hold a community meeting in front of the hardware store at 1:00 p.m. We will do our best to explain what is going on locally and in the country. Tell people to go to their neighbors and those to the next and so on and so on. We need the word to spread to everyone in Agua Dulce and Acton as fast as possible."

A few more comments, questions, and answers went back and forth. Lee then asked the neighbors to head back to their houses and start spreading word of the meeting. As people moved away, other curious residents were showing up. Lee could tell by the actions and gestures word would be spread quickly. Those on ATVs and motorcycles roared off, saying they would start getting the message further into town.

With the first meeting ended, Lee and the group walked to the front gate of the property. Lee directed the couple in the old car plus others who had gathered to spread word. A few minutes later, the second small group disbanded and headed off to tell others of the meeting.

Chapter 32

0800, Day 4, Sylmar, California

Dayyan and his army were growing in strength at a rapid rate. The raid at the National Guard base had netted a gold mine of equipment. The mortar tubes plus hundreds of rounds of mortar shells was a stunning find. Why the National Guard had a truck with army mortars did not make sense. Dayyan told his men, "This is a signal from God. He has blessed us, and we will win this war against the American infidels."

After quickly loading up the large weapons, such as the .50-caliber machine guns, and ammunition, they took the already loaded trucks plus two more. The small army left the yard with eight large trucks and six up-armored Humvees. His increasing number of trucks was starting to create a shortage of drivers. He continued the strategy of splitting up the group and moving to separate isolated locations. Some men returned to the original secluded truck parks to recover the excess trucks. He ordered his men to move to one of three locations. He kept to isolated locations in industrial parks and the foothills where the force could rest while Dayyan developed the next steps of his crusade.

The following day, their shortage of men versus vehicles would see a solution. Dayyan's handler told him over the satellite phone that a large group of loyal brothers had been making their way from central Los Angeles. They were rolling up Foothill Boulevard from Pasadena in a collection of trucks and old cars. Along the way, this group had attacked several planned targets and targets of opportunity. The group did have several rough battles with police and a group of Homeland Security soldiers, resulting in over twenty men killed. Even with those loses, their force remained over seventy-five men. Of those men, about forty were ex-military members of a Muslim motorcycle club. The club, formed after the first Gulf War, increased in size during the second Gulf War and the continuing war on terrorism.

The group met in a secluded location in the foothills up little Tujunga Canyon. Dayyan's massive stockpile of weapons and trucks plus new group's experienced soldiers was a perfect match. Out of the new veteran soldiers, four had experience with the Mortars from the National Guard base. The only negative to the new group, was a dozen women and six small children who came along. Dayyan questioned the leader, a Saudi emigrant named Hakim Ihab Albaf, about bringing along the women and children.

"I had no choice when I accepted the motorcycle members into my small outnumbered army. The leaders insisted on bringing along wives and children or they would not join. I considered the choices and decided to allow it. I can tell you that these brothers are fierce fighters. A minor burden of a few women and children may be worth it."

Dayyan was not happy about adding women and children to his army, but he accepted. His true thoughts included capturing a young infidel woman for himself. Or maybe even a young boy to fulfill his sexual wishes.

Why not? Dayyan thought.

The entire group now had close to 140 men and a massive collection of armored trucks, large 6×6 trucks, Humvees, and some odd civilian cars and trucks. Dayyan divided his forces into three companies. He spread weapons and vehicles around, mingling the military veterans throughout his forces. Arman who had brought his group from San Bernardino would lead 2nd Company. Adham would lead Third Company. Dayyan would be overall leader and would stay with 1st Company. Naseem would remain with Dayyan and was second in command. Dayyan decided to keep the truck with the mortars in his company and asked for the four experienced mortar men to join his group. The men agreed with one minor request. The man making the request was an experienced ten-year army veteran from the Eighty-Second Airborne named Jacob Alfarsi.

The man had approached Dayyan and asked, "General, I am honored to serve with you, but I would like to ask you to allow my young brother to also join your company. He is my responsibility. He is not a great soldier, but he is an excellent driver. His passion is racing sports cars and other high-performance autos."

Dayyan replied, "That will be fine, brother. I will use him as my personal driver. My officers and I are using the SWAT truck for our command car. Have him join us."

Jacob brought the skinny, nerdy-looking man over and introduced him to Dayyan and Naseem. "Thank you, my general. My name is Fawzi Sakhr Alfarsi. I am honored to drive for you."

Dayyan looked at Naseem, and it was obvious they shared the same opinion of the young man. This man was too small and wimpy to carry a pistol, let alone a large rifle. However, if the man's driving skill was as his brother said, he would be acceptable. Dayyan nodded and sent Fawzi to meet two soldiers who also rode in the SWAT truck.

Shortly after the morning prayer, Dayyan's satellite phone rang.

"Good morning, my brother," came the now familiar voice.

"God is great, my brother," Dayyan replied.

"You have done excellent. Your group is succeeding beyond our expectations. You daring raid against the infidel's most guarded base made news in the eastern United States and even overseas. Our people in other faraway lands consider you a hero of our war against the infidels."

"Thank you for the praise. God has been good to us," Dayyan answered.

"Unfortunately, because of your success, now large numbers of people are looking for you. You must keep moving and stay one step ahead. Sooner or later, the infidels may have no choice but to send their army and aircraft after you."

"I understand. As I was taught, I am keeping my units separate. It will be hard for them to strike a large single blow," Dayyan explained.

"Good. We have been given opportunity for an even more glorious victory, allowing us to flaunt our success to the world. A small group of our loyal brothers have captured six of the new MRAP trucks," his handler said, spelling out the letters of the acronym. "I also have information of a location of four of the massive American M-1 tanks. Unfortunately, our brothers had no one able to drive the tanks. Can you just see the publicity victory of your army driving these tanks through the American cities with our flags flying high above the turrets? When our war first started in Syria, the American circus media played the image of captured Iraqi tanks with our ISIS flags flying over and over. This simple video coverage, our leaders believe was a strong part of why believers worldwide flocked to our original battles in Syria and Iraq."

"I can see your point, brother," Dayyan replied.

Dayyan momentarily lost track of the conversation, thinking of himself riding in the turret of an American tank.

His handler had continued, "We have also contacted a group that may aid you. They are not true believers as you and I, but they carry deep hatred for the American authority."

"Go on, my brother," Dayyan answered.

"This group is a large gang with ties to the Columbian and Mexican drug cartels. Since the attack on the United States, they have lost their source of revenue. They are greedy and looking for ways of enriching themselves. They are willing to join your fight if there is value to them. I believe the term the leader used is 'loot and booty.' They are clearly infidel scum of the worse kind, but they may be helpful for a short time. At some point, we may decide to wipe them from the earth, but they may be useful to your army perhaps as fodder against the real enemy."

Dayyan smiled to himself. People he hated worse than the non-believers were drug addicts and their dealers. The new world law would have no place for these dogs. He would do as his handler has said. He would use them. Eventually, he would find a way to destroy them when they no longer have value to his fight.

Chapter 33

1300, Day 4, Downtown Agua Dulce, California

The morning was filled with reunion, explanations, and a recap of Lee's adventures. The Garrett family recounted what had been taking place at the Garrett home. Lee and Jake told the story of their exodus from Las Vegas to Madison and the other family and friends. Specialists Kirwan and Sanders with help from Richard, Mike, and Barry unloaded the ATVs and used them to shuttle the other gear down near the house. They secured the gear in the backyard to hide it. They placed some critical items in the house.

Lee then explained his role and the purpose of the town hall-type meeting. He planned on setting up specific groups of qualified people, and he would temporarily use family members in that effort.

Jake officially swore Lawrence and Richard back into the army. Some kidding and joking was part of this impromptu ceremony. It still astounded Lawrence his dad technically outranked him. Lee joked to the family, "First order will be to learn how the proper way to make a bed and clean your room." This idea quickly received a "second" motion from Madison.

After swearing into the army, Jake told Richard, a Marine veteran, "It is about time you get a real military job."

Richard joked back, "I will try to forget all the real training I had as a Marine Sarge. Should I spend some hours playing Call to Duty to learn how to be an army man?"

New multi-cam uniforms in the supplies brought from Fort Irwin were given to the two new soldiers. Lee and Jake wanted their small squad to look organized and professional. Each man received patches and emblems, including Sergeant Stripes.

They considered swearing in Barry, but he stated, "I got out about thirty years ago. I have a bad foot, and I don't want to look like I am a member of the AARP brigade."

Everyone laughed and decided if they formed an AARP brigade, Barry would be the commanding general.

They decided that seven of them would ride into town for the meeting. Lee, sergeants Rodriguez and Wilde, Lawrence, Madison, Melinda, and James. Specialists Kirwan, Sanders, Richard and his wife Sandra, Barry and his wife Holly, Mike and his wife Janet, and daughter Addison would remain to provide security. After early morning arrival of the military choppers, which certainly woke up the entire town, there was concern people might try something stupid. Those going to town would only wear side arms to lower tension of the army showing up with assault rifles and machine guns mounted on ATVs. It was a mutual decision to make a good first impression for the townspeople. One of the boxes bought from Fort Irwin contained printed briefings of the basics of the crisis. The plan was to give out the printed documents plus provide a verbal briefing to the town.

At around 11:30, the group loaded up and headed to town. It was obvious the message was getting out. Dozens of people were heading toward town or were already gathering when the Garrett group arrived. It was only about a five-minute ride. Many people were walking or using some other form of working transportation. There were old cars and trucks, ATVs, motorcycles, and even one old motor home with about thirty people crammed inside. At least thirty people were on horseback.

The team assessed the layout of the town. Lee suggested their group stand along the edge of the street. The townspeople would have room to gather on the slope and sidewalks in front of businesses on the east side of Agua Dulce Canyon Road. This group of buildings were elevated slightly, and the lawn and porches would create a natural amphitheater type arrangement, allowing people to see the speakers at street level. As people arrived, they were directed to take a spot in front of the small shops existing of the world famous hardware store, small café, and a gift store.

Lee spoke briefly to some people he knew but kept the conversations short, not wanting to explain things repeatedly. When the clock hit 1:00 p.m., he went to the front of the crowd and asked everyone to quiet down.

Lee started, "Ladies and gentlemen. Thank you for coming out. I know you are all concerned about the situation. I hope to shed some light on what is going on and how we need to work together to help our little town survive this ordeal. I know everyone has a ton of questions. If you can, please hold your questions until we finish with the basics of the situation. After that, we will have a question-and-answer period."

"My name is Lee Garrett. Some here may know me. I have lived in Agua Dulce for over twenty-five years. By now, most of you know an EMP, or electromagnetic pulse, nuclear weapon was used against the United States by North Korea. It detonated at high altitude near the California Oregon border. Four days ago, I was in Las Vegas when the EMP went off. To make a short story, I made my way to Fort Irwin, in the middle of the desert northeast of Barstow. On the way to Irwin, I met Sergeant Rodriguez here on my left, and once at the base, Sergeant Wilde." Lee pointed out Jake and then Liz to the crowd. "Additional soldiers arrived with us today in the two helicopters," Lee explained, leaving the total number of added soldiers untold.

"Other people here with me are my family. This is my son, Lawrence. He recently left the army after serving eight years as an Army Ranger. He and our friend Richard Silva, a Marine, were sworn back into the military this morning. Their reinstatement into the military is part of a sweeping federal proclamation of martial law. I am going to explain to you. I will also explain why I am here in army uniform, but first, I want to layout the situation."

Lee then went on to explain the events of the past four days. He told the people about the nuclear bomb in Washington, DC, the injury to President Harrold, and the other attacks by North Korea and Iran and the resulting actions by the United States and the rest of the free world. Most people looked shocked or stunned, and lots were noticeably crying. Lee told the crowd about the retaliatory strikes against North Korea and Iran. Lee explained how widespread damage to the power grid and vehicles was a result of the EMP.

Lee continued, "This devastating action has set into play a preplanned federal response known as a MACRO event. The term stands for 'Mass Casualty Relocation Operation.' Specifically, our event is a MACRO-7 event. MACRO events range in scale 1-10 with one being the least damaging and ten being the worst. This event is a seven on that scale. That alone will give you an idea of how bad it is. I am going to let Sergeant Rodriguez explain some of the portions of the MACRO Event."

Jake moved closer and started speaking to the crowd. "The Macro Event includes comprehensive preplanned actions based on the severity of the event. The entire plan was approved secretly in advance by presidential order by each of the last 3 Presidents. President Harrold also signed the MACRO Presidential Order. The Vice President and the majority and minority speakers of both houses were briefed in advance of the MACRO Events. It was done under strict secrecy to keep the plans away from our enemies.

"The MACRO-7 Event provides for a countrywide martial law. The law incorporates a set of rules and temporary law designed to help federal, state, and local governments. The authorities need control to keep or gain control of the crisis, which is on us. The goal is to first contain the event damage. Second, allow for relief efforts and relocation efforts to advance as quickly as possible. The efforts are large-scale and needed throughout the United States.

"We have a limited number of printed summaries of the MACRO event. But I will explain some of the most important points now."

Jake then started to read, "The prime order of all military, federal, state, or local authority is...

"One, by necessary means including extraordinary methods allowed by the MACRO document, authorities of all federal, state, or local levels shall deal with the threat or source that is the cause of the MACRO event. The federal government shall use all available resources and power to neutralize the source of the event, or the country or persons responsible for the event."

Jake looked up and added, "I think the counterattacks on Iran and North Korea have done a lot to that end."

He went on, "Two, aid the civilian population with immediate medical needs in any method possible with all the resources available.

"Three, immediately provide security and safety for the civilian population in those areas where possible. Then develop continuing operations to extend security and safety into wider portions of the country.

"Four, provide relief efforts directly in locations where possible, or provide relocation support to displaced civilians."

Now Jake again spoke freely to further explain. "So to summarize, all available resources of the federal, state, and local governments are tasked with stopping the problem and helping those they can where they are and setting up massive relief and relocation efforts. This is the reason Agua Dulce is vital, as we will explain later.

"Now about martial law, I will give you the basics. A national curfew is in effect from dusk to dawn. Rioting, looting or assault is now a crime that can be dealt with in any means necessary, including deadly force. Our legal system has some aspects temporarily altered. The purpose is to allow the authorities power needed for dealing with the scum of our society, which will take full advantage of our dire situation. The major cities are in meltdown. Looting and rioting is occurring on a massive scale. Law enforcement needs to deal with the criminals immediately and as necessary. Jailing hundreds, or perhaps thousands, of thugs is impossible with the country in a virtual shutdown. Adding to the mayhem, there are groups taking advantage of the power outage and dire situation. It is obvious by their actions some groups were set up in advance by outside terrorist organizations.

"Intentional hording or price gouging is forbidden. The value of the American dollar by government order is frozen at the level the day before the event. It is illegal to raise the price of goods or services simply for more profit. If you raise costs for profit, the authorities can seize the products. Seized products will be distributed to the public. For example, if the store across the street wants to ration what food remains they may. However, the store is not allowed to increase the cost of the food.

"Martial law does not allow for confiscation of food from peaceful civilians who have planned for emergencies. On the contrary, the government is counting on some people having stores of food. This will allow those people to take care of themselves, family, and friends. These people will not need food help immediately, allowing the authorities to concentrate on those that do not have stores of food and supplies. In other words, the doomsday preppers are less of a burden on society than non-preppers.

"On a similar note, there are no orders to confiscate weapons from peaceful law-abiding civilians. There are thousands of bad people with guns. Other bad people will try to get guns by stealing them. These thugs are out of control in many metropolitan areas. The police and military are struggling to contain the violence. Peaceful civilians able to defend themselves and willing to help the police can be part of the solution."

Lee interrupted Jake, "I assure you I would not have signed up for this job if guns were to be confiscated. And I promise you that if the government changes the rules, my guns will not be given up without a fight."

Lee's comment got a round of applause from the crowd.

Jake continued, "Summarizing the national transportation situation, all aircraft, trains and trucking are now under direct control of federal agencies. This is to allow for moving relief supplies on a massive scale. It also allows the relocation of refugees to safer parts of the country. No government agency has authority to seize private cars that are still running."

The last comments got a buzz from the crowd.

When the crowd quieted back down, Jake said, "Starting yesterday, massive truck convoys are being formed on the east coast to bring large amounts of food and supplies west. Progress will be slow because from the Mississippi River west, the road conditions are bad. It gets worse and worse further west. Cars and trucks blocking the highways are a huge problem for convoys to deal with. And it will not be popular trying to move large amounts of supplies past other parts of the country also in dire need."

Jake took a break, and Lee started to explain the financial crisis. "The government has also set up financial orders as part of the MACRO plan. As I stated, the US dollar will remain as legal currency at the current value. Inflation will be slowed any way possible. All personal and public financial debts are temporarily frozen. This includes mortgages, rents, car loans, personal loans, etc. All government-based fees are also temporarily suspended. This includes things like power, water, and all taxes, including federal, state, and local. Few people in affected parts of the country will have paying jobs. So it is impossible to expect them to keep paying debts, taxes, or fees. With loans and fees suspended, no one needs to worry about losing their house or other belongings any time soon. The suspensions will last nationwide for a minimum of one year. Possibly longer in the most damaged parts of the country."

This statement got another noisy reaction from the assembled crowd.

Lee went on, "With the financial system shut down, expected paychecks, and government-issued checks such as social security or welfare are not going to happen either. Temporarily, the entire country will be using the value of volunteer labor to pay for food and other services."

Small talk was going on around the crowd.

Lee waved his hand to settle the crowd down.

Jake continued, "Public employees, including active duty military, federal law enforcement, and local law enforcement, are ordered to return to their units. If not possible, they shall report to other units of military or law enforcement who have orders to absorb them into their ranks. Added to that, anyone who discharged honorably from the Armed Forces within the last three years is now officially reactivated. They shall also be absorbed by local units. If you were an officer in the Armed Forces within the last five years, you are considered reactivated."

These statements created comments and much talk among the crowd.

Lee pointed toward Lawrence and Richard and stated, "These reactivations are why you see my son Lawrence and our friend Richard Silva back in uniform and assigned to this local unit."

Jake then explained Lee's position, "The orders also provide Armed Forces generals the power to commission civilians who bring expertise or value to the command. Mr. Garrett is standing here at the rank of captain because the commanding general of Fort Irwin commissioned him to a liaison position for Agua Dulce. His job is to act as a go-between and adviser for the army command of Fort Irwin and the civilian population of Agua Dulce and Acton. Because of his long-time residency and knowledge of Agua Dulce, the general felt he would be useful and helpful to set up a relief effort here. The fact he happened to show up with me at Fort Irwin right when the general was trying to figure out a plan for Agua Dulce was 'right place at wrong time.' Mr. Garrett's commission is only as liaison, not a combat soldier. But let me say, I am confident after my experience getting from Las Vegas to Fort Irwin with him, that he will fight if needed."

Jake went on, "The Area of Operation, or A-O-R, assigned to the command from Fort Irwin includes Santa Clarita, Agua Dulce and Acton, and most of the Antelope Valley west of the 15 freeway. The base is in the early stages of setting up relocation centers at Edwards Air Force Base, Palmdale Regional Airport, and the logistics base north of Victorville. Those centers will allow large numbers of aircraft to haul in supplies and to transport out civilians to safer areas of the country. Agua Dulce is a vital choke point to people trying to get out of the Los Angeles basin. Thousands of those refugees will be on foot. Walking to Palmdale will be impossible for the elderly, ill, or out of shape."

Jake explained the primary task given to him and the others of the team. "You need to understand, the government, the army, the police, and all federal workers combined are a minor percentage of the overall population. There are inadequate resources to send large numbers of soldiers or police out to every affected part of the country. There is about one soldier per 250 civilians. You will be sadly disappointed if you expect a squad of soldiers to show up at your house personally with food for you and/or to evacuate you."

The crowd again was talking loudly.

Lee took over. "The government needs all help possible to bring this disaster under control. Estimates by the experts say it will take at least two years to restore the power in all parts of the country. Power in the western states, which suffered massive damage, will be the last to come back online. The United States did a crappy job planning for this massive damage. The stockpile of spare parts such as large transformers is pitiful. Ironically, most parts will need to come from China. The government and the power companies sold us out to the cheapest bidders."

Lee continued. "Everyone has a choice to make. You can sit in your house and live off your own supplies taking care of yourself and hope to stick it out. Your other choice is to help with the relief efforts. People who pitch in will be the ones who bring this country back from the brink of death. If you choose to help out, you will be entitled to help and supplies when they start to come in. If you decide to stick it out on your own and not help, you will be on your own indefinitely."

Lee let his last statement sink in before continuing, "Everyone needs to understand, there will be thousands of refugees trying to escape total chaos in the city. We saw groups of refugees on the ride over here. Agua Dulce is an important choke point. Securing Agua Dulce and Acton and helping the needy is the right thing to do. It is also important for our own protection. We need to provide aid to people coming in and start the relocation to safer parts of the country. This effort will not happen without volunteer help from us. The attacks have turned the entire country inside out. We need to do the right thing. There will be plenty of people doing the wrong thing."

Lee moved on to the most important part of the meeting. "I would like to outline the plan our team will be putting into action. We hope we get large-scale participation from everyone in Agua Dulce and Acton. This plan has three major parts. One, develop a security team for Agua Dulce and its residents. Two, help refugees with food, shelter, and medical care. And three, develop some long-term actions that will allow us to cope with the crisis for many months and perhaps years."

Lee then asked, "First I would like to know if there are any current or past members of the Agua Dulce or Acton Town Council. If there are, please raise your hands."

Two people to the right raised their hands, and a woman on the left raised her hand.

"Wonderful. I am hoping that all members of the council will remain in their positions to provide the core organization of our team. I would like to meet directly with you three so we can discuss specifics. I am hoping for your support and your leadership. I will work directly with the council in my liaison position with the army, but I hope the council can provide valuable help."

Lee looked out over the crowd and asked, "Now I would like to see a show of hands for anyone who is active duty military."

Only two people raised their hands. One was a tall stocky man with and obvious "high and tight" haircut.

Jake asked, "What branch and what unit are you from?"

A young man said, "Marine Corp Sir. Second Recon Battalion out of Camp Lejeune Georgia. I was home on leave when the attacks happen."

"And your name and rank?" Jake asked while taking notes in a small pocket-size tablet.

"Corporal Nolan, sir," the man stated.

Jake then said, "Okay, Corporal, I hope you are ready to work with this command. By order of the President, you are now in the army. You are now working directly with me and Sergeant Wilde."

Jake pointed at Liz and said, "When we finish, come on over and meet with the sergeants Rodriguez and Wilde. They are forming our defense unit."

Nolan replied, "Yes, Sergeant. I am glad to get back to work. Even if I need to lower my standards and join the army."

The entire crowd laughed.

Jake said, "You are the second 'Jar Head' that said that in the last couple of hours. We will be glad to have you."

Lee pointed at the other man, who was an older, taller man. "And you, sir?"

"Lieutenant Fitzgerald. Eighty-Second Airborne. I was home for my mother's funeral when the power went out."

"Sorry about your mother, Lieutenant Fitzgerald. I hope you are willing and able to work with us," Jake said.

"Absolutely, Sergeant," the lieutenant replied but continued, "But if I can get a ride out back to my unit, they may need me."

"I guess a ride will sooner than later be available for you to get back east, but meanwhile, your officer status will be valuable. Would you also please form up with the security team?" Jake replied.

The lieutenant and marine corporal made their way to Liz and the other defenders.

Polling of the audience continued. Jake called out for anyone recently dismissed from the military. By the presidential order, this gained them seven more enlisted soldiers and two more officers. Three of the enlisted were ex-army, one ex-Air Force, and one recently retired from the Coast Guard. One middle-aged man was a retired army major. Another stocky short blonde man was a Marine Corps Lance Corporal. Every man agreed to join the new group. The defense team gained four others who had been out longer than the presidential order prescribed. They volunteered regardless. The new unit was glad to have them.

Next, Jake polled for current police officers. There were three current Los Angeles Police, three Los Angeles sheriffs, plus one California Highway patrol officer. In addition, a Kern County Police Captain had found himself in Agua Dulce with family the day of the EMP. Again, everyone agreed to volunteer. This would bring the new force to twenty-eight. The small force was now loaded with years of experience and various skills.

Finally, Jake asked, "Are there any willing, able-bodied people that feel they have the skills and courage to join the security group?"

Lee joked, "For on-the-job training like I am getting."

Four more from the audience raised their hands. They varied in age from a man appearing about twenty-five to another in his late forties. One was a mid-twenties female. All were welcomed.

After the men formed up behind Jake and Liz, Jake asked, "By the way, gentleman, if you have your own private weapons to use temporarily it will help. We did bring some M4s and other tactical gear. But not enough to outfit everyone."

After developing the security force, Lee went on to other important groups needing volunteers. Next up were medical professionals.

Jake explained, "We expect a supply of medical equipment and some medical experts within two days. The army is deploying all army combat support hospitals, but there are way too few. One unit will deploy to Los Angeles International Airport as soon as security forces can put the airport under full control. Another combat hospital will be set up at Palmdale regional airport. Also, evacuation of some LA hospitals is occurring by helicopter with medical personnel moving to secure zones.

Out of the crowd, fourteen people raised hands and volunteered. Most were nurses, but there were three doctors of various expertise. A short discussion took place, and someone suggested to set up the temporary medical unit at the veterinarian clinic in town. The clinic was the only medical facility in the small town. Lee agreed with the idea, and he suggested the medical volunteers meet after the main meeting to start.

A man standing in a small group of six people raised his hand. Lee acknowledged him. The man said as he pointed to the ground around him, "Hi, my name is Garth Hudson. Myself and the others are with the Agua Dulce Ham Radio Club. We have trained for years for emergencies. We have already been successful with communication with many parts of the country and are starting to set up a network to gather information and get out messages. Does the army want us to help out?"

Jake answered, "Not only does the army want your help, we are counting on it. We have brought some military communication equipment, but we would really appreciate some help with manning our equipment and helping to establish coms to all the major areas of the country. Your assistance in locating friends and relatives will be invaluable. We will get together and figure out the logistics after this meeting."

Garth replied. "Great. We have quite a few people in town willing to help and we have hundreds of connections across the country."

Next, Lee asked for any water well experts. He explained that getting as many water wells working as possible was a top priority. Some people had solar power that was still working. Several people spoke up and pointed out, similar to the cars, the older solar systems were still working. The newer more sophisticated stuff had suffered damage. One man in the crowd spoke up, telling Lee he had found a work around on his nearly new solar system. Lee asked him to stick around and share that knowledge with others.

Lee was looking for alternatives for the water wells without solar backup power. A man came forward that was the owner of the local water well company. He said he would be glad to form up a team and start working on the problem. He knew several people he was sure would be glad to help.

Lee asked for any horticulture experts or anyone willing to help the town setting up gardens. He explained getting the water wells working was important for growing local food. This was an important long-term solution to help with food shortages countrywide. Colonel Braxton had told the team there was stockpiles of sealed metal cans of heritage seeds in the emergency containers. They would share the seeds if gardens were set up. About twenty people, mostly women, volunteered.

With all the major "departments" first filled with volunteers, Lee then said he would now have a question-and-answer period. Many people raised their hands, and Lee started from one side. "You, sir, what is your question?"

A fiftyish-looking man asked, "So why would the government choose Agua Dulce for what you called a choke point? Why not Santa

Clarita or Newhall? It seems Santa Clarita is the real choke point for people pouring through Newhall Pass."

Jake responded, "Excellent question. There are several reasons for the decisions made by those who created the MACRO event doctrine. Santa Clarita and Newhall are just an extension of the San Fernando Valley. With city water, sewers, and dense populations, they are in the same bad situation as the valley and the rest of Los Angeles. Likely, Santa Clarita will become part of the refugee problem. And most importantly, we have the small airport, which allows us to be supplied by air and evacuation of some of the refugees."

Lee pointed at a woman just in front. "You, ma'am."

"What is the plan for housing all the refugees you say we will be swarmed with?"

This time, Lee responded, "Another good question. Our original team has already discussed some ideas. As you know, along Agua Dulce Canyon near the freeway, there is an old campground with some buildings, an equestrian center, and a special event facility where they hold weddings and such. We intend to contact those owners and managers and gain use of their property and buildings. Just past the special event facility is the old mobile home park. It is empty with many large shade trees. We can set up tents. We also can use the Vasquez Rocks and its large flat grounds."

Jake turned the pages on his large copy of the Macro Event document and spoke. "Another section of the MACRO Event order, says—and I quote—structures, housing, fixed or mobile including travel-type trailers or motor homes not currently occupied by the legal owners and not claimed by the owners within seven days of the original event, may be appropriated for use for temporary housing or administrative use. End quote."

Lee explained further, "There are several RV storage lots in the immediate area. After a seven-day period, if the real owners do not take possession of the RVs, we may appropriate them. We can tow the trailers to the sites I mentioned. I am confident we can find a way of moving the motor homes even if they are dead from the EMP. Actually, if there are mechanics in the crowd, I would like to call on you to come forward to help with getting vehicles moved and maybe even running."

A man that was with several older-looking people all hanging out in one group said, "We are all mechanics and off-roaders. We can help out."

Lee said, "Thank you, that will be very helpful."

A man burst out loudly, "I have a motor home in the lot on Davenport, and it is dead, but I don't want to just abandon it."

Jake answered, "Not a problem. If you or anyone else rightfully owns a motor home or trailer, just let our teams know. We will mark it off limits and maybe even tow it to your house when we figure out how to move them."

"What about empty houses?" a woman on the right asked.

Lee responded, "If after seven days houses void of the rightful owner may indeed be used for housing a refugee family. We discussed saving the houses, motor homes, and trailers for families with small children. We will use tents and community buildings to house adults without children. If the rightful owners show up, we will move out the refugees and turn the house back over to them."

"Yeah, after they trash the place like what happen after Katrina." A rough-looking older man said.

"We share your concern on that issue. We will clearly order refugees to care for the property, and we will check often to ensure they do. We will send in a team ahead of time to remove valuables, which will be categorized and stored. If anyone trashes a place we have put them in, we will boot them out. No crap will be taken from disrespectful refugees," Jake said sternly.

Lee spoke up. "I would like to point out something to everyone. I imagine many of you have family or friends you have not been able to contact. Perhaps they live in Los Angeles, the San Fernando Valley, or other cities. Perhaps they were unlucky and somewhere far away from home when the attack occurred. They themselves might be a stranded refugee right now in some other town. Would you not want your friends and families to be able to get help? You need to keep that thought in mind when dealing with this. What goes around comes around. The people we will try to help in our town are all family and friends of someone else. We need to do everything possible to help everyone we can. And anyone not wishing help from us will be allowed to continue on their journey to some other place. We will not hold anyone against their will."

Lee continued, "We want to ask each and every one of you to help further. If you have extra room at your house and can take someone in, think about doing so. My family took in an older couple a couple of days ago. They were attacked not too far from here. You should also consider the help others can provide. If there is only one or two of you at your home, you will probably need help. Maybe you can take in a young couple with a baby or an older couple. Many good-hearted people will be trying to escape Los Angeles. If you can help, please try."

Lee finished speaking and pointed to another person.

"How many people are you expecting to come walking into Agua Dulce?" a man sitting on the porch railing asked.

"According to the study portion of the MACRO plan, we may see as many as two hundred thousand over the first thirty days. Maybe even more, depending on how the stabilization efforts in Los Angeles succeed or fail," Lee answered.

The crowd became agitated. Everyone was talking and loudly commenting. Most the comments were concerns of Agua Dulce being overwhelmed by refugees.

Lee and Jake did their best to calm the crowd. Their effort took a minute or so.

Then Lee said, "That sounds like a huge number and it is. This is why we need everyone's help."

Lee continued, "As the refugees come in, we will screen them for skills needed such as medical, or other past or present military. We will expect every single able person to work or help in some manner. No one is getting a free ride."

A man in the back shouted out, "How do you keep track of everyone?"

Lee pointed toward Liz and said, "I will let Sergeant Wilde explain the ID system which has been provided."

Liz moved forward. She had some plastic badges like the kind worn around the neck for events or conventions.

Liz spoke up. "We have brought with us several thousand of these badges. We will get more as we need them. This is a completed badge."

Liz held up a plastic laminated badge and showed it to the crowd. "As you see, it has a sample driver's license laminated into it."

The badge contained a sample ID in the center and a number in bold letters along the bottom edge.

"This is an unfinished badge," Liz said, holding up a new badge, which was twice as long with a crease near the middle.

Liz showed the crowd how the badge had a center nonadhesive section. This center rectangle was a size which would fit normal IDs, such as a driver's license. The rim around the badge had removable protective paper covering the adhesive. To use, you would place the ID in the center and the adhesive covering removed. Then you folded the badge over pressing the adhesive together, capturing and sealing the ID. This instantly created a photo ID badge with a new tracking number. Liz explained the color coding on the badges for certain expertise such as medical or security.

"We would like to issue everyone including residents and refugees a badge. This will allow us to track people, find their loved ones, and record voluntary work. When the badge is created, a form will be filled out containing information about the person, including age, social security number, address, and skills. The form also has places to write relatives' names and phone numbers so other volunteers can try to connect missing family members or move refugees to safe locations where they have family or friends. We will log the information here. We will send the information to a large database on the east coast. The database should help people countrywide who are searching for family and friends. The badge allows tracking of voluntary work and distribution of aid and supplies. People who help the effort and volunteer their time will be the first to be eligible for the supplies when we start receiving them. People choosing to sit home waiting out the disaster will not be eligible for aid."

"So we are all getting a number like the Jews in the concentration camps!" someone yelled out from the crowd.

Liz answered back in a harsh tone, "Numbers already track everything in life. Your driver's license has a number. You have a social security number. Heck, many of you were already blasting your entire life all over the internet. This badge is to help you, not oversee you. As Sergeant Rodriguez and Captain Garrett pointed out, we are all in this giant mess together. Everyone has a choice to make. Help to rebuild this great country, stand alone, or worse, become part of the problems we face. Make the right choice, people."

Most responded well to her statement. A few stormed off.

Chapter 34

1400, Day 4, Lake View Terrace, California

Dayyan had moved his three companies during the day. He sent them to three secluded locations in the foothills and industrial centers north of Hanson Dam. 2nd Company moved their trucks and armored cars inside a large movie sound-stage North of the 210 freeway. 3rd Company scattered their vehicles among hundreds of storage containers, trucks, and equipment stored in various lots on a hilly area west of the Lopez Canyon Landfill. This unique spot was a hodgepodge of buildings and parking lots. Dayyan wanted to hide his armored trucks among the variety of trucks, trailers, and containers. Dayyan's men quickly captured the few unfortunate individuals who ventured up near his army. After an interrogation for information, his men would kill the unlucky souls and bury their bodies in the soft hillsides.

Dayyan's company had driven up Kagel Canyon past the Shalom Chapel and large cemetery. A large densely packed housing track was and the end of the canyon. He ordered some of his force to block the road into the housing track. Then he sent his large armored vehicles to the far end, where the road turned into a truck trail. With all the residents trapped, the army went house to house and took what they wanted and tortured and killed most of the residents, only allowing the women and teenage boys to live. Those unfortunate ones would be tonight's rewards for his men. He left alone a few houses occupied by devout Muslims. Dayyan offered the young Muslim men the opportunity to join his force. He allowed the older Muslim men, women, and children to remain, and he even supplemented them with more supplies his force took from the nonbelievers' homes.

He was now waiting for an arranged meeting with leaders of the drug cartel gang. His handler had told the gang leaders to meet Dayyan at an industrial building further south on Kagel Canyon. Dayyan was impatiently waiting with Naseem and two other soldiers. He felt safe. In the hills behind was his entire 3rd Company. Eight men were in secluded positions with rifles and high-power scopes. In addition, his own 1st Company was two minutes away up the canyon road.

After a twenty-minute wait, Dayyan and the others heard the distinctive sound of multiple Harley Davidson motorcycles coming up the hill from Foothill Boulevard. Four of the old bikes pulled up followed by a sixties Chevy Impala. Each rider carried a shotgun or rifle across their back or in a scabbard across the handlebars. They dismounted and held the rifles in a ready but relaxed position. The car pulled up, and four men climbed out. The leader was obvious. He was a short squatty Hispanic in his late thirties wearing a pair of baggy prison pants and a dingy white "wifebeater" undershirt. Around his neck was a ridiculous number of gold chains, and he was sporting what looked like Rolex watches on both arms. Adorning all his visible skin, including his neck, arms, and head, were various tattoos. To Dayyan he looked like a fucking moron.

The man and two of his shabby companions walked up to Dayyan and Naseem. Dayyan and Naseem were both wearing their black combat clothing versus the more traditional Islamic ropes and garments.

The short leader walked up and said, "Yo. You must be the man."

"My name is Dayyan Imaad Shalah. This is my trusted soldier Naseem Jinan Amjad. I understand we may share some of the same wishes," Dayyan said in a calm voice and manner.

"Yo. If you mean taking whatever the fuck we want and fucking up the man, I guess you might be right. My name is Charro. Charro Velazquez. These are my bros, Hector and Raul."

Dayyan replied. "Our goals may overlap in a manner useful to us both. We take only what we need, but we are clearly intent on, as you say, fucking up the man."

Dayyan was trying hard to not just take out his Glock pistol and shoot the idiot between the eyes.

"So assuming we join our forces, what would that arrangement be bro?" Charro said.

"You and your men would join our force as an added company of soldiers under my leadership. We can provide you with superior weapons and armored cars and military trucks. You may continue your pillaging for gold trinkets and such. However, you shall join us in our battles with the police or military."

"Under your leadership? But yo man, my boys are my boys. I will be the only boss man giving orders to my bros," Charro replied.

"You may run your company directly. You will just take large tactical direction from me, as I will coordinate and plan our movements, strategy, and targets. We work together, but we remain separate to keep the authorities from catching all of us in one big net," Dayyan explained.

Charro looked straight at Dayyan without smiling and said, "I might be down with this little partnership. We will go join your little war, but for my boys, I will call the shots. If I decide it is not working, me and my boys will be gone like the wind, *amigo*."

"I will not stop you from leaving. However, you must know that once you join us, you will become part of the most wanted group in the United States. Every cop and solider will be looking for us and trying to kill us. At some time in the future, we may also fade into the wind. For now, we have our own mission. I think we can both help one another get what we want," Dayyan said, staring straight back at Charro.

Charro turned and walked back a distance and spoke quietly to two of the men. Dayyan could not tell what they were saying. After a minute or so, he returned. "Okay, Dayyan, my man. We are in. Sign us up, bro."

Dayyan, Naseem, Charro, and his two "lieutenants" went into the office of the industrial building. They sat and discussed the details of the partnership. Dayyan decided for Charro to bring his gang consisting of seventy-five men to the soundstage where 2nd Company was. They would split up the tactical vehicles and provide Charro and his men with military weapons, ammunition, and supplies. They would train some of Charro's men on the use of the tactical radios. Dayyan insisted that two of his own men go with the new group to act as liaisons between the companies.

When the meeting ended, Dayyan and Naseem walked back to their armored car. On the way and out of earshot, Dayyan said, "I hope to personally shoot that pig at some point. But for now, his extra numbers will be helpful. We can use them as bait and diversion if we play it smart. Charro is a naive idiot and will never figure out we are just using him."

As Charro slid down into the lowered Chevy, he said to Hector and Raul, "Those rag heads must die. We do not have the manpower right now, so we must play stupid to his fucking game. When the time is right, we will fuck those camel jockeys up. I will be the one to put a cap in that fucking arrogant asshole's skull. Fuck, man, we might even get a medal from the government if we kill all those goat fuckers."

Chapter 35

1430, Day 4, Downtown Agua Dulce, California

After answering dozens of added questions from the crowd, the large outdoor meeting ended. At that point, the volunteers assembled into teams. Lee met with the three council members plus a fourth who had recently showed up. First on the agenda for the new HQ Team was finding a location for an office. One of the council members found the owner of the small café right behind the town meeting location. The restaurant business would be impractical with the severe food shortage, so the owner agreed to allow the council team to use the dining room. Lee asked for volunteers to staff the HQ, and six people from the town said they would be glad to help.

Jake and Liz started to assemble their new security force outside. The manager of the pizza shop across the street offered to let them set up in his restaurant. The group reassembled and started to make plans for security. A map of Agua Dulce helped to decide the important points for the teams to secure. Agua Dulce Canyon Road just off the freeway would be one manned checkpoint. Davenport and Sierra Highway would be the second location. Jake figured their team would grow in size, so they would expand their checkpoints as they gained personnel. Jake and Lee guessed many residents had heard of the first meeting, but word would spread. In addition, they would try to recruit any refugee that was active duty or ex-military.

They would divide the security force into three teams. Teams would man the two road checkpoints 24-7. They would set up a third team as a "Quick Reaction Force." The QRF would occupy the woman's club building just south of town. The central location would allow the QRF to respond quickly to either checkpoint or other parts of town if needed. Each team would be divided into two shifts. A and B. Each group would do a 12-hour shift. Shift A would be from noon to midnight. Shift B from midnight to noon. The HQ staff would overlap the shifts providing support and logistics. They would also work with the airfield staff.

Some of the reactivated soldiers held higher ranks, but the team unanimously decided the active duty soldiers should keep command over the reactivated soldiers. After some evaluation of new soldiers, the command structure was open to change.

They selected personnel and started a roster for the six groups.

As selecting the teams was occurring, three more volunteers showed up. They had heard about the meeting and the needs for security team members. One of the new shows had left the army only four months earlier. He was a sergeant and an M1 tank driver named Jesus Benson. Both other men had been out of the military for over four years, but both were eager to help out. One was from the California Army National Guard with corporal rank named Johnnie Fisher. He had been a weapons technician. The last was a retired Marine Corp Gunny Sergeant with the name of Moses Pierce. Everyone saw the humor or good luck of the coincidence of gaining Jesus and Moses. Maybe it was a signal from God. Roz did a great Dan Aykroyd impersonation when he quoted the line from the Blues Brothers film, "We are on a mission from God." The place erupted in laughter, and several others followed with different Blues Brothers lines.

As an added value, the new people all came in with various military uniforms and weapons. Two had civilian AR15s and the tank commander had an AR-10. They added the new men to the ranks of the teams. Jake split up Moses and Jesus. He felt it would be better to spread around the good luck charms.

The initial roster was finished:

Headquarters Command (Restaurant)
    HQ Liaison = Event Captain Lee Garrett
    HQ Commander = Major Mitchel Hicks (Previous National Guard)
    HQ Vice Commander = Police Lieutenant Chris Moss (LAPD current)
    HQ Vice Commander = Captain Adam Tate (Kern County Sheriff current)
    Petty Officer First Class Dean Barton (Volunteer Ex-Navy)
Quick Reaction Force (Woman's Club)
    QRF-A-Shift Commander = Lieutenant Randolph Fitzgerald (active duty army)
    Staff Sergeant Jonathan Starker (National Guard)
    Sergeant Vince Padia (volunteer, ex-National Guard)
    Volunteer Mack Black
    Volunteer Bobbie Singleton
    Volunteer Pablo Goodman
    Volunteer Gilbert Russell
    QRF-B-Shift Commander = Corporal Thomas Nolan (active duty Marine Corp)
    Staff Sergeant Quincy Holstein (National Guard)
    Sergeant Terrill Hudson (volunteer, ex-army)
    Deputy Sheriff Willard Morales (LA county sheriff, current)
Checkpoint Alpha (Agua Dulce Canyon)
    A-Shift Commander = Sergeant Lawrence Garrett (reactivated Army Ranger)
    Gunnery Sergeant Moses Pierce (reactivated Marine Corp)
    Corporal William Sanders (active duty army, promotion expected)

Lance Corporal Roy Wilson (reactivated Marine
  Corp)
Police Lieutenant Wilbert Moody (LAPD, current)
Officer Lorena Fox (California Highway Patrol,
  current)
B-Shift Commander = Sergeant Rodriguez
  (active duty army)
Corporal Jeffry Jarvis (army)
Sergeant Jesus Benson (reactivated army)
Sergeant Victor Martin (volunteer, ex-army)
Police Officer Kelly Price (LAPD, current)
Checkpoint Delta (Davenport Road)
  A-Shift Commander = Sergeant Wilde (active
    duty army)
  Corporal Robert Kirwan (active duty army, pro-
    motion expected)
  Specialist Manny Solario (reactivated army)
  Lieutenant Pam Watkins (LA Sheriff, current)
  Deputy Sheriff Darin Sanchez (LA Sheriff,
    current)
  B-Shift Commander = Sergeant Richard Silva
    (reactivated Marine Corp)
  Sergeant First Class William Ballard (reactivated
    army)
  Corporal Blaine Keystone (reactivated National
    Guard)
  Corporal Johnnie Fisher (reactivated National
    Guard)
  Specialist Tracy Wilkins (reactivated National
    Guard)

There were several immediate tasks needing attention. The HQ
team needed to visit the airport and assess the status. The military
would like to start bringing in C-130 aircraft tomorrow and the
big CH-64 Helos. The first loads would bring the combat support
hospital equipment with trained orderlies to set it up. Some early

supplies of food, tents, blankets, cots, and other needs for refugees would also be part of the first loads. The team scrounged up a couple of old pickup trucks. An old Ford Crew Cab belonging to Sergeant Starker and an antique Chevrolet owned by one of the Town Council members were loaned to the HQ team.

B-team members went home to gather weapons, clothing, and other gear and rest. Everyone felt setting up checkpoints in the dark was risky. The leaders decided to have the B-teams plus some A-team members set up the two checkpoints at daybreak.

Uniforms were a mismatch of old desert camo, forest camo, and even blue navy camo. Extra current multi-cam clothing retrieved from the Garrett house was issued to anyone of the correct size.

Weapons were another potential problem. Most new team members owned a rifle and side arm of some type. Four extra M4s brought from Fort Irwin were provided to anyone not having a military rifle. Roz and Liz took notes of sizes of clothing and other needed gear. They would request what they could from Irwin using the satellite radio Kirwan had working.

The B-shift team for checkpoint Delta would go to the planned location first in the morning and decide the needs and the best approach. The team would also visit the large movie vehicle ranch near the corner of Davenport and Sierra Highway. The movie ranch contained a huge assortment of military vehicles. Lee knew there were jeeps, trucks, M-RAPs, Bradley fighting vehicles, and even M1 Abrams full-size battle tanks. Everyone was hopeful the surplus military vehicles had survived the EMP. Any military truck or armored vehicle would be a welcome addition to the team. Lee would go with the Delta team to act as official liaison. He hoped someone was at the movie ranch. The B-Team for Checkpoint Alpha would also survey their planned location somewhere on Agua Dulce Road near the freeway.

But there was an immediate problem. After the town meeting, several town members had approached Lee and the team. They said there was a band of gang members who moved into a house on Soledad Canyon near Agua Dulce Canyon Road. The gang was causing problems and blocking Soledad Canyon Road. People nearby were hearing gunshots often. The townspeople feared for refugees or anyone unlucky who approached the roadblock. Lee, Jake, and Liz discussed it with the local townspeople.

"How many do you think there are?" asked Jake.

An older man named Bill answered, "I got close the other day, and I counted about twenty people out milling around the McDonald house. I did not see the McDonalds. I am not sure if they were home when the power went out or have left or what."

"Do you know what weapons they have?" Liz asked.

"Yes, they have what looks like those Chinese rifles, AK something or another. They are always shooting—we can hear the shots from our house further up the road. They also have several working cars. Most are old Chevys and a couple of Cadillacs. They are those lowered kind with all kinds of stupid-looking paint jobs, little wheels and crap. I guess the old age of the cars kept them running though," Bill answered.

Lee looked at Jake and Liz and said, "They might be the people who shot at Barry and Holly."

"Good bet on that," said Liz, and she continued, "I don't think we can leave them be. Who knows how many people will come along and run into the road block? I think we need to take care of this right away."

Lee and Jake agreed. They rounded up the security team members who were still in town. Jake briefed the group of the situation. He suggested putting together a group to recon the location. They studied the location on a large topographic map that someone had. Bill pointed out the exact house. It was on Soledad Canyon Road just past the railroad crossing to the east of Agua Dulce Canyon road.

Three men would go on the recon mission. They would move along the ridgeline of the hills that lined Agua Dulce Canyon on the west side. The recon team would stay along the backside of the ridgeline and move carefully to a point where they would be able to see the roadblock. They would use the radios to report.

Chapter 36

1825, Day 4, Agua Dulce Canyon Road, Agua Dulce, California

The recon team was hastily but carefully organized. Marine Gunny Sergeant Starker would lead the recon team with Lance Corporal Wilson and Corporal Jarvis. All three would take AR10 rifles. Lee would provide his custom-built sniper version. The AR10 rifles would give the recon team a little more "reach out and touch someone" ability. They were heavy, but the team would not be taking much other gear, so they agreed with the larger caliber weapons and shared ammunition. Starker would use the sniper version, so Lee went over the setup of the thermal imaging riflescope currently mounted on the rifle. Lee explained how he had zeroed it at 200 yards. He explained other features of the large 308-caliber rifle. Starker was expert with several of the military sniper rifles, and he felt comfortable with the long-barreled AR-10. It was heavy, but Starker said it was light compared to a Barrett .50-caliber sniper rifle. "Piece of cake," he commented as he slung it over his shoulder while putting eight full twenty-five-round mags into his vest pockets.

The team took an extra radio for redundancy. Corporal Wilson would act as primary radioman. When the three men were ready, one of the civilians offered to drive them in his 72 Ford Squire station wagon. He would take them to a point past the 14 Freeway. He knew of a place hidden from view where they could unload. From the drop point on the road, the three-man team would hike up the hill to the ridgeline. The recon team would use the call sign "Batman." They assigned the name "Oz" for the gang house. The three soldiers and driver loaded up and headed out, while the rest of the town security team put together an assault team.

The team worked quickly, giving out weapons and gear and deciding on assignments. The two ATVs had top-mounted M-240 belt-fed machine guns. Specialist Sanders would be the top gunner on the first ATV. Sergeant Rodriguez would drive with Lieutenant Fitzgerald riding in the TC position. *Tank commander* is the name used by military for the person riding in the passenger seat of any vehicle. Lieutenant Fitzgerald would have command over the operation as the highest-ranking active duty officer.

The second ATV gunner was Sergeant Vince Padia, who had used the M-240 extensively during two tours in Iraq. Lance Corporal Wilson would drive, with Sergeant Wilde riding TC.

Jake suggested they should use Barry's red panel truck to follow the ATVs. The rest of the team would consist of those active duty soldiers and a quickly assembled group of volunteers or reactivated soldiers. No one knew what to expect, so all the help and firepower possible was welcome. Jake told Lee to drive the panel truck with Sergeant Silva in TC position. Sergeant Ballard, Corporal Keystone, Deputy Morales, Police Lieutenant Moody, and Sheriff Lieutenant Pam Watkins would all ride in the back. As they were getting ready to pull out, Corporal Nolan showed up riding on the back of an old dirt bike his wife was driving. They looked shaky and off balance with Nolan hanging on to his gear and rifle while she kept control of the old Honda.

"Got room for one more?" Nolan said.

"It is cramped, but get in," Pam Watkins responded.

Everyone was dressed in military camo except for Watkins and Morales, who both wore Los Angeles sheriff uniforms. Everybody carried assault rifles and most had side arms. The oddest gun in the bunch was an Israeli Bullpup Tar-21 that Sergeant Ballard owned. The Bullpup was a different arrangement than most battle rifles, having the magazine behind the trigger, making the entire weapon shorter than a standard AR15. The TAR-21 used the same 5.56 × 45 ammunition as the AR15s and M4s. Lee had brought along his M&P 10, 308 assault rifles. The other AR-10s, including Lee's sniper version, had all gone with the Recon team.

Each TC was given a handheld radio. Two more went to the group in the panel truck. Kirwan and Sanders had also brought four sets of NODS, or night optical devices, from the supply at the Garrett house. Three others had gone with the Recon team. Roz, Wilde and Sanders were wearing Kevlar vests, and the police and sheriffs had standard police-type bullet-resistant vests, but no one else on the team did. Wilde decided to give Padia her Kevlar vest and helmet, as he would be the most exposed as a gunner on the ATV.

As Padia struggled to get the too-small vest and buckle it up, he commented, "Jeez, Wilde, how do you fit your tits inside here?"

The comment produced laughter from the entire group.

Liz replied back, "Enjoy it. That's as close to my tits as you will get, Padia."

Sanders geared up with his own issued Kevlar stuffed combat vest and Kevlar helmet. Various side arms abounded. Jake loaded two large trauma kits into the truck. Although the team did not have a true military medic, all GIs had extensive first-aid training. Corporal Keystone and Corporal Ballard would carry the trauma kits.

The small three-vehicle convoy rolled down Agua Dulce Canyon Road about thirty minutes after the Recon Team had left. Robin would be the large team's call sign. They pulled up, stopping at the freeway overpass and waited for "Batman" to call in. They did so about fifteen minutes later at 1950 hours. Darkness was setting in now, but the recon team should still have good visibility.

"Robin, this is Batman," came the radio call from Corporal Wilson.

"Go, Batman," Lieutenant Fitzgerald replied.

"We in position and have eyes on Oz and the Yellow Brick Road," Wilson said, using the agreed name for the gang checkpoint.

"Three Tangos at the road. Roughly fifteen to eighteen Tangos confirmed outside Oz. Unknown number inside Oz. There are at least four RVs or trailers of various sizes with lights on inside. The number of Tangos inside the RVs is unknown. We have also spotted more Tangos at the house on our side of ADC road. Estimate about eight at what we now are calling Kansas."

"Roger that," Fitzgerald replied. "Eighteen plus at Oz, another eight plus in Kansas."

"Robin, we have a car moving eastbound below us on Soledad heading toward Brick Road. Hold."

"Roger. Holding."

Suddenly the team heard four gunshots from the distance. A few moments later, Wilson came back, but he was speaking with a more upset and hectic voice.

"Robin. The unfriendlies stopped the car. They forced four civilians out of the car at gunpoint. Two males and two females. The Tangos shot the two men without warning. They are now slamming around the two females. We cannot take a shot without possibility of hitting the girls."

"Roger that, Batman," an agitated Fitzgerald said as the entire team started closing in to hear the transmissions from Batman.

"Robin, multiple other unfriendlies have arrived at the road. They are dragging the two women back to Oz. Another unfriendly is driving the car to Oz."

There was a slight pause, and then Starker continued, "It looks like they are bringing a front loader tractor down to get the bodies of the two men."

Everyone was upset and pissed.

Jake said, "Fuck, if we had gotten here sooner, we might have saved those people."

"We did not know," Lee replied. "But now what should we do?"

Wilde spoke up. "If we storm the place, we most likely will be outnumbered. We do not know how many are inside. Plus, unknown number of Tangos are scattered in other buildings, RVs, and houses. It's too late for the two men. We might endanger the two girls even more. A frontal attack could turn into a shit sandwich quickly."

The group discussed a few different ideas. They could just rain down sniper fire from the hills. Or just storm in with the ATVs and their belt-fed machine guns. The ideas so far discussed had high risk to both the team and the two girls now held hostage.

Lee spoke up, "You know, you guys think too much like military. These assholes are nothing but unorganized gang members who drove their shit bucket lowered cars here from LA. They probably killed the owners of that house. We don't know how many other people they have killed or how many hostages they have? But they are not a military unit, and I doubt they will respond in any military manner. You need to think un-organized thugs, not an opposing military force."

Sergeant Wilde spoke up. "Lee has a point. I bet if we hit the barricade with a few shots, they will empty both houses like a bunch of cockroaches heading to a trash dump. If we get them into the open, a small assault team can enter the house from the rear and secure the hostages. The main team can pass out cans of whoop ass from the hill and the two forties." Her last comment was referring to the two M-240 machine guns.

"That might work. Who has the most experience clearing buildings?" Fitzgerald said to the group.

Sergeant Rodriguez spoke up. "Well, Sergeant Garrett is ex-Ranger, and of course that is what we teach daily out at Irwin, so me and Sanders know how to work it."

Wilde then spoke up. "I did close assault training in Ranger School. I would like to go with them.

Fitzgerald agreed and outlined the plan. "Okay, so you four make your way around the back from the same side as Batman. Do not go as far out on the ridgeline as Batman so you do not risk their position. It will probably take you about an hour. Meanwhile, we should call back to town for more help. We're outnumbered. If they spot us and decide to hit any of our groups, it could turn into one hell of a firefight. When the rear assault team is in position, the boys on the hill will open fire at the assholes manning the roadblock. The gunshots will remove the roadblock and bring the other cockroaches running."

Sergeants Garrett, Rodriguez, and Wilde plus Corporal Sanders geared up for the trek around the back of the house. Garrett had the most experience knocking down doors, but Roz was the highest-ranking active duty and would take command of the assault unit. They put on tactical dual channel radios from the house equipped with throat mics, allowing them to communicate easily with one another. Specialist Kirwan had brought over the radios and other gear in Lee Garrett's 71 Mustang. He would remain adding to the force. He also brought Richard Silva and a few more rifles from the supply at the Garrett house. Lee instructed Madison and the other women remaining at the Garrett house to stay armed alert. There was concern for the large supply of equipment still at the house.

Jake radioed the HQ team at the pizza parlor. They would send more help including Major Hicks and Petty officer Barton, LAPD police lieutenant Chris Moss and the Kern County Sheriff Captain Tate. All showed up a few minutes later riding in an old beat-up crew cab Dodge pickup loaned by one of the town's people.

A few minutes later, a beautifully restored 64 Lincoln Continental Convertible, top down, rolled up under the freeway overpass. Jesus Benson was driving, and Moses Pierce was riding in the passenger seat. They were sitting down low and had their arms over the side, looking cool.

"Yo! We hear you boys need a little help with some low riders?" Jesus said to the group.

"You dudes almost look like the bad guys," Lee Garrett replied.

"Yo bro, we is undercover. How you like our ride?" Moses said.

"Man, that thing is as close as we have to a tank," said Richard Silva.

Chapter 37

2045, Day 4, South of Soledad Canyon, Agua Dulce, California

Lawrence, Jake, Liz, and Sanders made their way toward the back of the "Oz" house. The four-man assault team, using call sign "Joker" had hiked over the ridgeline on the west side of Agua Dulce Canyon and down a small ravine to Soledad Canyon Road. They crossed the road in darkness and continued south across the railroad tracks. Once over the tracks, they started moving toward the east. They could see other houses in the area. But other than the house labeled as Kansas, they did not see any lights or people. Oz was brightly lit. They could see glow from a large fire pit in the front yard. They assumed the lights must be running from generators. As they closed in, they could make out voices. They could hear screaming and crying from inside the house. It sounded like more than one person. They could see a small outbuilding or barn ahead to their right. To prevent getting in a cross fire, they decided to clear it first.

The team moved silently toward the south side of the building. They stopped and listened. They heard nothing from inside the building. Jake moved up to an opening on the south side with Liz and Sanders moving to each side. As Jake got close, he could see it was a wood storage building or barn. He carefully leaned around the corner and peered inside with the night vision goggles. The rancid smell hit him.

Jake immediately knew the stench. Rotting corpses. Nothing else that smells that way.

He silently slid into the opening and moved carefully through the junk. Sanders, Garrett, and Wilde followed expertly searching every inch of the building with their night vision goggles.

Jake passed through the building to other side where he found the source of the smell. There were several piles of at least twelve to fifteen bodies. The bodies unceremoniously piled. His goggles allowed him to see that most of the bodies were clothed. As he moved closer and he could see several naked females. He wanted to turn on a flashlight but doing so could alert the gang members in the main house.

"Do you see this?" Jake said quietly into the throat mic.

"Fucking bastards," Liz replied.

"This is where they dump the bodies after ambushing and killing them on the road," Sanders said.

"They must rape and use the women for sick fun before killing them also," Jake said.

"These motherfuckers are going down," Liz said in a commanding voice. "Let's finish this."

The "Joker" team moved silently toward the main house. It was on a graded level about ten feet higher than the outbuilding holding the bodies. The team moved close enough to survey. The team did not see any movement in the backyard. They paused for a few minutes. They all heard many voices coming from the front yard and a few from inside the house. Suddenly, loud screaming came from the house mixed with hysterical crying and evil laughter. The words coming from inside were a mix of Spanish and English. Remaining hidden, the four soldiers moved up close to one another. They pointed out various items in the yard and any threat they added.

Sergeant Rodriguez spoke in a whisper. "When the shooting starts, we go in the backdoor and clear it. Once cleared, Garrett you stay with me to guard the front of the house. Sanders, you go back out the rear and secure the right side. Wilde, you secure the left side. Sanders, pay close attention to that large travel trailer there. I heard voices from it. Keep any cockroaches from making an escape to the rear of the house."

Roz used the radio to outline the plan. He made sure to have Robin tell all the attackers.

"Robin, make sure everyone is aware of our location. Do not direct fire into the side yards or the house. Let's not have any friendly fire incidents."

Robin replied, "Roger that, Joker. Everyone is aware of your position."

Roz answered, "Robin, Joker is ready."

"Batman, you can deal the cards when ready," Fitzgerald said.

After responding to the call from Rodriguez, Fitzgerald passed the word of the Joker's plan. Now he gave Batman the okay to fire when ready.

The two ATVs were two hundred yards up Agua Dulce Canyon from the Soledad Canyon Road intersection. The assault team carefully and quietly pushed the lightweight tactical all-terrain vehicles the last five hundred yards to a close position around the bend of the road and out of sight of Oz. ATV riders were in their positions and ready. Members of the attack team not riding in the ATVs moved forward silently into the dry riverbed within one hundred yards of the roadblock. The Rescue 8 truck was in the original position with Lee Garrett driving and Major Hicks riding in TC position. If there were any radio calls of casualties, Lee would move forward. Otherwise he would wait until the shooting died down. After Batman fired the first round of shots, the ATVs would race directly into the fight and open fire with the 240s. Fitzgerald worried how the eight tangos inside the house on the right would react. He directed Batman to do everything possible to keep those tangos from getting the ATVs in a crossfire. ATV 2 would guard the teams six as the two buggies went past Kansas. Targets emerging from Kansas who engaged in the fight would receive a hail of M-240 machine-gun rounds from the tail ATV.

Since the original drivers and gunner were now part of Joker, Richard Silva was in the gunner position and Kirwan was driving. The new TC in ATV 2 was Corporal Nolan. The gunners checked the weapons again for the tenth time to ensure they were ready. The infantry units locked and loaded their variety of rifles and pistols. Rodriguez had dealt out a dozen fragmentation grenades to the most experienced soldiers. He carefully directed each man to only use grenades in the direst of circumstances.

Chapter 38

2300, Day 4, Ridgeline above Soledad Canyon Road, Agua Dulce, California

Starker got the call from Robin. He told Jarvis and Wilson to get ready. They had agreed on targets below. The three sentries would not know what hit them. Starker lined up the big long barreled AR10 on the furthest man to the left. Lee had told Starker the scope had been zeroed at two hundred yards. The tangos were about 350 yards, so he compensated slightly. A slight breeze was blowing right to left. To compensate, he would aim one body width to the right. He was not making any scope adjustments but simply moving the crosshairs and using simple seat-of-the-pants skill.

Jarvis and Wilson also lined up and they were ready to go. Starker called it, "On my count. three...two...one..."

The three AR-10 rifles went off in near perfect synchronicity. The sound echoed from the canyon walls. Starker's shot hit his target dead center in the chest killing the thug instantly. Jarvis's target was leaning sideways against the concrete barrier. It was a more difficult shot, but the heavy 308 round passed through the man's arm and into his chest cavity where it tumbled, ripping through the man's heart and lungs. Wilson's shot was not great. The bullet slammed into the man's right hip and spun him around and to the ground. Nevertheless, before the man even figured out what had happened,

Wilson squeezed off another round, hitting the man just under the chin and nearly taking his head off.

The thundering echo from the shots did just what Lee had said. The house and trailers emptied. About twenty men poured from the buildings and RVs at Oz, and nine men ran out from Kansas. Some men ran out half dressed, but they all had weapons. They all sprinted toward the roadblock.

Chapter 39

2301, Day 4, Behind OZ, Agua Dulce, California

When the Joker team heard the thundering shots, they sprang from their concealment and headed to the back door of the house. Lawrence hit the door on the run, not even testing the lock. The door flew inward. Jake immediately had his weapon up and moved in far enough behind Lawrence to allow Wilde and Sanders to enter. Lawrence and Jake kept moving straight, and Wilde rotated left and Sanders right. The experienced soldiers moved as a unit passing quickly through the dining room into the center of the house. A man came running from a hallway to Jake's right. This man had the same response as many do when a soldier wearing night vision goggles suddenly appears. Shock. Jake never gave the man time to think twice. He simply swung the butt of the M4 around and hit the man direct in the forehead. The blow was powerful and square enough to knock the man out or perhaps kill him. The tango slumped in the hall. Jake turned back to the main room and front of the house. The front door was open, and he moved toward it. Looking around the edge of the door he spotted five men running away from the house toward the gunshots at the roadblock. Two other figures were not running. Jake could tell they were women, and both were holding large pistols. Jake moved behind the doorframe remaining hidden.

Garrett, Wilde, and Sanders moved down the hall clearing three bedrooms. They came to the last room, which was larger. The door was open. As Liz had trained, she expertly rolled in, intending to scan the entire room. She saw the forms of two naked women lying side by side on a large bed and it momentarily started her. Sanders moved past her and checked the bathroom finding it empty. Liz and Lawrence could now see two naked women tied down on the bed. Both women had their arms stretched behind them and tied to the headboard. One woman's left leg was tied to the other's right leg. Three ropes went over the edge of the bed to the frame.

Liz could not stop to deal with the scared and crying women. She needed to stay in the fight. She leaned over and said, "We are here to rescue you, but you need to stay put and stay quiet until the fighting has stopped. Do you understand?"

The two slowly nodded, agreeing.

Lawrence spun out of the room followed by Wilde and Sanders. Being careful not to trip over the body in the hallway, they all saw Roz kneeling by the front door. Lawrence moved up next to him and gave him the "all clear" sign. Wilde and Sanders headed out the back door to secure the side yards as planned. Then the world lit up.

Chapter 40

2303, DAY 4, RIDGELINE ABOVE SOLEDAD CANYON ROAD, AGUA DULCE, CALIFORNIA

The gang members had done exactly what Lee Garrett had predicted. They ran down to the roadblock, thinking some brave soul had put up a fight with their guards. The first of the gang arrived at the roadblock and found their three friends dead. They stood in shock for a moment before turning to tell the rest of the gang. That was the exact moment the first ATV came roaring across the railroad crossing. At seventy-five yards, Richard Silva aimed the M240 at the main pack and squeezed the trigger. His was the second ATV to leave the hidden spot on Agua Dulce Canyon, but the first one slowed at Kansas allowing number two to pass and move toward Oz. ATV 1 engaged eight startled men running across the yard at Kansas. Padia fired on them and six went down immediately. The snipers of Batman shot the other two as they tried to retreat to the house.

Now the second ATV pulled next the first, allowing Sergeant Padia to add to the carnage of lead pouring into the scattering gang. The two M-240s combined were capable of spitting out about 1800 rounds a minute of the big 7.62 mm rounds. The effect was devastating. The gang members did not have time to do anything but panic.

Starker and his team added more fire into the fight, throwing the same caliber bullets from their AR-10 assault rifles. The snipers picked targets who were trying to hide from the ATVs devastating firepower. The gang had made a serious mistake of leaving on lights. This allowed the snipers to see the hiding men without the need for night vision goggles. Few of the shocked and terrified thugs had any real chance of making it to a place of cover. They ran at full speed, trying to get out of the hail of bullets ripping their fellow gang members to pieces.

Chapter 41

2301, DAY 4, BEHIND OZ, AGUA DULCE, CALIFORNIA

When their world exploded in gunfire, the two women in front of the house turned and ran back to the front door. When they crossed through the threshold, the first received the same butt stock Roz had used on the man in the hall. She went down hard, and the second woman tripped and fell over her, dropping the big pistol she had been holding. Lawrence moved up to her and using the butt of his rifle tapped her on the back of the head putting her out for the count.

Roz and Garrett both then turned back to the door in time to see two terrified baggy pants wearing shirtless idiots with long rifles running at full speed toward the house. Rodriguez and Garrett were not going to give them the same consideration given their female companions. Roz pointed his M4 at one, and Lawrence pointed his weapon at the other. With expert marksman double taps from the two, both gang members stopped in their tracks with stunned expressions on their faces. They crumbled to the ground and died.

A third man holding a rifle and a fat woman with a shotgun were heading around the left side of the house. Liz met them both. She aimed and put a 5.56 mm round direct between the man's eyes blowing the backside of his head off. She quickly slid the sights to the fat chick and shot her twice as the woman clumsily tried to raise the shotgun in Liz's direction. Liz moved cautiously forward checking to ensure they were both dead, keeping behind the house so as not to become a target for friendly fire. She did not see any more people moving toward her side of the house. The first ATV moved into the large open yard in front of the house. The big M240 machine gun was silent but Vince Padia kept moving the gun around in a wide arc looking for any remaining tangos. The second ATV appeared a moment later alongside the first. The one-sided firefight was over, having lasted a mere ninety seconds.

Sanders was standing behind a large RV that parked along the right side of the house. Before he could stop them, two men ran and dove into the door of the RV.

Sanders keyed his throat mic and said, "This is Joker four. All units…two Tangos went into the RV on the right side of the house. I am behind the RV, so hold fire. I will try to flush them out."

"Roger that, Joker four. All units hold fire towards house and RV."

"This is Joker one. Joker One and Joker Two are moving out of the front door to help Joker four," Jake said into his mic.

"Joker four. I am going to use smoke to clean the rats out. Stand by."

"Roger four. We are waiting."

Sanders moved carefully around the rear of the RV. He could now see it was a large front-engine motor home. The large flat window on the rear had a covering of cardboard, so he moved over to the left side where he found a smaller window. He removed two smoke grenades from his vest and pulled out his large combat knife outfitted with a pointed glass breaker on the end of the handle. He smacked the glass, and it shattered. Immediately, he pulled the pin on one grenade and tossed it through the broken window following with the second. Sanders then hit the ground and slid under the motor home.

Shots rang out from inside the motor home in all directions. Sanders could hear the bullets tearing through the thin aluminum sides of the motor home, but his position underneath the heavy chassis and steel provided some protection.

Jake was at the corner of the house, pointing his M4 at the side door of the motor home while Lawrence covered him to the front. Smoke was starting to pour out of the open roof hatches. He could hear shouting and more shooting. The front door of the motor home erupted with bullet holes and splinters. The door flew open, and a man started out coughing and choking. A second man stumbled down the short stairs behind the first and rolled onto the ground.

"Drop your guns and get down on the ground or you are fucking dead!" Jake yelled at the top of his lungs.

Both men did as commanded, releasing their pistols, sprawling out wide in the dirt.

Sanders moved rapidly between the motor home and house. Shoving the barrel of his rifle into the back of one of the men, he yelled, "If you move, twitch, or fart, it is lights out. Get it?"

"Yeah, man. Like okay, we give up, man," one prone gang member said.

"How about you, fuck head?" Sanders said as he poked the other man with his rifle.

"Yeah, I surrender, bro. Quit poking me okay, bro."

"I am not your fucking bro dipshit," Sanders replied.

While Jake kept the men covered Sanders used large nylon straps to bind both men's wrists.

Jake radioed the rest of the team, "Robin, Joker One here. House is secure. We have four maybe five live ones and a couple of female hostages. We do not see any other threats. All tangos are down except the ones under our control."

"Roger, Joker. Ground units are moving up your way. Hold your fire."

A minute or so later, the Robin team members on foot came up to the house. Fitzgerald kept the buggies back to ensure they were not a target for any assholes hidden among the variety of cars, RVs, and other crap on the left side of the house. The first men up to Jake and Sanders were LAPD police lieutenant Chris Moss and Kern County Sheriff Captain Tate. A short distance behind came jogging Jesus Benson and Moses Pierce.

The two police officers expertly searched the two thugs, finding a large knife on one and a small 22-caliber revolver under the pant leg of the other. Roz and Liz went back into the house. Liz started down the hall where she found the limp body of the thug Roz had taken down. She leaned down and checked his neck for a pulse. Nothing. She then went to the backroom and untied the two crying women. The terrified women sat up, crying and hugging each other. Then both did their best to hug Liz, assault rifle and all. Liz found a pile of clothing the women said was theirs. Water in the bathroom was not running, and the toilet overflowed with solid waste. Liz could barely keep from vomiting from the smell. She went out to the kitchen while the women put on clothing where she found a case of bottled water. Scooping up four bottles, she returned to the room. Liz looked for anything clean in the room. She ripped the curtain down, causing the metal rods to clank onto the floor. Using the relatively clean curtain cloth and bottled water, Liz tried to clean up the women and their various cuts and wounds. She cracked open a chemical light, providing a subtle glow. The light allowed Liz to discover one woman was older than the other.

"What are your names?" Liz asked.

"I am Donna Stevenson, and this is my daughter, Denise," the older woman answered.

My God, Liz thought. *Those fucking bastards tied the mom and daughter to each other so they could rape them both. And those evil bitches in the other room allowed it.*

Then Liz spoke into the radio after pressing the small button on her chest rig. "Robin, Joker two here. Can you send up the van? I have two female hostages I want to get out of here."

"Roger Joker Two. Van is on the way," came the reply from Lee Garrett.

The had remained on Agua Dulce Canyon Road, but it was already running, so Lee sped off toward the target house.

Liz decided to have the two women wait in the room until the van arrived. She felt the trauma, death, and destruction would further destroy their already devastated emotional state.

She told them, "Stay in the bedroom until I come back for you."

The mother spoke up. "I cannot stay in this room any longer, please take us out of this house."

"Okay, I guess I can't blame you," Liz said and she moved over and helped the two women to stand and walk out of the bedroom. Lawrence came into the room and helped the younger girl.

In the living room, Rodriguez, Kirwan, and Policeman Chris Moss were standing over the two female gang members. Chris had bound their wrists with plastic cuffs. Roz used some of the bottled water to wake them both up. They were sitting on the floor near the front door.

One of the tattoo-covered gangbangers was spouting off non-stop. "You cocksuckers are going to pay when the rest of my bros get here, muthafuckas."

When Liz emerged from the room with the two women, the vulgar woman verbally attacked them, "Hey, GI Jane, where you going with my bitches? Hector is going to be really pissed if you take his mommy and baby girl away before he be done with them. That young bitch is a good fuck. Mamma is not quite as good, but Hector said she sucks…"

Roz slammed the toe of his boot straight into the gangbanger's mouth removing most of her front teeth. Blood spurted from her mouth and nose. She fell back against the couch, coughing and choking on her own blood.

Hector's woman spit out several teeth and mumbled, "Fuck you, fuck you. I get loose and I will fuck you up, dick for brains."

Liz took Donna and Denise to the front door, and she then turned to Moses Pierce and said, "Can you take them outside? The van should be here shortly."

Liz then walked over to the now toothless mouthy woman and knelt down close. "So, rat face, are you telling me that you and your cunt girlfriend here allowed those women to be tied down and raped after their husbands were executed?"

"Fucking right, GI Jane. Allow shit, I helped my man Hector fuck them both. Dumb bitches. And I will fuck you with that big rifle if I get loose."

"You mean this big rifle right here?" Liz said as she moved the barrel close to the woman's bleeding mouth.

"Yeah, cunt, that one. I will shove that so far up your…"

The gun went off, firing a single round straight into the woman's mouth and out the back of her head.

"Who fired, who fired?" Lieutenant Fitzgerald said over the radio.

"It was Joker Two, sir," Liz said back over the radio. "I was interrogating one of the perps, and she tried to take my gun."

Roz and Chris Moss were standing in the living room when the M4 assault rifle fired. Neither moved. They looked at each other, Liz, the dead woman, and the other shocked gang member who stared at the bloody mess on the wall.

"That was a powerful statement, Wilde," Roz said.

"I guess your loudmouth friend is not going to be raping anyone else anytime soon. What about you bitch?" Wilde said as she kicked the other woman in the leg, "You have any crap to say?"

"No" barely came out of her lips. She then threw up all over her chest and upper legs.

Roz pulled the living woman to her feet and out the door. The van pulled up, and Lee Garrett and Corporal Keystone helped Donna and Denise into the back. The two captured male gang members were sitting in the middle of the yard. Fitzgerald was questioning them but getting nowhere.

"I'm telling you, fuck head, this is my cousin's house, and these were all my cousin bros that you fucking storm trooping muthafuckas mowed down. You pigs are all going to pay for this massacre."

"And I suppose the people on the road attacked you," Fitzgerald said.

"Fuckin' A, General. We was just manning the roadblock to keep the neighborhood safe. You know we did not want any niggers breaking into the neighborhood," Hector spouted out while nodding his head at black police lieutenant Chris Moss.

Roz walked over and roughly tossed the gang female to the ground next to the two males.

She pointed at Liz and said, "Hector, that bitch GI Joe shot Lucinda right in her mouth."

"You cock-sucking bitch. You killed my Lucy? You are fucking dog meat when the rest of my bros show up and we do some serious ass kicking on your little fucking army here. I am personally going to skull fuck you bitch."

"What about the pile of bodies in the barn, shithead?" Roz said. "All of them try to attack you also? I am betting there are people out there who match the family photos hanging in the McDonald house. You scum bags just came here, probably running out of gas and took this house after you killed the rightful owners."

"Yeah, well, you heard the song 'Old McDonald had a farm, e-i-e-i-o. And on that fucking farm he had some Chicanos, e-i-e-i-o.'"

"Well, asshole, most of your Chicanos are dead and you are not far from becoming fertilizer yourself," Roz replied.

Hector replied, "Hey, fuck you, man. Just read me my rights. I want to call my lawyer when you assholes take me to jail. 'Cuz now you fucks is really going to pay. You shot my bitch. This is definitely police brutality. In fact, I am sure my Constitutional rights have been violated," Hector said.

Fitzgerald spoke up. "Listen, Mr. Hector, whatever the fuck your name is which really does not matter. You see, as far as I am concerned, you sacks of shit fall into the 'Including Deadly Force' category of the martial law order that this country is under. You are not getting any Miranda Rights. You are not getting a jail cell, and you are not going to be calling Saul, or whoever your slum dog lawyer is. Because, Hector, you are going to die right where you sit. The only decision for you to make is whether you want a blindfold or not."

The blood ran out of Hector's face. He got suddenly silent.

"Kirwan, can you drive that tractor?" Fitzgerald said.

"Yes, sir."

"Okay, unless someone has a very convincing argument as to why we should spare the lives of these pond scum bastards. I plan to dig a hole for them, and the rest of their dead friends and putting these three down like rabid dogs. We have no way to jail them. Food and security is going to be scarce. If anyone has another idea or has an objection to removing this trash from the planet, speak up now."

No one said anything.

Chapter 42

0720, DAY 5, DAVENPORT ROAD, AGUA DULCE, CALIFORNIA

When the assault team had finished the "necessary" things at the McDonald house, it was early morning. Lee Garrett, Corporal Sanders, Sergeant Silva, and some other team members left at about 0340. Madison was not happy at all. For days, she had no idea where Lee was or whether he was dead or alive. Then he showed up in an army helicopter. And since he returned, the two had hardly had time to talk. As mad as Madison already was, Lee did not think today would be any improvement for the two of them. He wanted to get down to Checkpoint Delta and start setting up. He was curious about the movie vehicle company on the corner of Davenport and Sierra Highway.

Sanders was driving the ATV, and Silva was manning the backseat or, if needed, the gunner position. Lee was riding in the TC position of the ATV, which was leading the small convoy. Lee signaled for Sanders to stop on the last crest of the road before the steep downhill along the front of the movie company property.

"Shit," Lee said out loud.

"Man, it looks like a real war zone in the movie car joint," Silva said.

The men stared down at the large lot, which days earlier had overflowed with military equipment. There had been Humvee's six-wheel trucks, Bradley Fighting Vehicles, and several M-RAP or Mine Resistant Ambush Protected trucks. Few vehicles of any type remained. There were a few partial vehicles, some antiquated-looking trucks, four M1-Abrams Main Battle Tanks, and a couple of older Vietnam era tanks.

The convoy pulled over. Behind the ATV of Lee, Sanders, and Silva was the big Lincoln Continental convertible and two of the confiscated cars from the low rider gang battle. The cars contained the members of the Checkpoint Delta B-shift team and others borrowed from the QRF team. The battle with the gang mob had changed timing and staff assignments of the A and B shifts. Lee pointed out to Sanders, "Any plan is only a starting point. It is surprising if a plan does not need adjustments."

One positive result about the gang cleanup was the large supply of guns, ammunition the security team gained. Twelve AK-47s, four AR15s, one AR-10, two Mini-14s, four 12-gauge shotguns, and various hunting rifles and pistols were all part of the weapons collected. The oddest gun of the lot was an old Thompson Submachine gun of 45 caliber. The security team had gathered thousands of rounds of ammunition from the McDonald house. The gang likely had brought a large supply of ammunition and guns. But some guns and ammunition may have come from unlucky people who met the gang roadblock.

Collecting belongings of the unfortunate souls whom the gang had killed was a somber task. They had recovered eighteen bodies from the barn. A cardboard box in the living room contained identification for all the murdered people. The HQ team would send the names to command during the next radio transmission. The men and women of the security teams and volunteers from town all pitched in to dig separate graves for the civilians. A Town Council member made temporary name plaques for each grave. A neighbor of the McDonald's offered to engrave more permanent tombstones using a simple pantograph which he owned. Any identification found for the gang members went with their bodies into a large common grave, which Kirwan dug with the tractor.

The gain in cars was a big plus. There were eight older Chevys and Cadillacs, which was obviously the original transport of the gang. All had way undersize tires and lowered suspensions. Scattered around the property were two older trucks, one Volkswagen van, one restored Dodge Super Bee, a diesel Mercedes, and a 1950 Oldsmobile. Several of the cars had suffered damage beyond repair by the heavy rounds of the M-240 machine guns. The running cars would be of great value for relief efforts.

Lee, Sanders, Silva and the rest of the security forces were all now staring down at the devastated lot below them. The entry gate was lying flat, having been torn from its hinges. An M1 battle tank sat sideways across the opening. It appeared someone had parked it to block the entrance.

Sanders commented, "That looks like an example of closing the barn door after the cows left."

Lee replied, "That is an understatement. I cannot believe how much equipment is gone."

As the team stood talking, two men came walking down Davenport road toward the group. A large property of undeveloped hills with sharp ridges isolated this end of Agua Dulce from the main part of town. But this area around Wagon Wheel road contained a lot of ranch houses on large pieces of property. The men most likely saw the convoy drive by and decided to investigate. A man looking to be in his sixties walked with a younger man looking about thirty. The two men had no weapons, so the team had no reason to worry as they approached.

"Hi there, are you guys part of that army group we heard landed yesterday in Agua Dulce?" the older man asked.

"Yes, we are. I am Captain Lee Garrett. I am also a resident of Agua Dulce," Lee responded while holding out his hand.

"My name is Brent Rollings. This is my neighbor Grant Cunningham. We both live in Davenport Estates at the top of the hill," Brent said.

Lee introduced Sanders and the others. All the exchanged hardy handshakes.

"What happen to the movie ranch, Brent?" Lee asked.

"Well, morning after the power quit, one or more stranded motorists must have figured out the military stuff might still be running. Someone climbed the fence and took a Hummer. Just drove it right through the gate. Bunch of other people then followed suit, and before you knew it, the place was overrun with people taking anything they could drive. But I can tell you some vehicles are not far from here. Some locals said 'What the hell' when the looting started," Brent replied.

As Brent was talking, he pointed up into the community over the ridge.

"Even good people will turn desperate if there is no control," Lee replied.

Brent said, "Yeah, I heard about you army guys flying in from one of the locals who borrowed a Hummer. He had taken an exploratory ride into Agua Dulce and heard the news. I may have a chat with him about his new truck now the army has arrived."

"So what happened to the bigger stuff like the Bradleys and the M-RAPs?" Lee asked Brent.

"Well, that is the really weird part. About 7:00 p.m. that same day, a group of men arrived driving a couple of old trucks and vans. They were armed to the teeth. They fired some shots and scared off other people at the yard. Then they took four of those big ugly trucks, which I guess must be the M-rips or whatever you called them."

"A group? Were they in uniform like police or army or what?" Lee asked.

"Not police or sheriff, but they did have a collection of army uniforms like you guys are wearing. Looked more like a hunting party or maybe a militia," Brent answered.

"So who moved the tank in front of the gate?" Jake asked.

"Oh, that's Marcus, one of the owners of the yard. Him and a couple of guys showed up after the place was looted. They put the tank in front of the gate to block the opening." Brent said, pointing at the yard. "I think they are down there, want me to call out?"

"Sure, Brent, if they know you, give it a try," Lee said.

Brent moved over to the side of the road and, cupping his hands around his mouth, yelled as loud as possible, "Hey, Marcus. Are you down there? These guys are from the army and they want to talk to you."

A few seconds passed, and a man came out from behind the M1 tank. He was holding what looked like a standard M4 rifle and yelled back, "How do I know you are not just another bunch of terrorist assholes?"

"Terrorist assholes? Why would he say that?" Lee asked.

"Oh, I did not tell you. Marcus said the people that took the M-RAPs wrote some stuff on his buildings like 'God Is Great' and other stuff in Arabic writing. But none of us know what it means."

"Oh, that is good news," said Sanders. "We graduate from Cholos to terrorists overnight. This shit gets better by the moment."

After a few back-and-forth exchanges, Marcus agreed to allow Lee plus one other come down to talk. Lee and Sanders walked down the hill on foot. Jake and the rest of the team remained. Lee and Sanders approached a middle-aged man fully dressed in recent military gear. He was holding an M4 rifle and sporting a pistol on a leg holster.

"Marcus, my name is Lee Garrett. The military command at Fort Irwin appointed me to act as a liaison to the civilian population of Agua Dulce and Acton. This is Specialist Sanders. Your neighbor up on the hill told us what happened."

Marcus moved his rifle to his left hand and extended his right. Lee and Sanders accepted the handshake and relaxed.

After handshakes, Marcus said, "Yeah, I guess some stranded motorists were the first ones to hit the yard and take some Hummers. Then some locals just pilfered the yard. The crappy part is a group of terrorists came later and took the M-RAPs and a couple deuce and a halfs."

Lee and Sanders understood the old common name for a large six-wheel drive military truck.

"Those assholes having M-RAPs is troubling," Marcus related to Lee and Sanders.

"How do you know they were Islamic terrorists?" Lee asked.

"Well, they left a bunch of terrorist graffiti in my office. Shit like 'God Is Great,' 'Down with America.' There is a couple of families living in their motor homes next door. They said the assholes were all talking in some Arabic language. And according to the people next door they had those black flags with the rag head writing on them. You know, like the ones we have been seeing on the news for the last several years," Marcus added.

"There are people living in the RV lot?" Lee said as he looked over to the large lot of trucks, RVs, trailers, and storage containers.

"Yeah, maybe two or three different groups or families. I am not sure if they own the RVs or not, but to be honest, I don't really care. Shit has hit all over the fan blades, and as long as they are peaceful and not causing me any further ill, I am not going to screw with them," Marcus answered.

"So why do you figure they did not take the tanks?" Lee asked Marcus.

"Probably did not want to burn the massive amount of fuel those M1s use. And the old M60s are not real fast down a paved road. Besides two of the M1s are not running. They have some transmission problems and we were waiting on parts."

"I guess that makes sense. I wonder where they took the M-RAPs?" Lee asked to Marcus and Sanders.

"I doubt it was just a bunch of boys out on a joyride," Sanders replied.

Marcus told Lee and Sanders his last name was Hogan. He relaxed and set down his rifle. He told Lee it would be fine to have the rest of his team come down. Marcus had his son Michael come over. He had been standing behind the tank since Lee and Sanders arrived. The twenty-five-year old came up and introductions were made. Lee pointed out the group had an army M1 tank driver named Jesus.

Marcus said, "Heck, my son is better at driving the big M1s than most army drivers. He spends hours moving the beasts around and, most of the time, drives them for the movie productions."

"That is a great thing to know," Lee said.

Marcus lead the team around the remnants of the yard showing them items left over after the looting. They did have about a dozen large military tents that would be of great help to the relief effort.

Lee said, "Look, Marcus, I am going to do everything I can to get some of your stuff back. I also hope we can count on help from you. If we find some of your Hummers and trucks, we would like to 'borrow' them."

Marcus replied, "Well, Lee, at this point I doubt there is going to be any real moviemaking happening for a long time. So unless I plan to form my own army, whatever vehicles you can find will be better off with you guys. We will help out with whatever we can. I would like to go back home in Acton. So what would you guys say if I asked you to just make yourselves at home here at the yard. If you are here, Michael and I could head back home in my World War II German staff car behind the office. I guess no one could figure out how to start the German relic."

Lee answered, "Well, we planned on having a team round the clock at the intersection of Davenport and Sierra Highway. We could just set up a local camp right here in your yard. And we will protect what is remaining, including those tanks. Hell, who knows, we may need them, but I sure hope not."

Marcus pulled Lee and Jake aside and said, "So, Lee, let's just say that you stumbled on some military stuff that might not have been too legal for me to have before this war. How would the army deal with it? Would I be in jeopardy of getting arrested?"

Lee and Sanders looked at each other and nodded.

Lee answered, "Marcus, I can tell you that right now the entire country has bigger problems than worrying about what some-one might have been doing or had in his possession before the war started. We are not going to do anything. And if you're willing to lend something you may have to the cause—well, no one is going to mess with you."

"Well then, come with me, Lee, and bring along Sanders if you want," Marcus said as he turned and headed for one of the storage buildings.

The three men entered a visibly ransacked building. Right in the middle of the building was a huge tank engine near two large overhead A-frames. The engine was sitting on a large metal pallet. Marcus pushed one of the rolling A-frames over the engine. He attached the hook from a chain hoist to a large eyelet on top of the engine. He then started to pull the chain raising the hook and removing all slack. Eventually, the motor started to rise up. Marcus worked hard and continued to lift the huge motor. Surprisingly, the large metal pallet went with the motor, which was a surprise. The entire motor and pallet lifted slowly, and as it did, an opening in the floor was revealed. Eventually Marcus, along with some help by Sanders got the motor up off the floor and the rough opening by about four feet. The concrete floor had been broken out and a large hole had been dug under the huge tank motor.

Marcus then asked for help, and the three men hoisted a large plastic case out of the hole. After getting it out, Marcus pulled a long strip of sealing tape off the seam of the case and opened it up. Everyone knew instantly what they were looking at. Four perfect condition Vietnam era LAWS rockets were carefully placed inside.

"Holy crap," said Sanders.

"I never seen one up close, but these are LAW rockets, right?" asked Lee.

Marcus answered, "Yep, genuine article. They were manufactured in 1968. These are fully functional. They might be just the thing to stop those assholes in my M-RAPs if they come back this way."

"They would definitely do some serious damage to an M-RAP," Sanders said.

Marcus then said, "Yeah, this goes back to what I was asking about being in trouble for having something I am not supposed to. I actually got these by accident. About two years ago, I was buying out a lot of old Vietnam era tank and vehicle parts. There were four complete M60 Patton tank engines fully crated. They had never been opened supposedly. All the paperwork was in place. Crates were still sealed. They had their serial numbers on the crates. I paid $750 for each of them. They loaded them onto my flatbed, and me and my son drove them down from Northern California. Well, lo and behold, the last one they loaded was the first one my son and I opened. We found a few extra parts that had been carefully placed inside the crate with the big engine."

"How do you think these rockets got inside the tank engine crate?" Lee asked.

"What I figured out looking at the paperwork on the crate serial numbers was that they had all originally gone to Nam. Then when we were clearing out, they all came back. But for some reason, someone hid the extra stuff inside. I don't know if someone had something dirty in mind or someone in shipping was just filling up all the boxes. Nevertheless, the crates sat in storage for about thirty-five years before the army finally sold them as surplus. Because the boxes were sealed up tight, the army guys got lazy and did not open them for inspection. So someone packed the crate full of extra stuff, and it came back to sit at a weapons depot for years and no one ever knew what was inside the crate."

"So what else was in there besides these LAWs rockets?" Sanders asked.

"Help me lift out the second box," Marcus said.

They all reached down deeper in the hole and pulled up another plastic case and unsealed it like the other, and Marcus opened it up. The case contained six odd-looking rifles that were lying side by side inside wooden blocks. Marcus pulled a rifle from the case and handed it to Lee and then another which he gave to Sanders. He then gave them each an empty magazine from the pile stacked up in one end of the case. Lee and Sanders both slammed the mags into the mag well of the odd-looking weapons.

"What the heck are those?" said Lee.

"*Heck* is almost correct. These are Heckler and Koch HK33 assault rifles. These were rare in Nam. They were only used by Navy Seals and Special Forces. These exact ones were produced by Harrington and Richardson under license by H&K. These are full auto capable with forty round magazines, and they fire the .762 by 51 same as the AR-10s."

Then Marcus explained the rest of the story. "So when we found this stuff with the engine, I called my contact at the army. I started to tell him what I found. He hung up the phone, and a few minutes later, he called me back from someone else's cell phone."

Marcus then replayed the conversation. "Look, Marcus, this is a crap storm of crap storms. If I let my people know what you found in that engine case, you will turn the entire surplus industry upside down. They will have us opening every case and box in our supply. That is more than five million crates and boxes."

"So what do I do with them?" I asked.

And he told me, "I don't give a shit what you do with them. Dump them in a mine shaft in the desert, toss them into the ocean. Just don't report this to me. If you do, I will put your name to the bottom of the most bottom list forever getting any surplus from us again. Do you get it?" And the army representative hung up the phone.

"So we did not want to destroy them and we did not want to risk selling them, so we just buried them under this engine. Now with the country in such a state, who cares? If these will help your cause, gentleman, you are welcome to them. By the way, I have over ten thousand rounds of .762 ammo in another hidden spot. You are welcome to that also."

Chapter 43

1100, Day 5, Undisclosed Medical Facility, Undisclosed State

President Pauline Harrold had awoken from her unconscious state two days after the nuclear explosion had leveled most of Washington, DC. After freeing her from the wreckage of the helicopter crash, the president was taken to the military hospital at Andrews Air Force Base for immediate treatment. A team of doctors and nurses stabilized her. A large convoy of armored trucks and armored SUVs formed up around several ambulances. The convoy of vehicles quickly and safely transported the president and her staff to a top secret hidden location.

The hidden location was one of the most closely guarded sites in the United States. Similar to the fashionable facility built under Greenbrier resort in West Virginia during the Cold War, this newer site was state of the art and massive. Its labyrinth of tunnels connected multiple large areas separated by rapid closing blast doors. The housing was large enough for all the top Washington, DC, politicians, their staff, and immediate families. In total, the site could house over five thousand people.

Besides the president and surviving staff members, the presidential secretaries, including the Secretary of Defense and Secretary of State were located and taken to the location by security forces. Also moved to the location were all surviving members of the US Senate and House or Representatives and all seven surviving members of the Supreme Court including the Chief Justice. Staff members not immediately available for transport had planned pickup locations. When they arrived, they were screened, put into windowless buses, and driven to the facility under heavy army escort.

The late-night occurrence of the nuclear explosion allowed many of DC politicians to survive. Many who lived outside the central district of Columbia were safe at home when the blast went off. However, the death toll was still horrendous. Special security forces found and picked up seventy-eight out of the one hundred senators. The search teams also found or accounted for 390 of 435 Representatives from the House. Security forces transported those in the Washington, DC, area to the same site as the president. For those outside Washington, other secure sites were available nationwide. The remaining members not located were assumed dead. A major impact was the change in politics. Before the attack, the Republicans controlled both houses by small margins. For no reason except dumb luck, the death toll was harder on Republicans than Democrats.

The secure center became the new capital for the US government. The president and both houses plus the Supreme Court all lived and worked from a location nearly four hundred feet below ground. Four days after the nuclear attack, roll call would show that both houses now had Democrat majorities that would remain so until special elections replaced the missing or dead members. The shift in the balance of power could clearly affect the actions of the government in the coming days, weeks, and months.

As it turned out, the president's injuries were fairly minor. The hard landing resulting in a hard hit on her skull had caused the temporary coma and following concussion. She also had a minor fracture in her right forearm and several cuts and severe bruises. She woke up feisty and as demanding and irritating as she typically was on any normal day. After a few hours of shock when told of her husband's death, she demanded a briefing on the state of the country and insisted on reinstatement as president.

The doctors and lawyers agreed that after another forty-eight hours and continuing medical testing, she would be able to perform in the POTUS position. To no avail, Republicans desperately tried anything to keep the Speaker of the House in power. With the Supreme Court justices living in the same site, it took only minutes for an unofficial ruling. The Republicans knew a full legal challenge would create more havoc in the country at this critical time. So they consented to the forty-eight-hour rest period before Speaker of the House Baylor would step down. So as long as he held power, President Baylor pounded the Iranians and ISIS locations with everything the military could muster up.

The Chief Justice reinstated Pauline Harrold as president on the afternoon of Day 5. She immediately made it known of her extreme displeasure in some of the actions of the acting President Baylor including the complete destruction of North Korea and the near destruction of Iran. She made a TV appearance in which she expressed her displeasure with the decisions made by Baylor. She even offered a weak-handed apology to the rest of the world. The United Nations Security Council was up in arms and considering actions against the United States, so her apology had some calming effect. Some of the actions the UN was considering were war crimes and sanctions. Several of the American-hating members had even proposed a declaration of war by NATO and/or OPEC against the United States. Some of the demands from the UN had been so outlandish that seven of the major members all but resigned, including England, Spain, Japan, South Korea, Israel, Australia, and remarkably, Russia. Fourteen other countries also boycotted and threatened to resign with the major members.

Evacuation of the United Nations building in New York occurred immediately within days of the attack. Most dignitaries transferred to an alternate UN facility in Geneva Switzerland. President Baylor pushed back hard on the UN and told them to go to hell as politically correct as possible. Baylor had been in constant contact with the Russian Prime President Vladimir Putin. The two of them had astonished the world with their newfound friendship and a pact of protection which Putin provided. Of course, this action enraged the Chinese. Recent events by the Russians in Ukraine and other hot spots worldwide already had the Chinese, most of Europe, and the

UN on edge. So the Russian-American allegiance dumbfounded the Chinese and many other nations. When questioned about his deal with Russia, Baylor explained how the two countries had historically become allies in desperate times. The United States had come to the rescue of Russian during World War II, so it was finally time to repay that debt. Russia was responding with massive relief efforts and offering military support if asked.

Meanwhile, the Chinese economy crashed the day after the attack. China had become so reliant on selling tons of goods to the United States, and cutting off that supply line had massive and devastating effects. Economists expected unemployment in China to hit 40 percent within weeks.

President Harrold did not share the fondness of Putin, and this was a big sore spot after the briefing on the agreements between Putin and Baylor. She was on the phone with Putin later that evening. She immediately started back peddling on most of the "handshake" agreements. After about twenty minutes on the phone, Vladimir Putin, in calm and nearly perfect English, told her, "Madame President, the United States is in dire need of a powerful friend. Russia is willing to stand with you now, but if your attitude does not improve rapidly… how is it you Americans say it? You can go pound sand." And he hung up the phone, leaving Pauline Harrold speechless for perhaps the first time in her life. The other high-ranking members of the cabinet all looked shocked. Baylor smiled and walked from the room.

President Harrold then sat down and started barking off a list of demands and orders. After she composed herself, she asked her aids to set up a phone call with the Chinese president. The next day, she met in private with many of her closest Democrat friends and allies. When the closed-door meeting ended, Madame President once again called China. Harrold no doubt had something planned. The Republicans and other moderates considered these meetings with the Chinese very troublesome.

Chapter 44

1430, Day 6, Budweiser Plant, Van Nuys, California

D ayyan spread his four companies out in several locations in and around the Budweiser Brewery in Van Nuys. Again, the units moved in separate convoys on different routes to prevent becoming a large target to the American military. Dayyan positioned some of his trucks along residential streets. Having his men mixed in with civilians would hopefully give the army pause about any large-scale air strike. The heavy smoke and haze that now blanketed the entire San Fernando Valley basin was a godsend for Dayyan and his army of thugs. He knew normal drone cameras could not see through the smoke. Infrared cameras or radar would not be acceptable for coordinating any aggressive military actions without risking civilian casualties.

They were starting to have more and more fights with military and police units and just large bands of well-armed civilians. In all the battles, his men prevailed with few casualties. Four of his men were killed. Three other men were severely wounded and not expected to live. Treated as martyrs, they were as painlessly as possible finished off. Dayyan knew that any captured soldiers would be brutally treated, interrogated, and then shot as the countrywide martial law allowed.

Dayyan and Naseem were planning their most daring attack. The day before, he had sent some scouts to the large National Guard Base in Van Nuys. The scouts reported on a massive refugee center created at the base and the fire station next door. The base and the fire station located on Sepulveda Boulevard backed up against the now abandon 405 freeway. This famous freeway was now a parking lot, littered with dead cars.

The scouts had used the tree-lined freeway. The trees and shrubbery provided a perfect observation point to watch the base. The scouts brought interesting news for Dayyan. They had spotted at least four of the large Light Armored Vehicles, or LAV for short. The large armored vehicles had eight road tires with small turrets and an infantry compartment.

Dayyan thought about the danger of hitting this obviously heavily guarded base. But Dayyan knew an attack on this base would make the news worldwide. He would show the infidels that even the army could not keep them safe. Using sketches and notes the scouts brought back, he and Naseem studied the layout of the base and had developed a daring plan.

Just after dark, Dayyan ordered all his companies out on different routes to different locations. He held some units in reserve to create blocking units in case the main forces had to make a run for it.

Dayyan's 1st company moved up onto the 405 freeway and made their way as close as they felt safe to the base. They would stay in the southbound lanes, using the center divider as a natural noise and visual block. He would set up his mortar teams behind the concrete K-rails.

2nd company, under the command of Arman, positioned their trucks in the large Sepulveda flood basin near the Burbank Boulevard overpass. They hid the trucks as best they could and left half of the men to guard them. The remaining men used the darkness to move south below the east side of the raised freeway along the heavily landscaped slope. They moved into position near the National Guard base and waited silently.

Dayyan had directed 3rd and 4th companies to move toward the base and approach it from Sepulveda Boulevard and Hartsook Street.

Hartsook was a small residential street running east and west which ended at the National Guard base on Sepulveda Boulevard.

By 2215 hours, his men and vehicles were all in place. Using night vision binoculars, Dayyan could see most the civilian refugees, police, fire, and national guard were in the fire station complex. The National Guard base appeared lightly occupied. Humvee's with turret mounted machine guns sat at the entry driveway on Magnolia Boulevard and along the fence line on Sepulveda. Dayyan could not see any signs of security placed along the freeway.

Dayyan watched as one of the experienced artillerymen triangulated the distances for the mortars. He ordered the teams to use all four launchers. Dayyan wanted the first volley to cause as much confusion and chaos as possible. Hundreds of refugees scattering like ants would be a massive problem for the outnumbered soldiers and police.

Chapter 45

2230, DAY 6, FIRE STATION NO. 88, VAN NUYS, CALIFORNIA

WNN reporter Bree Wilkins had arrived at the refugee center with Mike Bolingrass about two hours earlier. She had flown in on one of the military transports arriving at Van Nuys Airport earlier in the day. She had gotten a ride in one of the military trucks taking supplies to refugee center. The trucks would leave the badly needed supplies and return to the airport with civilians seeking transport to safer parts of the country. Bree and her camera operator were shooting a video of the center and doing interviews with civilians, police, fireman, and National Guard soldiers. The stories were consistent. The authorities felt overwhelmed by the sheer numbers of Los Angeles residents in dire need.

Mike turned on the camera, flipped the record button, and signaled it was ready. Bree started, "This is Bree Wilkins reporting from Fire Station 88 in Van Nuys, California. I have with me Los Angeles City Fire Captain Carl Park. Carl, can you tell me the situation here at the refugee station?"

The Captain started to explain, "We opened this refugee center the day after the EMP attack. We are taking in hundreds of ci—"

Captain Park stopped short in his sentence. Bree nor her cameraman understood why. Having never been war correspondents, they heard the loud, shrill noise but thought it to be some odd siren.

Captain Park suddenly tossed Bree to the ground and covered her body with his. His movement stunned her, and she landed hard and heard men crying out, "Incoming."

The first four rounds landed within two seconds of one another. One round hit in the middle of tables and chairs, which were part of a makeshift dining area. Luckily, few people were sitting at the tables this late at night. The tables and chairs exploded into hundreds of pieces. The second round hit square in the center of the main National Guard parking lot. The third hit only feet from the Humvee guarding the Magnolia gate. That round caused the gunner to duck inside the armored car. Moments later, both the gunner and the driver jumped out and ran for cover inside the main building. The last round also landed inside the fire department compound, exploding a section of a parked ladder truck. Shrapnel flew at ballistic speed in all directions, and many people were down, screaming and dying.

As the mortar teams dropped the rounds for the second volley, 3rd and 4th companies roared up in the armored trucks. Turret-mounted .50-caliber machine guns raked devastating fire into the Humvees and the main building of the base. Civilians in the fire department yard able to run were running as fast as possible south to any large cover.

Dayan signaled his attack team to go. The men had already cut holes in the freeway fence. Now ten men of the assault team took off on foot toward the row of parked LAVs. The LAVs were the prize Dayyan wanted. The diversion and chaos would add a spectacular public relations win for his cause. As the murderous machine gunfire was pouring in from Sepulveda and Magnolia Boulevards, all action by the defenders was in that direction. Some army veterans now in the National Guard had experience with artillery backed assault, but most did not. The men who had never experienced artillery had no idea how to respond except look for cover.

As the second and third volleys fell, none of the defenders noticed the ten men sprinting toward the LAVs. Dayyan's men had arrived and were opening the first two eight-wheel tanks, when battle-hardened Sergeant Wilford M. Jenkins came out of the back of the main building. Jenkins saw the men going after the LAVs. He shouted at two of his soldiers to get help, and then he ran for the dirt-covered Humvee sitting by the gate. He climbed into the right door and made his way into the turret. As the fourth volley hit, he paid no attention and spun the big .50-caliber around and racked the slide back. "Not on my watch, you fucking pricks." He opened up with the .50-caliber and started spraying the men that were surrounding the armored eight-wheel tanks.

Sergeant Wilford M. Jenkins was a battle-worn veteran of the war on terror. The burley 6'6" farmer from Kansas had seen so many conflicts and firefights that he had become cold to the fog of war. He held onto the large machine gun and poured the big rounds out at the men surrounding the LAVs. He ignored small arms fire pinging off the Hummer and the turret. Dayyan's other soldiers along the freeway were desperately shooting at the big man with the big machine gun. The armored trucks on Sepulveda and the side streets had moved south and no longer had a line on the sergeant's Hummer. Dayyan shouted into his radio to take out the machine gun in the truck at the North Gate. The fog of war was causing confusion for the terrorists. So far, none of the truck mounted guns on Sepulveda had directed fire at the lone brave and crazy sergeant.

Jenkins pounded the ten men around the LAVs. He killed three of Dayyan's men outright and ripped a leg clear off a fifth man. Ricochets of metal severely wounded two more. The remaining four men climbed two each into the rear ramps of the first two LAVs and moved forward into the drivers' compartments. There they started the procedure of firing up the tanks. The sergeant finally noticed the intensive AK-47 fire coming from the freeway so he spun his .50-caliber in that direction, spraying along the trees and walls. Cars on the freeway burst into flames as the huge shells hit gas tanks.

Suddenly, large rounds hit behind Jenkins, tearing apart the Hummer cab, hood, and windows. He felt multiple hits of sharp metal on his legs and lower torso, but he did not slow down. He spun the turret and pointed the big weapon at the armored car, which had backed into the intersection on Sepulveda. Jenkins was clearly the more experienced gunner and it showed immediately. His rounds tore into the makeshift turret Dayyan's men had added to the top of a Brinks truck. Jenkins's carefully placed shots ripped the terrorist gunner to pieces, and he slid back into the opening into a pool of his own blood. A second armored truck backed into the intersection behind the first, and the sergeant redirected his fire on it also destroying the cab, turret and occupants. But as the rounds started tearing the second truck apart, the last few inches of the ammo belt slid through the gun, and the devastating roar stopped. "Fuck," Sergeant Jenkins said as he dropped into the cab to bring back another box of ammunition.

The men inside the two LAVs got the motors fired up. The first one lurched forward as the driver slammed it into gear. The second followed closely behind. Both tanks moved forward leaving the injured men where they had fallen. Just as Jenkins came back up in the turret with a new case of ammo, the first LAV came roaring up. Jenkins had nowhere to run or hide, and the big tank slammed into the lighter Hummer, shoving it sideways away from the gate. Tossing him like a rag doll, Jenkins fell back into the truck as it spun ninety degrees. The Hummer was clear of the gate, allowing the LAVs to exit. Jenkins pulled himself back into the turret and expertly reloaded the gun in seconds. He slammed the breach door open, inserted the new belt, and then slammed it back down in record time. The AK-47 rounds were still pinging off the turret and cab as he pulled back the slide and loaded the first round. He did so just as the second LAV reached Sepulveda and started to make the turn. He managed only a few rounds at the back door as the tank headed north. "Motherfucking assholes," Jenkins yelled.

The sergeant spun the turret back at the second armored car and finished devastating the turret. The driver somehow managed to back the heavily damaged armored car out of his line of fire, so Jenkins spun around toward the freeway and engaged the AK-47 shooters.

Convinced they had done all they could do, Dayyan yelled for everyone to retreat out of the fight. He had lost a dozen or so men and at least one armored truck, but he had won a huge public relations battle. The two LAVs roared down Sepulveda, heading for the planned rendezvous in the hills above Sylmar. Dayyan, Naseem and, the mortar crew all beat a hasty exit north along the freeway.

When the smoke cleared, and the damage tallied, the death toll would be thirty-two civilians, four fireman, and three National Guard soldiers. An added forty plus had severe wounds. But the gruesome video played continuously on national and international TV would be far more devastating to the United States. The public relations victory was great for the terrorist army. But one piece of video captured by a brave WNN camera operator would become a calling for Americans. It showed a black flag with Arabic writing flying above a destroyed Brinks armored car. But as he filmed, an inspiring scene unfolded. A badly limping American soldier walked up the street from a destroyed Humvee. He was using an M4 rifle as a crutch as he approached the torn-up Brinks truck. As he neared the truck, a gun appeared from one of the small gun ports in the passenger door and multiple shots rang out.

Sergeant Jenkins slowed while looking at the rounds hitting the asphalt around him. He slowly raised the M4 and limped forward, firing round after round at the small gun port and glass. He kept moving closer. Rounds kept coming out the port, but the sergeant did not waver or stop. His fire was clearly preventing the terrorist inside from taking careful aim. The sergeant kept firing carefully aimed single rounds as he neared the truck. Jenkins dropped the rifle as the thirty-round magazine spent its last round. He limped closer to the truck while pulling an IMI Desert Eagle from his leg holster. The war-torn American Army sergeant pointed the huge pistol at the shredded window and squeezed the trigger. The .50-caliber round of the Desert Eagle blew the badly damaged glass away, forming a beer can-sized hole. Sergeant Jenkins calmly stepped up on the running board, pointed the gun in the hole, and fired six more rounds into the cab. "This is for America, you pricks."

Chapter 46

2140, Day 7, Oakland Police Headquarters, Oakland, California

C aptain Harold Martin was meeting with the top commanders in the boarded and barricaded police headquarters basement. The situation at his station was dire. At last count,
they had about 140 police, 130 firemen, 18 Army and Air Force
Reservists, 14 National Guard troops, and about 75 civilians and
politicians including the Mayor of Oakland Cecil Washington. They
were discussing choices while the gunshots rang out at random inter-
vals outside.

Oakland was a war zone. From day 2 after the EMP, its citizens
started looting, killing, rioting and converting into a caveman out-
look of "Only the strong survive." Like Los Angeles, a massive gang
army was forming and forming fast. By day 6, that army was close
to a thousand strong. They had taken every running car, truck, or
bus and had gone door to door, taking what little food people had.
The evil animals would kill the home owners mostly. Sometimes, if
lucky, young men had the choice of joining the Sharia Law Army or
perish from a gunshot wound to the head. Young women had few
choices. The savage soldiers took the girls and women they wanted,
kept them as slaves, or discarded them like dirty dishes.

The Oakland police and government had limited manpower
and few running cars or other vehicles. They fought hard as best they

could. But it felt like a hopeless effort to the few defenders of the city. The terror army would overwhelm any small groups of police or Homeland Security and mostly beat and kill them. Police patrols sent out sometimes never returned. Eventually, the entire police force retreated to the downtown police headquarters bordering the 880 Freeway. Remaining civilian workers and politicians joined the outnumbered police. Joining the police was a handful of military reservists and National Guard units. The occupiers hastily built a perimeter from barbwire and dead cars. The rest of the city fell to looters and gangs.

The barricaded men and women hoped the rioters and looters would not attack and eventually help would arrive. The National Guard, Homeland Security, and the NSA were trying desperately to carve a path to downtown. They had a convoy ready with help and supplies. They made several tries. Ambushes by gangs and hordes of civilians pleading for help thwarted all attempts. The mass exodus from Oakland, Berkley, and San Leandro clogged every road. A retired Army Ranger involved in the incident in Somalia known as "Black Hawk Down" said the likeness was astounding. Dead cars or intentionally created barriers blocked many intersections. Many small neighborhoods barricaded their streets trying to keep out the hordes of looters. As in Somalia, the convoy made detour after detour but never found an open path to downtown.

Captain Martin was in constant contact with Travis Air Force base. The base was the major military command in the Central California area. It had received reinforcements. Three battalions of Army regulars from the 10th Mountain Division 1st Brigade from Fort Drum New York had arrived by C5A transports on Day 5. Two transports carried extra equipment including AH-64 Apache helicopters. With the limited supply of Blackhawks, the military brought then along as surveillance aircraft.

Oakland was running out of time. The 880-freeway bordering the police headquarters was providing a cover for at least forty riflemen who were raining down semiautomatic and full automatic gunfire into the building. The terrorist army had overrun a nine-story condominium building to the south and had a dozen or more snipers using the top floor and roof. The high perch also allowed easy throwing of firebombs onto the police headquarters roof. Teams of men would go outside to fight fires and come under heavy fire from the snipers. Going onto the roof was becoming suicidal. The few military soldiers had the best firepower to fight back snipers and onslaughts of people, but ammunition was running dangerously low. Reports from two different rescue convoys were bad. And last reports from any rescue convoys were not good. There was little progress moving toward the besieged protectors of the peace.

Landing a helicopter full of reinforcements onto the roof would be impossible. Two tries both fell to a hail of rifle and machine gun-fire. Both choppers barely survived with severe damage and many injuries. A huge gang of attackers successfully captured the jail across the street from the courthouse. Remaining guards made a quick retreat across two pedestrian bridges connecting the jail to the court-house. Freed black prisoners usually joined the terror gang. The mostly Islamic leaders of the small army of thugs provided no such choices for the white or Hispanic prisoners.

Martin knew if help did not arrive in mass, they would all face capture and brutal execution. Using the radio, he pleaded with Air Force General Randal McCoy and the 10th Army Colonel Cliff Blankenship. Not wanting the blood of hundreds of brave men on their hands, the two military officers decided to act in direct violation of their rules of engagement. The two battle-hardened officers shook hands and agreed to take the heat together.

Four fully armed Apache gunships took off in formation. The pilots used maximum power and flew at low altitude in a direct line toward downtown Oakland. The pilots knew time was short. As they were heading southwest from Travis, the horde of rioters and gangs on the west side of the 880 freeway were starting a massive attack. Using the freeway center divider and all the dead cars and trucks as shields, they moved forward. At the same time, the gang army occupying the jail was attacking through both pedestrian bridges.

Travis told the defenders the attack helicopters were on the way. He asked if they had smoke or better yet infrared strobes with which to mark the police building. Luckily, some of the National Guard troops had infrared strobes. Sergeant Felix Hill and Oakland Swat Lieutenant James Allen volunteered to place the strobes on the roof. While the other defenders used their precious ammunition providing as much cover fire as possible, the two men took strobes to the corners of the building. They set them in places which would be visible to the oncoming choppers. Allen took two rounds to his Kevlar vest, stumbled, and fell, but Hill helped him into the roof access door.

The flight of four Apaches was named Condor with each ship being Condor-1, Condor-2, etc. Army Captain Jason Howard, call sign "Gator" for his Louisiana background, was the squad leader. His gunner was First Lieutenant Jaime Aguirre, call sign "Trashman," for the fact he once blasted the crap out of a dumpster on a training run. They led the other three ships in at high speed following the 980 freeway in a south west direction. The pilots and gunners had only ten minutes before takeoff to study the map. The police station, jail, and court building were just past the turn of the 980 onto the 880 freeway. They could see how the freeway ran along the right side of the target. The unique jail building would be first up. With such obvious markers, the crews were confident they could hit the target on the first pass.

With the few minutes of study, Captain Howard had to make quick choices. His training and experience was far different. But he knew there were a couple hundred cops and soldiers counting on his flight of attack helicopters. On the flight in, he continued to study the maps as best he could while Trashman flew the bird.

Using the radio, Howard gave Condor-3 specific orders. "Condor-3, lean left after the freeway turn and line up on 7th street. Hit targets of opportunity along the street. Turn left out of your gun-run."

"Roger one," Second Lieutenant Pete Lind replied.

"Condor-4, stay back and wait for targets of opportunity."

"Roger."

Howard had decided 7th Street was too thin for two gun runs along its length. The big 30 mm cannon shells would wreak havoc on the street and the buildings along both sides.

Captain Lilly Whitmer, call sign "Bambi," piloted Condor-2. Awarded the call sign by an instructor because of her "deer in the headlights," she was a fierce combat veteran of three deployments. Her gunner Captain Rex Sliger, call sign "T-Rex," for obvious reasons. Condor-2 followed close behind Condor-1.

"Bambi. Stay to my right as we make our run along the freeway. T-rex, target hostiles to our right. Try not to shoot off my tail rotor."

"Roger, Gator," came the reply from Bambi.

When they were getting close, Howard flipped the radio to the frequency used by the defenders at the police station.

Howard used the call sign for the police station. "Earthquake, Earthquake, this is Condor-1, do you copy?"

The reply came mixed with the sounds of gunfire and hectic disorder, "Condor, this is Earthquake. Copy you."

"Earthquake, we are thirty seconds out. Pull back from the sides of your building. We are coming in hot and danger close. Do you copy that?"

"Roger that, Condor. We are moving back and getting down. Give these fuckers hell for us. Over."

As the four birds made the turn over the freeway interchange, Howard could see strobes on the top of the police building. He could also see hundreds of heat signatures and bullet flashes along the freeway behind the center divider, or "K-rail."

Howard keyed the intercom, "Trash, target the line of tangos along the center divider. Looks like a hundred or more shoulder to shoulder. Bambi, T-Rex target right of the divider. I bet they run that way when the shooting starts."

Gator lined up above the freeway and tilted the deadly Apache attack helicopter into its predator position. Trashman threw one last arming switch then confirmed the synchronization between his gun and helmet sight. He pressed the button and the big thirty-millimeter chain gun came to life. The spray of cannon shells started immediately, and the tracers provided a nearly nonstop laser beam effect as the exploding rounds screamed to the ground in microseconds at 625 rounds a minute. The Gatling type rotary cannon was overkill for personnel. The primary use for the gunship was a tank and armored vehicle killer. But the main gun was the only gun choice on the vicious attack bird.

M789 explosive dual-purpose thirty-millimeter rounds do not have to be accurate. As they spattered along the K-rail, the explosive heads detonated obliterating anyone within twenty feet. Fragments from the rounds continued along the concrete barrier and pavement taking out added Tangos. The rounds shredded the cars near the center divider. Most cars burst into fire as hot particles hit fuel tanks.

The center divider was a death zone with no chance of survival. A few of the quickest thinking thugs jumped and ran for the right side of the freeway. But few made it. T-rex had their gun lined up with the center of the number four lane. Those making it to the right lanes met another stream of exploding cannon shells. Cars and trucks exploded as the two Apaches flew overhead.

Condor-3 was inflicting similar damage on the much thinner 7th Street. Second Lieutenant Pete Lind, call sign "Shaky" for his constant leg shakes when sitting flew Condor-3. His gunner was Colonel Jeffrey Ramos, call sign "Blue Sky." The colonel outranked the entire flight team, but he was in the front gunner seat. Lind's usual gunner was down with food poisoning. Captain Barnum Blackman, call sign "Whiteman," because he was not black but white, worked the controls in Condor-4. His gunner was Lieutenant Matt Lee, call sign "Bruce" for obvious reasons. Whiteman pulled back power as they approached and was riding about a quarter mile behind the other three Apaches.

As Condor-1 made their gun run, Howard felt more than heard a couple of pings off the canopy or metal around it. Through the night vision goggles, he could see nearly a continuous line of flashes emanating from the top floor of the building south of the police station. He knew it was the condominium building full of bad guys who had been raining agony down on the station from sniper positions.

Howard keyed the mic as they blasted past the building. "Condor-4, the tall residential building past the police building has multiple gunners blasting from windows on the top floor and the roof. Sweep them out."

"Roger that," replied Whiteman. He then lined the bird direct over the tall jail building and headed straight at the condominium tower. "Smoke the top floor and the roof, Bruce."

Gunner Matt "Bruce" Lee aimed his helmet display at the top left widow of the building. As he did, he saw the rapid flash of several automatic weapons, which were all he felt were pointing direct at him. He pressed the button on his stick, and his General Electric motor-driven gun spun to life. Rounds spewed from the gun splintering the window and large portions of the building.

Bruce moved his helmet sight across the line of ninth-floor windows and watched as the line of shells carved a slot along the wall. Tilting his head slightly, Bruce moved the helmet site across the edge of the roofline in the opposite direction cleaning off snipers, who had hunkered down behind the wall. When he released the trigger after finishing the one back and forth sweep, all gun flashes had stopped. Whiteman banked slightly left and followed Condor 3 around in a counterclockwise turn to await further orders from Howard.

Chapter 47

2230, Day 7, Broadway Towers, Oakland, California

Najid Saif al Din, perched behind the ninth-floor window of a private residence overlooking the Oakland Police Station across the street. His followers had taken the condominium building that morning. They had entered the side opposite the police station and went door to door and floor to floor taking what they wanted and killing or brutalizing the remaining occupants. Before the police knew what had occurred, his snipers had taken up positions on all sides of the multistory building. His men shot anyone foolish enough to move in the streets surrounding the police station. He had no concerns about armored trucks. Employing "value engineering," the Oakland City Council decided to save the nearly five thousand dollars per vehicle for EMP proof electronics. That money, one far left liberal Council member argued could be spent on social programs. He did not even want to spend the money on the large costly armored trucks anyway. If there were other costly "toys," as the self-proclaimed progressive called them, which were not necessary, he voted against them. So none of the Oakland police assault trucks had survived the EMP. Now the trapped Oakland Police had few "toys" in their possession, which could save them from annihilation.

Najid, like an unknown number of brothers had also been an ISIS plant. However, unlike many ISIS believers who traveled to

Syria or other Mideastern countries, that was impossible for Najid. His police record was long, and it was certain he was on a watch list. So his training was all done locally. Six months ago, a radical Muslim cleric from Sacramento contacted Najid. After intensive scrutiny to find out his true faith and loyalty, Najid joined an organization he knew little about other than they were true believers of God. He carefully attended clandestine meetings and gatherings and received training in many fields. Some subjects made perfect sense such as weapons and strategy. Other classes covered odd subjects such as electronics. Najid did not know the plans, but he remained loyal and obedient waiting for the day he would be part of the brothers who would wipe the infidels from the planet.

Najid, like others, had received a coded message the day before the event. He did as directed, preparing for what he knew not. But his preparation had advantages such as having several older trucks that survived the EMP. Najid received various weapons, which he kept hidden within the subfloor of his small office of his electronics store near City Hall in downtown Oakland.

The day Najid got the call to prepare, he did so gladly. He was eager to start the campaign against America. His handler phoned him on a satellite phone delivered that morning by courier. The man on the phone provided him with contacts and a meeting location. Eight more followers of radical Islam met him the afternoon before the blast. Like Najid, they had specific tasks and training. All the brothers had older cars or trucks and separate lists of believers to contact. The night of the EMP, the group of men drove to San Leandro and hit all three of the gun stores in the city. Those raids netted the group hundreds of rifles and pistols and thousands of rounds of ammunition. The often stranded or walking police could do nothing to stop them.

Najid and his top lieutenants contacted several gangs in the East Bay and, without much convincing, added them to their force. When the gangs saw the weapons won by Najid and his army, it was easy to draw them into the fold. With added manpower, Najid ordered the men to attack major stores including a Costco, gaining more and more supplies. As they grew in size, the attacks became easier. Soon, they were hitting any police or Homeland Security units at will. Some of the prizes for those attacks included armored trucks and more weapons and tactical gear. His men had killed dozens and dozens of police and federal soldiers.

Najid's army had been attacking the Oakland Police for several days now. His army had been growing and absorbing more and more willing brothers of Islam. Each time his men attacked, others would join his army. There were thousands of young brothers in Oakland that hated the police and needed little excuse to riot, loot and kill. Najid took advantage of their passion and recruited them by the hundreds. Most street thugs and drug addicts were worthless as fighters, but a few had some surprising skills. Najid even found some men with military experience. The ex-military Najid placed in leadership roles over the various squads and groups he was starting to form. He was careful to keep his various squads from being too large in one place at one time. Doing so would provide a target for the American military. His men stayed mobile and separated but in constant contact using various radios and codes.

Today was the day Najid hoped would be a huge victory for his army. His army had the police surrounded at their own headquarters. Now he now called all his followers to join him here so they could attack and destroy every last one of them. It would be a huge victory, further strengthening his army and allow him the needed manpower for more attacks in Berkley and maybe Livermore where many rich infidels lived.

Najid ordered his two most trusted lieutenants to form up several hundred of the followers across the freeway and make a daring attack using the dead cars and barriers for cover. His plan was to draw the police to the west side of the large building. Then Najid would order attacks from other directions.

Two more of Najid's lieutenants and about twenty of his best soldiers had attacked the jail a few hours ago. The men took along local gangs, thugs, and anyone who hated the police. In total, about eighty men attacked the north side. After using a small car bomb to clear an entrance, they quickly overran the remaining guards who fled over the pedestrian bridges into the court building and police station. Those soldiers went cell to cell and gave some the opportunity to join. Hispanics, whites, and non-clean races were either shot in their cells outright or forced at gunpoint into large holding rooms near the two bridges. Those unlucky souls were now human shields as his men fought their way over the bridges. So his plan was working at first.

Najid looked out of his window and saw something coming. Helicopters. He looked closer and could tell these were not the larger police helicopters such as the two they had nearly shot down earlier in the day. These helicopters were the sleek and small attack helicopters used by the American Army. Would the army use attack helicopters on civilians? Najid was pondering the question when the vicious gun on the left helicopter started raining fire onto the freeway below.

The stream of gunfire emanating from the helicopter was devastating. He could follow the tracer fire from the large caliber machine gun and see it ripping his brothers to shreds.

Najid keyed the radio, "Everyone, fire on those helicopters. They are killing our brothers."

Najid heard the sounds of dozens of weapons go to full automatic. The AK-47s and his other machine guns all poured fire at the approaching helicopters. Now he saw another helicopter following the first one on the left and a third coming down 7th Street spewing death on that side of the building.

Najid keyed the mic again. "Brother Hassan, you must push the attack over the bridges. We are under fire by American dog helicopters and you must get into the building where they dare not fire at you."

Najid heard a mumbled reply from Hassan. But he did not have time to worry about the reply. He picked up a different radio and keyed its mic, "Fariq. It's time to inflict the fire of God on the infidels."

"I hear you, my brother. I will do so," came the reply from Fariq.

Fariq was sitting in the cab of a liquid propane truck on Webster Street two blocks from the police station. He fired up the truck. Leaving it running, he went to the back and checked on the explosive charges Najid had rigged to the truck earlier that day. Duct tape was holding four standard fragmentation grenades securely around the liquid propane pipe where it exited the tank at the bottom rear. A rope laced through the pins of all four grenades. The end of the rope was tied to a large round barbell weight. The weight was currently securely taped to the truck bumper. Fariq untaped the weight and carried it, unrolling the rope as he went back to the front of the truck. He climbed back into the cab and brought the weight with him.

The plan was simple. Fariq would drive the truck as quickly as possible up 7th Street, heading toward the police station. When close, he would drop the weight from the side window of the truck. Najid told him it should land and eventually pull on the rope, releasing the pins on the grenades. Although the grenades would never be able to penetrate the thick steel tank, Najid was confident they would destroy the pipe and valve. This would allow the volatile liquid propane out where it should explode, causing the entire tank to blow. The five thousand gallons of liquid propane would create an explosion that would be massive in size and power. It should easily flatten the large tall portion of the police building on 7th Street, causing it to collapse on itself.

Najid looked out the window and saw the fourth helicopter now headed straight at them. He knew what was going to happen. He turned and ran out of the living room of the high-end condominium. But Najid was not fast enough to escape the fury of the American monster. As the Apache helicopter's 30 mm chain gun made the first sweep along the windows, he had just reached the door. The explosive shells screamed into the room at six hundred rounds a minute tearing apart everything.

The noise and concussion of the rounds expelled Najid through the entry door into the hallway. Shrapnel rained all around him coming through the thin walls in all directions. He rolled over and tried sitting up, but something kept him down. Najid looked down to his waist and could see his abdomen was torn open, and most of his internal organs had spilled onto the hall carpet. There was not much blood, but he felt faint, dizzy, and light-headed. Pulling his intestines and other organs up off the floor he slid to the opposite wall where he leaned. Najid knew he was dying. He could only wonder if his brothers would be successful.

Chapter 48

2235, Day 7, Over Oakland Police Headquarters, Oakland, California

Howard banked the chopper right and circled over the freeway. Looking down, he could see the damage, but he was mainly looking for other threats. He saw plenty. On the back side of the condominium tower was about a dozen trucks of various sizes with men running around them. Some of the men were climbing into the trucks. Two of the trucks had bed-mounted machine guns, and they both started firing at his bird. He jerked the stick to the right forcing the Apache into a tight high G-force turn clockwise back out over the freeway again. His wingman Bambi was right with him following him around. "Bambi, did you see the truck park down between the buildings?"

"Roger that, boss," Captain Whitmer replied. "We're with you."

Howard made the 360-degree turn and lined up on the street behind the condominium building. He tilted the nose of the Apache down to an attack angle, increased throttle, and headed toward the tangos. "You ready, Trash?"

"Locked and loaded, boss."

Howard replied. "Let's wipe out those machine guns and trucks. If any of these terrorist assholes plan escaping this mess, they are doing so on foot."

Howard led the two bird Apache flight back in lining up with the side street and the parked trucks. He kept the nose down to allow Aguirre easily to spot targets. And as soon as the first truck lined up with Aguirre's helmet-mounted targeting reticle, he squeezed the trigger. The heavy cannon rounds streamed out of the gun into the mess of trucks and men, ripping apart both. Howard flew up the street, and Aguirre kept moving the sight slightly to take out truck after truck. He was just about to release the trigger when a large truck roared into the intersection moving at a right angle toward the police station. He kept the trigger down a second longer and moved his sight over the truck. As he did so, he saw the big red letters that said "Suburban Propane."

"Shit, *pull up, pull up!*" Aguirre screamed into the mic.

Howard pulled the stick as far back as he could. He had also seen the big letters on the truck. He tilted the helo so the bottom was facing the unavoidable explosion. He knew the armor-piercing rounds fired by the General Electric gun would easily cut through the mild steel propane tank. The blast wave slammed into the bottom of the helo, flinging it violently backward. The rapid direction changes of the helo slammed both men into their seats with a massive force. The chopper motor started to stall. Howard assumed loss of air was the cause, so he backed off the throttle hoping this would lower the air intake need for the turbine motor. The boldest efforts by Howard would not save the Apache from the unavoidable and certain crash. It slid backward, losing valuable lift. The massive explosion blast wave was propelling the chopper toward the freeway. But it would not make it that far. It plummeted down into a three-story Salvation Army building. The Apache hit the building and exploded in a fireball. But compared with the propane truck, the fireball was hardly notable.

Whitmer was further back. She also heard the call from Aguirre over her headset. She yanked the stick with all her strength and turned the attack helicopter hard right. She applied full power and tilted the bird for maximum forward thrust. The bird screamed down 6th Street, parallel to the freeway. Out of the corner of her eye, she saw Howard's Apache slam into the building on the corner. Bambi dropped the helo below the building, lessening the power of the blast wave. When she made it to the end of the block, the turbine was overrevving, lights and alarms were sounding, but she kept the throttle pegged. Condor-1 just managed to race away from the rapidly growing ball of fire and debris.

The blast from the propane truck was massive. The blast wave crumbled and leveled every building within a block of the epicenter. The Salvation Army had been taking in homeless and stranded people since the EMP. Over three hundred refugees plus volunteer workers were in the building Condor-1 had crashed into. The damage by the chopper, instantly followed by the massive explosion of the truck ripped the building apart, collapsing it into a pile. Not a single person in the building would survive. The seven-story condominium building collapsed with the main part of the structure falling north across the street onto the Police Building. Anyone still in the high-end residential building died as well as twenty-five defenders in the police building.

The death toll would climb into the thousands. Flames engulfed everything for blocks in all directions except west. The freeway provided a great barrier protecting those neighborhoods. The police station defenders evacuated what remained of the building, dragging the wounded and dying as best they could.

The devastating blast would have occurred anyway had the suicide truck attack succeeded. But only a few of Najid's men knew of the planned suicide bomb. Those few were dead. So the army would take the blame for the horrendous blast and killing thousands of civilians. The national and international news outlets would discuss this story for weeks. Both Air Force General Randal McCoy and 10th Army Colonel Cliff Blankenship were arrested. Politicians called for a quick court-martial and execution of the two men.

Chapter 49

0900, Day 9, Command Center, Agua Dulce, California

L ife in Agua Dulce, as best possible under the circumstances, was settling down and entering into a rhythm. For the last few days, the teams had started to work into the original planned schedules and assignments. The security team decided to divide Checkpoint Alpha into two locations. One at the planned location where Agua Dulce Canyon Road crossed under the 14 freeway. And a second checkpoint at the house where the fierce one-way battle with the gang had taken place. Security teams and volunteers from town cleaned up the McDonald house. They buried the victims of the vicious gang in individual graves in a field near the house. They buried the gang members in a common hole using the McDonald tractor. The house became a local command location for both Checkpoint Alpha roadblocks.

Checkpoint Delta was set up and running at the corner of Davenport and Sierra Highway as planned. That team used the motion picture movie ranch as a local command for that checkpoint. The RV lot next door made for convenient housing of refugee families with small children or those too weak to continue.

The number of refugees started to increase exponentially. The situation in the Los Angeles basin and the San Fernando Valley had degraded over the last few days. People who originally just hunkered down and were living off limited food supplies now realized help was not coming. People could move to an overcrowded, understaffed, refugee center in Los Angeles or get out of Los Angeles. Many choosing to leave the city were streaming into Agua Dulce by the hundreds.

Many people were riding bicycles. Some lucky people were driving old cars or trucks of some kind. Those driving mostly reported coming over Little Tujunga Canyon Road. It was a winding two-lane road connecting San Fernando with the Santa Clarita Valley. The Newhall pass was still a clogged mess of dead cars in both directions. Reports were coming in of ambushes of people, their supplies, and any running cars along the clogged freeway. On the contrary, some drivers said there were local militia along Little Tujunga Canyon who were aiding evacuees to get over the mountains safely. Many of the young and fit were hiking with large backpacks, sometimes pulling carts or wagons. Most refugees were carrying little in the way of supplies including food and or water. All those who made it were glad to discover Agua Dulce was the first sign of an organized relief effort.

The checkpoints mostly performed triage. The checkpoint team would evaluate the condition of the refugees assessing immediate medical issues. The checkpoint teams encouraged those in decent shape to continue to the large refugee camps. People unable to continue waited for the military trucks or one of two running buses to ferry them into town. Once refugees arrived in town, teams of townspeople gathered information and queried of skills, which could be helpful. Those with needed skills were encouraged to volunteer. The medical group added two more doctors and a dentist. The security teams added two dozen men to their ranks. Two were active duty, and eight had been out a short time and were by martial law, reactivated. Retired career soldiers and many who left the military years before eagerly signed up for the security teams.

Someone suggested using the Agua Dulce elementary school for the HQ and other organizational teams. It was a great idea, so the security and HQ teams moved. This allowed the HQ team to work closely with the other teams. The medical team even created a small emergency room at the school.

The good people of society shined in the troubling time. The outpouring of volunteers from the Agua Dulce community and the refugees from Los Angeles was promising. Nearly everyone was eager to help somehow. Dozens of the local women handled the interviewing of refugees and creation of their profiles. An important question asked of refugees was names and locations of family or friends outside the badly affected parts of the country who could take them in. Radio links set up by the Agua Dulce Ham Radio Club facilitated the transfer of data back east where other volunteers would contact family and friends. Once contact was made with family or friends in secure and safe parts of the country, the refugees names and destinations went onto evacuation lists. Most people rode out on returning cargo planes. It was a tedious task sorting out the flights and cities, but some of the volunteers excelled at matching up names and places.

The small airport was a hub of activity. Four or five C-130 military cargo planes had been landing daily for the last three days, bringing badly needed food and gear such as cots, blankets, tents, and other crucial items of survival. A Mexican Army cargo plane landed on Day 8. The plane left Mexico City stuffed full of extremely desirable fresh food. Added to the cargo was about two thousand enchiladas the locals in Mexico City had cooked up and sent in boxes of ice. The enchiladas were a huge hit. The plane returned to Mexico with twenty-five Mexican citizens who had evacuated Los Angeles.

One exciting event was the birth of a child on Day 7. The woman, her husband and three other young children had hitched a ride from Panorama City with an elderly couple in a 1975 Cadillac Coupe Deville. Although a tight fit in the old Cadillac, the group made it to Checkpoint Alpha. The security team stood back in awe watching so many people climb out. When a large German Shepard and a fifteen-pound calico cat got out of the Caddy, the team fell into hysterical laughter. The lady was already in labor, so they rushed her to the medical building in town, where she gave birth two hours later. The proud and thankful father and mother decided to name the baby girl "Dulce Deville." When asked the last name, the father responded, "Vasquez, just like those rocks you have here." Baby girl Dulce Deville Vasquez became the first child of Agua Dulce since the EMP. The simple sign of humanity enlightened the spirits of the town and its ever-increasing number of residents.

It amazed Lee and Jake, only eight days had passed since the EMP event. Considering the escape from Vegas, the journey to Fort Irwin, the flight from Irwin in the Blackhawks and the major battle with the gang members, it seemed like months had gone by. The local citizens of Agua Dulce were responding in astonishing ways. Lee and Jake hoped the rest of the country was doing as well. Lee was reading a printed copy of a command report sent to the group from Colonel Braxton. A secured computer system recently received from Fort Irwin was now working and receiving coded messages. The new computer included an attached printer, allowing paper printouts of messages and reports.

The Fort Irwin command had moved nearly all its people from the base to other locations within its assigned area of operations. After spending five days rescuing thousands of stranded motorists on Interstate 15 and other roads in the area, the staff packed up and moved out. The general and most of his staff, including Colonel Braxton, were running the AOR command from Edwards Air Force Base. That base was a beehive of activity with as many as forty large cargo or transport aircraft arriving and leaving daily now. Edwards and the large air freight logistics base at the former George Air Force near Adelanto were the two primary air relief bases working in Southern California. Spreading the large quantity of supplies by truck became the most immediate problem.

A high school in Victorville became a secondary supply depot at first. But a local police captain told the Irwin team about a unique building in Victorville. It was a new distribution center with a massive solar panel array. Products such as rubber goods and air conditioners filled most of the massive building. After finding an owner of the largest company that occupied the warehouse and with his blessing, the Irwin team moved the supply depot there. Several sections of the building were empty. The team decided to use the massive industrial building for the stockpiling of supplies. Having power from the solar panels was a huge benefit to the new location.

From the new location, a team of army regulars, reactivated soldiers, and volunteers set up a checkpoint in the Cajon Pass. They used a fleet of natural gas buses to shuttle refugees from the checkpoint to four locations in Victorville. If screening produced names and places for relatives in safe parts of the country, refugees moved to the logistics airport in Adelanto. People remained at the base until room was available on one of the returning transport aircraft. Homeland Security was trying to set up a refugee, supply, and evacuation center at Ontario International Airport. But that effort had seen limited success. It was proving difficult keeping the airport secure, allowing supply aircraft to land and take off. They were in desperate need for added troops.

General Stollard contacted central command and sought permission to go beyond the Cajon Pass and clear a path to Ontario Airport. Upper command denied the request several times. Finally, after passing on statements from refugees who had been assaulted and or robbed coming over the pass, command consented to allow Fort Irwin to extend its AOR to Glen Helen Park. The park was south of the Cajon Pass and was a large multipurpose venue suitable for a relief camp.

So on the evening of Day 7, two companies of 1st Squadron, 11th Armored Infantry rolled at high speed through the Cajon Pass. The convoy consisting of various vehicles including Humvees, M-RAPs, and trucks and buses headed south pushing a path to Glen Helen Park. Another company of Marines from the Twenty-Nine Palms Command used their eight-wheeled light armored tanks, known as LAVs, providing flanking cover. Several short-lived gunfights occurred. The convoys would reach a roadblock, starting a firefight. But when the gangs and thugs determined who they were attacking, the fight ended quickly with the ambushers running as fast as possible into fields or housing tracks. Marine Recon units found two large gang camps along the freeway. More marines moved in surrounding and attacking the gangs who were easily and swiftly defeated. The marines found tons of loot and personal belongings in both camps and trails leading to large piles of corpses. Police and military officers interrogated captured gang members. Soldiers had little remorse for the vultures who were exploiting the already devastated civilians. Execution by firing squads of volunteer soldiers ended the short reign of terror by the vicious gangs.

Homeland Security forces at the Ontario Airport received orders to run north and rendezvous with the military teams at Glen Helen. So seventy-five HS agents plus over forty National Guard Reservists headed north and immediately faced the clog of dead cars on Interstate 15. The convoy left the freeway and used surface streets in an attempt to move ahead. Constant attacks by random sniper fire or massive groups of locals pleading for help, food, and water slowed progress to a snail's pace. The force made it six miles, but numerous casualties, including two fatalities, forced them to turn back.

Glen Helen made for a great camp, but it would now be a constant fight to keep a corridor open over the Cajon Pass to Victorville and George Air Force Base. The Marine units using their LAVs would fight daily to keep the road open and to escort relief convoys back and forth.

Closer to the Agua Dulce was the Palmdale Regional Airport. One company from the Fort Irwin Regimental Support Squadron had flown into the airport on day five and worked round the clock clearing runways and securing the airfield. But they, like most groups of authority, had to deal with hundreds or thousands of civilians. Most people were begging for food. Others were willing to kill for it. Similar to Agua Dulce, the soldiers in Palmdale used local help and were starting to get control of the airport.

Two squads of soldiers were deployed by Black Hawks to Green Valley. This was a small community northeast of Santa Clarita. Expectations were that refugees would use San Fransisquito Canyon Road or Bouquet Canyon Roads in a desperate attempt to exit Los Angeles or Santa Clarita. Green Valley was a small, secluded community similar to Agua Dulce. The teams set up to create a largely volunteer effort just as Agua Dulce had done. The plan was working fine, but the number of refugees fleeing in that direction was lower than expected.

Remaining troops of the Regimental Support Squadron, including 1st Squadron and 2nd Squadron, were sent to Castaic Lake north of Santa Clarita. The small town of Castaic straddled Interstate 5 at the south end of the Grapevine Pass. Expectations by the MACRO Event planners were that Castaic would see a massive number of people leaving Los Angeles by heading north. Heavy lift choppers set large water purification units from Nevada in the parking lot near the boat ramps. The American Red Cross sent a large contingent to the Castaic camp. Unfortunately, Castaic Lake lacked an airport, so all supplies would have to come by helicopter. General Stollard was concerned the lack of an airport would doom Castaic from providing the help necessary.

When the EMP had detonated days earlier, Fort Irwin did not have many troops on base for desert warfare training. But there were two companies from the 4th Infantry Division from Colorado. The expectation was the visiting troops would return to their home base as soon as possible. General Stollard kept at Central Command, asking to leave them under his command. This wish was finally granted on Day 6. On the evening of Day 7, a frantic plea for help came from a group of sheriff deputies and volunteers in Santa Clarita. The makeshift group had, from the first day after the event, taken to guarding the massive amount of supplies at the Costco store on Via Princessa near the 14 freeway. Four sheriffs were on a disturbance call at the gym next to Costco the night of the event. With their cruisers dead, they remained and took to guarding the large wholesale outlet. Four more sheriffs plus three Los Angeles police officers arrived to help over the next two days. They realized the massive stockpile of food at the Costco would become a huge target for looters. County sheriff commanders decided to keep them at the store and turn it into a makeshift food distribution operation. The store held one of the largest stockpiles of food in the Santa Clarita Valley. Dozens of volunteers from the neighborhood showed up, offering to aid defending the store. Usually, the volunteers came better armed than the sheriffs. The food was evenly and slowly rationed to locals.

On day 6, Agua Dulce security forces sent a team south on Sierra Highway who met the makeshift militia. They provided the Costco defenders with a military radio, allowing them to remain in contact with the Agua Dulce group and the Fort Irwin command.

The security detail returned to Agua Dulce with some welcome food supplies.

The next evening the frantic call came in. Hundreds of determined rioters were trying to take down security at the Costco. The group defending Costco barricaded the doors and took up positions on the roof. The ever-growing crowd threw rocks, shot at them, and repeatedly attacked the doors. The defenders saw a group what they described as organized instigators who appeared of Mideastern descent wearing military combat clothing and tactical gear. The small heavily armed group had running military Humvees. From positions on the warehouse roof, defenders could see a black ISIS flag above one of the trucks.

Two Black Hawks quickly took off from Palmdale airport with soldiers from the 4th Infantry unit. The two big choppers carried twelve soldiers each plus a door mounted M240-H machine gun. The choppers flew at top speed of 160 mph, making it to the Costco in twelve minutes. They came in low without warning just above the ground. The Black Hawks landing gear barely cleared the parking lot light posts as the rotor blasts sent the crowd running. As the first chopper passed over the front of the store, gunshots rang out and bullets banged into the left side door area. One soldier received a minor wound to his left thigh from a ricochet.

The pilot, Captain Jerome Silvers, call sign "Quick," slammed the stick back and left and applied full power. The big bird did a nearly vertical bank around to the left. Silvers screamed into the headset, telling the gunner there were hostile Humvees sitting on the street near the Jack-in-the-Box. Several men were out of the Hummers firing what looked like AK-47s rifles. The flashes from the rifles gave them away instantly. Silvers banked the Black Hawk back to the right, angled down thirty degrees, and flew along the opposite side of the road. The gunner leveled the M240 and lit up the two Hummers. Tracers highlighted the path of the .762 shells that poured out of the gun at five hundred rounds a minute. Even without a direct hit, the massive amount of lead banging off the metal of the hummers created a No Man's Land. Within seconds, all six tangos were dead and both Hummers destroyed.

With such a powerful show of force, the remaining civilians took off running in all directions. The siege of the Costco warehouse was over. The two Black Hawks set down in the Costco parking lot and all, but the wounded soldier jumped out. The defenders inside cleared the door and welcomed in the real soldiers. Two 4th ID medics stabilized two wounded civilians and one sheriff deputy and the other soldiers loaded the wounded men into the helos. It amazed the 4th Infantry soldiers to see how much food was still in the warehouse. The rationing was working well. Leaving the newly arrived reinforcements behind, the two Black Hawks returned to Palmdale at a much slower pace. The new call sign for the Costco warehouse would be "Alamo."

The bigger picture for Southern California was a mix of good and bad. Smaller cities such as Santa Barbara, San Louis Obispo, and Santa Maria were coping well. Locals were standing strong and helping one another. The larger cities, however, were chaos. Most sections of Los Angeles and Orange County had little control or organized relief. Trapped civilians struggled to defend what little food or water they had. Thousands of armed people were willing to kill for what they needed. Neighbors killed neighbors. Housing tracks banded together for defense or to go on the offense against other housing tracks. Few stores survived looting and, often, torching. Luckily day 6 had brought heavy and constant rain showers, which helped put out fires which had been burning for days. Entire portions of Los Angeles had burned, including most of San Fernando and Sylmar. The only reason the fires staring in the valley did not turn into a massive brushfire was that a massive fire had burned the foothills nine months earlier.

Authorities for the city led by Homeland Security could not determine who was leading the large heavily armed groups. Brutal attacks were coming more often by ever increasing numbers of terrorist soldiers. Attacks took place against two more National Guard armories, stripping them of badly needed equipment and weapons. A dozen American soldiers died at the armory in Sylmar and fifteen others in Van Nuys. By the time Homeland Security responded, the attackers would disappear into the massive residential parts of Los

Angeles and the San Fernando Valley. The organized army of thugs was smart in the way they moved around, staying in smaller more scattered groups. Drones would, on occasion, spot one or two vehicles, but never a large convoy. Heavy smoke from the hundreds of fires and now dense cloud cover provided the terror army perfect cover from aerial surveillance. The attacks were well coordinated and from all directions. Homeland Security and other forces had barely scratched the groups who moved about as they pleased.

Unlike the Costco in Santa Clarita, most large stores lacked any security forces and fell under the siege of the organized groups. The terror army attacked a Costco in North Hollywood one morning and a large food distribution warehouse in San Fernando later that same day. The group was gaining military vehicles, trucks, and dozens of armored cars. Why they had so many running armored cars was baffling to Homeland Security. They were newer units, so why did they survive the EMP? Reports came in that smaller gangs or groups were joining one larger group in the San Fernando Valley. Many witnesses reporting seeing black ISIS flags flying on many of the group's trucks and armored cars.

The ports of Long Beach and San Pedro were a disaster. When the EMPs hit, most workers and security left and went home on foot. By day 3, hundreds of civilians broke down the fences and started breaking open the recently unloaded sea containers. They scattered unwanted debris all over the isles and spaces, making vehicle travel impossible. On day 5, navy ships arrived in both ports and sailors and US Marines landed and tried to secure the ports. Dozens of cargo ships were en route from Hawaii and other Pacific countries, including China. It was urgent to secure and open the ports to receive relief supplies.

The Army Corp of Engineers arrived, with the task of getting cranes and other heavy lifting equipment running in some manner. On the morning of day 7, a Los Angeles attack submarine, the USS *Jacksonville*, docked in Long Beach. Engineers ran heavy electrical cables from the ship to the dock, planning on using its nuclear power as a generator for dock use. The hundred-plus sailors went to work as security or any other job needed. The first large ship arrived that day from Pearl Harbor with badly needed food and supplies. Lacking heavy equipment, the only choice was to unload it by hand. The navy called on hundreds of healthy volunteers from the local community. Reward for hard work was food and other needs.

San Diego was in slightly better shape than Los Angeles. The ports avoided looting because of the presence of the navy and Marines who quickly secured the cargo terminals. Massive generators from the navy yards provided zones of power around the ports. Some of the newest navy equipment was EMP proof. The port was ready and waiting for the first two cargo ships arriving from Hawaii on the morning of day 7. The navy moved one of the moored aircraft carriers from its location in the navy yard to the cargo terminal. Like the submarine in Long Beach, the carrier would become a massive nuclear generator.

San Francisco and Oakland were in pandemonium. The city locals on average stored only a few days of food. Few of the uber liberals fell into the prepper category. The few that did were subject to attack by the starving masses. Stores and distribution centers fell under attack immediately by anyone and everyone. By day 5, over one million people became part of an exodus south. The city became a ghost town with only hordes of homeless remaining. Once the rightful owners evacuated, what remained became open game to vandals, thugs, and criminals. Fires spread out of control. Several tall skyscrapers burned and finally collapsed. Hundreds of thousands perished.

Oakland was the worst place in the country. The major event at the police station the night before shocked the government and public around the country. Although exaggerated, the death toll infuriated President Harrold. She used the event as an excuse to sign several emergency executive orders suiting more her liberal agenda. She also had very close ties with the Department of Homeland Security and would use the events to empower the agency further. She was only a few steps away from banning all guns. This would be a dream come true to the far-left antigun advocate. Only with continued persuading by Republican and the military did she forgo a complete gun ban. She made it clear, however, that if the situation continued degrading, she would issue an executive order banning every firearm nationally.

So not getting her way with guns, President Harrold took out her frustrations on the military. She wrote new orders and rules of engagement for distribution nationwide. All the commands received copies and spread them through the ranks.

Lee had just arrived at the command center. He looked at a printed summary sent by Colonel Braxton.

> Summary: Emergency Executive Orders
> Effective Immediately
>
> 1. Effective immediately, all military and police are banned from using against United States citizen/s or within the territories of the United States, any aircraft originally designed exclusively for offensive operations. This includes helicopters such as the army Apache type aircraft such as the AC-130 Gunship or any other offensive attack aircraft or fighter aircraft.
>   a. No other aircraft of any type shall be equipped with automatic weapons such as door mounted machine guns or pod mounted weapons. Nor shall any weapon capable of discharging more than 1 round each trigger pull by the operator (i.e. machine guns) be fired from aircraft against civilians.
>   b. No explosive type weapons shall be fired from any aircraft such as rockets, grenades, missiles, etc.
> 2. Effective immediately, all military and police units are forbidden from using any explosive offensive weapon against any United States citizen/s or within the territories of

the United States. This shall include weapons such as hand-thrown grenades (except for smoke grenades), gun-launched grenades, standalone grenade launching units, rocket launchers, mortars of any type, and any type of artillery standoff weapon. Also banned is the use of large explosive weapons such as Claymore Mines or ambush-type weapons or any weapon composed from C4 or other high-grade military explosive.

3. Effective immediately, all military and police units are forbidden from using any armored vehicle equipped with heavy weapons, including machine guns or cannons against any United States citizen or within the territories of the United States. This includes armored personnel carriers, trucks, tanks, etc.

   a. No vehicles used by military or police shall be equipped with mounted machine guns.

   b. No tanks or heavy armor equipped with offensive weapons such as cannons, rocket launchers, machine guns, flamethrowers, etc. shall be operated with the offensive weapons in place.

4. Effective immediately, the possession or use of military weapons or ammunition by private civilians is banned. A military weapon is considered any of the following:

   a. Any weapon that fires more than one round each trigger pull

   b. Assault rifles or any rifles with removable magazines

   c. Rifles capable of holding more than 5 rounds of ammunition

    d. Any rifle that uses any standard military or NATO ammunition.

    e. Any side arm that uses a removable magazine

    f. Any side arm that contains more than 6 rounds of ammunition

    g. Any side arm that fires ammunition larger than 25 caliber

    h. Any shotgun that fires rounds larger than 20 gauge

    i. Any shotgun that holds more than 5 rounds of ammunition

    j. Any shotgun that has a pistol grip

    k. Any weapon that was previously illegal or is unregistered

    l. Any weapon constructed by the owner or someone other than a mass-producing manufacture and is unregistered, or any personally constructed weapon which falls into any of the categories above.

5. Effective immediately, all civilians shall turn in to an appropriate government authority all weapons and ammunition as listed above. Failure to do so within seventy-two hours of local notice of this order shall constitute a federal felony, and so persons shall be subject to detention and confinement.

6. Government authorities, local, state, or federal, are authorized without written warrant to enter and search any building, residence, vehicle, etc., for weapons and/or ammunition if there is reasonable belief persons associated with the location or vehicle may have banned weapons or ammunition.

    a. All seized weapons and ammunition shall be turned over to the Department of Homeland Security for storage or disposal or other use as deemed necessary by the DHS.

b. Other agencies may be instructed by the Department of Homeland Security to act as agents to carry out this order. However, those agencies shall upon seizure of weapons or ammunition, immediately make all attempts to turn over seized weapons and ammunition to the Department of Homeland Security

7. Effective immediately, the President of the United States shall, in the best interest of the safety and security of the United States and its citizens, be allowed to negotiate temporary or long-term security assistance from sources outside of the United States, including foreign sources.

Lee stared in amazement at the list of presidential orders. He was sitting with Jake, Lawrence, and Liz at the command center main conference table sipping coffee. Obviously, the hand tying of the military was a direct result of the Oakland mess and perhaps events such as the local battle with the gang members. But orders had gone way beyond overstepping of the government. No automatic weapons, no explosives.

Lee spoke up after reading the entire order. "Okay, this sucks. The bad guys are not going to follow these rules. We know there is at least one large gang army running rabid in Los Angeles using both automatic weapons and explosives and armored trucks. Now it finally happens, the government is going to collect our weapons and screw the Second Amendment."

Jake answered, "I will tell you one thing for sure. If anyone thinks I will be part of a door-to-door search for weapons from honest Americans, they can go to hell. We need help from a well-armed militia now more than ever. Fuck Harrold. She just wants to disarm America while she has the excuse."

Lawrence spoke up. "Well, at least those of us born-again soldiers can keep our weapons."

Lee replied. "We do not have enough actual soldiers to put up a real fight against a large force. We need the civilians who have volunteered to help."

Jake spoke up. "That is the key, Lawrence. These orders do not cancel the original MACRO event orders. General Stollard could swear in more civilians and they could keep their weapons. And for the rest of the people, need I remind you what Charlton Heston once said, 'from my cold dead fingers.'"

Jake turned and went straight toward makeshift radio room. As he got close, he spun around and said, "We need to get all our security people over here. They are all joining the army."

Chapter 50

1345, Day 9, Granada Hills, California

The San Fernando Valley was becoming a difficult place for Dayyan to keep his forces. More and more, his units or companies came under attack from DHS, police forces, or even gangs of civilians. Usually they were small forces and his units repelled the attacks easily. The outnumbered and outgunned attacking forces typically would retreat rapidly to prevent total annihilation from the ISIS Army. Sometimes, the armed civilians were more dangerous. Dayyan started to realize how heavily armed many Americans were. Some had large-caliber snipers or hunting rifles. Usually, long-range sniper attacks had limited effect, but it kept his men on edge constantly. Over the last four days, his forces had suffered about a dozen killed or injured, but they had also gained about forty more men who had found the calling to join his army.

Another large attack on a high-value target had not occurred for a couple of days. Dayyan had to assume at this point, the army would be carefully protecting the National Guard bases and police stations. The nerd Walter, his electronics wizard, had wired together a satellite TV system from parts they had taken from raids. The American News was broadcasting twenty-four hours a day on the situation, and his army was one of the top stories. A video from their daring raid against the Van Nuys National Guard base played over and over. The black ISIS flag flying from one of the armored cars made Dayyan and Naseem proud of the daring raid.

But the American media in self-defeating ways was working against the government. The massive fight in Oakland was the other major story. The civilian casualties from the fight and propane tanker explosion were staggering, that was true. To Dayyan, in the big picture, Oakland was a minor problem. That did not stop the news media from showing the devastation round the clock on all the TV networks. Somehow, they managed to get dozens of reporters into Oakland to conduct interviews with survivors. Most people cried about the murderous army helicopters. This negative publicity was playing right into the terrorist's hands. Dayyan's group was not the only group causing destruction, but by far, he had seen the most success. But he wanted more.

Dayyan had been in contact with his handler. The unnamed ISIS coordinator had contacted two brothers who had stolen four huge M-RAP trucks from a movie yard in Agua Dulce. Currently, the trucks remained carefully hidden in a large barn just north of Santa Clarita. Gaining M-RAPs would be a large prize for his ever-growing army. But even better was the possibility of getting his hands on American Abrams tanks the brothers said remained in the yard. This was just way too tempting to let slide. He also considered that his time in the San Fernando Valley was becoming too difficult for both security and supply reasons. His men were finding less and less food and water when they invaded houses or neighborhoods. Many local people were running out of food, water, and medicine and were starting to evacuate the valley. They were using any method of transport including bikes or just walking. After discussing the situation with Naseem, they decided to make a move into Santa Clarita.

Dayyan sent scouts to the Newhall pass to assess the condition of the roads. The scouts reported the freeway was completely blocked by dead cars as well as Sierra Highway. But they told Dayyan of a large bulldozer dealer in the pass which had new and used equipment. Dayyan was confident Walter and a few of his technically savvy soldiers could get an old or even new dozer running and use it to clear a path through the clog of cars. He sent a small group of men to the equipment dealer the night before to start working on the problem, and they had reported success. Dayyan passed the word his army would move tonight after dark. Dayyan ordered his companies to join for strength long enough to get over the pass. After clearing the pass, he would again split the army into multiple companies to prevent a large-scale attack.

The weather had turned cloudy with occasional drizzle. Not having the thick smoke overhead providing cover added a worry. However, low cloud cover and rain would help hide his force from the evil eyes of the American drones. The commanders from all four companies made their way to Dayyan's location in the hills above Granada Hills where planning was occurring. Dayyan had scattered his own company in the gas and oil well sites along winding roads above the San Fernando Valley. 2nd Company spent the last day hidden within large industrial buildings south of the Newhall pass. 3rd and 4thCompany had hidden within a similar industrial complex further south in the mostly burned-out city of San Fernando. Many of the large concrete buildings had survived the fire, but nearly all the civilians had evacuated the surrounding communities, providing a safe spot for the fighters.

Just after dark, Dayyan sent the order for his units to move out. But they would not leave the valley quietly. He had one more large surprise that he intended on launching on the infidels.

Chapter 51

1410, Day 10, Command HQ, Agua Dulce, California

The HQ team would typically receive a radio call and transfer documents at 1800 hours each day. Today, however, a call came over the radio about four hours early. Earlier in the morning, the team had spent time on the radio doing an en masse swearing in of almost the entire Agua Dulce security team. Jake's idea took some persuading of the general, but it was obvious without making all the members official army soldiers, they would not have the rights to any real weapons. Most of the volunteers said they would quit the team if forced to comply with the new anti-gun rules. A few said they would continue and they would defy anyone to seize their weapons. Sparky, the radio man from Fort Irwin, completed the normal call in confirmation. Then he told Lee and Major Hicks that Colonel Braxton wanted to speak to them directly.

The two men and several others in the HQ room at the school gathered around the radio.

Colonel Braxton jumped right to the point. "Guys, you may have a class 5 shit storm headed your way. I am sending you a scrambled burst message that you can print and digest, but make sure your scrambler is on, and I will give you the update."

"Roger that," said Major Hicks.

Petty Officer First-Class Dean Barton made sure the radio secure system was active.

The computer started beeping, signaling an incoming message. Barton hit the Print icon, and a document started rolling off a printer sitting next to the computer.

Braxton started to explain the situation, "A large gang, army, or group of ISIS sympathizers has been creating havoc all over the San Fernando Valley and parts of Los Angeles. Now, according to multiple intelligence and eyewitness reports, this gang of assholes is heading over the Newhall pass and into Santa Clarita. Our drones have spotted multiple trucks and armored cars. Current cloudy weather is restricting our drones, so we are relying on civilian spotters passing us information by HAM radio.

"This is the force that we believe hit a National Guard base in Lake View Terrace, killing several guardsmen including the officers in command. Then they attacked another base and refugee center in Van Nuys, where they killed forty-plus people and made off with two Marine light armored vehicles.

"We also know that this hostile force has managed to get multiple bulldozers working from a Caterpillar dealer near the pass. They are using them to clear Sierra Highway of dead cars so they can transit the pass.

"At 1700 hours yesterday, these terrorists attacked the refugee center just set up a few days ago at the Lake, what is the name...?" The signal stopped for a moment.

Braxton came back on. "Van Norman Lake. There is, or was, an LAPD training base there. Some LAPD officers, firemen, and about a dozen Homeland Security troops got the place up and running a few days ago. They were getting some supplies by helo out of Van Nuys airport. There were nearly two thousand refugees waiting or resting before continuing out of Los Angeles. Are you still getting this?"

"Roger, loud and clear," Hicks answered.

"Okay, so this makeshift bunch of Islamic wannabes has grown to over three hundred. They rolled up on the camp and, without warning, just opened fire on the cops and DHS guys using machine guns and mortars. This is the same approach they used at the Van Nuys base a few days earlier. Why DHS and the National Guard have not tightened security is a mystery. It seems they have done little to prevent these attacks. So the attack at Van Norman forced the defenders to flee to the hills. The base lost about a dozen killed and another dozen wounded. The refugees just ran in all directions. The bad guys just went in and took all the food, medicine, and other supplies and hit the road in several directions. A couple of helos from Van Nuys scrambled immediately, but the ISIS army was long gone when they reached the center. Of course, without any heavy guns or weapons, the two helos would have probably been nothing but targets and a pending crash scene."

"So how do you know they are heading our way?" Hicks asked.

"Couple of brave-as-hell ex-army LAPD trailed the Tango vehicles to a Caterpillar dealership along the I-5 freeway. There they saw the running bulldozers heading down Sierra Highway along the freeway. They were using the dozers to plow dead cars off the road. They had a dozen or so heavy trucks providing security as they moved through the pass. The two ballsy cops followed along and waited until one of tail trucks stopped. They jumped the idiots when they got out to piss. The cops captured the truck and two prisoners," Braxton explained.

"That is ballsy," said Major Hicks to the room.

After another acknowledgment of the transmission, Braxton continued, "So the two cop soldiers dragged the two terrorists to a safe location, and they used 'enhanced interrogation,' as some would call it. The two dipshits spilled the beans about the plan. The leader of this army, an Iraq immigrant named Dayyan Imaad Shalah, somehow knows the exact location of six working M-RAPS somewhere up near you guys."

Hicks replied, "Those could be the M-RAPs stolen from the movie ranch."

"It seems this Dayyan asshole has a hard-on for the M-RAPs. His idiots said he is planning on going back to that movie yard and get the M1 tanks that he believes are still there. The two captured soldiers were glad to get out of his army according to the cops."

"Shit," said Lee out loud.

The major asked, "What is the estimated size and status of the force?"

"That is what we just sent you," Braxton replied and said, "and I have some extra crappy news to dump on you. All of our Black Hawks have been grounded."

Hicks asked, "Is that another order by Madame President?"

Braxton came back with, "No, not connected. Just shitty luck. In the last week, at least a dozen Black Hawks out west have had complete hydraulic failures. Several have crashed, killing several dozen. We had two of our birds lose hydraulics while on the deck. So the tech gurus were able to isolate the issue. There is a complex electronics module, which apparently was damaged by the EMP. The army added the modules two years ago to improve fly-by-wire capability. Obviously, they were not one hundred percent EMP-proof."

Hicks answered, "So what is being done?"

Braxton replied, "There are not enough spare parts back east to retro fit all the West Coast birds. So we are getting new unaffected birds from back east. But it will be two days minimum before they get here. And of course, we are banned from using out Apache aircraft. Sorry to dump such a load of bad news on you guys. Take a look at the brief and call us back in five. Out."

The message finished printing. Lee laid it on the table, allowing everyone to read it.

> Opposing Force Status Intelligence Update
> As of 14:45 Event + 10 Days
> Force Name Designation: ISIS-LA-001
> Force overall area of operation, previous seven days: Burbank, Glendale, Sylmar, Van Nuys, and San Fernando
> Estimated Force Size (fighting age, male): 200–250
> Estimated Force Size (non-fighting, or female): 40
> Estimated Vehicles:

Heavy Military (eight-wheel LAVs taken from National Guard Base in Van Nuys) = 2

Heavy Civilian Armored (armored police assault vehicles taken from Pasadena Police) = 1

Light Armored Military (up armored Humvees) = six taken from National Guard base

Light Armored (Armored cars [brinks] taken from various locations) = 12–16

6×6 Military trucks of various configuration (Most taken from National Guard base) = 12

Other non-military or non-armored vehicles = 30+

Estimated and Known Weapons:

Artillery or Stand Off: (Mortars stolen from National Guard Base) = 4 launchers and 200+ rounds HE

Heavy Cannon-Type Weapons: None known

Anti-Armor Weapons: Possible small number or RPGs. No other type known

Anti-Air Weapons: Possible small number of RPGs. No other type known

Heavy Machine Guns: (stolen from National Guard base M2, .50-caliber) = 8, Rounds of ammunition estimated 6000+

Light Squad Machine Guns: none known

Full Automatic Weapons: (estimate approximately thirty converted AK or AR type)

Grenades or other explosives: (fragmentation grenades stolen from National Guard Armory [200+])

Current Location Lead Units: Newhall pass

Other Location Units: various locations in Sylmar, San Fernando, Granada Hills

Objective Via Latest Intelligence Appraisal: Link up with Tango Friendly Force to acquire additional heavy vehicles, including possible six M-RAP type or possible four M1-Abrams

Lee spoke up. "This is terrible news."

Hicks looked at Lee and said, "Shit, these guys are better off than we are. They have more vehicles and more machine guns and mortars. We are going to get our ass kicked if we try to stop them with our mostly volunteer army. Especially if we have to follow the new rules of engagement and are not allowed any automatic weapons or true air support."

Lee replied. "You're right, but their army is probably mostly volunteers and amateurs. I bet their percentage of trained ex-military is less than our forces."

"I would bet you are right on that, but we still are going to need some heavy weapons of our own," Hicks said. "Dean, call Roz and Wilde and get their asses down here right away. And then get Braxton back on the horn."

In the meantime, the bulk of the HQ team came into the radio room to hear the rest of the conversation with Braxton. This included Major Hicks, police officers Chris Moss and Adam Tate, plus several of the local civilian volunteers. Most were now officially working for the army.

After making the radio connection, Braxton asked, "So, guys, I assume you have seen the report?"

"Roger that. How are we supposed to deal with that army if they head our way?" Hicks said.

"First big problem is the new order by President Harrold, which is forbidding us from sending you any serious air support or any heavy weapons or even machine guns. General Stollard has been on the horn to US command for several hours pleading the case. So far, the president's cronies are stomping on him. The president is bent on giving Homeland Security the job of fighting the terror groups and leaving the army to run the relief camps. Seems completely back-ass-ward to me. She does not want the image of the army fighting on American soil."

Braxton continued, "Speaking of DHS, there is a new bizarre plan. It seems our glorious leader has made a deal with the devil. DHS has been trying to assemble enough forces to confront this ISIS gang headed your way but has not been successful. So yesterday, she farmed out the job."

"What do you mean?" asked Hicks into the radio as he looked around the room with a questioning look on his face.

"Harrold has made a deal with the Chinese. They sent a couple of military ships with their relief ships. First dumb act she did two days ago was allowing them to enter US territory. Then she told our navy to let them go all the way into Long Beach Harbor. Now she has decided to use them as reinforcements for the DHS group working out of Los Angeles. The Congress and Senate are going nuts, and there is a huge fight going. But meantime, the president contracted a company of Chinese soldiers to go with the DHS force to chase down the ISIS army. None of us at Irwin can figure out what the hell is going on.

"So where is this Chinese-reinforced DHS Military School army at now? Will they be able to intercept the terror army before they get to our front door?" Hicks asked.

"Progress is slow. Last report was the convoy was still on the south side of the Sepulveda still twenty miles from the San Fernando Valley. I don't think you can count on them saving the day."

"Well then, we assume you are sending us more ground troops at least," Fitz asked.

"We are flat running out of real troops. We already moved most of our fighting forces to other centers as you know. The president has also sent nearly every available unit to her hometown of San Francisco and Oakland. We have few trained fighters left at Edwards or in Palmdale. Most our remaining forces are same as you, volunteers, and reactivated troops. General Stollard is working on some plans right now. First, the twenty-four soldiers at the Costco near you are going to fall back to your location. They are shutting down the food distribution, and they have scrounged up an old bus to get to your location. They handed out most of the food anyway. We ordered a couple of squads from Green Valley to make way to your location to aid. We have a call in for more troops, but the entire western United States is still a massive problem. It is also obvious the president is concentrating available forces on the San Francisco bay cities, Portland and Seattle. She is obviously taking care of the heavy Democrat cities. Plus, few of our deployed troops from the middle east or Korean theaters have been sent home because of the fighting going on in those regions.

"Refugees are pouring out of Los Angeles on every road and trail now. Big Tujunga Canyon is nearly a nonstop stream of people. Convoys bog down with starving, begging people, blocking the road, and surrounding the trucks. We sent four trucks your way this morning, and they did not make it past Avenue S in Palmdale. The refugees swarmed the trucks, forcing them to stop. We cannot expect our soldiers to fire onto innocent starving men, women, and children."

Hicks keyed the radio microphone and said, "The Costco and Green Valley units will help, but even with them that boosts us to around seventy-five experienced combat troops, including those we have reactivated. And about twenty-five civilians with little or no combat training. We may confront an army of at least 250 with armored trucks, automatic weapons, and mortars. Even if the enemy is a group of poorly trained fighters, a real battle with them could be a high-casualty mission at best and suicide at worst."

"Let me see if I can scrounge up some armor and send it your way. Our orders forbid using our tanks and Bradley's until we remove all the large weapons. But let me work on it. Meantime, do what you can to slow down these dipshits if you cannot stop them. Use their own Taliban and ISIS tactics on them. Hit them and run. I will check to see how the search for reinforcements is going and let you know. Out," Braxton said to end the conversation.

"Roger that. Agua Dulce out," Fitzgerald replied.

Chapter 52

1730, DAY 10, COMMAND HQ, AGUA DULCE, CALIFORNIA

Jake Rodriguez, Liz Wilde, Lieutenant Fitzgerald, Corporal Nolan, Lawrence Garrett, and Richard Silva had all come to the HQ building. They, with Lee Garrett, Major Hicks, and about six others, sat around a group of pushed together tables in the makeshift conference room inside the cafeteria at the Agua Dulce Elementary School. Major Hicks held a briefing, and everyone present was well aware of the threat from the ISIS army heading toward Agua Dulce. Now Hicks opened the meeting for discussion and ideas. Most of the strategy suggested involved hit-and-run ideas. No one thought an all-out head-to-head fight was possible without many casualties.

New intelligence reports pointed out the ISIS army kept split up into groups except during an attack. They also knew Dayyan would send out small patrols ahead of the main assault. It was obvious he wanted to ensure his army was not going to meet overwhelming forces. Jake suggested that perhaps there was a way to make Dayyan's MO work for the Agua Dulce defenders.

"What we need is an IED or two," said Richard Silva.

"I agree. I can tell you firsthand that if you set off a large enough boom in the middle of a column, everyone instantly loses their heads. No pun intended," Liz Wilde replied.

"From what I hear, everyone but you, Liz," Jake said, looking at her.

"Believe me; my Afghanie panties were not dry when the blast went off," Liz replied and added, "I just happen to screw my head back on quicker than some of the others."

Liz's remark got a chuckle from the group.

Hicks spoke up next as the group calmed down. "Well, any high explosives are out per Madame Dipshit's Presidential Order, so unless someone has an idea how to make an IED without explosives, that will not work."

Lee spoke up. "Okay, so we cannot use explosives, but does the order that say we cannot make a big-ass explosion with something besides explosives?"

Roz said, "How do you blow shit up without explosives?"

"Same way our diesel engines run. Fuel and air. I may have a crazy idea of a method to provide a big-ass boom using the same principle," Lee said.

"Let's hear it, Inspector Gadget," Roz said, smiling at Lee.

"Okay, I have a couple of large air tanks on my property. We were using them for some effects a couple of years back. I think they are about 250 gallons. So we put about five to ten gallons of gasoline inside. I have some ignition coils and spark plugs. We insert a spark plug into one of the tank fittings. Then we use an oxygen bottle from a welding setup, which we connect to the tank with a valve."

Everyone was listening to Lee closely as he continued. "Just before the bad dudes come down the road, we open the valve *very slowly*." Lee stressed the *very slowly* part.

"Once the convoy is next to the tank, we trigger the coil and boom. This tank will go nuclear. I have seen air tanks blow up from only over pressure and the explosion is massive. Add the correct ratio of gasoline plus oxygen, and the blast will be large enough to wipe out vehicles for hundreds of feet in all directions."

"Why did you say *very slowly* when you talk about adding the oxygen?" Major Hicks asked.

"Well, what I don't know is the exact pressure that oxygen and gasoline will spontaneously ignite. I think it is around four hundred plus. I'm not sure if it's possible to do more exact engineering without the internet or an engineering library. If you open the valve wide and let the oxygen go in fast, it can create heat and the pressure limit drops drastically and it goes off early," Lee answered.

The major and the rest of the Agua Dulce security team were listening closely.

"Is there a way to open the valve remotely to prevent vaporizing someone?" Liz asked.

Lee thought for a moment and then said, "Well, if we use an electric valve and run wires to a battery, I think we can open it and trigger the spark from a distance. Long wires can create a line loss or voltage drop, so there is a limit to the distance. I guess we could up the voltage by adding another battery. High-voltage typically damages the valve, but when it does, parts of the valve will probably be in Orange County," Lee answered.

Lieutenant Fitzgerald spoke up. "Okay, so assume we were to open the valve just as the lead trucks get to the tank. If it goes off early, well, we might still kill a couple of lead vehicles and some assholes. If it does not go off early, we get the middle of the convoy and this splits them just like the Taliban did to our boys many times. Then hit them while they are split, and we might do some serious damage, while they are looking for their heads to screw back on as Sergeant Wilde said."

Roz spoke up. "Worse case, we keep our troops back and protected with escape routes and we flee for the hills if this does not work and we hit them later. I think Lee might have something here and I trust him. So what will it take to set up, and where will we place the ambush point?"

After a few more minutes of intensive discussion, the team laid out a large map of Agua Dulce and started working on the rest of the plan.

Chapter 53

0825, Day 11, Sierra Highway at Davenport, Agua Dulce, California

L ee Garret sat on a hill above Sierra Highway with Lieutenant Fitzgerald. They were just south of the movie vehicle yard on Davenport at the corner of Sierra highway. He had been up all night working with Lawrence, Logan, Barry, and Richard Silva getting two air tank IEDs ready. They had moved them before daylight from the Garrett house using one of the five-ton trucks to its current spot right on the southeast corner. One of the huge tanks sat in the industrial building lot among odd equipment, trailers, I-beams, pallets, and other junk. It fit right in with the junkyard look of the place. After placing the tank, the men piled junk on top, making it less noticeable. Hopefully not noticeable to the ISIS soldiers.

Lee and the others did not have time and necessary parts to outfit the second tank with automatic valves and ignition. So that tank became a backup weapon. They placed it in the middle of the movie yard, surrounded by 250-gallon plastic NATO tanks filled with gasoline and diesel fuel. Some of the men siphoned fuel from motor homes inside the RV storage yard next door. The backup tank had a simple ball valve, connecting it to three full-size welding-type oxygen bottles. If it became necessary to evacuate the yard, someone would simply turn on the valve and haul ass. At some point, massive pressure should rupture the tank and all hell would break loose.

The triggerman for the tank on the road was Police Lieutenant Chris Moss. He sat inside a heavy walled twenty-four-foot sea container two hundred feet away. Lee wanted to keep the distance down ensuring the wiring would not create extra resistance and cause a problem. Chris volunteered to be the trigger as he had badly torn ligaments in his right knee a few days earlier, jumping out of one of the five tons. Sealed inside the container, Chris had four layers of bed mattresses surrounding him. He had earplugs and a set of hearing protectors and a tactical radio microphone inside one of the earmuffs. A second radio lay near him just in case. Nevertheless, he tested the radio several times.

The Agua Dulce force was divided into five main groups. The five groups used the standard army designations of Alpha, Bravo, Charlie, Delta, and Echo companies, although they were short of standard army company size. Jake suggested calling them companies just in case the bad guys had the equipment to listen in on radio transmission during the battle. Hearing radio calls to companies versus squads might afflict more fear.

Alpha Company lay hidden in the hills on the west side of the intersection of Davenport and Sierra Highway. Sergeant Moses Pierce was leading Alpha. The company had the recently promoted Corporal Sanders, plus Lance Corporal Wilson, Corporal Jeff Jarvis, and Sergeant Victor Martin. They also had four specialists from the Green Valley unit. The experienced soldiers showed up just after midnight, boosting both the number and morale of the defenders. The rest of their team consisted of police and sheriffs and six civilian volunteers. Behind Alpha company were three volunteers manning a first aid station just in case. Two of the men were fire department EMTs and the third was Madison Garrett. She had insisted on being part of the help. She tired of sitting and worrying. Her and Lee had argued about it, but Madison won out. Madison took an AR-15 and Lee's LC9 pistol. The EMTs took medical emergency kits and the three volunteers used two ATVs to climb to the top of a trail near the ridgeline above the intersection. They would assist with wounded if the troops on the west side of Sierra had to retreat.

Bravo Company led by Sergeant Wilde was on the same side of the road but further south along Sierra Highway. Wilde's unit consisted of Sergeant Kirwan, Specialist Manny Solorio, Sergeant Ballard, corporals Keystone and Fisher, and Specialist Tracy Wilkins. Adding to Bravo were four Green Valley soldiers including Sergeant Nick O'Brian and three more specialists. Like Alpha Company, Bravo also had four police or sheriffs plus five civilians. Further back and well-hidden in the hills were another three medical volunteers.

Alpha and Bravo Companies' mission was simple. They would pour ravaging fire into the convoy after the makeshift IED exploded. But only if Lee Garrett's accumulator bomb had the devastating effect he promised. Two shooters in each company had one of the HK33 Assault Rifles Marcus had provided them from the movie yard. The large-caliber rifles with forty-round magazines would add some extra punch for the snipers. Everyone knew of the president's new order banning full automatic, so the shooters would use semiautomatic, unless "shit gets out of control," as Jake told them. The company would remain in dug-out positions protected from return fire. If the ambush went bad, they had planned escape routes through the steep hills. The uphill trails would force the enemy to dismount to follow. No one felt Dayyan would abandon the safety of his armored trucks.

Charlie Company was the entire group of twenty-two 4th Infantry soldiers from Costco. They had rolled up in a bright yellow 1960s era restored bus at around 1300 hours. They made the drive crammed in the bus with a quantity of leftover supplies from the Costco. Their commander was Lieutenant Boyd Murphy. The battle-trained soldiers all loaded into a collection of vehicles, including one of the ATVs, two Hummers, and two of the five-ton trucks. Two of the men were medics. Their mission was to attack at high speed from further north on Sierra Highway if the battle started well for the defenders. Otherwise, they would provide a blocking ambush further up Sierra. They would stay out of sight unless called in by Major Hicks or Lieutenant Fitzgerald. Being the most experienced company, they had the critical role of QRF, or Quick Response Force, if needed to help out the other companies. Lengthy and sometimes heated discussions took place about how to use the only full combat soldiers company. Many, including Major Hicks, Jake, and Liz, felt the other companies with less experienced men should provide the ambush from protected positions in the foothills. Everyone finally agreed a better use for Fourth Infantry was mounted cavalry charging into the belly of the beast.

Lee Garrett was part of Delta Company. Their position spread along a long line on the east side of Sierra Highway. Delta Company was covering a longer stretch with the one group. Like Alpha and Bravo, the company was close enough to the road to rain heavy rifle fire into the enemy but far enough away for protection and a head start if needed. Sergeant Rodriguez was leading the company with Lieutenant Fitzgerald tagging along providing communication with the other units and Major Hicks. He would provide front line leadership. Major Hicks would provide overall leadership from the large hill behind the movie yard. Delta also had Sergeant Lawrence Garrett, staff sergeants Jonathan Starker and Quincy Holstein, and sergeants Vince Padia and Terrill Hudson. Two policemen were part of the company. Deputy Willard Morales and an LAPD SWAT Team member named Lieutenant Preston Gardner. Delta was smaller but contained more experienced soldiers. Their mission was to ensure the bad guys did not retreat south or, worse, east into the hills toward Agua Dulce. Also, they would, if possible, get behind the enemy convoy and hit the end vehicles with sniper fire. Most of the men in Delta had larger and longer-range AR-10 weapons. Lee had his huge AR-10 sniper rifle.

The younger men joked and harassed Lee about the heavy weapon. "Can you even carry that, old man?" or "Do your eyes even work at your age?"

All was in jest, and Lee would respond, "Well, I was shooting when your daddy was trying to get to first base with your mommy" and "With this gun, I just need to find a nice cozy place to lie down and shoot. I don't plan to hiking around all day with it."

Lee also was carrying one of his custom M1 bull-pup 30 caliber carbines as back up. He had it slung over his back in a custom compact pouch. The small lightweight bull-pup carbine was a creation using the older M1 carbine from WWII with a modern bull-pup kit.

In the movie yard stood the bait. Four M1 Abrams tanks sat behind the closed and locked gate. Two of the bait tanks already had occupants. Driving one of the massive American battle tanks was the experienced tank driver Sergeant Jesus Benson. A Civilian, Bobbie Singleton was riding with Benson. Driving the other tank was the yard owner's son Michael. He had insisted on driving one of the tanks if they were going to use them.

Michael had said that morning, "Hell, I can drive one of these better than any army dirt digger."

His father Marcus, was not healthy enough for an intense battle, so Petty Officer Dean Barton would ride along "shotgun." The tank crews outfitted the tanks with rifles, pistols, and ammunition. The movie tanks were no longer equipped with their weapons of war. With the new order from POTUS forbidding the use of tanks equipped with the original main guns, they were nothing more than protected battering rams. But the size and weight of the tanks alone could be a devastating weapon, plus the psychological impact could create terror among the enemy ranks.

Michael added as he climbed in the tank that morning, "Shit, this is going to be like demolition derby."

His father called up at him, "Michael, watch your language."

"Hell, Dad, I'm going to war with a bunch of terrorists. Don't you think a little swearing is in order?" Michael replied.

"Well, if you put it that way, what the fuck." Marcus said. "Make me and your mom proud, son."

Michael saluted and lowered down into the tank.

Evenly spread along the ridgelines surrounding the movie yard were the last of the defender's forces. It consisted of twelve volunteer civilian snipers who would engage the convoy and try to stop them on Davenport at the yard entrance. The basis of the hastily developed plan was to engage the front of the convoy, forcing their leader Dayyan into the fight. Major Hicks was at the far-right end of the sniper line, and he would lead this ragtag group of civilians. The major would be making time critical decisions as the operation unfolded. The civilian snipers had an odd collection of rifles, mostly hunting types. Each sniper had created three different concealments.

They would fire a few rounds from one spot, back up, and move quickly to a different camouflaged location. Moving the men would prevent return fire from zeroing in and might make the enemy believe the force was larger. This would discourage an outright assault.

During the night, other civilian helpers blocked the top of the hill on Davenport with three large semi-truck trailers. Staggered positions of the heavy trailers fully blocked the road. All the trailers had deflated tires, making it harder to move them out of the way. Behind the semi-trucks were two Vietnam veterans from the local VFW. The men were concealed with two each of the Marcus provided LAWS rockets. Both men had been trained and had used the rockets frequently during their multiple tours in Vietnam. They were a last resort as the use of the weapons would be a violation of the Presidential order. Seventy-four-year-old Wayne Green, a short thin black army vet, sat in his motorized scooter cradling one of the single shot rockets. He had a plastic nasal canula plugged into an oxygen bottle mounted on his cart and a vintage 1911 forty-five in a holster duck taped to the chair. The slightly older and taller Claude Plemons, Marine Silver Star recipient, lay under one of the trucks on an old mattress with his two rockets. He told the team of defenders, "I used to tell my late wife I wanted to die in battle. She said, I would die in bed. Well, this way, we can both be right." Both men made it clear, "Two shots each and we are done." Both men also had a half dozen fragmentation grenades. They planned on just rolling them down the steep hill if needed and keeping the last one for themselves. The men would not be retreating."

Every soldier and volunteer who passed by them that morning had saluted them proudly.

The two dedicated and brave American war veterans were given the call sign "Benghazi" as an honor to the two Navy Seals who had defended the American Embassy with their lives.

Also during the night, reports came in the ISIS army had split up into several groups while making their way through Santa Clarita. One group estimated to be fifteen vehicles including one of the Marine LAV eight-wheeled armored tanks was close. The last known location was near the intersection of Sand Canyon and Soledad

Canyon. The rest of the army had moved in several directions around Canyon Country. Spotters positioned in a several locations using simple civilian radios. One of the spotters reported vehicles on Bouquet Canyon near Plum Canyon. Assumptions were the group had moved over Plum Canyon during the night. Plum Canyon Road was an important thoroughfare running from the two main east-west roads, Soledad Canyon Road and Bouquet Canyon Road. Both of the spotted convoy groups stopped for the night remaining until morning. The soldiers were just milling around. A worry was that no one had seen any sign of the M-RAPs described to the two LAPD officers during the intensive interrogation.

Suddenly Fitzgerald's radio sprang to life. "All companies, be advised, Tango force is moving toward our location. Confirmed four-teen Tango Vehicles various types. One LAV."

Replies came from each company in order.

"Able, Roger."

"Bakers, got it."

"Charlie is ready to rock and roll."

Fitzgerald chimed in the correct order: "Delta is ready."

"Wake up, Claude…oh…yep…Benghazi is locked and loaded gents."

"Nuclear is ready."

Nuclear was the call sign given to trigger man Lieutenant Chris Moss. Everyone including Lee Garrett hoped it was a good sign and should not have been something like "Dud."

Fifteen minutes later, Russel Thompson spotted the convoy again. His hiding location was inside a faux cell tower designed to look like a pine tree. It was on top of the small hill right at the end of Vasquez Canyon Road where the two-lane rural route dead-ended at Sierra Highway.

"This is Verizon. Tangos confirmed at my location and continu-ing north," Russell said into the small ham radio.

Russel made the broadcast while tucking himself in tight behind the steel and fake tree limp structure. He prayed his full green moun-tain camo would hide him from dozens of men riding in the enemy convoy. He held his breath as the convoy drove by fifty feet below him on Sierra Highway.

Hicks sent out another notice after getting the call from Thompson. He smiled, thinking of the call sign Verizon given to him because of his spot in the cell antenna.

The convoy moved along Sierra Highway at thirty miles an hour. Baker Company and Delta lead elements could both see the convoy now. Suddenly, the convoy slowed and turned into a large gated driveway leading to a huge ranch style estate on Sierra that was nicknamed "the Ponderosa." Used often for special events, the estate had many buildings and items strewn around its property.

The LAV moved forward at the gate, pushing it off its mounts, sending it to the ground flat. Liz Wilde was watching, and she knew volunteers went along the road last night, telling residents to clear out. She hoped the people at this house had headed the warning. The LAV moved into the massive yard followed by armored cars, trucks, and six-wheeled military transports filled with soldiers.

Liz Wilde called in on the radio link, "This is Bravo. Tango convoy pulled into the Ponderosa. They sent a team to clear the house. They are off loading women and children from their vehicles."

A moment later, she came back on the radio, "It looks like the Ponderosa residents did not all clear out as told. Tangos just brought out three men and two women at gunpoint. They are walking them across the yard to the creek…fuck…"

Everyone heard the sound of multiple full automatic AK-47s rifles firing. The gunfire lasted about ten seconds and stopped. The sounds echoed off the surrounding hills multiple times.

"Bravo here, I guess you heard the shots. I don't need to tell you what happen."

Lee looked up at Fitzgerald. "Fucking scumbags. I see no reasons we should give these assholes any slack. If we capture them, I say smoke 'em."

Fitzgerald replied, "I agree with that."

Chapter 54

0835, Day 11, Lombardi Ranch, Bouquet Canyon, California

Dayyan looked at the impressive M-RAP armored trucks sitting side by side inside the large barn. The small band of true believers from the Santa Clarita valley had done well getting the four huge trucks and five Humvees from the Movie Ranch. Sadly, however, was most of this local cell had died during the helicopter attack at Costco several days earlier.

He spoke to the new leader of the group. "Kamil, you have served God well by taking these impressive machines from the infidels and keeping them hidden. I am sorry to hear about your true brother and your other warriors."

"Thank you, my warrior brother. Yes, I am saddened by the loss of my older brother Aakif and his eight brave friends. My brother did not expect the massacre from the American helicopters at the Costco. Aakif's plan was to stir up local civilians to the point of overrunning the Costco. He and his men would follow the greedy infidels into the warehouse and take most the supplies. I remained here to protect family members and guard the American war machines. I feel ashamed I have let down our God by not being with the other brave soldiers who died."

"You have no reason for shame Kamil. War has many needs, and only God knows how the battles will end. By staying here, you have saved these valuable trucks for a larger purpose. We shall unleash the power of these machines onto the infidels who designed them to kill our people. I feel there is going to be a large fight today, and these trucks shall strengthen our army and allow us to slaughter the unclean."

Dayyan watched as his men finished mounting .50-caliber machine guns to the turrets of two of the four M-RAPs. The trucks originally had enclosed turrets and heavy protective glass view ports and even periscopes to protect the gunners. But the movie company had replaced real guns with a worthless fake. Unable to install the guns into the turrets and make them work with the electric drives, Dayyan had his men do the next best thing. They removed most of the heavy turret top and sides and simply added a pivot mount for the older machine guns. He had only two of the large guns in his company, so they put those on two of the trucks. The other two trucks would simply have open turrets, which would allow a man to use a standard rifle or perhaps one of the fully automatic AK-47s. He did not expect the Americans to use any large explosive weapons as the liberal American president had forbidden them after the huge loss of civilian life in Oakland.

Dayyan had already given orders to his other company commanders a few hours earlier. The entire Army had moved over the Newhall pass last evening after the daring attack on the Van Norman Reservoir refugee camp. After taking supplies and moving north his forces gathered in the pass where 5, 405, 210, and the 14 Freeway all joined, using bulldozers, they moved cars and trucks to clear a path for his army. As they moved through, a trailing bulldozer pushed the same cars and trucks back into piles of worthless metal, blocking the path for anyone trying to follow. They piled the cars and trucks and stabbed holes in all the tires, making moving them even more difficult.

As the terrorist army moved through the pass, they found hundreds of refugees walking or riding bicycles trying to escape the Los Angeles area. At first, the unlucky refugees would think his army was part of the relief effort. The fleeing civilians would find out different. Dayyan's army chased them off, or worse, robbed and killed them if they made the mistake of approaching for help. After taking any items of value including food, water, or weapons his men would kill the men in front of the women and children. Normally, he allowed his men to capture some of the younger girls and teenage boys as prizes, but last night, they did not have the time for such celebration.

One exception was the gang leader Charro and his company. They went after anything of material value. They wanted money, jewelry, silver, or gold. His men were brutal, searching and stripping people, searching for valuables. Most refugees left their homes on foot or bikes and carried their money and jewelry with them. Charro's men were ruthless in relieving anyone of any valuables. They would even cut of fingers of men and women to get gold or silver wedding rings. Anyone who protested died slower and more painfully. The terrorist army left a trail of dead and grieving civilians as it moved along.

When the army arrived at the intersection of Newhall Avenue and Sierra Highway, Dayyan again split up his forces for protection. He sent Charro and his pig gang members west on Newhall Avenue, telling him to move his company to the massive large buildings on San Fernando Road. The old warehouse complex was originally a massive glass factory, but now was a collection of businesses. He ordered Charro to stop for the night but move and join back with the army at the planned rendezvous point.

Dayyan directed 2nd Company and 3rd Company east on Placerita Canyon Road then to move north on Sand Canyon Road. Sand Canyon had large-estate type property, and they should be able to find suitable locations to hide out until morning. At daybreak, they were to continue up Sand Canyon back onto Sierra Highway and do the first scouting of the movie ranch. Dayyan had assigned the one running LATV to 2nd Company, providing a heavy tank for the early assault on the movie company. Unfortunately, the second LATV had to be abandoned. During the battle to capture the LATVs, several tires had been shot many times. Civilian snipers added holes to the constantly leaking tires. Eventually, the self-inflating compressor system on the armored truck could not keep up.

Dayyan led 1st Company north on Sierra Highway to Golden Valley Road. His group continued up Whites Canyon over the rolling hills and on to Plum Canyon, straight to the location given to him by his handler. There they found the loyal ISIS brother in the barn with the four M-RAPs as expected.

Now with the M-RAPs ready to go, Dayyan gathered his squad leaders to give them orders.

"My Brothers, 2nd and 3rd companies are already moving toward the objective at the movie yard. Our scouts reported most houses around Vasquez Canyon and Sierra Highway empty as if the occupants recently evacuated. This gives me a feeling the infidels for the first time may be preparing for us. I want to turn a possible trap for us into a trap for them."

Dayyan laid out a detailed map of Santa Clarita. It was a large-scale topographic hybrid map showing both the terrain and the local roads. He then pointed out how Vasquez Canyon Road, which turned west from Sierra Highway, turned back north and was nearly parallel to the road for a mile or so. Scattered between Sierra Highway and Vasquez Canyon were ranches and rolling hills. These hills would be his hiding spot for his company.

Dayyan spoke to his mortar squad leader Daysean, "Place half of your mortar team and two launchers here in this small recess behind the hills along Sierra Highway. Naseem and I will find a vantage point along the ridge and provide spotting for their shells. Take your remaining men and one squad of riflemen further north. Use this power line road to move back toward Sierra Highway and find a suitable location where you can rain down fire on the road but also have adequate visibility for spotting. You will be too far north for us to help you target your shells."

Daysean agreed and moved off to instruct his squads.

Dayyan then set up his own version of a QRF, or Quick Response Force. He ordered most his remaining riflemen to take three 6×6 trucks and an armored car and park along Vasquez Canyon and wait for his orders. He then broke the M-RAPs into two groups with one .50-caliber machine gun each and pointed to locations for them to wait. Dayyan was expecting any opposing forces if they were out there waiting to ambush and chase his army south on Sierra. If they did so, he would block them with the M-RAPs and then use the riflemen and mortar squads to devastate the infidels. Once he had them trapped, he would send the pig Charro and his gang in full force to hit the defenders while they were under attack.

At any point, Dayyan and his men could retreat from the hills and go east back to Bouquet Canyon Road. If he left that pig Charro and his band of thieves here to die with the Americans, that would be a win-win in his mind. The overall plan was to still get the M1s if possible and use them for a PR victory. If not possible, his army would evoke death onto any opposing forces they met. Only he and Naseem knew that he was planning on splitting up the forces into even smaller groups and heading to the hills to lie low and regroup. Dayyan felt an attack on his large force by the powerful American Army was imminent. Today, cloud cover provided his forces some protection, but when the rains ended, satellites, drones, or aircraft would surely find them. The split-up groups would make their way into the Antelope Valley. There they would join another large force west of Lancaster. This new location would be near most of the large military buildup and relief efforts, including the famous Edwards Air Force Base. The location could indeed provide Dayyan with the chance of spectacular victories against the infidels.

Chapter 55

0922, Day 11, Sierra Highway, Canyon Country, California

Sergeant Liz Wilde watched as only four vehicles roared out of the Ponderosa gate and headed north on Sierra Highway. After executing the residents, the four trucks had stayed at the Ponderosa only a few minutes. Most of the terrorist vehicles remained as the lead trucks left and were off-loading their own women and children. The four that left included two up armored Humvees, one of the armored assault trucks, and one five-ton truck with twelve men. The LAV stayed at the Ponderosa, which greatly concerned the defenders.

Liz used the radio to tell Hicks and Fitzgerald what was going on. "Four Tango trucks heading your way, but the LAV is still here."

Hicks radioed Chris Moss. "Nuclear, do not jump the gun on ignition. Arm only and wait for my command."

"Roger that," Moss said back.

The LAV was the target they most wanted to destroy with the air tank bomb. Now Hicks hoped the snipers could draw the LAV into the fight.

The four-vehicle convoy drove the short distance in less than two minutes. The lead vehicle was one of the armored Hummers with a turret gun that looked like one of the stolen .50-caliber machine guns.

Liz told Hicks of the gun.

"Well, that sucks," Hicks replied.

As the convoy came close to the corner of Davenport, Hicks gave Nuclear the call to arm the tank. Police Lieutenant Chris Moss flipped the switch that would open the oxygen valve and start over-filling the large tank.

The Tangos made the turn, oblivious to the big air tank behind the chain-link fence. The lead Hummer continued up the incline on Davenport slowing at the driveway to the movie yard. The other three vehicles lined up behind the lead Hummer. All four were on Davenport.

Hicks called out a command on the radio, "Echo team, commence firing." He waved his hand downward.

The man closest to Hicks could see the wave of his hand. He aimed a Remington 700 30-06 (30 odd 6) hunting rifle with an adjustable 4.5 to 27 × 56mm scope on the forehead of the gunner in the lead Hummer, held his breath, and squeezed the trigger. The man's face exploded, and he fell down into the Hummer.

The other eleven snipers all opened fire. The turret gunner in the armored car took a round in the neck just above his protective vest. He too fell inside. As told, the snipers fired a few shots and then moved back and into new positions. The enemy started returning from the last Hummer. The men in the five-ton quickly unloaded and scattered along Davenport, taking up firing positions behind trees or other objects. New gunners appeared in the lead Hummer and the armored truck. The .50-caliber opened up, creating a horrendous noise and spewing out its massive rounds at the positions along the hill.

Major Hicks was considering giving the fire command for the IED, but he wanted to do more damage from their one large weapon. He wished they had placed both air tanks near the road, but time had been short. They had only one air tank bomb, and Hicks wanted to do as much damage to the attackers as possible. If the LAV did not move forward, Hicks would explode the tank and order a retreat. He would rather not have civilian volunteer casualties, and they could all live to fight another day.

The radio came alive with the sound of Liz Wilde's voice. "Bravo here, I think they took the bait. All the other tangos have loaded up and heading your way. The LAV is leading the pack."

That was perfect in Hicks's mind. The enemy had probably decided it was just a bunch of locals taking potshots at them, and they could just roll in and wipe them out quickly.

Hicks keyed the radio, "Nuclear, are you armed and ready?"

"Roger that," said Chris Moss.

The lead LAV rolled up Sierra Highway at forty-plus miles per hour. The huge eight-wheeled behemoth slowed to make the turn onto Davenport.

Hicks held the radio close and waited. "Nuclear, fire now. Repeat, fire now."

Chris Moss flipped the second toggle switch forward and ducked his head deeper into the pile of mattresses.

To Major Hicks, it seemed like several seconds from his command to fire to something happening. But it was only a split second. The LAV had made the turn with the turret gunner pointing another .50-caliber machine gun at the defenders along the hill. The unsuspecting gunner had just squeezed the trigger when his world vanished.

The air tank exploded in two phases. Hicks could see the tank start to grow in size for a millisecond and then disappear. A massive growing fireball erupted where the tank had been. Hicks and all the snipers dove for cover. The fireball rapidly grew in size. The dark red and orange inferno spread out in all directions and three or four hundred feet high. The concussion wave rolled over the men on the hill a short second later, followed by the massive noises of the explosion.

Normally, the Marine Light Armored Vehicle would be a fairly safe place to be to ride out an explosion. Unfortunately for the men inside, the LAV was twenty feet from the air tank when the improvised weapon vaporized into a fireball. And the turret was open, adding devastation to the occupants. The highly volatile mixture of gas and pure oxygen created a thermobaric blast. This type of blast increased atmospheric pressure ten to twenty times normal. The gunner in the turret turned to dust and bloody mist, milliseconds before the intense flame and heat consumed him and his equipment. Blast pressure penetrated into the open turret of the heavy armored body. Men inside were subjected to a pressure great enough to collapse their rib cages into their body core, crushing their hearts and killing them all instantly. Their brains were also crushed by the pressure penetrating their ears, nose, and mouth. All five were dead before they could even begin to process what was happening.

The blast wave continued in all directions. It rolled over the soldiers who had unloaded from the five-ton truck, ripping them to shreds and tossing their bodies hundreds of feet. Like the men inside the LAV, they did not live long enough to even finish a single breath. The five-ton military transport lifted into the air and violently rolled on its left side. The driver and right seat occupant also died from the intense pressure invading the interior. When the truck rolled over, their bloody gore spilled onto the pavement of Davenport Road.

The next Hummer up Davenport Road suffered the same fate as the LAV. The wave of pressure obliterated the gunner, and his bloody corpse slid inside as the force of the blast flipped the lighter vehicle rear over front. The Hummer landed upside down. The armored truck in front also lifted and flew forward; otherwise the Hummer would have landed upside down on it. The weight of the armored assault vehicle helped to keep it upright. But the blast and debris tossed it forward and left into the ditch along the road. The back doors were still open after two men from inside had dismounted to find firing positions. That decision was fatal to the two men inside. The blast force entered through the rear opening and roared forward, ripping the two men in the front out of their seats and pulverizing them against the dash and windshield.

The replacement gunner in the last Hummer was using the .50-caliber with great effect against the snipers on the ridge. Although the gunner had not hit anyone directly, two men had injuries from flying debris from the explosive impacts of the giant machine gun shells. The civilians were getting leery of sticking their heads out. But when the powerful blast happened and because of his distance from it, the gunner had just enough time to turn around. This was fatal for him. When the powerful tsunami of flame and debris slammed into the Hummer, the man's body doubled over backward around the .50-caliber machine gun, instantly shattering his spine. He might have felt some pain or thoughts, but like the others, the massive pressure and heat pulverized his head, and he was dead before slipping down into the turret opening. The remaining driver in the Hummer survived for the moment, but he was unconscious and doomed to death from multiple brain bleeds.

The trailing portion of the convoy had made the amateur mistake of lining up closely in formation behind the LAV. When reaching the corner, the trucks had stacked up tightly with only a few car lengths of separation. The vehicle directly behind the LAV was a sixties vintage Dodge Pickup with two men riding in front and two more in the back. The old truck was so close to the blast it instantly turned to five thousand pounds of shrapnel. The heavy metal parts of the old Dodge dislodged as it was flying backward. The truck slammed into the pavement, rolled several times, and stopped in the ditch on the far side of the road over three hundred feet from the explosion. Those dislodged parts went flying back along the road, pounding into the rest of the convoy.

An armored-up Humvee was right behind the old Dodge. Although the Hummer had bullet-resistant glass, the upper body was not strong enough to withstand the blast hitting the widow straight on. Both windshields pushed through the mounts, slamming into the two men in the front seat decapitating them. The high-strength bulletproof windows continued back, carrying the heads of two men, and slammed into the rear occupants.

The next Hummer riding in convoy was almost far enough from the blast for the thick armored windshields to hold. But once again, the open turret spelled doom for all four men inside. The front window held the first blast, but then it rebounded from the pressure coming down the hatch, and the already weakened frames tore apart, allowing the windows to fly out. The blast was tossing the Hummer backward, and the front end was lifting. None of the men were wearing seat belts. This doomed them to becoming loose debris inside a metal can. All received fatal injuries, including broken necks and crushed sternums. The doomed Hummer and crew continued flying backward and crashed into the five-ton truck behind it.

The heavy five-ton truck did not move much at its distance from the blast. But the large flat windshields did not hold. Both laminated glass windshields blew in, killing all three men in the front seat. The eight men in the back of the truck died outright by pressure or flying debris or would internally bleed to death in minutes.

Ten car lengths from the truck another Hummer was the first vehicle far enough from the blast and with satisfactory protection to save the occupants. Or it should have been. However, when the air tank exploded, the heavy hemispheres on each end of the tank became high-speed, heavy steel missiles. Both hemispheres blew straight off horizontally. The one on the south end flew at hundreds of miles an hour in a straight line down Sierra Highway. Unaffected, the steel tank end had ripped through the chain-link fence without slowing, its flight path aimed right at the Hummer behind the five-ton truck. Flying dome forward, like a space capsule returning to earth, it slammed into the right front corner post of the Hummer. The 250-pound steel hemisphere tore through the steel post, ripping the man in the right seat in half. All the metal debris tore the other three men to shreds as the projectile passed through the cab exiting the rear. The flight through the Hummer's cab launched the dome upward and started it to tumble. Flying another five hundred feet and just missing another truck, it came back down on the left side of Sierra Highway. Careening and bouncing, the barely damaged dome finally stopped a quarter mile from the blast site.

The opposite end of the tank pointed at the RV yard. That hemisphere took off like a rocket, leaving a smoke trail behind. It hit another large RV in the back and blasted through like a hot butter knife. It hit a large RV and tore through, causing the internal fuel and propane tanks to explode. It continued through the yard, destroying two more RVs and damaging three semi-truck trailers. Thankfully, the refugees who had been using the RVs had all been evacuated during the night.

Chapter 56

0935, DAY 11, FOOTHILLS ABOVE SIERRA HIGHWAY, CANYON COUNTRY, CALIFORNIA

"Holy crap!" Sergeant Moses Pierce said while lifting his head and shaking off layers of dust, sand, and rock. The sergeant looked at other members of Alpha Company and saw them doing the same. The devastation caused by the air tank IED stunned the battle-hardened veteran. Pierce thought how he had doubted if the thing would even work. He had imagined nothing at all or, at best, a big thud from the large air tank. Pierce even pictured in his mind the ISIS soldiers all getting out of their trucks and laughing and rolling on the ground. But that was surely not the case.

Moses and Alpha Company had watched the first four vehicles roll up Davenport and the snipers opening fire. He heard Sergeant Liz Wilde report the rest of the convoy was heading to help the scouting party. Moses had not bothered ducking down when Hicks radioed the command to Nuclear to set off the bomb. But the blast grew quickly and to an enormous size. As the first shock waves hit him and the rest of his company, he yelled out, "Get down!" His people crawled as deep as possible into their dug-out positions. The first impact was a massive blast of sizzling hot air. Then came a tsunami of sand, dirt, and rocks. Because of the IED being on the road and terrain slanting uphill, the inferno and blast picked up an enormous collection of debris and sent it rolling toward Pierce's position. Sand, dirt, and anything loose rolled over Alpha company, and finally a shower of metal and rocks fell from above. One large chunk of steel from the air tank landed inches from Corporal Sanders's head. Another large section of chain-link fence landed behind Corporal Jarvis.

Moses shook off dirt and sand and looked at the scene below. Trucks and Hummers lay scattered about the road like toys. The damage was intensive. One Hummer was lying backward atop a 6×6 truck hood. There was no movement in the center section of the enemy convoy. The original four vehicles of the scouting party looked destroyed. From the LAV back, six trucks suffered such severe damage the sergeant knew the men inside would not be mounting a counterattack.

He then heard the call from Major Hicks, "All units execute full out assault. I repeat, execute full-out assault. We have what's left on the run. Go get them, boys."

Chapter 57

0936, Day 11, Foothills on East Side of Sierra Highway, Canyon Country, California

Lee Garrett was staring down from his position on the east side of Sierra Highway. The heavy damage from the IED astounded him. Unable to see all the destroyed convoy from his position, Lee could see enough to know the air tank bomb had worked better than even he had hoped. Delta Company, like Alpha had hit the dirt when the blast went off. But with the industrial buildings and other obstacles in the way, they did not experience the wave of dirt and sand like Alpha Company. When Lee heard the radio call from Major Hicks ordering everyone to attack, he knew the bomb had worked.

Delta Company opened fire on the remaining vehicles which could try a retreat. It appeared only four vehicles were moving at all—two Hummers, another 6×6 truck, and one of the Brinks Armored Cars. All four were trying to do U-turns when Delta opened fire. Lee lay prone on the edge of a hill. He pointed the big AR-10 sniper rifle at the windshield of the front Humvee as it started to back up, making a reverse type U-turn. The heavy 308 bullet smacked into the glass, cracking it out from the impact point.

Not armored, Lee thought. He squeezed four more rounds off in quick succession. Both windshields were now sporting spider web patterns of cracks.

The Hummer continued backward, out of control. Lee knew his rounds must have incapacitated or killed the driver. The driverless Hummer continued back, slamming into the Brinks truck behind it. The driver of the Brinks truck was trying to make a forward to the left U-turn when the Hummer hit the right rear side hard. This caused the Brinks truck to lunge off the paved highway. It now wallowed in the soft dirt, which the overweight two-wheel drive truck could not manage. It sat spinning the rear tires for about forty-five seconds before the rear doors opened and four men spilled out and started running down the road.

Bravo Company had also opened fire on the remaining trucks. Lee could hear the sound of at least two of the HK-33 assault rifles donated by Marcus from the movie yard. Rifle fire from both sides of the road was pelting the last two vehicles in the convoy. An open-top 6×6 truck with eight men in back was a sitting duck to the overwhelming rifle fire. The men spilled over the sides and took cover around or under the big truck to no use. The accurate fire from both sides made it impossible for anyone on the road to find acceptable cover. All the terrorist soldiers were dead or wounded within sixty seconds.

Suddenly, the radio came to life in Lee's ear. "All units, Verizon just reported, three 6×6 trucks full of Tangos and another Brinks truck just rolled by at high-speed heading our way."

"This is Charlie. We are inbound. I say we keep going and hit them head on. We have the momentum, let's keep it."

"This is Tank 1, we are already making the turn onto Sierra and Tank 2 is right behind us. I say let us clear a path and let Charlie finish the job."

Lee had forgotten all about the two Abrams tanks in the movie yard. The planned mission for the sixty-ton beasts, if the IED was successful, was power up, charge out, and confront the enemy. The Abrams outweighed any of the Tango vehicles including the almost thirteen-ton LAV. Without guns, the drivers would simply ram the enemy trucks and even the LAV if necessary. That was all they could do. But there are few ways to stop an M1 Abrams tank armed or not.

Lee thought the resistance on Davenport must have been light if the tanks were already turning onto Sierra Highway heading south.

"This is Charlie. We are falling in behind the tanks. I say let's keep going and wipe these shit-bags off the planet."

Major Hicks came back on the radio. "Delta actual, what is your opinion? Do we press or fall back?"

The Major was directing his question at Fitzgerald who looked at Lee. It shocked Lee that a West Point Army officer with two Middle East deployments would ask for a recently conscripted military wannabe's opinion. Lee gave him a thumbs-up.

Fitzgerald pressed the transmit button Velcro'd to his rifle and answered Hicks. "We are good with pressing on. I agree with Charlie. Let's hit them while we have the momentum."

Hicks came back. "All units, press the attack. Alpha and Bravo, move to the road and mop up any remaining Tangos. Then do the best you can to double-time toward Verizon. Delta, keep to the ridgeline trail and head south also. Recon the Ponderosa for threats. Then head to Verizon."

Major Hicks impressed Lee. He made decisions quick, and he was cool as a cucumber. He was a born leader who gave quick orders. He was careful not to disclose details in case the enemy, although doubtful, had cracked their radio frequency. Lee stood and started jogging with the rest of Delta Company. Now the weight of the AR-10 sniper rifle was really notable. Lee considered tossing either the AR-10 or the M1 carbine. The carbine was slung over his back with a small assault pack crammed with assorted stuff. But he reconsidered, mainly to prevent any harassment for dumping his load. He moved as quickly as he could with the younger men.

Lee was double-timing the best he could behind the rest of Delta. He looked over to his right and saw the two M1 Abrams tanks thundering down Sierra Highway. They were moving at about fifty mph. The small ATV behind the second tank looked like a small bug chasing a rhinoceros. Behind the ATV came the two Hummers and then the two 6×6 five-ton trucks.

He crested a small rise and could see the Ponderosa just ahead. Lee saw a group of women and a couple of young children out near the highway. As the two tanks and ATV roared by, the women were yelling and shaking their fists. Suddenly, one of the women raised an AK-47 from her side and started firing at full auto at the first Hummer behind the ATV. The Hummer swerved to the far right. The driver of the second Hummer saw what was happening. So did the gunner in the center turret. The solider raised his M4 rifle and, with a well-trained shot from a high-speed moving vehicle, shot the woman dead. She slumped to the ground. Two other women dropped rifles they were holding.

The first soldiers of Delta team ran up behind the gang women. One yelled out, "Get down. Get down. Get down on the ground now."

It took a few seconds, but the stunned women dropped to their knees. A smaller group of women with two young kids in tow also sat down. A woman told the young boy and young girl of about ten to be quiet. They sat sobbing. The men of Delta came up and pushed the women face down. Then prodding with their rifles, they ordered the women to stretch out their arms. When the winded Lee finally arrived, the women had their arms bound behind them with plastic wrist cuffs. Sergeant Padia and ex-SWAT member Preston Gardner returned to the house and performed a search. They did not find any more terrorists.

Lee noticed an old Dodge flatbed truck sitting by the house. He thought it might belong to the gang, so he headed over and checked for keys. There were not any keys, but he found a couple of toggle switches duct taped to the dashboard. Flipping first one switch and then the other, the old clunker Dodge sprung to life. He drove over to the group.

"Hey, look what the bad guys left us. Anyone else want to ride?" Lee said.

Rodriguez answered, "Well, all be," in a Gomer Pyle accent.

Jake then said loudly so the women would hear, "Morales, Gardner, you two stay here and guard these bitches. If they do anything that you dislike, you have my permission to just shoot them.

They are in direct violation of martial law and are part of a murdering bunch of ISIS-loving fucks. We could just shoot them now. If by some far chance we don't come back, kill them and hightail out of here."

"What about the kids?" Morales said.

"Lock them in a bathroom or somewhere in the house," Roz answered.

The rest of the team jumped into or on the old Dodge, and Lee gunned the motor, spinning dirt and rock, heading out the gate toward Verizon.

Chapter 58

0937, Day 11, Casey Residence, Agua Dulce, California

Dayyan was frantically calling on the radio to find 2nd and 3rd companies. So far, he was not getting any reply. He had told Fawzi to park the big Pasadena SWAT team truck in a barn off Vasquez Canyon Road. He told his young driver to wait with the truck and guard it. He also knew, however, that any real threat would probably cause the skinny boy to run and hide or, worse yet, relieve himself. Dayyan, Naseem, plus two soldier bodyguards walked the short distance to where the four of them now sat over-looking Sierra Highway.

Dayyan and his small command group had arrived in this spot before he had ordered the 2nd company scouts to the movie ranch. When the sniper fire attacks started, the squad leader Badr el-Haque told Arman and Dayyan it was likely another case of locals defending their property. Taking sniper fire was becoming more common over the last several days as the rogue army had moved around the San Fernando Valley. They even had some civilians attack them last night while moving through Sand Canyon. Arman suggested he lead the rest of his company to quell the locals and seize the M1 tanks, which Badr confirmed were in the movie yard. Dayyan consented so Arman and Adham loaded up their companies and headed the short distance to the objective.

But then a massive blast occurred. Dayyan could see the fireball from his location over two miles away. Now he could not reach anyone using the tactical radios. The sound of a raging battle could be heard from the distance, so he expected his men were at least still fighting. Not knowing what was going on was giving Dayyan a bad feeling. He did not share the feeling with Naseem. The situation was bad enough, and they needed to concentrate. Besides, the big explosion and unknown status of 2nd and 3rd Companies, the idiot Charro and his band of drug dealers and thieves was late. Dayyan was able to contact Charro on the tactical radio. His company had held up at a roadblock manned by a small force of sheriffs and locals. He and his men had to shoot their way through. They were en route but still twenty to thirty minutes out.

Dayyan's first mortar team was in place as well as his QRF people, but his second mortar team had taken the wrong power line road. Now they were in a dead-end canyon a half mile from the ridgeline above Sierra Highway. The second mortar team should have already been in place and ready to fire. But they were in the wrong canyon, trying to backtrack to the correct road.

Dayyan decided to send in his QRF force. He ordered the men in the trucks and the armored car to head down Sierra Highway and help 2nd and 3rd companies. He had the M-RAPs move up closer to Sierra and standby just out of sight. If the attackers moved further south, he wanted to use the M-RAPs to box them in. Dayyan screamed at Charro to hurry up, and he cursed the second mortar team for their incompetence.

Dayyan spoke to Naseem. "My brother, we must remain ready to move out. I still think we may have the final surprise, but if not, we will quickly return to our truck and take the M-RAP squads with us to a safe location."

Dayyan turned to his right when he heard the three 6×6s and one armored truck make the turn off Vasquez Canyon onto Sierra Highway and speed up toward the fight. He slid forward to the corner of the house and used powerful binoculars to look north on Sierra Highway. What he saw turned his face white. He turned to Naseem, who could sense the look. "My brother, they are using my tanks against us."

Chapter 59

0948, Day 11, Sierra Highway Near Vasquez Canyon, Canyon Country, California

L ieutenant Boyd Murphy was in the right-hand seat of the small ATV. Specialist Jackson Cosby was driving. They were right behind the two monster M1 Abrams tanks rolling at high-speed down the two-lane highway. As they made a big sweeping turn nearing Vasquez Canyon Road, Murphy spotted the first of the 6×6 five-ton trucks heading straight for them. The rears of both trucks were full of men in shooting positions. The tanks moved closer, and the men in the trucks opened fire with semiautomatic and full automatic rifle fire.

"Get this buggy off the road and behind something," Murphy said to Cosby.

Cosby turned the buggy left onto a dirt road leading to a house slightly off the main road. A small ridgeline ran down from the main hill nearly to the highway. Murphy told him to stop behind the hill and both men jumped out with M4s and moved up the hill to a shooting position.

Murphy got on the radio and called his men. "1ˢᵗ and 2ⁿᵈ squads dismount and take up defensive positions. Let the tanks do some work. If the tango trucks get by, open fire. 3ʳᵈ and 4ᵗʰ squads stay in the trucks and move forward carefully. If they turn and run, you give chase."

Just as Murphy got to the hill, he could see the lead M1 slam into the first of the Tango trucks. The idiots in the back had been firing full auto at the oncoming tanks, somehow thinking an AK or AR rifle round was going to pierce several inches of hardened steel.

"What a bunch of dumb shits," Murphy said to Cosby.

The truck driver, however, saw the futility in going head to head with an Abrams and was trying to turn the truck around. He managed to get halfway around at a right angle to the fast-approaching M1 tank. That was the worst possible position. The sixty-ton tank hit the truck broadside at nearly 30 mph. The truck tilted up as the tank pushed it sideways. The tank rode into the air at nearly a forty-five-degree angle running up the side of the truck. The men in the truck bed desperately trying to jump out before the impending crash had no chance. Either side they jumped from resulted in either the tank or the rolling over truck, horrifically crushing them to death. Those remaining in the truck died of the crash, tank, road, or maybe just from sheer terror. But the huge overbuilt military truck was hard on the movie tank. The tank had been retrofit with a lighter weight rubber-coated set of road tracks. The heavy metal framework of the truck tore into the lighter tracks, breaking the right-side track, leaving the tank immobile straddling the 6×6 truck.

Only two men managed to climb out of the truck alive. Cosby took aim at nearly five hundred yards shot them both multiple times. They staggered, crawled, and fell.

Murphy commented, "Nice shooting, Cosby."

Sergeant Jesus Benson and Bobbie Singleton opened the top hatch of the tilted tank and slid down the turret and onto the pavement below. The second tank, driven by Marcus's son Michael with Petty Officer Dean Barton, used the right shoulder to pass by the crash. The second ISIS 6×6 truck in line was trying a different escape tactic and backing up. The terrified soldiers having just witnessed the gruesome fate of their fellow fighters bailed out and as a group ran for the side of the road. The truck roared backward and slammed directly into the Brinks trucks behind it. The motor on the Brinks truck stalled from the massive impact, leaving it motionless. Four men from inside the Brinks truck exited the rear door, joining the three from the cab of the 6×6 and sprinted to join the other men looking for cover along the road.

The last five-ton driver must have seen the utter commotion on the road ahead of him. He suddenly veered off to the right and crashed through a chain link gate into the local baseball field complex. He drove into the center of the parking lot and stopped. The ten men in the back dismounted and started to move into firing positions. They started to pour fire out onto the road. Michael, driving the second tank, saw the truck turn into the baseball field. He did not stop or slow down. He roared the Abrams tank over the ditch, into the sporting complex, and headed straight for largest group of fighters. The now-dismounted enemy was firing down the road at the 4th Infantry trucks heading into the fight. When the reluctant infantry saw the oncoming tank, they took off at a sprint, heading into the hills behind the baseball fields. Eight of the ten men escaped to the safety of the ridge. Another twelve men from the other truck and armored car ran a different path into the same hills.

About the time the tank chase ended, the old Dodge flatbed truck showed up with Delta Company. A few minutes later, Sergeant Wilde and Baker Company jogged up. Everyone was surveying the carnage and celebrating the seeming victory over the terrorist army. Kudos and high-fives abounded. Fitzgerald brought everyone back into reality when he began barking out orders to secure the perimeters. Fitzgerald voiced concern for the twenty or so Tangos who escaped into the hills as being potential sniper threats or a lasting danger to civilians. He ordered his men to give chase and capture or kill them.

The lieutenant had barely issued his commands when the experienced soldiers in the group heard a loud screaming sound. The high-pitched noise was obvious. Mortar.

"Incoming!" yelled Fitzgerald, Wilde, Rodriguez, and several others.

The mortar round continued inbound as everyone hit the ground or shielded behind vehicles or other objects. The first round hit short on the west side of the road and blasted a deep hole in the field, throwing dirt and rock around. Seconds later, another round hit on the same side of the road but closer. The second round hit in near proximity to some Alpha Company soldiers throwing out rock and debris and deadly shrapnel. One solider took a hit to his lower body and fell to the ground. Another soldier leaned over and expertly hoisted the wounded man in a fireman's carry and started trotting further back from the rounds. Two 4th ID soldiers ran to the downed man's aid. They carried the injured man over behind the Abrams and laid him down gently so one of the medics could examine his wound.

Fitzgerald shouted loudly to those around him, "Everyone, take shelter. They were off, but I am certain their next rounds will be closer. Snipers, look for spotters in those hills."

Lee Garrett and Jake Rodriguez ran up and flung themselves under the oddly angled Abrams tank lying across the overturned five-ton. The two men positioned themselves behind the damaged heavy wheels and tracks on the right side. Lee slid his AR-10 out from between two load wheels, popped off the scope covers, and used the powerful scope to scan along the west ridge. Jake used binoculars and did the same. Both men searched the hills looking for a spotter who might be directing the mortar rounds.

The high shrill started again as two more rounds headed in.

Roz said, "They have two launchers. Those two rounds are too closely fired."

Jake just finished his statement when the first round hit past the road near one of the baseball fields. A moment later, the second round hit dead center in the road fifty yards north, just missing one of the parked Echo Company five-ton trucks.

Lee was thinking to himself, *What could get shittier?*

It did.

Suddenly, the distinct heavy thumping of a fifty-caliber machine gun broke the silence between mortar explosions. The gunfire was coming from the intersection of Vasquez Canyon and Sierra Highway. Jake crawled around to the left rear corner of the overturned truck. Lee kept up the vigil for the mortar spotter.

Jake yelled out to Lee, "Damn it, there are two M-RAPs at the intersection. One has a turret mounted fifty. A sniper is in the other turret."

Jake slid down next to Lee and used the radio to call Fitzgerald and Hicks. "We need to get the hell out of here."

Then the loud noise of a second fifty-caliber machine gun sounded from the opposite direction. Fitzgerald yelled back to Rodriguez. "There are two more M-RAPS at the intersection to the north."

The intersection was Vasquez Way. It was a smaller dirt road and a shorter route from Vasquez Canyon to Sierra Highway. Vasquez Canyon Road turned west off Sierra Highway but then curved back around to the north and almost parallel Sierra. Vasquez Way went from the larger road and intersected Sierra about a half mile further north. It was a rough dirt road through some large homes and ranches but would not stop the battle and off-road proven M-RAPs. Two of them had obviously come down Vasquez Canyon and the other two down Vasquez Way in a well-planned pincer movement.

"I guess we know what happened to the four missing M-RAPS," Roz said to Lee.

Two more mortar rounds screamed out as they flew an arc inbound.

Chapter 60

1002, DAY 11, HANGAR 14B, EDWARDS AIR FORCE BASE, CALIFORNIA

Colonel Braxton looked at the four ugly A-10 Warthog aircraft that sat inside a massive hanger at Edwards Air Force Base. The building was originally built to hold the custom 747 used to transport the space shuttles back to Florida after a landing at Edwards. The four small attack aircraft looked tiny sitting in the huge space. The colonel had flown one of the four A-10 Warthogs himself from Fort Irwin the morning most the Irwin troops had moved to Edwards. Braxton had talked General Stollard into bringing the four tank killing machines just in case.

"In case of what?" General Stollard asked.

Braxton replied, "Well, if World War III is going to break out, I want them so I can sleep better at night."

"Do you want to bring a couple of nukes also?" the general replied in jest.

In the end, the general approved the aircraft. Only three of the eight A10 pilots stationed at Irwin managed to return after the EMP attack, so Braxton offered to fly one of the planes to Edwards. Truth be told, Braxton jumped at the chance. As an Air Force officer, he had flown over 160 missions in the twin turbo prop ground assault planes in Iraq and Afghanistan. When the Air Force decided to retire the jets and turn them over to the Army, the colonel asked to go with them. The Air Force provided the opportunity to him and other A-10 Commanders, pilots and ground crew to transfer to the Army and keep their seniority and equal ranks. But his promotions and career choices had taken him out of the pilot seat and put him behind a desk. His experience with the Warthogs provided valuable training in the use of the attack plane for the new soldiers and pilots. General Stollard accepted Braxton with flying colors by at Fort Irwin, and they had become fast friends on and off the base. Now Braxton had been spending the final years of his career teaching Rangers and Special Forces. His job was educating the soldiers on using A-10 Warthogs or other types of airpower in support of ground missions.

Braxton had been in the command building all morning following the situation in Agua Dulce. At first, like everyone, he thought the battle was going well. But he had a bad feeling. He told the general, he had other matters, and he left the command center. He was still furious about the orders from POTUS and how little they could do to support the makeshift army. Leaving valuable soldiers and civilian volunteers without air support enraged the colonel.

Colonel Braxton went to the hanger where the four A-10s sat and found the crew chief Sergeant Grady Wagner. Wagner was a twenty-year veteran who loved to fix stuff. The crusty old sergeant had found his passion working on the odd ugly A-10s. This was after he had lost the lower part of his right leg by an IED in Iraq during Operation Enduring Freedom.

"Wagner, are my birds ready to fly?" Braxton asked right off.

"Of course, sir. The birds and I are always ready. I even scrounged up a new hydraulic valve for the sticky gun feeder valve on number 3," Wagner said.

"Great. The general and I want to run a drill right now. He is on the horn to Madame President at Centcom, begging for permission to use the birds. I want to see how fast you and the boys can have a bird fueled, armed, and pointed out the door." Braxton then pushed a button on his watch and said, "Starting now. *Go.*"

Wagner stood looking at Braxton for a few seconds and then said, "You're shitting me, right?"

"No, I am not shitting you. And if you stand here staring at me for much longer you are going to fail this test miserably," the colonel said.

Wagner snapped into gear. He yelled across the hanger at two disheveled-looking mechanics who were sitting feet up doing nothing of importance. "You two screw-offs. Get your butts up and do something. We are on the fast clock, and we need Bird One ready now."

The two men jumped up looking lost. Wagner helped them find themselves quickly. "Miller, go get those other two idiot retards and tell them to bring out the ammo loader and a full load of the bang bang stuff. Gomez, you call the gas farm and tell them to hightail their rears over here with a fuel truck."

Wagner then looked at the colonel and asked, "Sir, do you want any bottle rockets for this baby or just the big bullets?" Wagner was referring to adding air to ground rockets or just the massive thirty-millimeter cannon shells for the giant electric belt fed multibarrel gun the airplane was built around.

"Madame President will be lucky if she lets us shoot a pistol out the window, Wagner. I seriously doubt she is going to let us use any rockets or missiles. Just fill it up with gas and bullets and point it out the door. Just use the TP rounds. Get the auxiliary power unit plugged. Then stand by for me to return."

The colonel had asked for the TP or target practice rounds only. Although not explosive as the HEI, High Explosive, or API, Armor Piercing Incendiary rounds, he knew the less powerful rounds were still devastating on anything less than a full-size battle tank.

Braxton turned and headed out the door, going back to the command building to see what was going on with the battle in Agua Dulce. He entered the command building just as the frantic call came in from Lieutenant Fitzgerald. The ISIS army had the Agua Dulce fighters surrounded and were attacking with mortar and heavy machine gun fire. Several men were already dead and many wounded. The four missing MRAPs had them trapped on Sierra Highway and ISIS troops were now lining the hills to the west. It appeared a full-scale attack was imminent.

Braxton walked over to the large paper map of Agua Dulce and studied it for a moment. Then without saying a word, he turned and headed out the door. He arrived at the hangar a minute later. An A-10 was sitting outside the hanger, and a fuel truck was driving off.

The colonel walked up to Wagner and said, "Are you guys done yet, or do I need to call in some Air Force pukes to help out." Wagner and his other men were all regular army.

"She is ready to go, Colonel. What now?" Wagner responded.

"The test is not done until I start it up and make sure it's flight ready. I will be right back." Braxton said and he turned toward the rear of the hanger.

Braxton entered a ready room, went in, and opened a padlock on one of the lockers. He quickly slipped on his flight suit and grabbed his helmet and parachute. He returned in record time and went straight to the ladder, leaning against the side of the Warthog.

Wagner held the ladder as the colonel climbed into the cockpit. The sergeant climbed up and helped to secure the belts and attach communications equipment. The colonel reached down and pulled a safety pin off the ejection seat arming it. He handed it to Wagner, who was starting to look quite concerned.

"Well, Sergeant, are we doing a full test or not. Get down and pull the flags," the colonel said, referring to several safety pins attached to the aircraft with the famous "Remove Before Flight" flags. One flag secured the safety for the thirty-millimeter cannon.

"We typically don't do that for a test, sir," Wagner said as he stared at the colonel, who was going through the checklist and was getting ready to start the engine.

"Wagner, what is typical right now? This is not a test, Sergeant. We just got approval for a fly over. Get down off my ladder or you may get sucked into my left engine," the colonel said.

The colonel reached for the starter switch.

Wagner slid down the ladder and pulled the remaining safety pins. The motors started to whine and both started quickly. Wagner knew something was not right. He had no paperwork, no clearance from the tower. No official approval to load weapons on this plane.

Wagner said to himself, "Fuck it."

The old sergeant trusted Braxton and knew the man was honorable. He pointed to the wheel chocks and his other men slid them out. As the canopy came down, Wagner and the others saluted the colonel, who sharply returned the salute, let off the brakes, and pushed the throttles forward. Braxton steered the A-10, rolled left from in front of the hanger and down the taxiway. Braxton had the plane moving at a high rate of speed for a taxiway.

Wagner said to the four men standing with him, "Shit, he may just take off from the taxiway."

Gonzales one of the technicians responded, "I am not sure he really had permission for this flight Sarge."

Wagner replied, "Nah, I don't think so either. I will tell you that when they were passing out brass balls, that crazy colonel got himself some big ones. Godspeed, Colonel."

Wagner saluted the vanishing plane one more time.

Braxton did not take off from the taxiway. He was running the plane at nearly seventy miles per hour as he turned and steered toward the end of the shorter runway. The radio speaker blasted to life inside his helmet. "A-10 on taxi, what are you intending? You do not have clearance."

"Flight of one on emergency departure. I plan taking off south on Runway 22R. Advise me if you have traffic."

"A-10, you do not have clearance. Stop your plane immediately. Ground personal and security have been dispatched. Do you copy?"

"Tower, do what you want, but I am taking off to the south. If there is traffic, you better advise them. Over and out," Braxton said.

The colonel reached to the radio panel and flipped off the tower frequency. He could see several Hummers with red lights flashing heading toward the runway trying to cut off the agile jet. He gunned the throttles and made the big sweeping turn onto the southeast facing runway. He took the turn so fast Braxton thought the plane might spin out like a race car. If that was even possible. He completed the turn and lined up on center of the runway. Then without hesitation, the now renegade colonel slammed the throttles to their full position. He felt the massive power from the twin turbofans push him into the seat.

"Well, so much for a cozy retirement," Braxton said to himself.

The A10 accelerated quickly. Without rockets or missiles or drop fuel tanks, it was considerably lighter than its normal takeoff weight. It gained speed quickly, and before he was halfway down the runway, Braxton pulled back on the stick and lifted the bird airborne right over the tops of the two Hummers. He climbed to a few hundred feet and leveled off, staying under the cloud cover that had socked in the entire area. He would dead recon navigate, and he needed to see the ground. The Warthog screamed across the Antelope Valley at just over four hundred miles per hour, which was the rated top speed of the aircraft. At this speed, he would make the 40 mph flight in Agua Dulce in about six minutes.

Braxton thought, *Hopefully I'll make it in time.*

As the A10 approached the mountain range separating the Antelope Valley from Acton and Agua Dulce, Braxton could see the hilltops disappear into the overhead cloud cover. Not having ground following radar, he would have zero visibility over the mountain range. It would be tricky and dangerous and require simple seat of the pants flying. The plane did have an Inertia Guidance System. Braxton would have to trust his position to the IGS and guess on altitude as he cleared the mountain range. He pulled back on the control yoke, and the plane flew up into the heavy clouds. He kept climbing until he was certain he would clear the highest peak. When he was confident he had passed the ridgeline, he pushed the control yoke down and headed to what he hoped would be clearing under the clouds.

The colonel was sweating profusely as the plane dived toward the ground. Suddenly, he could see images breaking and then it cleared allowing him to see below the clouds. Braxton only took a second to pick out Sierra Highway as it rambled below him. He turned slightly to the right and took the Warthog down to five hundred feet above, following the road to the battle.

Chapter 61

1018, Day 11, Sierra Highway
Near Vasquez Canyon Road

L ee Garrett and Jake Rodriguez continued searching for spotters or enemy soldiers along the west ridgeline. The battle-proven soldiers were looking for shooting positions and fearlessly helping the wounded. Most volunteers had sought shelter among wrecked trucks, buildings, or anything solid within or near the baseball fields. The entire force was taking heavy fire from both the M-RAP mounted machine guns and the two mortars. A line of regrouped ISIS fighters had secured firing positions on the east ridge, allowing them to rain fire down at the trapped soldiers and civilians keeping anyone from escaping to the east. The Agua Dulce defenders were trapped and taking casualties.

Something had to break. And several things did.

Barry was positioned in the old Rescue Eight panel van on Sierra Highway at a safe distance. Barry and some other helpers had repainted the van with a bunch of browns, tans, blacks, and whites in a makeshift multi-cam. The hardware store in Agua Dulce had provided the paint in either spray cans or brush on latex. The paint job was terrible, but the van stood out less than with its bright, shiny red finish. Barry was not happy about wrecking the restored fire-engine-red paint job but preferred the stealth look over being such a noticeable target.

Liz Wilde and Bravo Company had been the last to arrive from the North. The .50-caliber machine gun in one of the M-RAPs at the north roadblock had her company pinned down. The second M-RAP at the north had a sniper firing from a heavy steel protective turret. He backed up the .50-caliber gunner while looking for targets stupid enough to raise their head. He had already killed one of Liz's men. A sniper round hit Sergeant Nick O'Brian in the neck while he was trying to get a position to return fire. Shrapnel from a .50-caliber round hit another one of her men in the shoulder and her civilian medics were treating him behind one of the wrecked five-tons.

Liz looked out from the side of her protective wreck to see the old Rescue-8 truck screaming down Sierra Highway at high speed.

"What the hell is Barry up to?" she said out loud to those around her.

The truck continued straight at the two M-RAPs which sprawled across the highway. It never slowed down, and it hit the M-RAP with the .50-caliber broadside on the driver's side. The old panel truck was no match for the heavily armored twenty-ton truck designed to resist massive IED explosions. But the inertia of the van slamming into the big truck rocked the truck nearly off its wheels. The crash shook the occupants including the gunner, slamming him into the gun and turret steel. The gas tank on the old van exploded on impact, and a fireball erupted around all three trucks.

Just after the van hit the M-RAP, Sergeant Moses Pierce and the two men from Alpha Company started firing at the M-RAPs from high positions above the intersection. Alpha Company was the furthest north on Sierra and had to hike south after the massive air tank IED arriving after the two M-RAPs blocked Sierra Highway. The rest of Alpha Company continued south along the ridgeline in search of the mortar positions. Moses and the other two men had quickly found secure firing positions. Caught in a cross fire, exposing the sniper in the turret, the non-burning M-RAP backed away from the flaming wreck. The frantic driver was desperately trying to move the beast. The heavy old steel of the crumbled van had embedded around the rear tires of the truck, locking the axles from rotating. The large truck rocked back and forth as the driver frantically tried to free it from the inferno. Frustrated, the occupants of the burning M-RAP opened the rear door to escape the inferno. They were easy targets for Alpha Company as they emerged. Four men desperately ran for the other M-RAP, but only one soldier made it without dropping from rifle fire.

Liz keyed her mic and exclaimed, "The machine gun is out on the north roadblock. We can retreat in that direction."

Fitzgerald replied, "We are still pinned down by the mortars. But all companies make plans to exit north."

A couple of minutes later, the other Alpha Company soldiers led by Sergeant Sanders spotted the mortars. Looking down from a hidden position on the ridgeline, the men could see two launchers and six men. Four men were bringing back cases of rounds out of one of the Brinks armored cars as the other two men adjusted the launchers and continued to fire off rounds. Lucky for the Agua Dulce defenders, this was very inefficient. Adding to the defenders' luck, one of the civilian volunteers was using a .50-caliber sniper rifle. The gun was a Barrett model M95 bolt-action sniper rifle. This rifle used the same large rounds as the machine guns in the M-RAP trucks. It was clearly illegal in California, but Billie Newton had bought the gun in Nevada and had kept it buried on his property "just in case." Well, "just in case" was here, and he was glad he had the long-range and powerful weapon.

Sergeant Sanders told the rest of the men to take up positions and to fire after Billie made the first shot. When everyone was ready, the skinny certified public accountant Billie Newton adjusted the sights for the seven-hundred-yard shot. He lined up the reticle of the Nightforce 5-25×56 long-range rifle scope on a case of mortar rounds sitting behind the gunners. The two men ferrying the rounds from the armored car had just placed the case there. He took his time and then held his breath and slowly squeezed the trigger. The heavy .50-caliber round screamed out at high velocity and in a split second hit the mortar shell box. It easily penetrated the thin metal box, slamming into the rounds in the box, piercing and tearing them apart

A huge explosion occurred. The blast created a massive cloud of dirt and debris. As the men from Alpha Company watched, one large object oddly spun through the air toward their position. It hit twenty-five yards in front of Sanders, tumbled over and over, and eventually came to rest within arm's reach of the sergeant. Sanders look down at a slightly beaten-up but intact mortar round. Thankfully the main explosive had not armed.

Sanders looked at the round and said, "Shit, talk about dodge a bullet."

When the dust cloud cleared, Sanders and the others could see nothing left of the launchers, crates, and most of the six ISIS soldiers. Body parts were lying around a large crater. Even the heavy armored car showed signs of severe damage. One well-placed .50-caliber round ended the artillery barrage.

Suddenly, a high-pitched screaming sound penetrated the canyon echoing off the steep hills. The men of Alpha Company turned toward the odd sound.

Sergeant Sanders exclaimed, "Hell yeah. The cavalry has arrived. That, boys, is the most beautiful airplane in the world."

Chapter 62

1026, Day 11, Over Sierra Highway, Agua Dulce, California

Colonel Braxton had weaved the A-10 up through the thin canyon north of Davenport Road. He was flying low. He stayed at five hundred feet above Sierra Highway to insure visibility of the road and battle. Now as he approached, he could see signs of the battle at the intersection of Davenport. Destroyed trucks, Humvees, and the LATV lined the road. Bodies lay in odd positions around the wrecks. Dark clouds of smoke rose from several burning vehicles.

Braxton had already adjusted one of his tactical radios to the frequency and security codes used by the Agua Dulce defenders. A few minutes before, Braxton had contacted Fitzgerald. "Sweetwater, this is Braxton. I am inbound in a flight of one. I will be on location in one minute. Do you copy and can you give me your situation and exact location?"

Fitzgerald answered immediately, "Braxton, Bird of one? One what? Hell, glad to see you whatever you are driving. We're pinned down on Sierra Highway between Vasquez Canyon and Vasquez Way. There are two tango M-RAPs at each end of our position firing on us with .50-calibers. We are taking mortar fire from the hills to our west. Our forces are scattered along the road and baseball field.

We also just got word of a convoy of Tangos coming down Vasquez Canyon Road."

"Roger Sweetwater. If you can, lay smoke. Otherwise, I will just look for the M-RAPS," Braxton said quickly.

Braxton was going through the final checklist, ensuring he was ready for an A-10 gun run.

"No way to lay smoke now. Look for the two M-RAPs on the north and don't fire south from that point. You are clear when you see the two M-RAPS on the south. They are past an M1 sitting on a five-ton truck."

The colonel concentrated on remaining above Sierra Highway. He saw the first two M-RAPs. Flames engulfed one of the large armored trucks, while the other moved away from Sierra Highway. Braxton throttled back power, dropping to two hundred feet above the road and moving south. Now he could see more damaged vehicles and many men using them for shields. Then he saw the odd sight of the M1 Abrams sitting at an angle on top of a turned over 6×6 truck. A few hundred yards past the odd wreck, he saw the other two tango M-RAPs. A turret gunner was firing a large machine gun at the trapped men. Tracer fire was visible. Suddenly, the gunner turned the weapon up and started frantically shooting in Braxton's direction.

Braxton worked the controls on the Warthog and lined up his sight on the M-RAP with the chain gun. He depressed the trigger, and the huge General Electric 30 mm gun swirled up, releasing a hail of the massive rounds. He held the trigger depressed for less than two seconds, and as he did, he jinxed the plane to the right. The 378-gram PGU-15 TP rounds left the gun at over one thousand meters a second, tearing into the armor and destroying both vehicles and whoever was unlucky enough to be inside. He saw men trying to jump out the rear door and run, but shrapnel from the rounds and metal of the trucks flew in all directions, killing them instantly.

Braxton pulled up on the stick and flew past the intersection. He looked to his right and saw Vasquez Canyon Road turning off and curving back north. He also saw the weird fake cell-phone antenna tree on a hill rising above Sierra Highway. He rolled the plane nearly vertical to the left putting it into a tight 5-G turn. The force of the turn pressed the colonel into the seat as the little stubby plane went around counterclockwise. As the attack jet came around and lined up with Vasquez Canyon Road, he straightened it up and pointed the nose down.

Vasquez Canyon Road curved slightly to the right and then back to the left. Past the second curve Braxton could see the terrorist convoy. It was an odd collection of trucks, cars, buses, and armored cars. Two trucks near the front had large weapons mounted in the back like the pickup trucks in the Middle East known as Tacticals. Those guns and every other exposed gun started shooting at him as he lined up on the road.

What a bunch of dumb asses, Braxton thought as he squeezed the trigger.

The plane shook as the stream of death poured from the belly of the Warthog. The cannon shells ripped into the concrete just in front of the first vehicle and the experienced colonel walked a line down the road cutting through vehicle after vehicle. The rounds tore the smaller cars and trucks into two pieces. Nothing or no one could survive this onslaught of firepower. As the colonel kept the nose pointed down, he adjusted his flight path slightly keeping in line with the curve of the road. He counted off at least fourteen vehicles, most which exploded into fire from the rounds hitting fuel tanks. This just added to the horrific scene below.

The Warthog was getting dangerously low to the road as Braxton worked the controls taking out the last couple of tango trucks. He was concentrating hard to keep the gun sight on the column. When his rounds took out the last trucks, he looked up to see disaster in front of him coming quickly. Large power lines crossed the Vasquez Canyon Road after looping from hilltop to hilltop.

Braxton cussed. He knew he screwed up. He pulled up hard on the stick and jammed the throttles full. He tilted the plane hard to the right trying to clear the heavy cables normally charged with thousands of volts. He almost made it over the highest lines.

The right-wing tip did not make it in time. The cable sliced through the aluminum skin and airframe about four feet from the end. Braxton worked hard keeping the plane from spinning sideways which would spell doom. He pulled the stick hard to the opposite side and worked the pedals. He did all he could to prevent a flat spin, but it was hopeless. The A-10 did not have much damage. Braxton had seen the tough little planes return to base in worse shape than this. With more altitude, he probably could save it and fly it. But he did not have room to work and stabilize the plane. He made one last move to point the nose up and add as much power as possible. The plane lost lift from the lack of right wing, causing a stall and sending it down. Braxton reached down and pulled the ejection handles, and he and his seat rocketed out of the plane.

Chapter 63

1028, DAY 11, SIERRA HIGHWAY, AGUA DULCE, CALIFORNIA

Lee and Jake had been concentrating on finding the spotter they assumed was somewhere along the west ridgeline. Lee had been using the high-power scope on his AR-10 while Jake scanned using a pair of army-issue binoculars.

Suddenly, Jake spoke into Lee's ear. "There, I got something. Next to that house on the ridge. Look at the left side."

Lee moved the scope over and focused it for the range.

"Yes, I see something," Lee said.

Both men could see at least two objects moving slightly. It looked like white head scarves. Jake saw another small object moving and pointed it out to Lee. An antenna. Someone was using a hand-held radio, and the antenna was moving around above them.

"What do you make the range?" Lee asked.

"I figure about a thousand yards, Lee. Slight breeze to the right. Tough shot. Can you do it?" Jake responded.

"You should take the shot, Jake. You have more experience," Lee said.

"You know the rifle better than me. You can do it," Jake responded.

"I don't have time and experience to adjust my scope. I am just going to have to wing it."

"Take a shot and then just open up. Once the first round comes in, they will duck or run. Do it, man," Jake said as he watched through his binos.

Lee lined up the scope reticle on the man on the right. Now he thought he could see three or four figures lying on the ground next to the house. Lee decided to line up to the furthest right figure and then move the rifle up and slightly left. He would be guessing, but Lee and Jake knew time was the essence. He moved back and forth a couple of times until he was comfortable on his rule of thumb sight adjustment, and he took a breath and squeezed the trigger on the long barrel AR-10. As soon as the first round fired Lee nudged the barrel back down and pulled the trigger again. Lee repeated the motion again and again, bringing the weapon down on target and squeezing the trigger. He saw dirt fly and pieces of the stucco on the house explode behind the men. He kept firing round after round until the entire twenty-five-round magazine was empty.

Just as Lee fired the last shot, he and Jake heard the roaring sound of the Warthog. They looked up to see it fly over them and then felt the powerful sound wave of the thirty-millimeter cannon going off just above their heads. They could see the line of tracers heading down Sierra Highway. The two excited men slid from under the tank and carefully moved to the rear of the overturned truck. They peered around cautiously.

"Fucking A!" Jake yelled.

Both M-RAPs were burning wrecks. There was no gunfire coming from that direction.

Jake and Lee looked over to the hills behind the baseball fields. They could see 4th ID soldiers had worked up the ridge and were outflanking the tango snipers who had been shooting down from the east ridgeline. Catching their attention again, the unique screaming noise of the Warthog echoed off the hills as the attack plane came around in a tight turn, nosed down, and lined up with Vasquez Canyon. Again, the massive multibarrel gun let loose a stream of instant death. Although Jake and Lee could not see the unlucky bastards on the road, they knew there was no escape from the agile little plane. The roar of the cannon continued for seven or eight seconds.

By that time, the plane was no longer visible because of the west hills. They kept watching, and they heard the plane throttle up. Then they saw it.

"Shit, something is wrong," Jake said.

The plane rolled over and started diving toward the ground. A piece of the right wing was missing. Then the canopy exploded from the body of the plane, and the rocket propelled ejection seat carried the pilot away from the falling craft. Jake and Lee watched as the ejection seat continued skyward before another small explosion occurred and the pilot separated from the seat. The parachute opened, and they watched it heading behind the ridgeline.

"Come on. That is Braxton, and he is on the enemy side of the hill!" Jake yelled.

Roz grabbed Lee by the shoulder, and the two men took off running across the road and into the dry wash alongside. Jake was again showing his military fitness as he easily ran ahead of Lee. As fast as Jake was running, he was still able to key the mic on his radio and call out.

"Colonel Braxton is down behind the hill. I am advancing on his location with Garrett. We need more support."

Lee looked to his right and saw Sergeant Lambert and three men from the 4th ID take up the chase behind him and Jake. Lee struggled to climb the hill carrying the heavy sniper rifle. He had only made it halfway when Jake ran over the crest and disappeared. Lee was still moving up the hill, and he could hear random gunfire from the other side. He reached the top and ran through the yard of a large ranch-style estate. Lee could see Jake ahead crossing a large corral heading toward the location where the parachute carrying Braxton was headed. Suddenly Jake turned to his right, and Lee could see three Tangos coming down the hill from further north on the ridgeline. They were dragging along a fourth injured person. The startled ISIS soldiers saw Jake about the time he saw them.

With composure, Jake shouldered his M4 rifle, and while continuing forward in a precise step-by-step movement, he targeted the group and fired off quick rounds one after another. Jake never missed his stride, and with only six shots, all three Tangos were down. Lee thought it magical to watch such expert marksmanship and training which had come together in such a professional display of American Army skill.

"Stunning," Lee said out loud.

Suddenly, Jake spun counterclockwise and fell over a small rise down a slope onto a lower field.

"Crap," Lee said.

Lee looked left and saw two more Tangos coming across the adjoining field with rifles raised and firing in Jake's direction. The sergeant was lying down below the hill, and incoming rounds were ripping into the dirt just above his head.

Lee was on the verge of exhaustion after the long uphill run, but he raised the heavy 308 sniper rifle and pointed it at the two threats.

"Goddammit," he said again to no one.

Lee had zoomed the scope so far in to make the thousand-yard shot he could not find the two men through it. Like looking across a small yard using a telescope, it was difficult, if not impossible, to center the target within the scope. Thankfully, Lee had also installed forty-five-degree side mounted hard sights for short range shots. He tilted the rifle sideways, lined up the first target in the fixed sights, and squeezed the trigger. Nothing happened.

"What an idiot!" Lee yelled out loud.

Lee had never taken the time to change out the empty magazine and load a fresh one after firing all twenty-five rounds at the observation post. He could pull another mag out of his vest and change, but then he remembered the M1 Bullpup still hanging over his back. He dropped the AR-10 unceremoniously and yanked the M1 over his shoulder. He pulled back the simple side-charging handle and aimed at the two Tangos who had yet to see Lee up by the house. The two men were moving close to the slope where Jake had fallen over. Lee lined up the now seeming-too-small of a weapon on the first target and started squeezing off the rounds. The M1 had a decent effective range of about three hundred yards. These men were about two hundred yards out from Lee. The rounds started hitting the lead Tango. He tripped forward and fell over, clutching his gut and chest. Lee shifted aim and started firing at the other man who saw his buddy drop. That man turned and dove into a small wooden building. Lee continued firing as the ISIS soldier fled inside. Lee emptied the illegal California thirty-round magazine into the small building, hoping the small thirty-caliber carbine rounds would penetrate the flimsy wood siding and find the target inside.

When no return fire came from the barn, Lee loaded a full mag into the M1, picked up the AR-10, and ran down the hill to where Jake had fallen. When he arrived, Jake was lying behind the small hill. At first glance, seeing a red color around Jake's left side, Lee thought he might have been hit.

Is it blood? Has Jake been hit? Lee worried as he ran up.

"Roz, are you okay? Did you get hit?" Lee asked.

"Not really. One round hit the lower receiver on my M4," Lee said as he held the weapon up.

Lee could see a hole in the left side and a bulge on the right side just above the grip.

"Inch lower and I might not have a thumb on my right hand. And the other round hit my rucksack. I am not sure what is leaking all over me. It must be my canteen of red Gatorade."

Jake removed the small backpack and held it up. Red fluid leaked out the bottom as they both watched.

"Dude, that asshole shot my canteen," Jake said in an amused tone.

"I can't believe you are running around with that pack on anyway. Shit, you still outran me by two hundred yards while carrying your dirty laundry," Lee said.

Jake replied, "Hell, after Vegas, I don't go anywhere without my bag. You're the guy who told me 'Better to have it and not need it than…'"

"Yeah, yeah, I get it. Glad those assholes are crappy shots," Lee replied.

Lee then looked over the small rise to ensure the guy in the barn had not come back out. A loud booming voice behind them startled both Lee and Jake.

"Well, what in God's name are you two miserable-looking bastards doing sitting in a ditch full of horse shit?"

Jake and Lee looked over to see Colonel Braxton walking up. "Are you guys down there playing find the weenie while this war is still going on?"

"No, Colonel. Lee and I were just looking around in this horse-shit to see if we could find your sense of humor, which I figured fell out of that perfectly good airplane that you seemed to have broken," Jake replied.

"That perfectly good airplane just saved your asses. And I am going to bitch out Edison on placement of their power lines. And I completed a study on power line strength versus wing strength of the A-10 Aircraft," Braxton said.

Suddenly, Braxton pulled a large semiautomatic pistol from his vest and aimed it toward the barn. Jake and Lee spun as Braxton fired three quick shots. The Tango from the barn was slowly limping toward the three men while trying to hold an AK-47 steady. The man dropped dead as the rounds from the colonel's weapon hit him square, exploding his chest into red goo.

Lee raised his rifle and was lining up the red dot tactical sight, but it was not necessary. The ISIS soldier fell into a heap near his already dead friend.

"After I fly in to save the local militia, get my ass shot out of an airplane, land in a bunch of cacti, and walk over here, I then have to save your asses from getting shot by a dipshit from Compton with a Russian-made crap rifle. It is amazing you two assholes are still walk-ing around," Braxton said.

The colonel slid the big pistol back into his shoulder holster. Lee could now tell it was a well-worn 1911 Forty-Five.

Just as Jake was going to make a sarcastic reply, a single shot rang out from a house on the other side of the large corral. All three men turned in that direction. They could see movement in the front yard of the house through the trees and bushes.

"If you two meatheads have finished jacking around, we better go see what is going on," Braxton said.

Lee handed the AR-10 to Jake. "Here, you carry this overweight cannon for a while, being your army-issue gun is toast." The three men took off toward the house where the commotion was taking place.

Chapter 64

1026, Day 11, Casey Residence, Agua Dulce, California

D ayyan, Naseem, Enrique, and the two other soldiers were still on the hill next to the house continuing to watch the battle scene below. They had been optimistic about victory once the four M-RAPs moved into position, blocking the infidel defenders at both ends of the road. And when the two mortars started their barrage tearing into the small and surprised army below, they thought things were finally happening with God's will.

Dayyan was furious. "That idiot Charro and his worthless drug cartel gang members not showing up as planned is allowing the infidels to escape."

He then told Naseem quietly, not wanting Enrique to hear that he was going to, "I will personally shoot that Cholo when he shows up."

The gang had finally arrived an hour late. Dayyan was certain it was due to another night of alcohol, drugs, and rape. He only kept the allegiance with them to strengthen his army. And now with so much of his army killed in the early ambush, he may need to keep the gang army, even if he did kill their leader. He would make the others fear him and follow him.

The five men suddenly saw a large black smoke cloud to the north. The house was blocking the direct view. Dayyan and the others, as slowly and stealthily as possible, slid forward to see the far end of the road. Dayyan could see one of the M-RAPS engulfed in fire and its .50-caliber machine gun out of commission. The driver of the other M-RAP was moving the truck backward, trying to escape the inferno. Dayyan watched as the gunner in the turret slumped forward as rifle fire poured down from the hill behind the two large trucks.

"Dammit," Dayyan said to Naseem. "There were still troops north of our blocking position. They have the last M-RAP in a cross fire."

Then suddenly, a huge blast occurred behind the hill to the west. Dayyan knew the blast was in the spot where he positioned the mortar teams.

Dayyan spoke again to Naseem. "The infidels must have attacked our mortar team with rockets or grenades. The American Army must be ignoring their president and using explosives. What else can go wrong?"

Dayyan had no sooner said the words when a huge noise came from the canyon to the north. It took only a couple of seconds for Dayyan to recognize the new threat. He leaned out even further, holding the radio in his right hand to brace himself with his left. He turned his head right to look at Naseem and Enrique who had also slid forward. As he did, Enrique's head exploded, releasing a torrent of blood and brain matter splattering on him and Naseem. Stunned and frozen, Dayyan could not quickly grasp what had happen. Before he moved, the radio ripped from his right hand. Dayyan looked down to see part of his hand was gone. A gooey mess remained where three of his fingers and part of his palm had been.

"Dammit, Naseem, someone has spotted us," Dayyan said as he dove backward.

Bullet rounds were hitting the ground all around the ISIS believers and smacking into the walls of the house next to them. The four remaining men slid and crawled back out of the line of the unknown sniper. As the A-10 aircraft screamed up Sierra Highway and opened fire on the south blocking M-RAPs, Naseem took the tribal scarf from around his neck and wrapped it around the bloody hand of Dayyan.

"You are badly wounded, my brother. We have failed. We must get to our truck and get you out of here."

"Yes, my brother. It is done. We are done. God has not blessed us today. The only bright spot is the annihilation of those idiot gang members by the American warplane. They shall all perish by the sword," Dayyan said.

Naseem carefully wrapped Dayyan's hand and trying to stop the flow of blood. "Help me to our vehicle, my brave brother, and we shall escape to inflict our revenge on the infidels another day."

The four men started down the hill. Naseem was holding onto Dayyan, helping to steady him as shock started to kick in. The other two soldiers followed along, holding their rifles. The bullet that hit Dayyan had destroyed the radio, so they had no way to call Fawzi in the armored truck to have him drive closer. The defeated terrorists had no choice other than walk to the barn where they had hidden the truck.

As they moved down the hill, they watched the A-10 bank around and line up with Vasquez canyon below. A stream of tracers poured from under the nose of the plane, ripping into the line of gang cars on Vasquez Canyon Road. The four watched in horror as the convoy of gang members were ripped to shreds. Vehicle after vehicle exploded in fire. Thankfully, they had hidden their truck in the barn. Otherwise, the Burbank Police SWAT truck would have become another target for the brutal attack.

"I made a mistake thinking the American government would not use aircraft to attack us, Naseem," Dayyan said.

"Yes, my brother. Our information was false or a well-planned lie by the American government," Naseem answered.

As Naseem helped Dayyan along, the cannon on the plane stopped firing. But then, suddenly, the plane turned sharply, trying to avoid the high-voltage power lines crossing over the road. The evasive turn was not enough, and the right wing hit a high-tension cable. Dayyan and Naseem stopped and watched as the pilot put the plane through some extreme maneuvers, trying to recover. But he had no chance as the nose of the small plane pointed at the ground. The canopy flew off, ejecting the pilot out of the doomed aircraft. The seat separated, and the pilot's parachute deployed. He sailed down, landing just over a rise in front of Dayyan and his men.

Dayyan turned to the two bodyguards. "Go and capture that pilot. We can use him as a shield and perhaps ransom him to save ourselves. Go quickly and bring him back to the truck. We will meet you there."

The two soldiers took off jogging to the north toward the pilot. The two loyal men had only been gone a couple of minutes when gunfire erupted from that direction they had gone.

"What now?" Naseem said to Dayyan.

The two friends kept moving slowly down the hill to the barn and their truck. Naseem worried about Dayyan passing out from blood loss.

Passing another large ranch-type house, they could see the barn holding their truck. The doors were open, which Dayyan thought was worrisome. Before either man could say anything, the large armored truck drove out of the opening, heading toward the main road. It turned right heading west on Vasquez, weaving around the burning wrecks of the gang convoy.

"Fawzi has fled and abandoned us," Naseem said.

"I knew that idiot was a coward. I only kept from killing him because he did make a decent driver," Dayyan replied.

"What should we do now, my brother?" Naseem asked.

"The house we just passed. Did you notice the plywood covering the windows?" Dayyan said as he turned around looking at the house.

"The owners must have left. Perhaps we can pry open the door and hide inside until dark."

Naseem steadied Dayyan, and the two men moved into the front yard approaching the front door. The windows were all boarded up, but the front door was not. The cheap deadbolts would not be difficult to bust open. Naseem had a huge knife in a leg holster. He could use it to pry open the door. They reached the porch, and Dayyan reached out and braced himself on the post support on the right side of the porch overhang. Naseem approached the door.

Chapter 65

1040, Day 11, Johnson Residence, Vasquez Canyon, California

Tom Johnson and his son Todd were staying quiet inside the living room of the large ranch-style house. They had been listening to the battle all morning, hearing the massive explosions which rattled everything inside. Then the battle had come closer. About an hour ago, watching through slots in the plywood window coverings, they saw the armored truck drive into their neighbor Jack's yard. Two men had gotten out and opened the barn doors and the truck backed in. Tom had cut slots in the plywood before placing the ¾-inch thick wood over each window. He and Todd had done it the first couple of days after the EMP. Tom wanted slots for some visibility outside, and if push came to shove, they would act as gun ports to defend the house.

The armored truck had the wording "Pasadena Police Department" on the side, but Tom knew these guys could not be police. Two men got out dressed in Arabic clothing. They looked like Afghanistan Taliban soldiers Tom had seen on the TV news. Three men had what looked like AK-47 rifles.

Tom told his son, "We better remain very quiet. Let's hope they only want to fight the army and leave once the battle is over."

"What if they defeat the small army from Agua Dulce?" Todd asked.

"Let's hope that does not happen, son."

Tom and Todd turned all lights off and sat in the dark house. They kept their guns with them and remained quiet while listening to the sounds of the fight. The rest of Tom's family left the night before. Army people had come door-to-door, warning the residents of the battle that may happen in the morning. All of his neighbors had taken the army's advice and had fled to downtown Agua Dulce. Tom sent his wife, Maxine, and three daughters to town in his 1970 Lincoln Continental. Maxine protested profusely, but Tom finally convinced her that he and Todd would be fine.

Tom had prepared well for this day. He had at least two years of food and supplies stored in the downstairs basement. He had solar panels, a large battery bank, and inverters for power twenty-four hours a day. He was also an avid gun nut with many rifles, shotguns, and pistols. Tom had given thought about volunteering for the makeshift army, but Maxine would not allow it.

Maxine made her point. "Look at you. You are overweight with a beer gut, you have high blood pressure, high cholesterol, and several other problems. You were never a soldier and have no training. Fighting in the volunteer army is suicide for you. You might as well just shoot yourself and get it over."

Maxine was right, and Tom knew it. But now he was not about to risk having someone loot his house of his survival stuff. Some people around his neighborhood who had nothing to survive knew about his stuff. His house would be a big target. He was staying, and he needed another person to help keep a lookout around all sides of the house. Todd had to stay.

But now, Tom was worried. The battle was fierce. Many enemy soldiers in trucks had passed by his property, moving to the hills up behind the house. The ones in the armored car parked in the neighbor's barn had walked right by, going to what Tom guessed was Frank Casey's property. But so far, no one had bothered the house or tried to break in. Then the large convoy came down Vasquez Canyon Road, but a few minutes later, the American Warthog flew over and strafed them, setting most on fire. He now also feared the fire spreading. Tom prayed the drizzle of rain would increase. He was scared, but he was trying hard to not let Todd know that. The boy was doing really good so far.

Todd called out from the back of the house. "Dad, two men are coming back down the hill. I think it is the two guys in the robes from the armored car."

Tom looked out the small peephole and agreed with his son. "I think you are right, son. Looks like the one prick has had his hand shot up. Stay here and watch the back. But stay very, very quiet."

Tom went back to the front window of the living room and peered out through one of the gun slots. The two men passed by the house but then stopped. Tom followed their gaze and could see the Pasadena Police armored truck pull out of the barn and take off.

Tom thought, *I wonder if that guy just took off and left these two assholes here.*

The men confirmed his assumption when they turned and the injured man pointed at Tom's house. They both started walking toward it.

Tom knew the windows would be hard to penetrate, but the two men might be able to kick in the front door if they tried hard. He and Todd should have pushed heavy furniture against the door, but it was too late now. He set down his Smith and Wesson AR15 and picked up the Mossberg 12-gauge pump shotgun. He tiptoed to the door and waited. The shotgun already had a chambered round, and he clicked off the safety and stood behind the door and listened. He then heard footsteps coming up the porch steps. He raised the shotgun to the view port on the door.

The view port was the type with a large opening, a metal grate over the outside, and a hinged cover on the inside. When the footsteps got right up to the door, Tom flipped the little cover up, stuck the barrel inside, and pulled the trigger.

Chapter 66

1144, Day 11, Johnson Residence, Vasquez Canyon, California

Naseem approached the door and pulled out his massive knife. He would pry open the lock, trying not to damage the door, making it obvious someone had broken in. Just as he neared the door, he saw the view hole in the door open. He froze which was Naseem's final mistake. Seeing the barrel would be the last thought to ever pass through his brain.

The 12-gauge "double-ought" buckshot obliterated Naseem's face. All ten of the lead balls hit him straight on, traveling 1,500 feet per second. The blast also brought along the small cast iron grate from the front of the peephole. At this range, the balls easily penetrated through his facial bones and deep into his brain and out the back of his skull. The force was also so great it severed his spine at the number two vertebrae, flinging his head back ninety degrees, nearly decapitating him. His brain was dead before his body slumped back and fell into a pile on the porch.

The shock of the gunshot and Naseem's body and pulverized face and head landing at Dayyan's feet caused him to fall backward off the two steps. He managed to stay upright but continued backward into the yard, where he tripped over yard art and landed against the side of a large concrete fountain. Trying to catch himself, he had put both hands back including his severely damaged right hand.

When he landed on it, the pain was so intense he thought he might black out. His vision was blurry, and he could just make out the door opening and someone moving out of the house. He reached for his shoulder holster with his left hand and pulled out the 9 mm Glock pistol and raised it up toward the blurry image.

The shotgun sounded again and the gun tore out of Dayyan's left hand. He looked down to see that his left hand was now gone with a good portion of his wrist.

"Well, shit head. Want to try something else? You are down to two limbs now. Move again and the next thing I will shoot off is what you are hoping you will have with you when they give you your seventy-two virgins."

Dayyan stared up at the man. He was a short, overweight man wearing a Dale Earnhardt NASCAR racing shirt and a black hat with large gold letters "NRA." It shamed Dayyan a gun-toting American redneck had shot him. It was a disgrace.

Dayyan thought, *Why is God doing this? He should be helping our cause.*

The man was standing over Dayyan, looking down at him. A young boy came running out of the house, also carrying a rifle. The older man spoke to him.

"Todd, go get a towel for this idiot so we can keep him from bleeding out. Isn't it ironic there, Akbar, that we are trying to save you after I shot your hand off? Who shot your other hand off?"

The boy ran back in the house and brought back a dish towel. The man spoke to the boy, "Son, point your rifle barrel right at his nose, and if he so much as farts, you blow his head off."

"Will do, Dad," the boy responded.

The man reached down and pulled the bloody stump up, causing Dayyan to cry out in pain.

"What's the matter there, Akbar? Can't take a little pain. Tough shit, dude. I am keeping you alive in case the army guys want to talk to you. If not, I will put you out of your misery personally."

"Fuck you, old man. When my other men get here, you will die a slow, painful death. We will rape your son while you watch and then kill both of you."

The man twisted the bloody stump, which caused Dayyan to scream out again.

"Well, your other men are not here yet, and it looks like the Air Force just toasted your convoy, so you best just keep your dumb-ass thoughts to yourself, Akbar."

"My name is not Akbar, you pig. My name is Dayyan. Quit calling me that name."

The man twisted the stump even harder. "Fuck you and the camel you rode in on."

Suddenly the boy spun around and called out, "Dad. Someone is coming."

The older man jumped to his feet and picked up the shotgun. The boy was already pointing his rifle toward the men.

"Hold your fire. We are with the United States Army."

Three men walked into Dayyan's view. Two were dressed in army camo and carrying rifles, and the third man was wearing a flight suit and carrying a large pistol.

Chapter 67

1152, DAY 11, JOHNSON RESIDENCE, VASQUEZ CANYON, CALIFORNIA

ee Garrett, Jake Rodriguez, and Colonel Braxton trotted up to the scene in the front yard. An older man was holding a shotgun, and a younger teenager had an AR15-style assault rifle. Sitting on the ground was a man dressed in Taliban robes. Both of his arms had large cloth towels wrapped around them. Both towels were red with blood. Another body lay prone on the steps of the house. A bloody gooey mess was all that remained of the face of the dead man.

"Jake Rodriguez, United States Army. This is Captain Garrett and Colonel Braxton."

"Tom Johnson, and this is my son, Todd," the man said.

Everyone exchanged handshakes.

"This guy and his prick friend there tried to break into our house. It did not work out so well for them," Tom added.

"Did you shoot off both of his hands?" Jake asked.

"Nah, his right hand was messed up when he got here. But he tried to pull that pistol on me, so I had to remove his other hand. I think dipshit and his dead buddy were walking back to an armored car parked in that barn over there," Tom said, pointing to the barn.

Tom added, "The truck took off though, and I think someone abandoned these two pricks. By the way, he says his name is Dayyan."

Braxton spoke up. "Dayyan is the name he told you?"

"Yep. He did not like me calling him Akbar. Did you, asshole?" Tom said as he kicked Dayyan in the right foot.

Braxton turned and spoke in a low voice to Lee and Jake, "Dayyan is the name of the leader of this army. Maybe this is him."

Tom spoke up. "To me, he looked like a leader or commander. Five soldiers including these two came out of the armored truck and went up on the ridge. Everyone but Akbar and his dead buddy had rifles. Akbar was holding a radio and a folded map. Only he and dead man came back."

Then four soldiers from 4th Infantry came trotting up.

Sergeant Lambert spoke up. "You must be the pilot from the Warthog."

"Yep. Colonel Braxton."

The sergeant saluted, and Braxton returned the salute. Meanwhile, Jake was on the radio getting a situation update from the other units. Fitzgerald told him the fighting was all over. A few terrorists had fled to the east, but elements of the 4th ID were chasing them. The M-RAPs were out of commission. Alpha Company had eliminated the mortar team.

One of the 4th ID soldiers was a field medic, so he knelt down next to Dayyan, but Braxton waved an arm in a "stay back" motion.

"Well, Dayyan. Looks like your little crap-sack army is all but wiped out," Braxton said as he knelt down near the now weak ISIS leader. He then frisked him, finding a notebook and a map. He also found an Iridium 9505 Satellite phone. He quickly thumbed through the notebook, finding what looked like readiness numbers for many combat units. But up in the front of the notebook, he found a list of what Braxton knew were satellite phone numbers. He stood back up and showed the book to Jake.

Braxton said quietly to Jake and Lee, "These might be phone numbers for other planted terrorist cells. This notebook is a great intelligence gain, assuming the other terrorist cells are not aware we have it. Knowing the numbers can allow the spy guys to track the calls easier and perhaps zero in on locations. We need to get this back east as quickly as possible."

Braxton then leaned down to Dayyan and said in a calm voice, "So, Mr. Dayyan Imaad Shalah, shall we stop the bleeding and then fix you up, assuming you are going to cooperate with us and provide us the names and locations of your other groups?"

Dayyan's eyes popped open wide when he heard his full name used. He looked up at the colonel in shock.

"Surprised we know your name, are you? Well, we know all kinds of stuff about you. Your men who we have captured in the last few days had a lot to say about you. Now it is your turn to tell us what you know," Braxton said.

"I will tell you nothing, you fucking infidel military clown," Dayyan said.

"Are you very, very sure about that?"

"You will get nothing from me. My brothers are killing your country, and you will all perish. America is done."

Braxton replied very calmly, "Well, okay then. I guess if America is done, then our laws mean nothing. And if you don't plan to be any help to us, well then, you can just lie here and die of loss of blood or gangrene."

Braxton stood up and addressed the rest of the group, "He is worthless. Leave him. We have important and pressing matters to attend. Mr. Johnson, you caught him. What would you like to do with him?"

Braxton was winking at Tom Johnson, who caught on right away to the scam. "You mean I can do whatever I want and no one will prosecute me?"

"Sure. With martial law in place, this enemy of the United States can be shot on sight. But if you happen to take a long and painful time killing him, that is just a minor detail," Braxton said.

Lee and Jake were getting a kick out of the colonel's game. They looked at each other and smiled.

Jake spoke up. "Tom, how about our medic sews up Dayyan's arms and stops the bleeding so he stays alive for a while."

"Nah, Dayyan Imaad FN Shalah will be dead before you guys have your lunch. But he is not going to die from these wounds," Tom Johnson said.

Tom stepped forward with the Mossberg shotgun, which he pointed down at Dayyan's crotch.

"I already told him I would shoot off his manhood."

Tom then chambered another round in the shotgun and lowered the barrel even lower between Dayyan's legs.

The gun going off surprised everyone. Tom had fired the 12-gauge into the dirt between Dayyan's knees. Dirt and rock flew everywhere, including all over Dayyan, who jumped and pulled back his legs while uttering a loud scream.

"Shucks, I missed. I am not sure of the spray pattern of this double-ought buck. Let me get a little closer," Tom said, moving the gun closer to Dayyan's crotch.

Colonel Braxton turned and told Tom, "Let us get out of here while you finish this game of 'hunt the pecker with a shotgun.'" And he started to walk away. The others took noticed and followed. Jake gave Dayyan the finger as he turned to go with the group. The 4ᵗʰ ID medic picked up his bag and followed.

Dayyan screamed out after the group, "Okay, okay, don't leave me with this fucking maniac. I will cooperate."

The group turned around, and Braxton headed back and addressed Dayyan again. "Okay, dipshit. We will fix you up and you had better cooperate *fully*. If you fail to answer a single question about anything, I bring your ass right back here and dump you on Tom's porch and tell him to finish your sex change procedure. You got that?"

Dayyan nodded. Braxton sent the medic back over, who started undoing the right-hand bandage after applying a tourniquet above the wound.

Braxton addressed Sergeant Lambert, "Sergeant, have your medic stabilize him. Sergeant Rodriguez, can we get a vehicle over here to pick up Dayyan and take him to your hospital in town? Make sure two men watch him constantly and keep him restrained. We will come and talk to him later after he is stable."

Both Sergeants nodded. Jake used the radio to contact Fitzgerald who informed him that help was already on the way.

Then Fitzgerald said, "And by the way, the ham radio club just got word from one of their spotters this side of the Newhall pass. DHS just rolled by with a dozen odd looking armored vehicles with red stars. I guess our Chinese backed Homeland Security forces decided to attend this party."

Jake replied, "Well talk about a little late. Oh well, if they had shown up earlier, we would have probably been restricted to rock throwing only."

Jake then turned and moved close to Braxton and Lee and said, "My bet is that you are in deep shit for stealing an A-10 and then wreaking it. But as far as we know, you went down with the plane. Lee, what say we go retrieve that ejection seat and parachute and see if we can make our savior Colonel disappear for a while? It may take some time to dig what is left of that Warthog from what I am guessing is a pretty big hole in the ground, but if a drone sees that seat and parachute laying around, the jig is up."

The three men turned from their private conversation in time to see the army ATV roaring up the dirt road with a five-ton truck loaded with 4th Infantry troops trailing close behind. As the ATV and truck approach it started to rain. Everyone was looking up and commenting on the perfect timing of the storm and how it would help to extinguish all the fires. A large flash of light was followed quickly by the clap of thunder.

Braxton replied, "No matter what Dayyan thinks, God is on our side."

Chapter 68

1155, Day 11, Sierra Highway, Agua Dulce, California

Sergeant Liz Wilde and her company were checking for survivors and assessing the damage. Fires were burning everywhere. The situation could get ugly quick. But no sooner had Liz thought about it, the rain started coming down. The welcome rain was coming down heavy, so it had an immediate effect on burning brush. The welcome rain was not doing a lot to put out vehicle fires, but at least it would stop them from spreading.

Liz moved up close to the burning M-RAP and looked down the street to see Sergeant Moses Pierce and Sergeant Kirwan walking along helping Barry. Barry was limping on what looked like an injured leg. Liz trotted up. "Barry, I thought you committed suicide with your truck against the M-RAP."

"Hell, lady, I might be stupid but I am not crazy. I propped the clutch down with a stick put it in high gear and put a big rock on the throttle. Then I carefully pulled out the stick tell she got rolling. The old babe took off like a rocket ship and knocked me on my butt. Almost ran over me. I twisted or broke my ankle falling into the ditch on the side of the road."

"That is unbelievable, Barry. How did it stay straight on the road?"

"Oh yeah, forgot to tell you, babe—I used my belt to tie the old steering wheel straight. In fact, my pants may fall down any minute, little lady, so try not to get all excited when you see my true self," Barry said as everyone started laughing heavily.

"Careful, Barry, old guy, I might have to tell your wife how you are acting," Liz replied.

"Shit, lady, she is going to kick my ass all the way to Timbuktu and back when she finds out I used the truck as an IED. Me trying to flirt with you is not even going to faze her," Barry said with a wink.

Liz got closer to Barry and put her arms around him and gave him a huge hug. "Well, I am glad to see you are okay, you old pervert you." She kissed him on the cheek.

Barry used one arm to try and hug Liz back, and as he did his pants fell down to his ankles like he had warned. Everyone started laughing hysterically when they saw his white boxer shorts which had red hearts all over them. Liz stepped back and started laughing hysterically with the rest of the tired and weary fighters.

Epilogue

aysean and one half of his mortar team were lying along the ridgeline on a hill overlooking Sierra Highway. His mission had turned to crap after he had placed the other half of his team in a spot further south. The first placement went well, and he assumed from the sounds during the battle those men had been able to fire dozens of mortar rounds into the enemy positions. Now his first mortars were silent as well as the gunfire from the intense battle.

While lying prone on the hill overlooking the valley and road below, Daysean started thinking back. In his thoughts, he revisited events responsible for him ending in a terrorist army trying to kick the United States while it was down. He had been the perfect candidate for Dayyan. Daysean was a typical South-Central Los Angeles youth. Child of a single-parent mother who balanced between herself between coke and heroin habits while trying to raise her son. Daysean also precariously balanced between good and bad growing up in the ghetto of Los Angeles. Mostly, he managed to stay out of trouble. He was one of the few in his "hood" to graduate from high school with decent grades. But sadly, not good enough grades for college. So at the age of eighteen, he took a bus to downtown Los Angeles and joined the army. Three tours with the 82nd Airborne in Afghanistan found him as a sergeant and in a position of reenlisting or getting out and returning to his mother and the projects. His distinguished service and recommends allowed him to ask for a shot at joining the Ranger Regiment. He received the "unofficial" okay. Two days after the approval, he received a call from his uncle telling him his mother overdosed on heroin.

He returned home to bury her but never went back. Days of drinking turned into weeks, and when he finally realized it, he was already a week overdue and essentially AWOL. Two days after the EMP hit. With nothing of any value and the city falling apart, he followed his recently found religion and walked to a neighborhood mosque. When certain people saw the well-toned and sharp-looking man wearing a set of army camo, they approached him with an offer. Days later, he was in charge of a mortar squad and running with a terrorist army. Now with his small squad of men, he was staring down at the total destruction of his army.

Along the highway, Daysean could see nothing but wrecks and dead soldiers. His own 6×6 truck was useless. On the wrong road, the driver had tried a U-turn near a large concrete drainage channel, and the truck slipped over the edge, rolled over killing two men in the back. The cargo of gear, ammunition, and mortars fell into piles around the overturned truck. He and his men tried to using their Hummer and the 6×6 winch to free the big truck, but all they succeeded in doing was breaking off the main driveshaft.

Freeing the truck was hopeless, so Daysean and the other five men decided to hike up the hill and survey the scene.

As Daysean looked down, he saw something else. Just below him and his men was a group of three people hidden in a small valley above the highway. Two men and one woman. They had backpacks and gear and a couple of Quad-type ATVs.

Daysean made a guess. "Was it an observation point? Or maybe a medical team?"

Daysean turned to his men, who were lying along the ridge. "Move into two groups, and let's see if we can put this group in the middle. I only see one rifle. I am not sure who these three are, but we may need leverage to get out of this shitty place. And we can use the two quads."

His team quietly moved down the hill in two groups and worked to surround the three people below.

Addendum: The Contents of Lee Andrew Garrett's Bug-Out Bag

Tasmanian Tiger TT Range Pack G-82 100+ liter Tactical Backpack

Rear Removable Pouch
First-aid kit, vacuum-sealed
Blue surgical gloves—4 pairs
Black "crud" gloves—2 pairs
4×4 gauze pads—16 packs
2×2 gauze pads—16 packs
5×9 extra absorbent pads—2
Quick-seal Celox packs—2
Kling gauze rolls—4
Triangular bandage—1
Adhesive bandages—12
Adhesive tape—1 roll
Eye patch—1
Eye wash—1 tube
Burn cream—3 single-use pouches
Insect sting relief—2 single-use pouches
Antiseptic towelettes—2
Alcohol prep pads—6
Triple antibiotic ointment—1 tube
Crazy glue—4 single-use tubes
Surgical masks—4
Pill box (various)—1
Emergency blanket—1
Carmex lip cream—1
Right side pouch

Headlamp—1
Lighters—2
AA batteries, plastic box—16
AA batteries, rechargeable—8
AAA batteries—12
AAA batteries, rechargeable—8
Nalgene water bottle, 32 oz—1
Mechanics wear gloves—1 pair

Left Side Pouch
9 mm leg holster—1
Lighters—2
Folding tarp (HD survival)—1
Folding multi-tool—1
Survivor series emergency sleeping bag—1

Rear Zipper Compartment
Map case
Sharpie markers—2
Pencils—2
Ballpoint pen—2
Rubber bands—assorted
Notepad, small—1
Signal mirror—1
Samsung tablet—1

Main Compartments (Upper or Lower)
Upper Compartment, Under Top Flap
Rain poncho—1
Bag rain cover—1
Tarp, water resistant—1
Wobbie blanket—1

Hygiene Bag: Zip Lock Bag
Small terry towel—2
Large terry towel—1

Toothbrush—1
Toothpaste—1 small travel tube
Body wash—1 travel bottle
Shampoo—1 travel bottle
Baby wipes—1 small package

Goodie Bag: Zip Lock Bag
Power bars—6
Energy-drink powder mix—6 sleeves
Instant coffee powder—12 sleeves
Other MRE drink mixes—6
Zenergize drink tablets—1 tube
Five-hour energy drinks—4
Gatorade Prime Energy Chews—2 packages

Silverware Pack: Ziplock Bag
Plastic silverware—2 sets
Salt and pepper—2 small bottles
Tums antacid tablets—4 rolls

Main Compartment, Loose Items
Boafeng BF-F8HP, portable radio—1
Boafeng extra battery pack—1
Boafeng AAA battery pack with batteries—1
Boafeng radio throat mikes—2
Large baby wipes—1 package
Titanium metal cup—1
Sol emergency blanket—1
Ditty bag—1
Life straw water filter tube—1
9 mm Luger ammunition—50 rounds
Garden twist wire—1 roll
Disposable lighters—4
Silver Eagle coins—10
Paracord—50 feet
Wire ties, short—25

Green trail marker tags—20
Samsung charge cord—1
Gorilla tape—1 compact roll
9 mm ten-round magazines—2
LED flashlight—1
LED glow stick—1
Jumper wires, with alligator clips—4
Electrical wire, 14ga—25 feet
Telescoping radio antenna—2
Solid fuel folding stove—1
Solid fuel pellets—1 box
Folding solar charger set with AA, AAA charger—1
Extra eyeglasses—1
Magnesium fire starter—1 ziplock bag
Para Cord—fifty feet
Survivor Series emergency sleeping bag—1

Clothing (Loose)
Desert camo long-sleeved surplus shirt—2
Desert Camo surplus pants—2
Hat Boonie, desert tan—1
Shemagh scarf—1
Tactical gloves—1 pair
Black hood—1
Long underwear—1
Long-sleeved quilted undershirt—1

Clothing Vacuum Bag, Sealed
Underwear—4
Socks—6 pairs
Moisture wicking T-shirts—2

Main Compartment Food
MREs—Contents of 6 removed from pouches
MRE Heaters—3
Tuna snack packs—2

Emergency food bars, 2,400-calorie packs—4

Chest Pack, Main—Attached to Front Straps
Rubber Bands—assorted
Clothespins—10
Shoelaces—3 pairs
Solar charging 5-volt battery pack, flashlight—1
Garden wire—1 roll
Lighters—3

Chest Right Outer Pouch
Steiner Binoculars, 8 × 30—1
Garmin Etrex GPS unit—1
Disposable lighter—2

Chest Left Outer Pouch
Boafeng BF-F8HP, Portable radio—1
Boafeng extra battery pack—1
Boafeng AAA battery pack with batteries—1

On Belt or Belt Pouch
Leatherman OHT one-handed multitool—1
Tactical straight-blade knife—1
Red/white LED flashlight—1

Attached to Bag Outside
Climbing rope—100 feet
Large tie downs (wrist cuff)—20
Syphon hose—1

Loose in Car
Smith & Wesson tactical waterproof side-zip boots—1 pair
Bass Pro Shop redhead hunting socks—2 pairs in boots
Extra hat (boonie)1
Water, gallon jugs—2
Water, Fiji 1-liter bottles—4

California map book
Las Vegas, Southern Nevada maps
Fanny pack
Emergency 400-cal food—2
Hand sanitizer—1
Foot powder—1
4×4 gauze pads—4
Celox blood clot—1
Sunscreen—1
Gatorade Prime Energy chews—2 packs
Compass, small—1
Chapstick—1
Disposable lighters—2
Krazy Glue, individual use—4
Tums antacid tablets—1
Shoelaces—1 pair
Wet wipes—1 small pack
Asthma inhaler—1
Lens cleaners—4

Water purification tablets—1 pair bottle
Glow sticks—2
Swiss army knife—1
LED flashlight, small—1
Paracord—25 feet
Gorilla tape—20 feet

About the Author

Andrew Adams has lived a fun, diverse and exciting life and career. Born and raised in the mecca of racing in Southern California, he raced off-road vehicles and developed a successful all-terrain vehicle company. He used his vehicle development experience as a spring board into the entertainment industry including film and the amusement park industry. Andrew is a highly respected designer of high-tech special effects and large equipment for installations worldwide. He has been involved in large-scale entertainment projects in numerous countries besides the United States, including Japan, England, Spain, France, India, Singapore, China, Panama, and more.

Andrew is a strong supporter of the United States military and our brave law enforcement. Andrew has worked closely with the military as a developer for certain vehicle-related projects. He could easily be called a doomsday prepper and has used that knowledge extensively in the creation of this book. Although this book is a work of fiction, the tools and skill of the main character are all based on real survival techniques and technology. Lee Andrew Garrett's bug-out bag can be considered as a good base for anyone who decides to prepare for the unknown.

Andrew has been fortunate to have lived in the diverse environment of California, with great friends of all ethnicities, religions, and sexual orientations. Nothing in this book should be considered as an afront to anyone or any group, only bad and evil people.

Andrew lives in Southern California with his wonderful, loving, and supportive family.